BLACK

Sometimes Good Guys Do Bad Things

RICKY
CONLIN

Dream Oak Publishing LLC
3000 Village Run Road
Unit 103 #233
Wexford, PA 15090

EIN: 81-4936946

Dedicated to Stacy, Caci, Charlie, and DJ.

I love you more than you know

A Note Before Reading

This book, and the story told within it, is a work of fiction. Names, characters, places, and incidents are the product of my imagination or are used fictitiously to build a believable representation of the Naval Academy and Ocean City Maryland circa 1995.

A drug scandal did take place at the Naval Academy in the fall of 1995. Those events led to the eventual expulsion of several midshipmen involved. The story characters' entanglement within this scandal and its aftermath is a work of fiction. I had neither involvement nor association with the actual Naval Academy drug scandal that transpired in the fall of 1995.

Though this book is a work of fiction, I tried very hard to construct a story representative of the environment and culture of the mid-nineties Naval Academy. As a graduating member of the mighty class of 1999, I wouldn't have it any other way.

Lastly, to the current Brigade of Midshipman, know that some of your best future heroes are currently on restriction.

Enjoy,
-Ricky

Prologue

Mid-Afternoon
Thursday, December 7th, 1995

"Attention on deck!"

A male in his young twenties blurted as he and all other room attendees snapped to immediate military attention. Each gathered occupant crisply stood upright in unison with the collective rigidity of an oak tree. The entire room's attendees, save the one individual wearing formal Marine Corp's garb, were meticulously dressed in cleanly pressed black suits known to Naval Academy Midshipmen as "service dress blues," an ironic name since the entirely black and white outfit did not have a speck of blue in it. Everyone in the room was wearing fastidiously polished shoes. A handful of those standing at attention felt too intimidated to look forward. They viewed the room's transpiring activities in the reflections of their neighbor's spit-shined shoes.

The large rectangular room had a sterile air of primness accented by a sparse array of oak and leather adorned furniture placed orderly throughout. Though the size of the room would likely support a large conference table under normal business settings, the sparse furniture was instead arranged as an impromptu courtroom. The large outwardly facing desk was currently unoccupied, but orchestrated in a way that would soon facilitate a pending trial. The many leather-bound chairs remained newly unoccupied as the room's participants stood anxiously firm in front of them, slowly releasing the seat imprints long after everyone stood. Aside from the furniture, there was little décor, save a few stock pictures of the Naval Academy's grounds. There was not a speck of dust in sight as the air still wreaked heavily of Pine Sol from a likely recent scouring of an already clean room.

The group's currently donned uniform was more formal than their regular standard working uniforms worn on a typical December Thursday, and were usually reserved for more formal occasions. This formality provided an air of gravitas to the room. While everyone's uniforms looked largely identical, most variation came in two spots: the collection of golden stripes on their sleeves, and the rows of military award ribbons pinned on the left breast of each person's suit coat. The amount of stripes designated seniority. The more stripes someone had, and the fatter those stripes were clearly indicated who the most superior rank in the room was. The more rows of "chest candy" pinned over someone's heart, the greater a person's acknowledged merit in military service.

The room was currently occupied by ten men. Three of those men were active duty military personnel. The first was a forty-year-old Navy Commander who looked as though his face had been affixed in its current state of perpetual sullen for at least the past decade. The second was a Navy Lieutenant in his mid-twenties who displayed the expected alertness of an over-stressed father of a newborn daughter whom had afforded him and his wife exactly two hours and seventeen minutes of sleep the night before. The third was a thirty-four-year-old Marine Corps Gunnery Sergeant with a flat top haircut shaved so high and tight that it looked as though someone had glued a black scrub brush onto Mr. Clean's head.

The other seven men in the room were various ranks of Naval Academy midshipmen. All of these midshipmen looked exceedingly young. Their sleeve stripes were really the only way to adequately determine rank amongst the bunch. Each midshipman in the room had varying degrees of knuckle whiteness. They anxiously tensed their fists anticipating the start of the oncoming festivities. There was nothing festive about the mood. One of the midshipmen had not a single stripe on his sleeve. This midshipman wore a shiny black nametag with yellow characters spelling "McGee '99."

As a large oak door swung open, a handsome gray-haired gentleman, with a sleeve full of thick gold stripes and a Crayola box's assortment of color on the many rows of ribbons on his chest sauntered into the room.

"At ease, gentlemen," said the room's new guest. Everyone shifted their hands to a seemingly more relaxed resting position, yet the stiffness in the room remained.

Entering the room was Navy Captain Ron "Vader" Clemens. "Vader" was Captain Clemens' call sign as a Naval Pilot of F-14 Tomcats, the Navy's elite dog fighter jet of the time. A call sign was naval lingo for nickname, much like "Goose" and "Maverick" of Top Gun, fictitious movie characters that piloted the same jet that Vader actually flew for nearly two decades.

Vader received his call sign not by his demeanor. Quite the contrary, he was a much more pleasant and approachable character as compared to the villainous moniker he retained. He was relatively well-liked by his midshipmen subordinates. This was quite a rare feat for a Naval Academy Commandant of Midshipman, a role typically forged in formality and intimidation. Vader instead received the name for the way he resembled Darth Vader when donning his flight gear. A helmet and reflective visor on his six foot six frame made him but a black cape and light saber away from appearing to be directly from George Lucas' darkest imagination. It was rumored throughout the Brigade of Midshipman that he had to get a special medical waiver just to become a fighter pilot because of his extreme height and potential difficulties in fitting within a space-constrained cockpit.

The proceedings moved forward in a haze. There were multiple midshipmen called to testify to Captain Clemens, all on behalf of the room's lone freshman, Midshipman Fourth Class (4/C) James McGee. Captain Clemens' demeanor was anything but jovial.

"Midshipman Fourth Class McGee," Clemens directed towards the room's lone defendant. While this was not a legal hearing, the formality of the proceedings certainly made it seem as such.

"Do you realize the enormous shit-pile you have created for this institution?" queried Clemens as his demeanor and inflection shifted towards uncharacteristic aggression.

"Sir, yes sir," sheepishly replied 4/C McGee as the line of questioning continued.

"Do you know the trouble created when *THIS* shows up on my morning doorstep?" screamed Clemens as he slammed two Washington Newspapers on his desk. Each newspaper was dated November 27th, each sporting a different photo angle of the same picture, and each providing provocative headlines.

"I am having a BAD FUCKING WEEK, SON!" he continued as voice volume built exponentially. His face turned tomato red.

McGee stood with an air of contrived meekness and sweat began to bead on his brow as though it was generated intentionally. Physically maintaining the visual balance of contrition and reverence was exhausting. Before he could muster a response that remained consistent with his physical posturing, 4/C McGee briefly thought to himself, *I hate this fucking place.*

Part I

Oceans

Chapter 1

I-Day Morning
Friday, June 30th, 1995
Mick, 0830 hrs.

"Barb, Mick, did you guys hear that Nan was riding a horse last week down in Pocomoke?" my aunt Nellie asked her car bound audience.

The traffic outside of the Naval Academy's visitors' entrance extended four blocks beyond the gate and entirely up King George Street. My mom, Barb, was in the front passenger seat and I was sprawled out in the backseat. Pearl Jam was on the car radio via a cassette jack connected to a well-used Sony Discman. In it a bootleg concert CD I recently received as a high school graduation gift, a fired up Eddie Vedder was scolding the audience to "shoe the shoeless."

"Now how the hell did she do that?" my mom replied, obviously surprised that my mid-seventies grandmother was remotely that nimble in her golden years.

"Well, she had a bucket or step stool or something," continued Nellie, "otherwise she would have had to be flexible enough to get her foot above her head to mount a horse from the ground."

"Ah, I remember when I was flexible enough to get my foot to my head," my mom mused, "but I wasn't getting on a horse."

"Fuck, Mom!" I yelled as both my mom and Aunt Nellie giggled like a couple of junior high teenagers. "Where are your boundaries?"

I didn't even bother to notice the beautiful surroundings of downtown Annapolis. I had seen and enjoyed them before, but I knew that I wouldn't be seeing much of them this summer.

Why bother torturing myself?

My summer adventure would transpire just beyond the Naval Academy's visitors' gate, on the other side of the ten-foot wall that surrounded the entirety of non-waterfront campus land. Newly minted Naval Academy dads sat anxiously in traffic, while the moms frantically paged through tourist guides touting which quaint restaurant had the best crab dip or the most delicious breakfast soufflé. Most of us plebes-to-be lucky enough to still be on the outside looking in actually welcomed the traffic pileup. It meant a few more short lived moments of civilian freedom.

Aunt Nellie drove my mom and I in our brown, two door '86 Oldsmobile Celebrity. We were within three cars of the gate's entrance. The car's engine wheezed like an asthmatic smoker on the homestretch of the Boston Marathon. "Yogi" I affectionately called it. I scrounged enough lawn mowing money between my sophomore and junior year of high school to buy it from Margery Watson, Aunt Nellie's eighty-year-old neighbor. I think I was doing the entire city of Ocean City, Maryland a favor when I took that vehicle out of the hands of old man Watson, Margery's husband of sixty plus years. Back then, he had a proclivity for running red lights, hitting mailboxes, and driving naked, sometimes all on the same trip.

"On the bright side, every day is a new day for him," Aunt Nellie used to say.

I begged his beloved wife to take my cash payment of $567 for the car. It was every penny I had. She refused to take it. We settled on making a hefty drop in the gift basket at her Catholic church that next weekend. From then on, I had cart blanche privilege to light prayer candles in "St. Mary, Star of the Sea" for the next twenty years. Yogi had since been a loyal friend over my past two years of driving. We spent many an early morning, longboard strapped to the roof, trolling down the Delmarva shoreline hunting for the best waves of dawn. After a while, I stopped trying to vacuum the sand off the floor. It reminded me that I lived at the beach.

Yogi had a "250" air-conditioning unit, meaning two windows rolled fully down driving fifty miles per hour was really the only way to stay cool in the summer. While we were hardly driving fifty anymore, the windows remained rolled down as a way to aerate the cigarette smoke emanating for the front seat bench. From my current vantage point two cars back from the visitors' gate, the dialogue between parents and the armed gate guard unfortunately standing watch on this busy and already humid day became audible.

"Which way to Alumni Hall?" questioned a father of an otherwise timid eighteen-year-old passenger. The gate guard pointed immediately left and then back towards the other end of the yard in what I assumed was a rough estimate of suggested destination.

The car in front of us pulled up to the guard. A WASP-y looking family in a BMW sarcastically queried, "Do we just drop him off here?" The cavalier humor did little to impress the surly rent-a-cop, an ill-tempered middle-aged man that looked beyond annoyed with his post and life in general. Again, he stoically gave the exact same visual directions as though his hand motions were being driven by autopilot.

Barely pressing the brakes hard enough to come to a complete stop, Aunt Nellie pulled up. The guard cautiously approached our vehicle secretly hoping that this crazy lady had the audacity to actually avoid the mandatory full stop. It would have been a nice excuse to draw his weapon and break up the routine of his otherwise monotonous professional routine.

"Which way to I-Day?" she asked as she exhaled her menthol cigarette without missing a beat.

I-Day was the abbreviated name for Induction Day, the check-in day of the Naval Academy experience. It was the day that hot-shit jocks, class presidents, valedictorians, and everyone in between instantly transitioned into life as a plebe. Being a plebe was the lowest form of existence on the Naval Academy yard.

My mother was a blubbering mess in the front seat. She had been crying on and off for at least the past hour. Mom still couldn't believe her baby boy was about to officially leave the nest.

Yogi continued following the steady flow of traffic as

my aunt spent the next twenty minutes scouring the area around Alumni Hall for a parking spot. I tried to enjoy the scenery, most of which came in the form of grieving girlfriends in short sundresses.

Eventually we settled on a spot at least a half a mile away from our Alumni Hall destination. It was almost certainly in a "no parking zone," and though no sign was visible, the red and yellow stripes painted on the space led me to believe my oil-leaking piece of crap car was not meant to be there. I closed the car door and temporarily said goodbye to Yogi. I tried to take notice of my luscious blond locks in the reflection of my car window. They would be a distant memory soon. I tried to relish every final moment of fading ownership.

The three of us finally made the long walk from our ill-planned parking spot. I digested my first lesson in the Navy: "Hurry up and wait." The snaking line continued to grow outside of the main entrance to Alumni Hall, an impressive basketball arena built upon the glory of David Robinson's Naval Academy basketball career. We approached a mass of humanity all waiting at the gateway to Naval Academy birth. It was I-Day ground zero.

The line extended at least one hundred plebes-to-be deep. While there were families of many different accents, ethnicities, and even citizenship, a good majority of these families were lily white. Of those white families, most were wearing slightly nuanced preppy looks. My long, curly, blond hair and generally baggy casual wear was enough to maintain some level of individuality for the time being.

The waiting families understood how difficult entrance to the Naval Academy was. Not only was the line just to get into today's festivities a long one, the entire year leading up to it was too. There were endless applications, essays, interviews, standardized tests, Congressional interviews, and if lucky, eventual appointments. For some of us, prep school or even previous years of civilian college had been part of the journey. For an even smaller subset of oncoming plebes, prior military service as enlisted Sailors or Marines was included in the price of admission.

The United States Naval Academy spent the previous year accepting and evaluating well over fifteen thousand applications from around the country, and even the globe, to one of the most prestigious academic institutions in the United States. All of this was to see which roughly twelve hundred students would get the privilege to attend the academy. Attendance was financially free of charge. All that value traded for just a five-year commitment of military service upon graduation, as an officer no less. It seemed like a good deal.

An hour passed in a blink of an eye. I was already beginning to sweat through my clothes. Not only was the temperature rising as late morning emerged, but my mom and Aunt Nellie both hugged onto me as though they were my pet koalas. In between the excessive amounts of public physical groping, they also managed to knock out about a half a pack of cigarettes between the two of them. They had the courtesy to step away from the crowds for each smoke, but that did not escape the occasional point, snicker, and stare from some of the more typical looking families in the crowd. Most of those folks had never been to a pool hall, bowling alley, or a laundromat in a few years, if ever. They just didn't know how to react to people like us.

Fuck these people.

Most of these plebes had other options. Some could have played college sports on scholarship. Some were smart enough to get academic rides elsewhere. Some showed up in German-engineered luxury vehicles. Those plebes had rich enough parents to go wherever the fuck they wanted.

I didn't fall into any of those categories. When my dad died, traditional college options disappeared. We couldn't afford much beyond community college. My grades were good, but not enough to get an academic ride. I was decent at sports, but Florida State was hardly beating down my door to play football. But the United States Naval Academy? They were just crazy enough to let me in. This was my "American Dream." It had to be.

Each plebe-to-be had a nuanced version of dread in their eyes. Some were dreading leaving happy hometown living. A few were dreading leaving pretty girlfriends. Most were just dreading what lay on the other side of the guarded doors ahead.

We finally reached the entrance doors. I felt sick to my stomach. It was a mix between butterflies and getting kicked in the balls.

My family needs me. Eventually somebody has to grow up and be an adult. I need to do this.

Upper-class Midshipman, easily identified by their shiny red nametags, ordered us to wait for two minutes and say our temporary good-byes to our family. We would have one more shot to say good-bye in six hours after the final oath of office and official entrance into the United States Navy. None of us knew exactly what to expect in between. I looked backwards and saw all but five other families standing behind me as our long line had finally dwindled down to a fleeting moment of its existence. I realized for the first time since joining the line that I was pretty close to the end of it.

I gave one last hug to my mom and Aunt Nellie. They had both been coyly sobbing for the past fifteen minutes, trying to avoid the possibility of getting me upset. I intentionally tried not to notice. By the time it was time to say good-bye, even I was a little choked up.

"Never let them see you cry," I remembered my dad used to say to me when I was a young child. He never felt that a man should allow himself the privilege of public tears, no matter how deep the scar was. "That's your burden to bear as a man, son," is how Dad would typically continue his lecture. There was something about that lecture that made me try to hold these moments in. It wasn't my privilege to let that slip.

I gave my mom and Aunt Nellie one last big kiss and hug. They both smelled and tasted of salty tears and menthol cigarettes.

"I love you guys. Thank you for," I unexpectedly paused as I stumbled for a word that could actually capture the breadth of my gratitude. "Everything," was the only word I could muster.

I bit the inside of my cheek just as my eyes welled up. It was the exact same way I held it together at my dad's funeral a few years earlier.

"Alright, ladies and gents," said the red name-tagged gent with the starchy white get-up, the excessively short haircut, and the look of annoyance. "Please step over the threshold, up the steps, and to your respective check-in table," he continued in the same loud yet monotone narration. "The check-in tables are in alphabetized clusters. Your check-in table will correspond with the first letter of your last name and its appropriate matching to a cluster of serialized letters associated with it."

This is going to be a long year.

Most of my fellow classmates in my entry cluster scurried like eager mice up the stairs leading up to their appropriate check-in table. Some scurried because of their excitement to initiate their Naval Academy experience, others did so only by sheer fear of being yelled at by the now ten plus non-plebe midshipman within our vantage point inside the entry doors. Our families, though literally just a few yards back, already seemed miles behind us.

The interior of Alumni Hall was buzzing with activity. The temporarily empty steps leading up to the check-in tables in the arena's main level were quickly filled with lines of the last check-in group. The folding tables and bountiful staff facilitating I-Day on the arena's main concourse made the inside seem more like a DMV than a basketball arena.

As I stood third in line, I heard the second repetition to a dialogue that I suspect had been on a replay loop all morning.

"Next! Welcome to the Naval Academy, shipmate, please recite your last name and social security number."

A few mundane and barely audible words were exchanged between the plebe and the upper-class midshipman sitting on the other side of the table. Some signatures were hastily made on a variety of documents. Once completed, the final package of paperwork was exchanged, and in a matter three minutes and forty-five seconds, the plebe was then hurried deeper into the belly of Alumni Hall. The next plebe two steps down awaited instruction and like clockwork the cadence repeated almost exactly as it had before upon hearing the order "NEXT!"

"Welcome to the Naval Academy, shipmate. Please recite your last name and social security number."

I stood in the on deck circle. My blood pumped anxiously. All I could observe on the other side of the table was seriousness. There was no smiling. There was very little emotion at all. Instead of the expected immediate intensity, I was chilled by the cold lack of any emotion. Everything on the other side of that table was mechanical.

"Next! Welcome to the Naval Academy, shipmate, please recite your last name and social security number."

"McGee, 221- . . ."

Mick, 1100 hrs.

The rest of the morning was filled with needles, paperwork, lines, instructions, signatures, measurements, more lines, and a shaved head, not exactly in that order. Our last stop in our first stage of plebe processing was to the uniform stations to receive our new plebe garb. With already uniformly shaved heads, the trade of civilian clothes for military uniform was the last piece of individuality lost. By the end of the process, every average height, average build, white midshipman male like me looked almost identical.

My physical appearance exemplified the strain and the general look of the day thus far. Most of the plebes around me had dark circles under their eyes from the double whammy of an early wakeup preceded by a night of anxious and minimal sleep. Sweat beaded on our faces and steadily dripped on our newly issued plebe "white works" uniform.

The "white works" uniform consisted of white pants and a similarly colored blouse styled in the likeness of the Cracker Jack boy. The sneakers on our feet were reminiscent of something Rose from *The Golden Girls* might wear within her fictional Florida retirement community. Literally topping all of this off was a blue-rimmed Dixie cup sailor's cap. We all looked like something out of a Benny Hill skit.

With the exception of the underwear I wore that day and the newly issued Dixie cup hat, nothing else on my body fit very well. My shoes were a half size too small and my garments were all at least one size too big. We collected our new uniform and other gear one piece and one painfully long line at a time. A cadre of little old ladies had been busy hawking us ill-sized clothes all morning long.

After what seemed like an eternity of lines, sweat, and anxiousness, I had collected what I hoped was a complete set of gear over the course of the morning in my newly issued sea bag. Pessimistically, I suspected this was not going to be the case.

The collective set of plebes in my final entrance group received our first breather of the day after two hours of "hurry up and wait." We were led to a seating area in the lower deck section of the Alumni Hall basketball arena where slowly but surely each plebe making it through the initial phase of I-Day festivities was corralled into their respective assigned companies. In civilian terms, a company was the group of midshipmen you would share the plebe experience with.

"Hopefully they didn't short me any important stuff," I randomly stated to the open air.

"Bank on it, homey," said a fellow plebe sitting two seats down the row from me. He had already peeled his white works top off and was sitting slouched in his chair with his feet up on the chair in front of him. I wasn't even sure if any of those activities were permitted. In a millisecond I knew who this plebe was.

A month earlier, I had received a list of two names in the mail via the academy. There was not much detail to the letter other than the name of my two future roommates and the company number I had been assigned.

"Nicky Gonzalez," said my newly found acquaintance, "but I guess you already knew that."

Instead of trying to politely reply with, "What do you mean by that?" I simply chuckled and replied, "Well, I'm no Sherlock Holmes, but it's pretty easy to guess which guy in this section has a name like Gonzalez."

Gonzalez's look suddenly became serious as he lowered his eyebrows in a visual display of scorn. "What the fuck is that supposed to mean?"

I was taken for a loss as my sweat began to sweat.

After a slow pause, just enough to garner the split second enjoyment of viewing my shockingly apologetic face, he broke the tension. "Ah man, I'm just fucking with you, homey!" He extended his hand outward for a firm hand-shake.

"My name's Nicky if you ask my mom," he continued, "but my friends call me Gonzo. You can call me Nick for now, the jury's still out on you, homey." He smiled, "You gotta earn Gonzo privileges."

"Cool, it's nice to meet you, Nick. My name is . . ."

"McGee," Gonzalez interrupted, "Jim McGee. I know all 'bout you, dawg."

You don't know shit about me.

If I hadn't known this guy was going to be my room-mate for the next year, I would have verbalized my inter-nal dialogue.

"My name's Jim, but I go by Mick," I replied.

"Wow, offering up the nickname right off the bat. I guess you can call me Gonzo then," Gonzalez replied with another coy smile. He could sense that I was put off by the initial dialogue so I presumed this was his way of getting things back on the right course without having to apolo-gize for coming on so strong. There was still a part of me that wondered if he even cared about that.

Gonzo was a tiny Puerto Rican, standing no taller than five foot six. Compared to the rest of our classmates, he was certainly on the pudgy side of physique. I was still pretty sure I could kick his ass if needed. Then I figured he may be scrappier than he appears as his bold mouth surely had him in fisticuffs on more than a few occasions.

"You see that big brotha over there?" Gonzo interrupt-ed my sizing him up and pointed two rows down to a ro-bust looking African American sitting quietly in his seat.

"Yo, N.D.!" Gonzo yelled and a light skinned, rather

large African American turned around to acknowledge the shout with a brief head nod before he stood up and headed our way.

I couldn't immediately guess his identity as I just did of Gonzo. While there was only one Hispanic looking company mate in my seating area, there were two African American classmates. The last thing I wanted to do was guess wrong and start on the wrong foot.

Okafor was a mountain of a man standing around six foot four. He had fists the size of bowling balls and forearms strong enough to carry those bowling ball sized hands. He and Gonzo had clearly met earlier, and though I initially wondered what the connection was, I figured Gonzo would end up telling me all about it soon enough.

"S'up, Gonzo," calmly replied Okafor giving Gonzalez a soulful handshake that would have looked ridiculous if executed by two white guys. He and Gonzo were the two guys in the seating area that didn't seem completely sweat drenched and stressed at the moment. I was hoping they could teach me their collective secret, if one even existed.

I had initially noticed Okafor earlier in the day while sitting in my last line for uniform pants. I surmised that he had entered Alumni Hall a few groups ahead of my entrance group. He was delayed in line as the uniform ladies scrambled to get their paws on the largest pair of white works pants they could find. By the time I received my ill-fitting garments, I noticed they had found Okafor a pair of well-fitting pants.

That figures. They can't find clothes for an average built five-foot-ten plebe, but they can tailor fit you if you're built like Godzilla.

"Hey N.D.," Gonzo continued. "This is your other roomie, Jim McGee." He added, "It looks like we are officially the room of racial equality now."

"My friends call me Mick," I said trying not to convey how utterly awkward I felt being the lone white member of the room. I broke the awkward silence and added, "It's nice to finally meet the two guys I'll be living with for the next year."

"Likewise, man. My name is Ndbuze," he started his formal introduction, "but my friends, and those that get tongue tied by traditional Nigerian names," he cracked a smile and looked over at Gonzo surely acknowledging one of Gonzo's previous transgressions, "call me N.D." At that exact moment, I made up my mind that I liked this guy.

"Good to meet you, Mick. I'll catch you guys at the room. I gotta holla at some of my teammates over there," N.D. said pointing two sections over to some other larger looking classmates. It didn't take a rocket scientist to figure out what sport they all played.

"Yo, N.D. is supposed to be one hell of a football player, dawg," Gonzo said interrupting my gazing. "Some of the enlisted guys I know that went to NAPS last year said he was the best football recruit Navy has landed in the past five years. He's a beast of a defensive end."

NAPS was short for the Naval Academy Prep School. A place where many of the prior enlisted and recruited varsity athletes spent a year in a "plebe-light" environment. For many of the enlisted guys, NAPS was a chance to beef up their academics since many of them, though extremely intelligent, enlisted in the military by route of fucking off in high school. They needed NAPS as a venue to demonstrate their previously unproven academic rigor. For the varsity athletes NAPS had academic intent, but it was also a "red shirt year." This meant that NAPS athletes were given an extra year to learn the playbook of their respective sport and beef up in the weight room. They were also simultaneously learning how to clean their rooms and polish their shoes in a military fashion one full year before the rest of us normal plebes had the chance. It was certainly an advantage, but it also meant a full extra year of military bullshit. They earned whatever advantage that garnered.

"My boys on the football team said this kid can flat out ball," Gonzo continued gushing. "He was Mr. Corn Husker in Nebraska his senior year and turned down major scholarships at Big 12 schools to come here right out of high school."

"Plus, get this, his pops is some crazy math professor at Nebraska, and he wanted his son to come to the academy for engineering," Gonzo continued giving me the remainder of the N.D. biography. "Can you believe that shit?" he queried, "a full ride to play football in a Big 12 school and you willingly come here to eat shit for a year."

It was the first thought Gonzo came up with that I could relate to. I then spent the next twenty-three minutes pretending to pay attention to Gonzo's sea stories of his enlisted days as a machinist mate. He also talked about his admission into the academy, which did not come via NAPS but rather some other program. It was a detailed story full of confusing acronyms and military jargon that I did not pay appropriate attention to. All the while, I was daydreaming about what life might be like for an eighteen-year-old starting at defensive end at a place like the University of Missouri or Texas A&M. My imaginations were a far cry from my current state of affairs.

Suddenly my happy daydreaming was rudely interrupted by a red name-tagged detailer. After a variety of unmemorable introductions and instructions, we were all shortly thereafter taken from temporary oasis. It was time to head back to the processing factory.

Chapter 2

Hanging with the Fellas
Saturday, June 24th, 1995
Mick, 1230 hrs.

I pulled Yogi into the first parking spot within sight. The suburban streets of a vanilla track neighborhood in Delaware's capital city of Dover were apparently the place to be. Nearly every bit of street parking was occupied on an otherwise sleepy Saturday afternoon.

My brakes screeched to a halt, and I cranked the parking brake by force of habit on a dead flat road. I took one last drag of my half-smoked cigarette and flicked it out of the window when I assumed no one was looking my way. Nicotine tended to help cool my jets.

My forthcoming social situation fueled my anxiety. I hated the thought of being the stranger at the party. By June of '95, I had been to plenty of graduation parties. This was the first that also included a Naval Academy send off. My social circle was a bit different from what I imagined I'd be walking into this afternoon.

I was one spot shy of a stop sign guarding the cul-de-sac's exit. Naively I had driven the full loop of the ten-home dead end. Thinking I could find a spot closer to my final destination was wishful at best.

The cul-de-sac looked as though a 4th of July block party was in full swing. American flags and blue and gold streamers hung from each of the home's mailboxes. At the end of the road was a home that looked ninety percent identical to the neighboring homes. The entire neighborhood was a massive collection of cookie cutter colonials that varied by little else than shutter paint and the occasional basketball hoop cemented beside the driveway. I didn't need to look at the street numbers displayed atop the mailboxes to figure out where I needed to be. The twenty bikes piled on the front lawn and the sign posted behind them was all the marking I needed.

"Anchors Away, Danny," I read aloud to myself accompanied by a sarcastic smirk and chuckle.

I pulled out the invite from my board short's pocket for one last verification. I had driven to the party directly from a morning surf session at the southside of the Indian River Inlet. I unfolded the postcard and could feel the slight graininess of sand on its corners. I visually scanned the details I was looking for: Graduation Party, Danny Hudson, Belmont Court.

I guess this is the place.

Dover, Delaware marked the middle of the state. It also made a logical initial rendezvous point for Delaware's eight future members of the Naval Academy's class of '99. Hailing from Delaware's shoreline town of Lewes, I was proud to be the lone beach dweller of the bunch.

I had lived the first half of my childhood in Wilmington, Delaware. It all happened within a typical "All American Middle Class Family." It looked a lot like where I was currently headed. White suburbs, summer vacations to the beach, and Hershey Park. We went skiing a few times in the Poconos. I even remember Mom and Dad mentioning they wanted to give me a sister. Those plans, along with the rest of my typical American dream, went to shit when he died.

Eventually I was knocking between Ocean City, Maryland and Lewes, Delaware after my dad passed. My mom permanently moved us to Lewes once she felt emotionally stable enough to do so two years ago. My aunt let the two of us crash with her in Ocean City in the interim.

Danny Hudson had agreed to offer his graduation party as a dual venue. Every fellow classmate invited to the party lived no longer than an hour drive from Dover. Most of us had gone to different high schools and had never actually met. This party was a convenient way for all of us to meet up.

I crumpled the postcard invitation and tossed it into a gutter. I almost never littered. My nerves were making me act out of sorts. I approached the home's car-packed driveway. I could begin to smell the hot dogs roasting on the grill. The twang of country music became audible from around the house's corner. Everything seemed to be emanating from behind the house.

I quickly tossed a few pieces of Trident gum into my mouth. I hoped the citrus orange flavor would cover up the stench of the freshly smoked cigarette on my breath. I had cleaned my hands back at the car with a McDonald's wet wipe. Again breaking habit, I tossed the gum wrappers into the small bushes in the mulched landscaping beside me.

I approached the front door opting for the more traditional arrival. I briefly considered walking directly into the action in the backyard. I opted against it. I didn't feel familiar enough to make that informal an entrance.

I pressed the doorbell button twice before realizing it was broken. I knocked on the glass storm door. Behind the glass, the main door was open. Inside I could see groups of children running around like a pack of wild monkeys.

Waiting on the front door step, I stood below three flags proudly flying on small posts attached to the window above the front door. Looking upwards, I immediately recognized the American and Navy flag. It took an additional few seconds to read the letters of the third. It was an Air Force flag. I imagined most of the neighborhood had some association to the Air Force. The Dover Air Force base was just a few miles down the road. It was one of the biggest bases on the east coast and by far Dover's biggest employer. Danny Hudson was likely an Air Force brat.

Great. One more classmate nothing at all like me.

About three minutes of waiting after my initial knock, a young blond-haired boy answered the door amidst a pile of toys and sporting equipment strewn about the hardwood floor. He looked like Dennis the Menace with a crew cut.

"Come on in, help yourself to whatever food you'd like," said the obnoxiously mature child. I assumed he was one of Danny's much younger family members. He quickly broke character and resumed running with the three other young hellions screaming down the hallway.

"Come on in and head to the back. We're all out here!" I heard a loud woman's voice scream from beyond the open sliding glass window in the kitchen. I could see her petite silhouette waving me outdoors while the other hand sported a wine glass. I took a deep breath and followed orders.

Despite the festive exuberance in the entry hallway, everyone inside the home looked like they were dressed for church. I brushed my T-shirt off to ensure I had wiped all of the sand off before heading out to the back deck. I was feeling more out of place by the second.

After a round of introductions to various family members and neighbors, I finally found my temporary social circle. Four guys and two girls that looked roughly my age were gathered together in one corner of the patio around a large round glass table. Half of the six people seated were wearing Navy T-shirts.

"Hey everyone, I'm Micky," I formally introduced myself to what I assumed was a group of future Naval Academy classmates.

There was a brief silence. My introduction was taking longer than expected to process. A few more awkward seconds passed.

"You must be Jim McGee," replied the lone male seated at the table not wearing a Naval Academy blazoned shirt. "Aka Micky." The friendly stranger had opted toward the more traditional white preppy look of khaki shorts, green polo, and a haircut meant for Sunday service.

Two other dudes seated beside each other politely smiled and nodded their heads. It had just dawned on them that I too was a future classmate and not just another one of Danny's high school friends.

"I'm Danny, Danny Hudson," the friendly prep said

getting out of his seat and waking over to shake my hand.

"Nice to meet you, and thanks for inviting me to your party," I said trying my best to fit in and generally be a gracious guest.

"I see that you met Micky," obnoxiously interrupted an older but attractive blond woman holding a well-used glass of white wine. She placed her arm over my shoulder and around me. Her perfume singed my nose hairs. It felt awkward. It was too friendly too fast. I had just been introduced to her moments earlier. She had been the waving silhouette from the sliding glass door. I quickly grabbed the open seat next to where Danny had just re-seated himself. The shade of the table's umbrella provided a welcome respite from the hot sun and artificial scent.

"Yeah, Sally, we're all good, thanks," Danny replied smugly wiping the sweat from his brow.

"Is that your mom?" I asked Danny once the woman had moved far enough away not to hear us. She had introduced herself as Sally when I met her with her arm wrapped around Danny's father. She appeared much younger than most moms I knew.

"Step-mom," he quickly clarified. "My mom still lives in Colorado."

I was about to ask what brought him to Delaware but I opted against it. My mind was already racing with assumptions to answer those questions. Danny's dad fooled around with a younger blond. Divorce followed, out popped a younger towheaded step-brother. Air Force Dad got the hell out of dodge. Welcome to Dover, Delaware. I kept my curiosities as to why Danny tagged along quiet. There was no sense in raising a likely sore subject.

"I followed my dad to Delaware because I thought it would increase my odds of getting into the academy. You know, Delaware being a smaller state and all," he explained as though reading my mind. "I guess it paid off."

Broken home, running away, maybe I'm not so different after all.

"So have you guys gotten a hold of Reef Points yet?" asked one of my other future classmates seated around the table to the general audience. He was tall and already sporting a neatly groomed flat top. I could still see the remnants of his morning haircut on his gold Navy Crew T-shirt.

I didn't answer the question. It was clearly posed as an opportunity for him to talk about his own experience with Reef Points. I had barely heard of it. I just knew it as something we'd have to study endlessly this summer.

"I don't know, I guess a little," replied Danny finally interjecting himself into the previously one-sided conversation. "I figured I would just learn that stuff for real when I get down there. They've shortened my summer vacation enough."

My three other classmates eventually chimed in to indicate that they had indeed been studying Reef Points diligently. They were at least polite enough to not obnoxiously boast about it like crew boy had moments earlier.

The more I listened, the more I felt the anxiety of being potentially underprepared. Despite this anxiety, I sided with Danny. Taking his blasé attitude a step further, I refused to waste even a moment of my remaining summer on studying to be a plebe.

"Plebe Year seems shitty enough as it is, why make it

any longer than in has to be by adding prep time," I finally joined the dialogue and piled onto Danny's initial sentiments. I had spent enough time listening to my other future classmates drone on about poems and other pointless shit they had spent their early summer memorizing. Everyone, save Danny, looked at me like I had a horn growing out of my head. I'm sure they had already written me off as someone that would be sent packing for home before the fall. I knew I'd prove them wrong.

In short time, the table crowd dispersed. I spent the next hour shooting the shit with the man of the hour. In that time, I learned that Danny Hudson had originally wanted to go to the Air Force Academy. His dad was a graduate of the Air Force Academy's class of 1975, and Danny had grown up with glorified tales of his academy experience. His dad's marital indiscretions with an Air Force Academy Gift Shop employee while he was stationed there quickly changed Danny's allegiance. The Naval Academy was a fair compromise.

"Anchors Away, Danny," Danny recited as we passed the sign on the front lawn. We were sneaking back to my car to grab a cigarette. Moments earlier I told him I needed to grab a smoke and to my surprise, he asked to join.

Danny quickly lit a smoke from his own pack just before getting to my car and leaning against it. Yogi was a shitty enough car that people automatically assumed they could lean and sit on it without asking. I never minded. Danny offered his Camels before I opened Yogi's driver side door. I politely declined opting toward my Marlboro preference.

"Can you believe that shit?" Danny queried within an angry laugh and a point towards his house at the end of the street.

"When I first saw that sign in front of your house I was worried that you put that up there," I replied.

Danny took an extra-long drag of his smoke and held it in. Shaking his head, he finally let out a long exhale. His white trash habit juxtaposed against his preppy look was comical yet endearing.

"No matter how bad this summer gets, it's got to be better than putting up with another summer of my drunken whore step-mother," Danny dictated to the open air in front of him within a cloud of cigarette smoke.

Quickly I tried to change the subject. Soon I was rambling on about the beach and my favorite surf spots. Within ten minutes Danny was convinced he needed to finally make the hour and a half jaunt from Dover to Ocean City, Maryland to see that part of the shore. I let him know I was having an informal get together with some family and friends at my aunt's house later that night.

Who was I to pre-emptively limit his interest in what I thought was an otherwise underrated place?

Mick, 2030 hrs.

A small party emanated a raucous from a screened-in porch on the side of an unassuming house on pilings. The roof was weathered. The gutters had piles of rotten leaves and sticks visibly protruding outwards. What was once a lone house on stilts fifty yards from marshland and two miles from the beach had since been accompanied by several other larger homes exploiting their bayside location. A stunning and unobstructed twilight view of the Assawoman Bay in West Ocean City, Maryland began unveiling a sparkling reflection of the setting sun. A motley crew of young adult males uniformly appreciated the respite and cool bay breeze of sunset within the dilapidated porch. The heat and humidity in early summer of '95 had been brutal already. Save for the handful of mosquitos that squeezed their way through the sporadic holes in the porch screen, the venue provided a perfect oasis from the heat of a few hours earlier.

"All of the movie stars are doin' it these days," said the Caucasian twenty-something sporting salt drenched red dreads on the porch rocking chair. His pale skin held the maximum mix of suntan and burn that it could. His leathery outer shell peeled like a snake shedding its skin.

"Peeing while sitting down. Dudes peeing in the hopper while sitting down," continued the peculiar ginger, "all the Hollywood types are doin' it."

"Bird, man, that sounds like some shit you just pulled out of your ass," said the bronzed yet portly stoner named Farm sitting on a mold encrusted bean bag chair. The well-used seat had been left on the screened porch one too many times during a Nor'easter.

The entire porch felt like a marijuana sauna with its combination of Mid-Atlantic Summer evening humidity and clouds of reefer smoke fueled by a large, blazing joint being passed around. I hadn't anticipated weed making such a prevalent appearance before nightfall. Knowing that military indoctrination was weeks away, I had no problem abstaining. I was pissed the porch couldn't hold off while Danny Hudson was my guest. He was made noticeably uncomfortable by the joint. I tried my best to hide my annoyance. I imagined at some point in high school Danny had seen a joint. I doubted he had seen one openly smoked at a family function in the waning minutes of daylight.

"Yeah? Where'd ya hear that, 'cause it sounds like your being facetious," said the surfer known as Turtle sprawled out on the porch floor. He had received his name from the beloved character and handsome blond-haired doofus featured in the cheesy '80s surf flick "North Shore." This Turtle was more doofus than handsome.

"Facetious?" replied Bird. "Nah man, I just took a shit fifteen minutes ago."

There were several surfers on the porch that evening. We were known as the "Fellas." The group name was born through the several hundred times Bird watched Scorsese's *Good Fellas*. There were eight of us. Seven of us processed our new guest with great interest. They were getting a slight glimpse into my future journey. I was the first midshipman they had ever known. This would be their second.

Danny had been intrigued enough by my descriptions of the Maryland shoreline earlier in the afternoon. After dinner, he made the southward bound trip down Highway 1. He wanted to see what this place was all about.

All of the Fellas were good surfers. Some were better than others. The Fellas hardly competed with each other but mostly relished in the fellowship of a small surfing community in Ocean City. The Fellas shared two key elements of commonality: surfing waves and smoking weed. I was the exception to that rule. They understood the Navy tested for drugs and were cool with my abstinence.

It is worth noting that most of the Fellas leaned to a particular side of these common elements. Guys like Shawn Devlin, aka Turtle, were great surfers and dabbled in marijuana. Farm was the exact opposite, a very serviceable surfer, but at his core, a stoner.

Bird was the only member of the Fellas that perfectly embodied both of these characteristics. He was a phenomenal surfer, perhaps the best of the bunch and one of the best on the Delmarva shoreline. He was also a consummate stoner. These traits made Bird the natural leader of the group.

"I read that peeing on the hopper story in the paper the other day," Bird continued his seated urination tale. "So you know it's gotta be true."

That was bullshit. I hadn't seen Bird read a newspaper in at least two years. The weather channel and the local radio surf report was about all the news he cared about.

"What paper was that, Birdman?" asked Danny, desperately eager to make small talk.

Bird looked towards Danny, his glassy bloodshot eyes fixated on this newcomer since he entered into the party ten minutes earlier. I cringed in anticipation. Danny looked like he had walked out of last summer's JC Penny's catalogue. He stuck out like a sore thumb.

I looked over to Bird and gave him a quick nod as if to say, *"It's okay, man, this guy's cool. Don't be an asshole."* The room's tension remained.

Under normal circumstances, if any of the Fellas had

seen this "barney" walking down Highway 1 they would have given him the typical Ocean City tourist welcome. This came in the form of an aptly thrown jelly donut to the target's head from their speeding car.

Why would this time be any different?

"Dude, his name is Bird," blurted Turtle from the floor.

"Oh man, sorry, Bird," Danny politely gestured towards Bird. A bead of sweat slid down the side of his face and ultimately dropped from his cheek onto his previously spotless golf shirt. "I thought I just heard that guy over there call you Birdman. I must have misheard him," said Danny as he pointed over to Farm.

"No, dude," responded Farm in a very relaxed voice as he exhaled a smoke cloud. "What I said was Bird, comma, man that sounds like some shit."

An awkward silence ensued.

Danny would have blended in anonymously in most traditional settings with his clean cut looks and mid-western vocabulary, but this was Bird's porch. There was nothing mid-western about it or its current inhabitants.

Technically the porch was Aunt Nellie's, who also happened to be Bird's mom. My mom and I lived there for the first few years after my dad passed, right up until I graduated junior high. This was not coincidentally about the same time it took my grieving mother to temporarily escape the grasp of her depression and alcohol. Bird still lived with Nellie despite his 1960ish birthday and a financially lucrative job as a top pharmaceuticals salesman. Pharmaceutical sales was just another term for selling weed.

Even before Bird became a full-fledged drug dealer, Farm and Bird were constant occupants of Aunt Nellie's porch throughout their adolescence. They often talked about the waves they rode that morning and speculated on what the waves the next day might look like. Bird even made Nellie get a cable connection on the porch so they could watch the weather channel for hours at a time. They would hang on the weatherman's report in a way their high school teachers could have only hoped for. Then, after a few tokes, the conversation would transition into discussions of what female cartoon characters they would like to fuck, and possible locations of Aunt Nellie's extra-large box of Fruity Pebbles. Many years had passed, but these types of conversations were a constant.

Aunt Nellie's head peeked through the partially opened door from the interior of the house leading to the porch. She typically left this door wide open to let some breeze into the house. She almost never utilized the central air installed a few years earlier and hence needed all help possible just to keep the interior temperature below 80 degrees. This evening the door was kept partially closed to avoid getting a contact high in the adjoining kitchen. She had been in the kitchen chatting with my mom since before I arrived hours earlier.

"Larry, you seen my nail clippers?" she asked Bird nonchalantly and totally un-phased by the people and smell occupying her porch.

"Yeah, they're in the oven where you usually keep them," quipped Bird in a smart-assed tone. The comment had been tongue in cheek for two reasons. First, Aunt Nellie had a tendency to stow her personal belongings in completely random places. Second, she rarely, if ever, cooked in her oven. These habits severely aggravated my cousin.

Nellie was the only person on Earth with modern day "Larry" privileges. Bird picked up his current name while wearing #33 on a junior high basketball team he had been forced to play on by his mother. Nellie had made him play on the team with Farm in fear that they were both getting too pudgy. Bird eventually slimmed down, Farm didn't. The nickname stuck.

After Nellie's temporary distraction from the awkward silence, Bird calmly closed his eyes and took a deep breath. It was audible enough to make everyone on the porch pause and look over towards Bird. Suddenly Bird burst out laughing.

"Hey, Bunkie, no worries," Bird continued through his stoned giggles and with the appearance of a strung out Ronald McDonald. "Any friend of Micky's is a friend of mine." He rose from his rocking chair seat and extended his hand for a soul shake. Danny obliged with his own extended hand. He looked horrified.

Most white guys didn't even know the meaning of the word Bunkie. Then again most white guys hadn't spent any extended time in prison. Bird had. Dealing drugs had its benefits, but it also came with obvious risks. "Bunkie" was actually a friendly phrase used amongst cellmates in behind bars. I'm sure most of Bird's actual bunkies weren't as amicable in tone. Good or bad, the phrase was embedded in his vernacular. It typically sounded lame if a white guy used the term "bunkie" regularly. When Bird said it, it actually sounded a little dangerous, at least to a Caucasian that had never spent any time in the pen.

Danny may have gotten more than he bargained for once he came down to the shore that day. It didn't take long to realize smoking cigarettes was about as much rebellion as Danny could handle. I should have figured as much.

Moments after his first interaction with Bird, he seemed quite eager to get off that porch. He went inside and asked Nellie if he could use her phone. Within minutes, he came outside to explain rationale for sudden departure. Apparently his brother unexpectedly needed a babysitter. It was total bullshit.

"What the flying fuck, man?" I laid into Bird, as soon as Danny left.

"What?" Bird asked in genuine curiosity.

"The weed. That shit could get my ass kicked out of the academy. I just met Danny this morning and now he just stormed out of Cheech and Chong's graduation party. If he were to tell the academy about that shit, I'd get booted before I ever got there."

"Relax, Bunkie," Bird assured. "It's not illegal to watch someone smoke fucking weed."

"That's not the point. You knew he was coming, and I told you he might be a little square. It's a respect thing, man."

"Sorry, Micky, I really didn't mean anything by it. You should've just asked." All of the other Fellas nodded. I could sense slight remorse.

"I shouldn't have to," I dejectedly replied. I was fine. I just hated that this type of shit was the norm. It was part of the reason I was running away from it.

Chapter 3

I-Day Conclusion
Friday, June 24th, 1995
Mick, 1530 hrs.

After a morning full of commotion, an eerie silence draped the yard. The frenetic energy of I-Day morning had reached a temporary climax back at Alumni Hall. After receiving seemingly hours of introductions and military instruction, the final portion of processed plebes were marched about a half mile down Stribling Walk. Stribling was the academy's brick paved thoroughfare, and the direct pathway back into the belly of the beast. By mid-afternoon, we had finally arrived at our future home, Bancroft Hall.

The tour guides of Maryland's historic state capital would routinely tell visitors that its resident Naval Academy Midshipmen would affectionately call their massive dorm room "Mother B." Even when I heard this a year earlier as an actual tourist, I knew that was bullshit. As I entered Bancroft for the first time as a midshipman, I found it far more likely that this holding cell of a dorm would be referenced as something a little more profane than the matriarchal visions that the local tourists were led to believe.

"Alright, plebers, once we get downstairs into King Hall, ya'll need to stuff your faces so I can get y'all into your rooms before you swear your life away to Uncle Sam," one of our assigned detailers commanded, emphasizing a sense of urgency as we prepared to eat our last meal ahead of being formally sworn into the military. King Hall was a massive T-shaped dining facility. It was large enough to host all four thousand plus midshipman at once during sit down meals that would occur once the full brigade returned home. It seemed cavernous with the sparse amounts of plebes dining.

"For those of you that don't know already," continued the nearby detailer. "This will be one of the few non-squared meals that you will have this summer. Enjoy it while you can."

As I would soon learn by observing the demonstrating detailer, squaring meals was the practice of lifting your food loaded fork straight up from the plate, transitioning fork trajectory at a right angle to the mouth, and then placing the fork on the table between each bite. It was a less than efficient way to eat. That was the point.

This was the first of many rules and restrictions the detailer continued to articulate. Judging by the volume of King Hall, detailers were prohibited from yelling at us during our last "civilian" meal. Depressing us with all of our soon to be restrictions and prohibited activities was a fair compromise. I assumed it was also a fun way for detailers to ensure that we hated the experience as much as they had two years earlier. We all sat dejected hearing about how television, phones, radios, and free time in general were all soon to be things of the past.

After about seven bites of a meal I was barely paying attention to, we were being hustled by every detailer within eyesight, obviously running behind schedule. The lines and ineptitude of the check-in process had us running at least an hour behind the anticipated schedule.

"Giddy up, plebers, time to go." We were prodded like cattle to get moving.

After eating lunch in total silence with my fellow plebes, we were reassembled for a quick exit. All of us were lugging mammoth sea bags filled to the brim with all of the recently issued crap the Naval Academy spent the entire morning shelling out to us. A few of the female plebes looked comical carrying these body-sized bags, but to their credit, they carried them without complaining or asking for help.

In addition to squared meals, being a plebe meant living within many crazy rules and regulations for personal commuting in Bancroft Hall. For starters, it meant that if plebes were in the halls of Bancroft between 0700 and 1900, they were running or as the midshipman call it "chopping." Second, when you did go chopping out of the room, you were to stay in the middle of the hallway or to the outside of the stairwell. Third, it meant that any time you turned, it would be only at a 90-degree angle and each turn would be accompanied by an alternating scream of "Go Navy" or a "Beat Army." This was all mandated as a way to demonstrate our love of the Army Navy football rivalry that in 1995 was rumbling towards its 96th occurrence.

There were many other rules thrown our way that day. Most of them I had already forgotten. We learned how to stand at attention, how to salute, and how to fold clothes in a military manner. Much of the crap we needed to know was spelled out in my hardly used copy of "Reef Points." Its contents were already being beaten over our heads by the detailers all afternoon. I finally understood why my Delawarean classmates back at Danny Hudson's party had studied its contents so thoroughly this summer.

Reef Points was a plebe's bible. It was one of the first things handed to every plebe checking into I-Day. We were required to carry it everywhere. In addition to detailed descriptions of naval basics, Reef Points also had a bunch of other random stories and quotes. I had already assumed detailers would be forcing us to memorize each and every one of them. Their mandated recitals I assumed would provide ample opportunity for detailers to yell at us for not learning them fast enough. I half-heartedly studied them while waiting in a few of the day's earlier lines. I was sure my motivation to study would increase shortly.

I checked my pants pocket for the seventeenth time fearing in typical form that I would lose my newly prized possession. Gonzo hadn't even opened his Reef Points yet. I'm not sure if that was calming or worrisome. I'd find out soon enough.

After being led through a maze of turns and staircases in the underbelly of Bancroft Hall, we were led up four flights of stairs and eventually arrived at our residence for the summer.

"Motherfucker," whispered a wheezing Gonzo as we finally reached the entrance to our room. We had the unlucky designation of being stranded on the top floor, which meant plenty of stairs to supplement the other many physical poundings of the summer. N.D, Gonzo, and I entered a room filled with additional boxes of gear.

"Fuck, it's hot as balls in here," I narrated to my new roomies. Even though I knew ahead of Plebe Summer that Bancroft lacked central air, the sweaty reality warranted comment.

The room's floor space was a bit larger than a standard prison cell to accommodate three large desks in the middle of the room. There was a small shower the size of a telephone booth and a sink area directly connected to it in the front corner of the room. Our toilet, otherwise known as the Men's Room, was twenty yards down the hall through a gauntlet of detailers. I would have rather pooped in the sink. The whole space smelled like a dusty church basement in hell.

"Alright, ladies and gents," said the Navy Lieutenant walking past us in the hall as we finally arrived on the 4th floor. "Everyone form up in the wardroom in fifteen minutes, don't want to be late." The detailers then scurried up and down the hallway conveying a menacing presence while softly but assertively rehashing the lieutenant's orders. "Fifteen minutes form up, form up in fifteen minutes, hurry up, and stash your trash." Part of this routine was informative, but I surmised the majority of it was just to rattle our collective nerves.

Though nothing was overtly said, we all figured out quickly in our time at Alumni Hall that the upper-class detailers weren't allowed to officially harass us until we took the upcoming "oath of office" in an hour. The "oath" was when we formally swore our allegiance and lives to protecting freedom in the United States Navy. Gonzo knew this before most of us did and used this opportunity to crack jokes and whisper smart-ass remarks throughout the morning. I was just hoping he wasn't painting a giant bull's-eye on himself when shit hit the fan in about an hour. The detailers so far were limited to indirect intimidation. That helped explain the cold and distant attitude of the day. I had a sinking feeling that things would be much more hot and heavy later in the day once we were sworn in and made official.

Most of the seven detailers that I had visibly counted thus far continued to silently yet frantically pace up and down the hallway. Occasionally they would shoot an intimidating glare into random plebe rooms. Though nothing was said, the look exuded the notion: *"Enjoy this temporary truce right now, shit bird, because tonight means war!"*

Gonzo, N.D., and I had been in our rooms for precisely two minutes. I imagined that we were intended to get more time to check into our new digs, but long lines and clusterfucks beyond my pay grade prevented that from happening. I did not get much of a chance to meet my plebe company mates outside of my roommates. I had noticed in the handful of rooms that I passed on the way to mine that most plebes had their sea bag and new boxes unpacked and on the way to full storage. This was likely because they checked in earlier and had extra preparatory time. The rationale did not help my building feeling of panic.

I dumped my bag on the floor and immediately began

to pack my stuff away. Gonzo and N.D. followed suit but not nearly in the same frantic manner. I then noticed we had yet to pick a bunk situation. I worried that my room-mates might take my sea bag's floor dump by the lone bed to the left of the room versus the bunk set on the right side as a sign of presumption and entitlement. It was the very last thing I wanted to convey in the room of "racial equal-ity."

"Don't sweat the racks, dawg," quickly chimed Gonzo. "They'll make us switch them up at least five times this week. Just one of the many ways they will try to fuck with your head."

Though Gonzo was a blow hard, his conviction in speaking towards anything remotely military, was surpris-ingly reassuring. At least someone knew what they were doing. Gonzo had already taught me that beds were racks, bathrooms were heads, and stairways were ladders. He was my long-winded and obnoxious translator of military vernacular.

Gonzo also knew exactly what to unpack, how to fold it, and where to store it. N.D. was smart enough to im-mediately follow suit without asking many questions. His football buddies had probably given him that good advice earlier in the day. I, on the other hand, was too frazzled to figure out Gonzo already knew a thing or two about prepping a military inspection-ready room. I spent the first seven minutes in my room randomly fiddling with my newly acquired clothes and gear. I was desperately try-ing to fold them but making very little progress. In the ten minutes since we'd entered our room, my roommates were completely unpacked and stowed while my pile of gear and half emptied boxes were still accumulated on the floor in a disorganized mess.

"Damn, Mick," said Gonzo, "you're all ate up, homey."

My initial reaction to Gonzo was continued scorn but quickly transitioned into gratitude. In less than five minutes, he had folded and stored a third of my stuff.

"All the stuff folded in the closet are necessities," said Gonzo as he continued, "the rest of this shit I'll just throw in your sea bag and we can hide it behind the locked portion of the closet and put it away later."

"Thanks, man," I replied with a newfound level of respect.

"No worries, homey," quipped Gonzo. "Just listen to my advice and we'll get you through this."

Perhaps Gonzo isn't such a bad guy after all.

In the last few minutes before we needed to gather in the wardroom, Gonzo and N.D. began putting out personal pictures on their desk's ink blotter. Each of us had one, and it was the only space permitted to display personal effects of any kind.

"Rule numero uno, Wonderbread," continued Gonzo, "if I catch you over here jerkin' off to this picture of my sister. I'll cut your throat while you sleep."

Great, one more rule to add to the list of one hundred and thirty seven already provided today. Maybe friendship is a bit of a stretch.

N.D. had remained quiet during this time. Once he mimicked Gonzo and got his stuff stowed, he spent the remaining time reading what I presumed to be a love letter, given the pink ink written on the multi-pages of accumulated loose-leaf paper. He was mesmerized.

He finished reading the letter. I assumed it was not for

the first time. He reached into his bag and pulled out a set of pictures. The first was of his mom and dad with N.D. in a cap and gown. It was seemingly from high school graduation a few weeks earlier. The rest of the pictures were of a rather attractive blond co-ed in a variety of short and skimpy outfits.

"Damn, N.D.," Gonzo blurted as he finished out filling his blotter with pictures, "I didn't realize that's how you roll."

My teeth clenched anticipating Gonzo to blurt out yet another blatantly inappropriate comment, but even he wasn't that stupid. N.D. looked up at Gonzo, smiled, and silently chuckled. "You know that's how I roll. That's my girl, Sara, from back home."

I, on the other hand, avoided saying anything about N.D.'s blond bombshell. I also avoided making any comments about the bevy of attractive Puerto Rican beauties on Gonzo's blotter. I feared any or all of them could be family and could subsequently get me knifed. I had but one picture. It was a family shot on the beach during the late spring of 1990. I was a pudgy and awkward thirteen-year-old at the time. It was my favorite picture because it was the last one taken of my full family. My dad died just two months after, in a motorcycle accident. For a fleeting glimpse, I was lost in that moment. I still missed him.
"Showtime, dawg," N.D. then interrupted as he stood from his seat and headed to the door.

As I entered the wardroom, a common television room within company area, I immediately appreciated the air-conditioning. The hurried nature of the fifteen minutes in my newly assigned room precluded me from noticing the 80 degree heat in the non-air-conditioned midshipman rooms. As soon as I entered, I was blasted with a cool caress of mechanically cooled air and the joyous hum of a window air conditioner unit. By the time all thirty plus plebes in the company filtered into the room, the temperature had risen ten degrees. The air began to smell like a dirty gym sock.

"Alright, guys," said the lieutenant, "this is your big moment." LT Chris Walker had formally introduced himself briefly when our partial plebe company was grouped together back at Alumni Hall. He actually seemed like a nice enough guy. He had graduated from the academy just four years earlier. This was his first time back to Annapolis. He had just started his job as our company officer, our senior officer representative ultimately responsible for our collective company's wellbeing, or at least to ensure nobody killed each other. After spending four years aboard various ships, he and his pregnant wife were excited about the oncoming shore duty.

A few brief introductions and rah-rah speeches were given by LT Walker and a few of the detailers. I paid attention to none of them. I was just trying to soak in the last few minutes of air-conditioning and quiet voices. I suspected both would soon be a big rarity in my life.

Finally, the wardroom's television was turned on. Other than for training purposes, plebe midshipman were not allowed to watch television during their freshman year, so this privileged visit to the wardroom would be rare.

LT Walker pulled a VHS tape out of its sleeve. It had a piece of white tape on the exposed edge with "I-Day Oath" sloppily written on it in black marker. Judging from the decrepit nature of the box holding it, I imagined the tape predated our arrival by several years. From what little I did pay attention to in the last fifteen minutes of instruction, this video was meant to fully describe the oath we were about to take and all of the formalities and legal implications induced upon saying "I do" to the oath.

As LT Walker fumbled to get the tape out of its box, he inserted it into a well-used VCR player. Multiple lines of thick fuzz appeared on the screen as LT pushed the play button. He then proceeded to fiddle with the tracking settings, eject the tape, blow on it, insert it again, bang it on the side of the television. It didn't matter. The result was the same.

After ten minutes of futile attempts, LT Walker gave up. "Well, unfortunately it is time to go," he continued semi flustered by his technical difficulties. "All you really need to know is to raise your right hand and say I do at the end of it."

"Nothing like swearing your life away on blind faith," I mumbled to myself, hoping I hadn't inadvertently said it too loudly.

"Don't sweat it, dawg," whispered Gonzo as he sat next to me. "This ain't nothing but a formality."

His response had surprised me. With all of his blabbing for the past four hours, I never had a chance to qualify his listening skills.

Mick, 1722 hrs.

I could not keep my eyes open. My heavy eyelids strained from squinting for the last twenty minutes. The June sun reflected intensely off the freshly obtained white works uniforms that all twelve hundred and ninety six class of '99 plebes adorned. The glare was too much for my eyes to take.

I did not want to have my eyes closed for the entire oath of office ceremony. I managed to open my eyes every few minutes to take mental snapshots of the moment. I was hoping my brain would stow the Polaroid in my own mental photo album, only to enjoy it years down the line when I wasn't so anxious. As it stood, those brief glances were about all I could digest.

In the short-lived moments I managed to glance up, I began taking it all in one frame at a time. There was the thousand plus classmates all seated and packed together in front of Bancroft Hall within the outdoor Tecumseh Court. There were the thousands of parents, family, and girlfriends observing from the perimeter and extending back throughout the yard. Most of them had enjoyed a distracting day of souvenir shopping and general tourist activity. At the head podium, atop the front stairs of Bancroft's main entrance, the Superintendent and the Commandant of Midshipman stood tall. They were the two guys that basically ran this whole outfit. Lastly, there was Tecumseh Court itself. While the massive brick enclave had quite a large group of midshipmen occupying it, there was still plenty of space to spare. Most of my snapshots of Tecumseh Court, however, were simply at the bricks beneath my newly issued white court shoes. I found that looking down was another alternative escape from the glare.

There sure are a lot of bricks here. I wonder how many?

My mind wandered back to the task at hand as I closed my eyes for the seemingly thousandth time. I speculated that Reef Points might just have that fun fact, but at this point, I was more worried about losing it than memorizing it.

All of the non-Naval Academy spectators were roped off behind Tecumseh Court. This was likely done to keep overly clingy mothers from running over to their child and smothering them with hugs mid-ceremony. I knew this would be the case with my mom and Aunt Nellie. Both of them were likely crying and smoking menthol cigarettes somewhere amongst the massive crowd behind us. Gonzo and N.D. flanked my left and right. There was something comforting about the immediate roommate solidarity.

Gonzo had been wisecracking the entire ceremony. He elbowed my side. "Hey Mick, there are plenty of hot white chicks out there today, remember what I told you about my sister, homey." He finished that statement by taking his right index finger and figuratively running the imaginary slice across his throat complete with associated sound effect.

He leaned forward to summon N.D. "Yo, N.D., keep your eyes on Mick, you don't want him eyeing up your girl, do you?"

"Shhhhhhhh!" ordered a fellow plebe a row behind us.

"Fuck you, bootstrap," Gonzo quipped to whoever had anonymously signaled for silence. "I've been through this rodeo no less than five times."

For whatever N.D. and I gained in an advantage from Gonzo's prior military experience as roommates, I worried that his outlandish mouth would counter the good we'd otherwise gain. I just tried my hardest to listen to what was being said over the loudspeaker.

"I wish I were in your shoes right now," said another senior official over the speaker. I had given up tracking who was talking.

That has to be some bullshit.

I was developing premature crow's feet and sitting in a pool of my own ass sweat.

Finally, we were all asked to stand and recite the oath. As LT Walker had highlighted earlier, all we really had to do was raise our right hands for a few minutes and say "I do" when told.

In what seemed like a mere blink of an eye, we said "I do" one last time as prompted. Our collective voices' assertion boomed off the stone walls of Bancroft in a loud echo. I could barely recollect what we had collectively agreed to do, but in that moment, we were official.

"Congratulations, Class of '99. Welcome to the Naval Academy," echoed the loudspeaker. "You now have fifteen minutes to say your goodbyes."

It took me twelve minutes to actually find my mom and Aunt Nellie amidst the swarms of family and friends that were crying, hugging, and kissing their respective plebe in unprecedented frequency. As soon as I found my fan club, all two of them, I was accosted with ferocity in a sea of their own hugs and kisses. When my mom removed my Dixie cover cap from my newly shorn head, she burst into hysterics. Aunt Nellie, on the other hand, could not avoid the temptation of constantly rubbing my newly cue-balled head.

In the two remaining minutes we had together, not much was actually said. The impending dread made the moment too difficult to enjoy.

"Good luck, Mick," my mom sniffled as we ended our final embrace. "You know you always have a welcome place to stay if things don't work out. Always remember that," she continued. I think she still secretly hoped that I would be back in a few weeks.

"Good luck, kiddo," Aunt Nellie added as she gave me one last peck on the cheek. "We're so damn proud of you. Give 'em hell."

This is finally happening.

I turned away from my family and headed back to the entrance of Bancroft Hall. As my mom and Aunt Nellie needed appropriate space to smoke and listen to the oath of office simultaneously, I had an extra-long walk back to where I needed to be. As I was one of the last plebes to head back into the hall, I could already here the voracious screaming from within the walls of Bancroft. With detail-er restrictions finally lifted, they all waited in the indoor company areas like a pack of hungry lions poised for the tasty wildebeests. They had waited two long years for this moment. They were itching for some payback from their own experience as plebes themselves. I could hear the drum and guitar solo of Metallica's "One" emanating from inside Bancroft. It was accompanied by screaming upper-classmen.

And so it begins.

Chapter 4

Rolled into Shorebreak
Tuesday, August 25th, 1992
Mick, 0530 hrs.

A red Toyota pickup truck screeched into Aunt Nellie's driveway in the waning morning darkness. Calling the vehicle red was generous. It could have just as easily been described as brown. There was almost as much rust as paint on the vehicle. It had well earned the nickname "Turd." The Toyota lettering on Turd's back tailgate had been peeled off to visibly spell "YO."

Farm popped his head outside of the driver's side window and laid on the horn. He smiled like Cheshire cat when he saw me accompanying Bird down the wooden stairways on the side of the house. From ten yards away, I could already see Farm had had at least one donut on the ride over. Jelly and white powdered sugar caked his unshaven scruff.

For the first time in over two years, I was a guest in Aunt Nellie's house. My mom and I had previously moved in with Nellie about six months after my father's fatal motorcycle accident. At the time, it was the only hope for maintaining any level of stability in life. As a roomie, Bird gave me his own bed to sleep on. He traded it for a shoddy mattress on the floor even after being extensively away from it during his incarceration. Two years after living with Nellie, Mom got her shit together and we moved thirty miles north to the Delaware shore. I decided to take up surfing as a way to stay close. Bird and Farm shortly thereafter wanted me to join the Fellas.

"Big day, Mick. Time to pop your cherry," said Farm as I helped Bird throw his short board in the short bed of the dilapidated pickup. "Hurricane Andrew is pumping all sorts of good shit in today."

I didn't even consider bringing my body board along. I wasn't allowed to ask questions. Though I wanted to, it would have been an automatic deal breaker for the trip.

"Initiation day, Bunkie!" Bird joyfully exclaimed. "Boogie boarding graduation day."

Body boarding had become all of the rage in the early nineties. Ocean City became a particular hub of body boarding interest. On typical surf days, the waves on the Delmarva beaches broke closely to the shore. Traditional surfboards were too dangerous to ride in these breaks during tourist season. Wipeouts and subsequent flying boards could pose a threat to the swimming tourists. These tourists constituted the lifeblood of the local economy. As such, surfing was prohibited between 10 a.m. and 5 p.m. during most of the tourist season summer.

As the body boarding trend began to catch on, various sundry shops that were obnoxiously scattered throughout the shoreline joined the trend. They hawked cheaply built thirty dollar body board impersonators, often called boogie boards, to tourist kids.

Ocean City lifeguards had no mandated restrictions on body boarding. The boards were light enough to avoid being harmful to tourists. This meant it was game-on twenty-four/seven. By June of '92, the ocean looked like a boogie board feeding frenzy. This came compliments of every kook in the Mid-Atlantic sporting their new foam floatation devices on summer vacation. This pissed Bird off to no end. Even though the at-large surfing community and the legitimate body boarding community favorably co-existed, Bird wasn't having it.

We hopped into the truck, three dudes and two boards. Though my body board was hardly a boogie board, Bird still viewed it as enemy territory.

Bird smirked with reassurance and slapped his hand on my back, "Don't worry, I got the perfect board for ya today, Bunkie."

"Big day out there, brah," Farm exclaimed as he backed out of the driveway. "East winds barely blowing out and incoming high with a big storm pumping off the coast. Heavy wave but lookin' glassy." He gunned the gas pedal and we were soon speeding like a bat out of hell within a 25mph neighborhood speed limit. Within seconds, I could see from the rearview mirror Nellie's asshole neighbor Rusty Gaskins. He was taking his dog out for a morning shit, pumping his fist and screaming obscene suggestions for reducing our speed in the residential neighborhood.

Good waves had a limited expiration stamp at 10 a.m. As it stood with our current pacing, we would have just about a four hour window of surf before the dick-head lifeguards kicked us out until after dinnertime when surfing could resume.

We made our way to the end of Route 50 over the draw bridge connecting land bound West Ocean City to the main island of Ocean City. Heading north on Baltimore Ave., we sped past the many motels housing Ocean City's temporary residents. The parking lots looked packed, but the streets were dead. Most people on vacation slept well past 5:45 a.m.

"Oh shit, Mick, there's your spot," Farm taunted as we passed 28th Street.

"They should call themselves a fucking boogie board shop," Bird interjected before I had a chance to say anything.

Bird and Farm were referencing a small board shop in 28th St. Plaza called "Shorebreak." Shorebreak was hardly the coolest surf shop. K-Coast, Chauncey's, and Malibu's were where most surfers wanted to be. The entire store-front of Shorebreak was owned and operated by a local Jewish family. The store had a long history as a sundry shop, selling beach blankets, flip-flops, and sun tan lotion to local tourists for generations. The owner's middle-aged son, Drew Greenstein, decided to do a little less local partying and a little more earning his keep within the family. He was industrious enough to convince his father to allow him to launch a surf shop within the existing store. Even though it was housed within the sundry shop, Shorebreak Surf Shop was run as a separate business entity. At least that's what I told myself. Bird hated Shorebreak. He especially hated that they deemed themselves a surf shop without selling a single surfboard.

To make ends meet that first summer we moved in

with Nellie, my mom had picked up some part time work waiting tables. She worked down the street from Shorebreak at the Salty Dog Saloon. I would occasionally go with her to work so I could play arcade games. These arcade games were scattered throughout the nearby pizza and sandwich shops. Eventually I would run out of quarters and go ogle at the body boards for sale in Shorebreak. Drew was a nice enough man to offer me the chance to work in the shop after finding me browsing several days in a row. I started out sweeping and stocking shelves. Shortly thereafter, I was selling boards. It was an especially sweet gig. No other shop would allow a thirteen-year-old to work a sales job. Everything was under the table. I used the extra cash to buy my first body board.

The Turd made its way to Route 1. We eventually hit 130th St. and peeled into the back of Montego Bay. It was neighborhood of trailers that housed tourists and a few of Bird's friends. Despite being a trailer park, the homes were generally well maintained. Our nan had owned a vacation home there until she bought a bigger one farther north in the '80s.

Farm peeled the Turd to an abrupt halt, screeching tires in front of the white doublewide on South Ocean Drive.

"You said 112, right?" asked Farm. "Fuck dude, get in there, we're wastin' time."

"Bunkie, here in the O.C., we treat Fellas mo' betta." Bird smiled, looking back for a quick smartass glance before he slammed the rusted red door hard enough to knock the small knob off the manual window roller.

I remained curled up, half asleep in the back cab. My

seat was about big enough for a three-year-old child. I assumed Bird was trying to secure me a board for the morning. Leave it to him to wait until today to find one. My guess was this was all a part of the initiation process.

After three minutes of anxiously waiting, I heard a loud argument erupt from inside the house. One of the voices was female. Shortly thereafter, Bird kicked through the trailer's front screen door with a very long surfboard in hand. He struggled with its heft. The board was quickly but carefully placed in the back bed with the other two boards. Bird leapt immediately into the passenger seat with a renewed sense of urgency.

"Fucking gun it, Farm!" ordered Bird.

Tracy Jenkins kicked the already broken screen door on the dilapidated front porch out of her path and screamed, "You bastard!" She was wearing a single flip-flop. Her half-adorned tattered pink bathrobe did little to conceal her broad daylight nudity.

Farm gunned the gas pedal. The asphalt pebbles of the worn pavement kicked backwards towards Bird's ex-girlfriend. She was brandishing a kitchen knife. In angered desperation, she threw her blade in the direction of the truck as it harmlessly clanked off on the street behind us.

"She was too high to call the cops. We're safe!" Bird yelled amidst the chaos. My heart was already racing.

"Fuck, dude," Farm calmly scolded Bird. "You could have just asked me to bring an extra-long board."

"No fucking way," Bird replied. "I'm not letting this guy off easy."

I looked from the cab into the truck's bed to visually inspect my new ride. The dinged up white board had a single red stripe running down the middle. It looked as though it had been stolen from the set of a Gidget movie. It was roughly twelve feet long and almost twice as big as the other two boards in the back.

In the ten minute ride from 130th St. to 50th St., I was quickly caught up to speed on just how my first surfboard was obtained.

"Tracy just moved into that shithole a month ago," Bird narrated. "She still owed me four hundred bones. She was just going to sell that board to buy more drugs," he continued. "I was just collecting on money I'd already get later. Her old man picked it up used while he was stationed at Pearl Harbor in the Navy back in the seventies. It's a torpedo, but quite a beauty."

Bird pulled out a joint and lit it as we sat at a red light two blocks from our desired 48th St. destination. Every year since I had lived down on the shore, the best surf spot resided somewhere around 45th St. Each year the previous year's collective storms would shift the sandbars underneath the ocean and would move the beach's best surf break up or down. This year 48 was the lucky number.

Eventually we hit 48th Street. The ocean block of parking was already filled up, but luckily, Farm had a handicap parking pass he had stolen from Nan.

"Best spot in the city," said Farm. He placed his car in park and set his car keys atop the driver side front wheel, ensuring his keys would not get lost in the ocean in the upcoming session.

"Damn, already chopped up," yelled Bird, the first of us to the high point of the sand dune path leading down to the ocean. He had jumped out of the truck's passenger side door before Farm had a chance to stop the truck. "Gonna be fun getting out there, Micky boy!"

"Choppy but big," said Farm who arrived where Bird stood about seven paces ahead of me. "Head to overhead," he continued. It was a big day by Ocean City standards.

"Micky, great day to be with the Fellas," Bird yelled out above the building wind gusts. My eyes widened.

"Bird, are you sure I can ride this thing out there?" I asked my cousin, trying hard not to sound like a total chicken shit. I had been in waves this big before with my body board, but this was a much different situation. Navigating a twelve-foot longboard on an arm paddle was going to be harder than kicking my way with flippers on a three-foot body board.

"That thing rides like a Cadillac," boasted Bird knocking on the board. "A real classic."

I was not sold.

"Here," Bird summoned. "Rub some more of this on it," he continued, handing me a chunk of Sticky Bumps wax for a board that looked as though it hadn't been waxed since the Reagan administration. "Initiation day, Bunkie. Buck up!"

"It looks like a shaved down wooden door with a fin attached," laughed Farm as he initiated his jog down to the water. The observation was not helping calm the intensely fluttering butterflies in my stomach.

Bird stayed behind. With Farm already paddling in the water, it was just the two of us.

"Just go out there and see if you can paddle out with us and watch us ride from in the lineup," Bird coached. "Just showing up with this gnarly board in that lineup,"

Bird continued pointing outward to the ocean, "will get you the thumbs up." At least he had indirectly admitted to the difficulty of the task.

I had heard enough gripes inside Aunt Nellie's porch to know that "barneys" and "posers" were not well received by the Fellas, especially on a big day of surf. I was just hoping not to make an ass of myself.

I quickly tossed the wax chunk back towards the truck and put on my rash guard. Running across the sand, I splashed my board out into the water to join the rest of the Fellas. Due to board's heft, I could barely get momentum generated as I hit the water in a poorly attempted glide. I started my paddle at nearly a dead stand still. The sea foam produced by the crashing waves was already splashing in my mouth and up my nose.

The Ocean City breaks were in shallow water. The wave was very top to bottom. It washed out frequently. Even on big days, the surf was breaking quickly and close to shore. On a big wave day, the best way to get past the breaking waves was to hitch a pull in the riptide. I scanned quickly and could not find any visible rips in front of me.

Unfortunately, the only alternative was a strong paddle and a series of well-timed duck dives through the thick of the breakers. It was a very similar exercise on a body board, so I was used to it. Long boards like mine, however, were too buoyant to perform a duck dive. My strategy was just to paddle as hard as I could and hang on tight through the beating.

I lifted my head and could already see Farm and Bird sitting atop their boards. They were already well past the breaking waves and scouting the choppy yet large incoming sets.

"Shit," I cursed aloud as I inched towards the kill zone of the crashing behemoths, gargling saltwater the entire way. What transpired for the next fifteen minutes was akin to a white water treadmill. I struggled paddling my canoe of a board ten yards forward as I became achingly close to the end of the breakers only to be rolled back to the shore by the breaking wave I could not get over fast enough. The sets of waves were unrelenting. I was getting pummeled.

As anticipated, my board was far too big and buoyant to duck dive beneath the cresting waves like Farm and Bird's shorter boards. I was perpetually getting rolled back to my original starting position. I was playing a real life version of Chutes and Ladders. Breaking up the monotony of this cycle was the occasional exceptionally large wave, which would break ten yards farther out than the rest of the sets and subsequently throw me into a washing cycle of a ride beneath the water.

After getting rolled under the choppy seas for the third time in twenty minutes, I was resolved to give my paddling excursion one last shot. I treaded water and pulled my leash to gather my temporarily lost board back within my reach. I pulled myself back atop the board and could see Farm and Bird. The loudness of the crashing waves and my heavy breathing precluded me from hearing exactly what they had to say. Part of me was relieved the ocean had muted their surely agitating comments. They would be busting my chops the whole way home. That was for certain.

I mustered enough strength within my spaghetti arms to give it one last go. Bird and Farm continued screaming my way, and as I paddled closer, I could begin to hear their then barely audible screams.

"Mick, big set!" was about all I could make out. Knowing what was now inevitably barreling my way, I paddled like a madman to get out of my predicament. I worked up to a frantic pace out of pure desperation as my muscles burned with lactic acid. The giant aqua mountain built before my panicked eyes as I ascended my way up it. Just as I reached the crescendo, I could feel the wave's force begin to toss me like a football. In an instant, I was sucked back over the falls. I tumbled back into the water with extra might and finally crashed under the white water with an exclamation point. The power of the breaking wave held me underwater. After a few disorienting flips in the drink, I couldn't think straight. I was disoriented and in desperate need of a breath.

My head finally broke the surface of the water as I attempted to suck in a giant recovery breath. Half of that breath was filled with saltwater. I began coughing and choking on the water without noticing the next large wave crashing atop my head. I was brought down one last time before I established an on the spot plan.

Gotta grab my board!

I struggled for my next breath. I managed to grab my leash. I simultaneously popped my head above water and yanked my leash as hard as I could. Though saltwater was stinging my eyes, I was shocked that I could not see my board yet. My head frantically turned left and right until finally looking upward.

The next thing I remember was a large thumping sound as my board slammed upon my head with velocity compliments of the third large wave of the set. I thankfully tumbled far enough out of the breakers to actually crawl atop my board and gingerly paddle to shore. I was just hoping I could make it to shore before passing out. The thud of the board had really rung my bell.

Though woozy, I finally managed to reach the wet sand at the water's edge. I immediately crashed forward into a fetal position rapidly gasping for breath, yet thankful that I had survived the series of recent tumbles.

"Fucking motherfucking Bird!" I finally cursed. It was about all of the words I could muster as I finally caught my breath. My tears were mixed with rage, pain, and ocean water. Mainly I was embarrassed. I really felt like an ass out there and wondered if I would get the thumbs up for my initiation.

My desperation for survival had kept me from checking my injury status. My head was throbbing from the collision. I could feel wet drips down my forehead being complemented by the throbbing lump surely growing from atop my head. As I wiped the drops from my brow, I wondered if my palm would show red. Thankfully it was just water.

"Hey dude, are you okay?" I heard from just above me. It was an unfamiliar voice. I knew instantly that it was none of the Fellas. Full out decapitation or cops would be about the only things to pull them out of the water on a big day of surf.

"Yeah," I replied calmly as I looked up. "I think I'm okay." As I made eye contact with the concerned stranger, I could see that I was actually amongst a small gathering of onlookers. My new friend was a large, bearded biker decked in a black Molly Hachette tank top that went well with his various tattoos of engines, eagles, naked ladies, and the like. The burly biker was out with his old lady for a morning walk with their Chihuahua. It was a humorous third wheel.

"Cool man, looks like you got jacked up pretty good out there," he continued. The various members of the impromptu group began to disperse once they realized that I wasn't in immediate need of medical attention.

"Yeah, I'm okay," I responded.

"By the way, dude, your pants are split pretty good too," he said holding back laughter. He turned his head to politely hide his smirk.

I reached back instantly. "Son of a bitch!" I said through clenched teeth.

"Good luck with that one," my new companion said finally turning away to continue walking his Chihuahua with a plastic grocery bag full of shit in his hand.

As soon as I realized my stark white rump was on open public display, I turned over quickly. I was going to be stuck in place until my ride home exited the water. That was almost two hours away. I sat in a cold puddle of salt-water and shame.

Mick, 1006 hrs.

Boards in hand, the Fellas reluctantly exited the water and headed towards their cars. I was still seated in my original hiding spot waiting for my initiation grade.

Thumbs up, thumbs down, I felt like an ass either way.

Despite the windy conditions, the weather was pleasant once I had dried off upon exiting the water. I considered going back in the water a few times but opted against it. Getting the long board out in those conditions was a lost cause, plus my ass would be hanging out. I was content keeping my bare ass temporarily shielded in the sand until the last of the Fellas were scolded by the lifeguards to get out. Another few minutes in the water, and the cops would have been called. The Fellas were excellent at pushing the limits.

"Farm, come on, man. Get your fat ass up here and let's go," Bird yelled. "I gotta get smokes and I'm jonesin' pretty bad." Farm was the fattest Fella and almost always the last out of the water and into the car.

"The keys are on the tire," Farm shot back slightly peeved. "Go across the street to the gas station and I'll meet you there with Mick," he continued quickly tossing his board in the back of his pickup. The gas station was across the highway and four blocks down from our car. He glanced backwards towards me as I initiated my careful walk back. He could see I was walking funny and knew that Bird's patience wouldn't last through my extended walk back to the truck. "Just make sure you get me a chocolate chip cookie," he yelled as Bird screeched the pickup backwards and then throttled immediately towards his tobacco fix.

My arms strained as I walked my solid wood board back to the parking spot. I knew my ass was exposed to the open air. I kept one hand tightly gripped to my board and the other held behind me holding my rash guard over my split bathing suit. There were towels in the truck, but that coverage option had already sped off. The extra three hundred yard distance to Bird at the store was going to make the walk extra difficult.

"Dude, you alright?" Farm called out.

"Yeah, I guess," I said with a dejected look.

"It was cool of you to get out there with the long board." He continued, "Just trying to get out with that canoe took some balls."

I worried that he might be patronizing me. His compliments did make me feel a little better to know that I didn't look like a total dipshit out there, at least not from the front.

"Dude, why ya walkin' so funny?" Farm queried.

"Farm, I split my pants," I confessed.

"No shit!" Farm said as his face lit up. He tilted his head to verify my previous statement and immediately saw my other occupied hand holding my rash guard. He snatched it out of my hand before I had time to blink.

"Hey, fuck you!" I yelled as Farm yanked my rash guard and immediately started sprinting towards Bird across Route 1 Ocean Highway.

I chased behind him as fast as I could. I quickly realized the strain of my board and prior injury would be no match for Farm. Despite his slovenly physique, he had already made it to Bird well before I could. I ended up stuck on a corner waiting for the next red light to disrupt traffic flow. When Farm arrived at his truck, Bird was already sitting on the hood smoking his newly bought pack of Marlboro Reds.

The steady stream of cars prevented any possibility of

jaywalking. Every local tourist in town not within a walking distance to the beach by 10:20 a.m. was desperately hunting for an ocean block parking spot. I urgently paced towards 52nd Street on the wrong side of the highway. I was mooning the entire ocean block of 50th Street. The commotion caused by my rash guard theft and subsequent footrace with Farm had ensured that everyone within an eyeshot was getting quite a show. Passing traffic pointed at the half-naked jackass with a long board on the corner of 51st St. My eyes frantically looked up and down the street. Naively I hoped that I might find a break in the speeding traffic. I had no such luck.

Traffic suddenly slowed then stopped as a traffic light a few blocks down the road flipped red. I immediately initiated my sprint across the street. In hunting for the break in the traffic, I hadn't noticed that Farm had already conveyed my situation to Bird during my two-minute wait on the other side of the highway. By the time my eyes made it back to the Turd, it was already peeling out of its spot. As I hit the road's median, I was just close enough hear Bird laughing hysterically. Other cars stopped bumper to bumper at the red light began to notice their mid-traffic entertainment and horns began to blare.

"Nice ass, Bunkie!" I heard Bird scream as he peeled out of the gas station's parking lot. He sped forward a block where he parked again in a prime view parking spot on the other side of the Candy Kitchen's parking lot. I was helpless and could only continue the chase. The comments and catcalls intensified until I angrily tossed my board in a bush within the gas station's landscape and sprinted the remaining block to a waiting Bird and Farm.

"Fuck you, guys, get me outta here!" I fumed as I finally reached the car.

"You gotta grab your board. We're not leaving without it," said Bird as he slowly reduced his laughing.

"Take this," Farm said tossing a damp and sandy beach towel.

I looked back towards the truck after securing a more modest cover. Bird and Farm each held their right thumbs proudly high.

"Pass!" they exclaimed in unison. I was officially a Fella.

Part II

Whipping

Chapter 5

The New Normal
Monday, July 3rd, 1995
Mick, 0457 hrs.

As one of the one thousand and ninety-six members of the Naval Academy Plebe class of 1999, I was likely the only plebe not deeply engaged in a sweat-drenched sleep. Even though we had been living in our new digs for almost three full days, most of us had yet to use the bathroom beyond urination. We were constipated from exhaustion, annoyance, and perhaps from just a little fear. For most of us, sleep was a rare, yet welcomed, escape from the typical verbal abuse that took place in our recent days.

"Click, clack," the mechanical minute hand transitioned to 4:58 a.m. on every one of the hundreds of clocks all synchronized within Bancroft Hall. Each minute hand first taking a half "click" backwards, and then a dreadfully assertive "clack" forward to the next menacing minute of the rapidly diminishing night of sleep. The sound echoed in the morning as all of the clocks hung in the now empty hallways. Most of my classmates had their own battery-operated alarms synchronized to this clock and alarms set to

4:59 a.m. This gave them a conscious breath of sanity, and a small fraction short of maximum night's sleep before reveille sounded and all hell broke loose.

I had been listening to this symphony for the past twenty minutes. For the life of me, I could not understand why I was up at this hour. Maybe it was because my current in-room temperature, largely due to a lack of air-conditioning anywhere in Bancroft Hall, was sitting in the mid-80s. Maybe it was because my mattress pre-dated the cold war. Maybe it was because I still missed my friends and family back home. Regardless of blame, I understood my last daily moments of personal peace and space were evaporating quickly.

"Click, clack." 4:59 a.m. and a symphony of personal alarms echoed throughout Bancroft Hall. I heard the faint rumblings of my two roommates awakening. Gonzo and N.D. lie momentarily awake, still in the rack like me, relishing their last thirty seconds of peaceful rest until the next bed time seventeen hours later. None of us had yet acknowledged the other.

The Naval Academy's newly minted class of '99 was three days into our freshman experience. I could already tell that we were aptly named after the Roman Empire's term "plebeian" for citizens of minimal social status. Us modern day "plebes" would gladly have swapped out the academy's version of this lowly rung of existence for any plebeian goat herding peasant under Caesar.

It was the start of a day almost exactly in the middle of summer yet the hope of swimming pools and bikinis had long since died out. Unfortunately, the occasional glance I would sneak in viewing the myriad of inappropriate pictures of bikini-clad women on Gonzo's blotter was about all the bikinis I'd seen. Gonzo's knifing threats be damned, as a sexually repressed red-blooded male, I needed something to get my blood pumping in the morning. Plus, I knew it would only be a matter of time before one of our detailers took time enough to notice their risqué nature and force them to be stored in privacy.

In my brief stay thus far I better understood the Naval Academy's own take on military boot camp. The Plebe Summer process involved taking roughly a thousand high achieving, eighteen to twenty-two year old boys and girls and embarking on the United States Navy's twisted take on summer camp for over-achieving youths. While I-Day had been the initiation into this madness, we were still very much in the early stages of a long summer filled with sweat, pushups, and insults. I-Day was a mere seventy-two hours ago, but felt like months had passed.

Plebe Year, which was initiated with Plebe Summer, in its entirety, was nothing more than a series of three hundred somewhat bad days compressed into about eleven months. Nothing about Plebe Summer was exceedingly sadistic, just ever slightly so. We were by no means getting tortured and rarely were we ever put into life-threatening danger. Meant to shape future toughness and decisiveness in war, Plebe Year most importantly meant eating the biggest slice of humble pie that anyone could possibly digest. Plebe Summer, the initial phase of the plebe experience, was the first dreadful bite of this menacing dessert. Thus far, I was already stuffed full of it.

N.D. remained his stoic self since we met a few days earlier, rarely complaining or even getting much attention from the detailers so far. He already understood the drill and had no problem laying low. Despite being such a physical specimen as compared to the rest of his plebe company mates, his intelligence and athleticism allowed him to float under the radar.

Gonzo left little to the imagination when conveying his impressions of the Plebe Summer experience. I imagined every muscle in his slightly older and slightly out-of-shape body ached at this point. Somehow, his mouth had endless stamina.

While Gonzo's mouth had already generated a few hundred extra pushups for our room, he definitely helped our cause by teaching N.D. and me virtually every dirty little short cut and trick in the book within a boot camp environment. I would have been in far worse shape without his help. This made his antics tolerable and kept me thankfully a little more anonymous to the seemingly constant scrutiny of our detailers.

"Click, Clack." 5:00 a.m. Alarms bells blared. Daylight was far from broken, yet morning had begun for the mighty class of '99. "Reveille, reveille, all hands heave out and trice up. It is now reveille," blasted out of the intercom system throughout the halls of Bancroft Hall.

Gonzo finally mustered up enough energy to sigh, "Fuck, this, shit." As he sat up in his already neatly made rack, he rolled back over to sleep atop of the covers so he wouldn't have to make it amongst the impending morning of chaos. Gonzo taught N.D. and me that trick just a day before and we had already implemented this best practice, amongst others, into our daily routine.

As I sat up, I looked back and noticed my body's outline in sweat remaining on the covers of the already made rack. Gonzo assured us that the suspicious evidence would dry up before the detailers could catch on.

I could already hear a hissing whisper matriculating down the hall towards our room.

"Al'ight, shit birds. Beauty sleep is over. Get your asses out of your racks and in formation, and you better make sure you make 'em real purtty," softly spoke Midshipman 2nd class Nate Severson in his thick southern accent. He was from some podunk Georgia town that I could not muster up enough coherent thought to recollect at 5:01 a.m. on a Thursday. I was supposed to have that information committed to memory two days ago.

"You betta be scrapin' those faces and scrubin' those nasty fangs," Severson continued. "Nobody better be stankin' up my P-way with pleber morning breath."

"Maconsville? Decatur? Athens? Shit, hopefully Severson won't ask me that question today.

I was too tired to ask my roommates. Gonzo would have likely just made fun of me anyway.

Severson's voice remained at an audibly soft tone, as yelling inside of Bancroft Hall before 0700 was prohibited for all midshipmen, even those responsible for training us plebes. This was a typically respected rule, as even the snarkiest of detailers did not want to risk waking any of the other few hundred upper-class midshipmen still asleep. While the full brigade wouldn't be back until late August, there were enough upperclassmen stuck in summer school or in disciplinary trouble to stay respectful early in the morning.

I also sensed that Severson's voice could use a few

minutes to warm up into its full tilt yelling mode. I'm sure Gonzo and I would give him plenty of opportunity. He had been screaming at us constantly for the past three days. Each new day took just a little bit more time for Severson to get the voice engine up to full throttle.

Mick, 0519 hrs.

2/C Severson was one of seven other detailers primarily in charge of training roughly thirty plebes over the course of the next four weeks of Plebe Summer. Upon completion of the fourth week, a new set of seven detailers would come in to replace them for the remaining half of training. This second half of summer training would lead us directly into Parents' Weekend, our only bastion of temporary hope for the summer. During this glorious weekend, we would get two-and-a-half golden days of temporary freedom to visit our families or whatever else we could sneak in outside of the constant supervision we were currently dealing with. Until Parents' Weekend, for the next six weeks, there would be no days off save Sunday mornings when we were permitted to attend religious services on the yard.

Detailers were the Naval Academy's version of drill instructors. Instead of the experienced enlisted sergeants that typically ran a military boot camp, the Naval Academy staffed this responsibility predominately to upper-class midshipman. They came in the form of 2nd class (2/C) midshipman juniors and 1st class (1/C) midshipman seniors. They were just a few years older than we were. They gave up their brief summer vacation between summer ship assignments to come back to Annapolis a few months early and beat on the oncoming plebe class. While a few junior Naval officers and senior enlisted men stuck around during the day to babysit, most of the training day of Plebe Summer was owned by the early twenty-something detailers. Gonzo was taking orders from many detailers that were actually younger than he was. His gripes about this situation were a continuous diatribe.

"Midshipman 4th Class McGee, Gonzalez, and Okafor," growled 2/C Severson as he nonchalantly paced by our now open door in the hallway. "You better get your ass out here on the double. You don't rate bein' late." I understood that most of this bantering was for show. I suspected Severson was taunting my room simply because he knew we were within an earshot of him inside our room. I cringed anytime there was an opportunity for Gonzo to reply with a snarky answer to such statements. It would have been made infinitely worse if Severson caught him mouthing off while still lying in bed.

"Yes, sir," N.D. and I belted out just loud enough for Severson to hear our acknowledged response without being too annoyingly loud for Gonzo, nor drawing undue attention from the upper-class detailers lurking the hallway. It was a delicate balancing act.

"Gonzo, come on, man. We gotta roll, man," N.D. said shaking Gonzo who still lay in his made bed.

Despite being a little older, and a little less in shape, Gonzo's primary reason for morning sluggishness was overwhelmingly due to his smoking habit. He could barely make it twenty-four hours without his trusty Newport Menthols. Typically he'd wait until an hour after lights out to sneak out of our window and onto the roof of Bancroft to get at least a small fix. It was the one lone benefit of residing on the top floor of Bancroft. I was glad he wasn't smoking too close to the window. I didn't mind the smell. It just reminded me of Mom and Aunt Nellie.

I scrambled to grab my neatly folded regulation physical training gear, otherwise known as "PT," from my con-locker. My last blue rim T-shirt was itchy with newness and neatly tucked into my regulation Naval Academy blue athletic shorts. I pulled my knee-high white athletic socks to my knees. My gray running shoes, which we called "go fasters," were neatly tied. Every last detail of the outfit would be scrutinized momentarily. An un-tucked shirt or less-than-knee-high sock spelled certain doom for any non-compliant plebe. I kept up my frantic pace to get dressed along with my roommates who were similarly scrambling around. I had already begun sweating through my shirt.

Gonzo and I grabbed our razors, taking turns running them under the continuously flowing hot water while we gave ourselves the best possible dry shave thirty-five seconds would allow us. N.D. did not have to shave. A few ingrown hairs and a subsequent permission slip from the medics had allowed him to grow the beginnings of a beard. As if his ethnicity and large frame didn't make him stand out enough, his sprouting beard made him look extra distinctive. Magically, N.D. still found ways to blend in anonymously.

As I left my room, following the lead of my two roommates, I shut off the lights and left my door open. Behind us was an inspection-ready room, as prescribed by normal midshipman fourth class protocol. I also admired just how neat and organized our room looked. "My mom would be proud," I whispered to my smirking roommates.

You can't frazzle me, you hillbilly munchkin son-of-a-bitch.

I passed by the 5'6" Severson ten yards farther down the hall. In formal military uniform, Severson was entirely shined, pressed, and starched. He exuded a sense of authority. In morning PT gear, however, he looked more like a dorky twelve-year-old anxiously awaiting the onset of puberty.

Severson obviously couldn't read my mind, but certainly didn't back off the opportunity to smugly lay one more dig on me as I caught his arrogant smirk in my peripheral vision. "Keep your eyes in the boat, McGee. I got my eye on you all doggone day," Severson said.

Mick, 0524 hrs.

All of the plebes in my company neatly filed out of their respective rooms, and quickly in an impressive unison of squared turns and precision, filed into formation. Formation was military speak for "meeting time." It was how our detailers corralled all of us in one place at one time. It was the same way a teacher handled a group of small kindergartners on a field trip to the zoo. It was also a convenient way to cluster plebes together and yell at them in the most efficient manner.

Formations happened about fifty-seven times over the course of a typical Plebe Summer day, and this was the first of many. A formation consisted of three squads of plebes. Each squad was supposed to consist of about ten plebes. One of the squads in my company was already short. One of their members had already decided to quit and was already out-processing in Tango Company. During each formation, all squad members would stand horizontally shoulder to shoulder and each squad would assemble in three rows. Some formations were more formal, accompanied by fancy uniforms and subsequent marching. Others like this one, an informal gathering meant mainly to ensure no plebe tried to escape Bancroft Hall during the night.

I looked to my right and saw my squad mate, Nathan Latimer, with a face full of shaving cream. Just yesterday, following an intense detailer interrogation from Severson, Nathan had admitted he hadn't shaved in over a week. His boyish features and late onset of puberty precluded him the need of daily shaving. I even wondered if he had begun shaving at all. I pondered the same thing about Severson. As a way to compensate for his lack of required "face scraping," Severson mandated that Latimer cover his face with shaving cream for every morning formation. I initially felt bad for him. Then I noticed virtually every other plebe male in my company, save N.D. and Latimer, had a full "blood beard" compliments of a hurried yet mandatory dry shave ahead of formation. None of us would sacrifice the sleep time required to actually shave properly with shaving cream. I was lucky as this activity was once a day for me. For Gonzo, who typically had a five o'clock shadow by ten in the morning, dry shaving happened three to four times a day. His face looked like a giant case of road rash.

"Foxtrot Company, ah ten . . . HUT," 2/C Scott McVane grunted out as he stood in front of the platoon. All of us snapped to attention. Even our collective plebe running shoes made a fairly audible "clack" as our heels unitarily clicked together to assume the ordered position of attention. We stood straight and kept our eyes "in the boat" looking straight ahead without exception.

McVane, unlike Severson, far more looked the part of intimidator. Despite sporting workout gear, McVane's 6'2" chiseled frame, icy blue eyes, and perfectly cut flat top buzz cut made him look like he had jumped directly out of the G.I. Joe cartoons I watched as a child. Even though some of us were too proud to admit it, McVane generally scared the crap out of every member of Foxtrot Company.

Not all of the detailers were up yet. While most were technically required to attend this 0530 formation, they usually rotated responsibility of this duty to a handful of 2/C detailers. This morning comprised of Severson and McVane. The 1/C detailers, or "Firsties" as midshipman otherwise referred to them, typically stayed in bed, playing hooky straight through morning PT.

"Squad leaders, report," grunted McVane.

"First squad, all present and accounted for," replied fellow plebe D.J. Green. D.J. was one of our room's three next door neighbors during Plebe Summer. He was a natural spit polish midshipman. He was also the only Jewish kid I knew from Nebraska, or anywhere for that matter outside of Drew and his dad back at the Shorebreak shop. D.J. naturally already hated Gonzo's propensity for being the company's overall lightning rod for attention.

"Second squad, all present and accounted for," belted out 4/C Summer Harris. Summer was a highly recruited women's soccer player. In addition to being a phenomenal athlete, she was also regarded by most of us as the most squared away plebe in our company. Hardly timid or shy, her walk had the swagger of a cowboy. It had already been rumored that she would routinely sneak a wad of spitting tobacco in her lip before bedtime. Gonzo would go on and on about how hot he thought that was. I never quite got that specific turn on.

She would actually be kind of attractive in the normal world.

I pictured her toned legs in shorts or perhaps a tight sundress as I stood about three feet behind her, catty-corner in my third position in 3rd squad. Soon thereafter, my mind wondered what her extremely athletic build might look like sans clothes. It was hard for my typical eighteen-year-old male mind not to go there on occasion.

Gonzo had been going on and on for days about how the academy put pepper-salt in our food to repress such feelings. Pepper-salt was slang for potassium nitrate, a salt the military used as an ingredient for explosives. It was also rumored to be used as an anti-aphrodisiac. If this King Hall spicing had been true, then I was certainly immune.

Save Gonzo's publicly displayed family album that I so fancied, formation views behind Summer were a rare spark of sexual excitement in my day. My libido was a caged dog being taunted by the slightest scent of a woman. There was definitely something about Summer I found intriguing beyond her physical attractiveness. Her confidence and strength were equally sexy.

"Third squad, ALL present," loudly replied Gonzo with a sly smirk and providing my dirty mind a figurative cold shower.

"GONZALEZ!" Severson interrupted after a brief pause, offering the most effective anti-aphrodisiac of the morning. "I guess you are such hot shit that you don't rate lettin' us know that everyone is accounted for too, huh?" he continued. "Did you account for 4/C Mason?" he continued harping on his nitpick. "Hard to be present while you're standing watch, huh?"

"Sir, yes sir," calmly responded Gonzo. "Third squad is all present and accounted for," he replied in a matter of fact manner that was far more snarky than any of the rest of the Foxtrot plebes had the guts to convey.

"Gonzalez, I really don't give a shit about how you did things in the fleet," aggressively chimed in McVane with a steely glare. "During Plebe Summer, you will do things our way, or we will make things much more difficult for you and your shipmates." McVane had a unique talent for sounding perpetually pissed off with every word that exited his mouth.

The detailers were great at leveraging potential peer pressure. Even McVane, with his arsenal of stone cold faces and laser beamed stares, knew he had little ground to stand on when trying to intimidate guys like Gonzo. Gonzo saw right through any phony façade of toughness and intimidation. Deep down almost everyone knew that midshipman with prior active duty experience were the only "non-pretenders" of the whole lot of us. For McVane, countering Gonzo's temporary immunity meant shifting the potential threat of punishment toward the entirety of plebes. Power in numbers was a notion that kept the most unflappable prior enlisted man in line. Even Gonzo understood the limits of pushing his shipmates too far. While Gonzo hardly felt intimidated by the potential scorn from his fresh faced plebe shipmates, he had felt enough loyalty to them already to not get everyone destroyed this early. It was going to be a long day as is.

The plebes of Foxtrot all stood tensely for the moment. I hoped that McVane would quickly downplay this potential showdown. The last thing any of us wanted was to be dropped for pushups directly before our morning workout.

"Pffft," a gaseous bodily release, likely induced by stress, broke the temporary silence. No one in their right mind would own up to it, but within five seconds, we could all smell it. Each plebe struggled to hold it together. The temptation to burst out in laughter was almost unbearable. I managed to not even give into a smirk.

"Well, I guess somebody's poop streak ends today," Severson chimed in temporarily lightening the mood. While being reminded of our stress-induced constipation wasn't my favorite topic, it was a welcome distraction from the momentary tension between Gonzo and McVane. We all uneasily chuckled along if only to acknowledge that we were listening to Severson's marginally good joke.

"Alright, fall-out," McVane continued smugly without breaking character. "Everyone muster up in formation in our usual spot in the parking lot ASAP."

Chapter 6

In the Shit
Thursday, July 13th, 1995
Mick, 0540 hrs.

All of the plebes of Foxtrot Company continued our synchronized ballet of precise and purposeful walking. We proceeded in a single file down the middle of the hallway, squaring our corners with each turn precisely as prescribed by our plebe rules. We were all on our way to our daily dosage of Plebe Physical Education Program, otherwise known as PEP.

What fucking day is it? They all feel the same—shitty.

Eventually we funneled down the stairs, maintaining our single file line amidst the other plebes. We were all hustling down to make our way to the second formation in ten minutes. Detailers manned the hallway and the staircase in a predatory fashion. They were waiting for the first errant plebe they could lay eyes on.

"Eyes in the boat," exclaimed one detailer. He kept his voice barely below the unacceptable level of yelling inside Bancroft at this hour. The intended aggression remained conveyed.

"Quit smoking and joking and get your asses down to the parking lot for PEP," barked another. He kept his commands a decibel below yelling.

A plebe one flight up was getting flamed before even making it outside.

"You're more ate up than a soup fucking sandwich, Hudson."

In a split second, it registered. My former summer-house guest, Danny Hudson, was getting lit up.

Sucks, but better him than me.

Once we arrived in the parking lot, we quickly made our way to our normal muster spot for PT. Though we had literally been through the same drill just minutes before, McVane initiated what had become a very repetitive practice. "Foxtrot Company, ah ten . . . HUT!"

The formation continued its normal cadence of activities with plebe squad leaders reporting, "Present and accounted for." Plus all necessary formalities. Even Gonzo played nice for the time being, seemingly learning his lessons from the prior weeks.

"Right face," barked Severson who had now assumed position of temporary platoon commander. Now that we were outside, the quiet voice constraint of pre-7 a.m. Bancroft Hall had been fully lifted. Each plebe upon hearing Severson's order turned uniformly right, now all facing in a marching position. "Forward, MARCH," continued Severson.

"At'a double time!" Severson loudly added, his voice still cracking from the intensity of two straight weeks of screaming.

"Oooooo Rah!" the plebe platoon replied, with just enough false enthusiasm to not get yelled at for lack of enthusiasm.

"March!" Severson commanded and we all immediately transitioned our march into a tightly cadenced jog.

The musical double time cadence began.

"Left, left, lefty, right, left, right!" went Severson as he too initiated his double time jog.

"Left, left, lefty, right, left, right!" the plebes yelled back in unison.

"Bullshit!" interrupted McVane, "not motivated enough!"

We all secretly grumbled, at least in our minds. We all knew that this was just the beginning of yet another very long day.

"Lo righty, left right!" Severson initiated another round of cadence

Foxtrot plebes screamed in return, "LO RIGHTY LEFT RIGHT!"

Morning PT was one of the few times that I could get away with not getting yelled at by my detailers. While I was not the most physically fit in my platoon, I was amongst the most physically fit. This meant during intense periods of exercise, I could relatively blend in. Guys like Gonzo and his black lungs were welcome targets for guys like McVane and Severson at PEP.

"Nothing but a peaceful morning jog by the Chesapeake," I whispered over to Gonzo taking a temporary moment in the run when I knew Severson and McVane could not see or hear me.

"Fuck off," he grumbled with a slight smirk.

At least we had ditched the rifles they made us run with the day before. Rifle PEP was one of the most dreaded forms of plebe existence. It was just like regular PT, only carrying rifles. The heft of the carried rifle over a three-mile jog was bad enough, but providing one more item for detailers to critique was another. Gonzo's limping jog reminded us all that we were a little extra sore today.

We eventually completed the half-mile trot to the "Rip Miller" football field where all members of the plebe class arrived, platoon by platoon, for their morning PT session. The rising sun glistened as one end of the field was juxtaposed against a panoramic view of the Chesapeake. By time of arrival, all of us had completely sweated through our blue-rimmed T-shirts. The morning bay breeze did little to help us out.

Shit, this is my last clean T-shirt.

I stopped in place, having finally arrived to our pre-determined spot on the AstroTurf. It felt vaguely like the surface of a putt-putt golf hole, only coarser.

One of the few luxuries of plebedom was found in Bancroft Hall's complimentary laundry service. The tradeoff was that it was terrible. Our previous laundry submission had been lost for three days and all of us, save Gonzo, were down to our last clean shirts. Gonzo had somehow finagled ten shirts during plebe issue versus the normal five. My suspicion was that he stole them. As I felt my last clean shirt drenched in sweat, I hoped he would front me an extra clean shirt. He had already delivered the same service to N.D. using his clean socks like bartering chips. I cringed at what he might ask me in exchange for a clean blue rim.

All of the final groups of plebe platoons set into position at precisely 6 a.m. Like clockwork, we began to hear a rumbling from down the road. It grew louder until we could all hear the slightly out of synch pistons firing off within a massive 1455cc V-twin engine. In a glistening show of chrome and steel, Senior Chief Spenato steered his turquoise Harley Davidson Fat Boy from the street and onto Rip Miller Field. As he hit the AstroTurf, he immediately torqued the throttle with the clutch in neutral. His sure to be non-street legal pipes erupted in a deafening roar. Every car alarm within a half a mile began honking. The audience erupted in cheer.

Is he even allowed to drive that thing on the field? I wondered to myself. If he wasn't, it really wouldn't have mattered. Senior Chief Spenato received celebrity status amongst the midshipman at the Naval Academy. Senior Chief was a decorated war veteran, having served in multiple combat missions over his nearly twenty-year career. This was made even more impressive by the fact that he spent this time as a Navy Seal. The Naval Academy welcomed Senior Chief with open arms and assigned him as the head of our PT regime throughout Plebe Summer. Two weeks in and he had already made us incrementally tougher.

Senior Chief Spenato dropped the kickstand down on his Harley with barrel chested authority, parking it just a few feet from a head-high platform with a megaphone already resting on its top. Spenato energetically climbed the wooden platform until he was standing on his temporary place of work.

His nimbleness was made even more impressive considering his large stature. He was thickly muscled but had a pronounced beer gut. I guess he had a few too many festive happy hours in his career. He grabbed the megaphone with authority and quickly shook it above his head like a trophy. The whole spectacle looked more like the entrance to a professional wrestling match than a military evolution.

"How y'all feeling out there this morning?" Spenato blared from the megaphone.

We all erupted in cheers and motivational yelps. Some of this was staged theatrics, but it was also difficult not to get caught up in the momentary excitement.

"Are you 100% motivated today?" Spenato continued stirring up the crowd.

"NINETY-NINE PLUS ONE, SENIOR CHIEF!" we all barked back in unison showing our class pride.

"Sure you're not ninety-eight percent?" Spenato continued.

"FOUR HOURS AND FIVE MINUTES, SENIOR CHIEF!" we continued our mandated mantras. The class of '98 had just completed their end of Plebe Year six weeks earlier. Their four-hour plus climb of the greased Herndon monument, a long-standing final tradition of Plebe Year, had been ridiculed from the moment we arrived for I-Day. Our detailers made extra sure we called that out any time we heard about the class of '98. It was yet another way the detailers ensured all upperclassmen, inclusive of the new ones, hated the plebes' guts.

"Alright then," he continued, "let's get this thing started. Drop and give me twenty-five motivational push-ups!"

And so the PT session began. We alternated between

pushups, sit-ups, flutter kicks, and the occasional set of jumping jacks. Intermingled within these exercises was the occasional roundtrip sprint from one sideline of the AstroTurf football field to the next as a way to break up the monotony. By the time we were through the fifteen-minute session of exercises, we all looked as though we had jumped in a swimming pool. The exercises were invigorating for most of us, challenging for a few others. Gonzo looked like death warmed over. No one could escape the blanket of humidity and heat summer had brought to Annapolis. Even before 6 a.m., it was already smothering us.

The PT session culminated with our Spenato-led three-mile formation run around the yard. There was something zen-like about the peaceful views of the Chesapeake Bay and the Severn River at dawn that morning. It had been rumored that Eric Clapton was staying on his yacht "Slow Hand" for the 4th of July weekend and had decided to stay a few extra weeks. Though no one could exactly qualify the rumor, it was a fun hobby looking at the collection of massive yachts parked on the bay and imagining which one might be his. I made a mental note that if I ever became a rock star that I would certainly enjoy sitting in my yacht laughing at the plebes getting the shit kicked out of them at 6 a.m.

The light of the early sunrise unveiled a reddish orange over our spectacular waterfront view. All of this serenity hummed along to a far less placid tune of "double time" cadence song:

And if I die in the Commie mud
Bury me with a case of Bud

Bury speakers all around my head
So I can rock with the Grateful Dead
Bury speakers all around my toes
So I can rock with Axel Rose

"McGee, sound off like ya gotta pair," screamed Severson following a less than enthusiastic singing performance somewhere around mile number two.

My lack of enthusiasm during our run wasn't being driven by exhaustion or fear. I was just lost in the moment, lost in the run. The exertion of physical exercise was a welcome bit of escapism. It was a chance to let my mind wander into thoughts of Budweiser and Guns N' Roses played on loud speakers. Even the morbidity of being buried and dead amongst these items did not taint the momentary joy it brought me just to think of them.

"Gonzalez," sternly blurted McVane midstride as he positioned his jogging path within inches of Gonzo. "Get your ass in gear. You are fucking with my platoon and making us all slow." McVane's voice lowered in conjunction with his use of profanity. While McVane swore like a sailor at nearly every possible opportunity, he always ensured that his profanity was meant for a private listening audience.

Our platoon made its last turn and double timed towards the final hundred yards of the run. Based on the amount of yelling accompanying this morning's run, most of us all sort of expected a pre-"fall-out" thrashing from our detailers.

"PlatOOON, Halt!" McVane belted out mechanically. "RRRRRRight, FACE!" He intensified his delivery and sounded a bit more personally agitated than normal.

Observation was not my strong point. I should have been patiently reading McVane's increased intensity and escalating temper. Instead I prepared to fall out before McVane could properly give the order. As everyone else stood deathly still awaiting what was sure to be a scathing pre-breakfast tirade from McVane, I was inattentive enough to prematurely step out of formation ahead of the order. Within seconds, the entire platoon was on the ground for an extra session of PT.

"One, two, three, seventy-eight!" our platoon shouted

"One, two, three, seventy-nine!" our platoon shouted again.

Oh good, only one hundred and twenty one of these four fucking count leg raises left.

I could feel my classmates' hatred burning holes in Gonzo and me with their scornful stares. Who could blame them? Gonzo and I each likely had a heavy hand in this. Perhaps this was already planned, perhaps I had nothing to do with it, or perhaps I was the straw that broke the camel's back. It really didn't matter as each classmate had their own verdict already determined in their heads. Though seeing each other get grilled was often funny, no one enjoyed getting mashed at another person's expense. If I had been in my classmates' shoes in that moment and not in my own, I'd be feeling the exact same thing.

We were eventually dismissed and sent off to prepare for morning formation and breakfast. Our platoon sprinted up the stairs frantically trying to make-up the ten minutes we lost in our morning preparation time from our platoon's punishment. Shower time would now have to be a thirty-second hose off this morning. My balls were going to stink all day.

Mick, 0712 hrs.

N.D. and I made it back safely into our room.
"MuthaFUCKA," N.D. screamed as soon as he crossed the threshold of our door. He sounded like Ice Cube. Nevertheless, it was the first time I had ever seen him lose his cool, and I knew that I was partially to blame. I remained silent and tried to let him vent without interruption. Although I considered myself a tough and scrappy guy, it would take N.D. all but about seventeen seconds to knock me out.

Our con-locker boomed as N.D. punched it off the tracks with one strike.

Correction, make that seven seconds to knock me out.

Gonzo was the last of us to make it into our room. He was struggling for our entire run. He was especially tired from our recent beating and could not join the rest of us in sprinting up four flights of stairs.

Just as he passed our doorway, he fell forward on his hands and knees panting like a wounded dog. He frantically grabbed for our garbage can. For a moment I worried that he might be initiating cardiac arrest.

"BWAAAAALLLLLTRRRRAAAAAALLLLTTTTH-HHH," he said

"BWAAAAALLLLLTRRRRAAAAAALLLLTTTTH-HHH," he said again

Soon our garbage can was half filled with its own bowl of stomach porridge. I wondered how Gonzo was getting so much food.

He must have a stash somewhere. That fucker has a trick for everything.

"Come on, man, we gotta hurry up and get shit goin,'" exclaimed N.D. "Gonzo, you gotta dump that shit somewhere. We gotta leave for formation in five minutes."

With that command, Gonzo immediately dumped the can's contents directly into the sink. The smell wafted to my nose and ignited my temper.

"What the fuck, man?" I aggressively queried Gonzo.

"You gotta fuckin' problem, man? The whole reason we got mashed is 'cause your green horn ass couldn't stay in formation," Gonzo replied, chunks of vomit were still on his chin. He tossed the garbage can my way, and I reluctantly caught it, fearful that any remaining contents would spill onto the floor, or worse yet, me.

"Fuck you, Gonzo, your slow ass got McVane all torqued up to begin with. Gonzo, for a guy that talks about being from the streets, you must be from Sesame fucking Street."

"What the fuck did you just say?" Gonzo angrily replied as his face turned red.

"I said I think you're a fucking pussy ass poser," I quickly antagonized while throwing the garbage can back in his direction.

Gonzo batted the steel can to the floor. It spilled the final remnants of vomit residue on our floor as it loudly clanged and rattled to a settled state. He then immediately charged while subsequently grabbing my shirt. I returned the favor with a punch directed at his face but instead grazed the side of his skull as he wisely dodged the punch.

Before we could grapple any further, N.D. grabbed each of us with one hand and slammed us against his personal locker. We immediately ceased our fisticuffs as we both knew we were powerless against a juggernaut like N.D.

"Cut that shit out," N.D. said, miraculously retaining his typical cool. "Get hosed down, get dressed, and get goin'. We got three minutes. Gonzo, you're given Mick a clean shirt, no fucking debate."

I was surprised that he hadn't just let us both beat the shit out of each other. Lucky for us, N.D. was the biggest man in the room, and not just by stature.

For a split second, I fantasized.

What if I just beat Gonzo's ass anyway? Eventually N.D. would just let us have it out. I'd kick the shit out of Gonzo, get kicked out. I'd be surfing within two weeks, just in time for fall's hurricane swells.

I squinted and clinched my teeth, forcing those thoughts to a silent place.

Don't quit now.

Gonzo and I begrudgingly obliged N.D.'s request. We grabbed our white work uniform and a clean change of underwear, before individually hosing off for thirty seconds in the cold shower to cool down. That and a few hurried swipes of deodorant was about all of the freshening up we had time for. My entire plebe class consistently reeked of b. o. throughout the day. It was an unfortunate side effect of Plebe Summer. All of the deodorant on the yard couldn't mask it.

Mick, 2130 hrs.

The day continued much the way it started, filled with formations, instructions, yelling, orders, waiting, sweating, pushups, yelling, formation, yelling, drill, marching, sweating, and pushups. After a while, it all seemed to blur together.

I couldn't get my mind off the morning. The more I thought more about my confrontation with Gonzo, the more I was disappointed with myself. I let my anger get the best of me.

By the end of the day, we were all exhausted. We finally made it back to our rooms and had thirty minutes of personal time ahead of our nightly mandatory singing of Navy Blue and Gold. The first bright spot of the day was only made better when we received a new round of "care packages" in the mail. Care packages were boxes filled with food, letters, and treats from back home. We had only been at the academy a couple of weeks, so we were just beginning to receive the initial care packages our friends and family had sent upon returning home from I-Day.

My initial boxes included Snickers, Twix, Doritos, and Gatorade mix stuffed as tightly as it all could fit into the worn cardboard box they were carried in. Nellie and Mom knew me well. I did, however, trash the brownies Bird had included. I didn't want to chance what special ingredients he may have added to the batch.

N.D.'s family outdid everyone. This was partially because they wanted him to keep his weight up for football. Dropping ten pounds over the summer wouldn't help him against the likely three hundred pound left tackle he'd be lining up against when Navy would open its football season on the road against SMU in two months. It took a man the stature of N.D. just to lift the massive box and store it in the closet, certainly a two-man job otherwise.

"Man, you don't even have any comments for these pictures, Gonzo?" N.D. taunted as he waved three new pictures of his hot girlfriend and her friends looking as provocative as ever in minimalistic bikinis.

Finally when N.D. was caught up writing his girlfriend a love letter, I mustered up the courage to approach Gonzo.

"Hey man, I am really sorry about this morning," I offered in as contrite a tone as possible. "I was pissed at you, but also at myself. We both fucked up out there."

Gonzo stared forward, took a deep breath, and looked up. "That's cool, man." I had wished the apology had been further verbalized and perhaps countered with a separate apology, but coming from Gonzo I recognized this was the best I was going to get at the moment.

"Look at you two muthafuckas makin' up and shit," chimed in N.D. dropping the love letter and joining in on the dialogue. "I guess the room of racial equality is back up and running, even from the Streets of Sesame."

We all had a good laugh. It was the first time this place felt remotely like home since we moved in. Truthfully, I was still a little angry with Gonzo as I am sure he was with me.

Isn't that always the case with family?

Our detailers quickly peered into our room to ensure no one had tried to escape or kill themselves before our mandatory bed time of 10 p.m. It was just a quick drill to cover their asses. Soon they'd be sneaking out on the town for a few beers before another day of training. Our room's bed-making scam stayed intact.

"Training day number fourteen," I whispered loud enough for our entire room to hear and with a dramatic pause continued, "flushed down the shitter."

"Amen to that," Gonzo said, quaintly validating the apology I had offered earlier.

Chapter 7

One Day Before Freedom
Thursday, August 3rd, 1995
Mick, 0459 hrs.

My alarm went off with the rest of my classmates. I rolled over in the bed and pounded the snooze button with my fist, relishing in my few remaining moments of horizontal joy.

This morning was happier than most. We were one day away from the start of Plebe Parents' Weekend. Through all of the training, marching, yelling, and countless push-ups, we finally had something to tangibly look forward to. Tomorrow and the two days following would be our first time off in over six weeks. Plebe Summer had seemed like an eternity. While brief encounters with rifle training and sailing offered a few glimmers of fun, this was the first big break of the summer. We were finally getting a well-deserved breather.

We had a busy day ahead before we hit our temporary finish line. We had a full slate of inspections on tap for the day.

The room seemed eerily quiet. N.D. had left the room a few days earlier to join his football teammates for training camp. He was one of a few plebes good enough to make the Varsity team as a plebe. This was made even more impressive since he had not even attended NAPS the year prior. As the upper-class football players had returned a few days earlier, N.D. would spend the majority of his remaining summer time prepping for the season opener against SMU.

As I looked across the room to the single bed, I noticed that Gonzo was suspiciously missing. I supposed he was either out on the ledge smoking a pre-PT cigarette or making a quick bathroom run. Within four seconds, my mystery was solved as our room door opened.

"What's up, homey?" Gonzo whispered in an excitedly silent tone. "I come bearing a gift."

In his hand was a yellow sheet of thin paper that resembled some sort of military form. We learned that these forms were often called "chits" and typically gave you special permission to do or miss something. N.D. had received one earlier in the summer to get out of shaving after a few ingrown hairs.

"What scam did you pull now?" I asked.

"I just bought us some extra prep time for uniform inspections with this sick chit," Gonzo replied. "Turns out I have the Hershey squirts, a dangerous proposition in this heat."

In other words, Gonzo had scammed the corpsman, the Naval Academy's version of a school nurse, into thinking he was sick with diarrhea and needed a day to re-hydrate in his room. The idea was genius. There was really no way to disprove he had diarrhea. Gonzo had essentially bought himself an extra day of rest and preparation ahead of Parents' Weekend.

Gonzo had already received a few get out of jail free cards from the corpsman with a yeast infection he had contracted in his ass a few weeks earlier. I wondered if Gonzo pleaded for similar mercy or just simply bribed the medical staff with cash. I wouldn't rule out either scenario.

"Now while you guys are out PTing this morning, I can catch up on some Zs," he continued, "and of course, when you get back from PT, you can spend your time prepping for the uniform inspection instead of the room. They're not going to force a Class Alpha inspection on a room with a sick classmate."

This was a needed advantage. We were well behind in prepping for our last "Class Alpha" room inspection, the most stringent of all room inspections typically conducted. In a Class Alpha, a white glove was used to thoroughly inspect for dust potentially residing on all room horizontal surfaces. A black sock was used to inspect the shower for camouflaged soap scum. While we were both super excited for N.D. and his pending football glory, we also struggled to make up for being one man down in prepping for inspection. This move was a great equalizer, proving yet again that despite his mouth and attitude, Gonzo was a strategic advantage as a roommate.

By the time reveille sounded, my optimism had grown exponentially.

"Holy shit, did you hear about the plebe from Alpha Company?" Gonzo continued. "Apparently this dude was so fed up with plebe shit that he snuck out of the yard a few nights ago and made a beeline for the highway. The cops picked him up at a gas station around midnight where he was trying to hitchhike across the Bay Bridge. He was headed to the Air Force base or some shit like that. Who the fuck would leave the Naval Academy to head to an Air Force base a week before Parents' Weekend?"

My heart sunk. I immediately knew exactly who that plebe was. I imagined there was only one guy in my class that would sneak out of the Naval Academy looking to head to the nearest Air Force base north bound on the Chesapeake Bay Bridge—Danny Hudson. Delaware was too small of a state to create statistical anomalies.

I avoided mentioning to Gonzo that I knew Danny or anything related to his story. The last thing I needed was his color commentary on the topic.

Mick, 1129 hrs.

There was a frenzy of energy in Tecumseh Court despite the current silence and stillness. Over one thousand plebes stood throughout the brick beach directly in the front of Bancroft Hall. All plebes were neatly aligned in thirty-six triple squad platoons. They were equally divided into two regiments assembled to the left and right of T-Court. A sea of white dazzled the viewing audience. Many parents watched attentively from the grass. They had already arrived in town ahead of formal Parents' Weekend kickoff the next day.

"REEEHHHHHH-JEEEEEEE-MEEEHHHHNT,

AAAAHH, TEEHHHHN, HUT!" The show formally began with a booming order to attention. The formal uniform inspection began.

Over the past few weeks we had graduated from our plebe "White Works" uniforms to our substantially sharper summer white uniforms. The summer whites looked very similar to what we would eventually wear as Naval Officers. It was a small yet motivating step towards making our way through the Plebe Summer experience.

I squinted my eyes and wiggled my toes. It was an unsuccessful attempt to distract myself from the uncomfortably hot stillness of our final formal uniform inspection before the weekend. The air felt like a sauna. My mind continually drifted to the topic of Danny Hudson.

I found some sorely sought commonality when I met Danny a few months earlier. Like me, he had yet to sweat the details of Reef Points or think much at all about Plebe Summer. Maybe he should have. Perhaps his lack of care before the summer was really an indication that he did not belong. That he really never wanted to be at the academy in the first place.

Was it only a matter of time that I'd come to the same conclusion?

I had thought about quitting plenty of times before. This was especially true during formation time in T-court. The mandated silent time gave my mind extra opportunity to mentally wander.

Not only did I think about quitting, I pondered every excruciating detail associated with it.

Who I would tell? What time? What day? When would I get home? How would I get there? What would I eat? What

TV shows would I watch? Who would I date? What would I tell friends when they asked me why I quit? Would I get complacent? Would I just end up being like Bird?

The train would halt right about there. Truthfully, I knew deep down that I would never fully end up like Bird. Still, it made me scared enough. I hated this place. I hated the majority of the people I shared it with. Still, voluntarily quitting was not something I could even begin to entertain.

I loved my mom deeply, but the last five years of her addiction battle had strained our relationship. Yes, she had come a long way, but she still had her demons. Eventually, she would need someone to lean on again. I had to be that person. Stability wasn't sitting back home smoking joints on the porch. It was right here, chasing my dreams, building my own stable world. There was no doubt it would eventually be needed by those I loved the most. I had to stick with it. It was during times like these that made me think of my dad the most.

"Quitting and crying," my dad used to lecture, "two things men don't do."

It was a message I would hear repeatedly as a child, often with resentment. It meant sticking through wrestling in 6th grade even though I lost all but one match. It meant forcing back tears every time I scraped my knee skateboarding, which was often. It meant being stoic when I watched my dad get buried in the ground before I had my braces removed. It was part of who I was as an individual.

The publicized intent of inspection scheduling at 1130 was to synch up the evolution with the eventual noon meal formation. This essentially killed two birds with one stone by having us remain outside for the entire time. It felt like that same stone was being shoved up my ass.

It was all bullshit. The real reason for the inspection's timing was to incentivize more pedestrian tourist traffic to help sell more trinkets at the gift shop that day. Parents' Weekend was just a day away. The entire yard was already swarming with obnoxious parents anticipating the big weekend. There were mom shorts and fanny packs for as far as the eye could see.

It was an academy mission to make the plebe experience as uncomfortable as possible. Starting the day with a morning inspection was bad. Waiting a few hours and having it at peak humidity was shit icing on poop cake.

Why did we have to eat "squared meals?" Why did we have formations fifty-seven times a day? Why did we have to chop in the hall? Why did we have to salute squirrels when we passed them on the yard?

My hypothesized logic was the only one that credibly answered the entirety of those questions. There was no other sane answer.

Always err to the side of shittiness. That's the only modus operandi that logically makes this place tick.

I grinded my teeth as that reality sunk in. Then I thought of Gonzo taking a wondrous nap while all of us were out here sweating. My annoyance grew exponentially. I knew this was a hypocritical emotion. How could I get mad at Gonzo for gaming the system when a split second later I'm cherishing him for weaseling us out of the afternoon's room inspection?

This was the most uncomfortable part of Plebe Summer. Knowing your character was being tested constantly and typically failing on a daily basis. It was a tough pill to swallow. The Naval Academy set an impossible standard for perfection, fully knowing that no individual could muster up to it. Dealing with those shortcomings was really what the academy was all about. Despite perpetually coming up short, a plebe needed to keep their grit tank full.

"This shit is all a game," Gonzo said repeatedly to N.D. and me over the summer. Even if it wasn't true, we heard it enough from him to believe it. That simple notion preserved the right perspective to get through this stuff. It made a difference.

I wondered if Danny Hudson had heard those words that things might have played out differently. The concept of mantra salvation seemed too far of a stretch. Perhaps Danny was simply living his father's dreams and not his own. There was a lot of that going around these days. This is what kept Tango Company, the temporary holding entity for all out-processing plebes, filled to the brim the entire summer. Just seeing Tango Company, who still made the plebes participate in all mandatory formations and inspections until their processing was complete, made me question my own intent and desire to be here.

Questioning my intent was not a rarity. Hearing about Danny and seeing Tango Company were hardly the only things that triggered these musings. I thought about intent constantly.

It was intent that made all the difference. No sane person would ever put up with the toils of plebe life without wanting to get through it. That, I resolved, was the key difference between Danny and me. I wanted to get through this. I had to get through this. Whether they knew it or appreciated it, my family needed me to do this.

Our platoon commander, 1/C Theisen and company officer, LT Walker, pivoted and purposely walked behind second squad. He checked their backside to ensure everyone was squared away with 360 degree coverage.

"Second squad," barked out 2/C Foster, one of the second set detailers to the left of the middle line of the platoon, "Parade, rest." The second squad simultaneously exited the position of attention to a slightly more relaxed stance of parade rest. Their hands crossed behind their backs. Their feet were now shoulder length apart.

"Third squad," followed 2/C Irving, "ah ten, HUT." All ten of my squad mates snapped to immediate attention. Our heels brought together in unison making an impressive clicking sound that echoed off the stone buildings collectively surrounding Tecumseh Court.

I stood tensely. I tried not to get too distracted or annoyed by my current state of physical discomfort. I could feel individual beads of sweat dripping from the back of my neck, down my back under my T-shirt, through the canyon of my ass crack, and into the swamp of despair in my nether region. It was no wonder I had to blow through about a can of Tinactin a week during my stay on the bay. I maintained an aggressive front against the variety of bacteria and fungus each day offered. My perpetual state of damp sweat did not help matters. Gonzo told us enough "crotch rot" sea stories to scare N.D. and me into buying and applying every antifungal ointment we could find. Our aerosol savior became the most common element of all of our care packages, surpassing cookies, potato chips, and Gatorade combined. Gonzo's tales nor the ointments helped me much. My testicles were as red as Christmas balls.

God damn, I'd kill for a scratch.

I wiggled my toes in an attempt to subtly adjust my boxers for temporary relief. It did not help one bit.

As I was on the shorter side of the mids in my squad, I stood third from left in our row, the second shortest male and taller than our lone female squad-mate. I had to wait for six other mids to get inspected until it was my turn.

1/C Theisen, the platoon commander, was first down the line. He would typically do a quick once over, pick some ridiculously tiny nit-pick on the uniformed plebe in front of him, then wait for the lieutenant to his right to finish his inspection. He'd then pivot left, take a long step, and pivot right to face the next squad member in line. This process would repeat ten times until all squad members had been inspected.

To the right of the platoon commander was our company officer, LT Walker, the senior ranking officer in our platoon and inspecting officer for this evaluation. To the right of Walker was 2/C Irwin, our detailer and squad leader who would stand by taking notes of the inspecting officer's various comments and critiques. All pivots and turns going down the line were completely synchronized as the three individuals slowly but surely made their way to my end of the squad.

LT Walker was a cupcake in these endeavors. Irwin had barely written two sentences in his notepad as there were very few noteworthy critiques coming out of our inspecting officer. While our "I want to be a Marine" platoon commander would typically shit on us for a nametag that was pinned an eighth of an inch too high, or a belt that was the same distance off center, Walker was quite a bit more relaxed. He played the "good cop" of our inspection team. I actually think he took a little pleasure in annoying the far more detailed obsessed platoon commander to his right. It wasn't hard imagining anyone hating that guy's guts. He was a fucking tool. A Joe Mid in every sense of the word.

Despite the relaxed standard for this inspection, Walker was still deliberately slow. All of the plebe platoons were being inspected at the same time. This meant that a few of the harder inspectors were taking their dear old time. This was especially the case with the attention to detail obsessed Marine Corps company officers. In order to avoid appearing blatantly lax, LT Walker merely slowed his pace down. This delay created feeble attempts for small talk to bridge the obsessive-compulsive timing gap.

I could hear the same repetitive dialogue repeated down the line of my squad.

"Midshipman fourth class, blabbity blah, how are you doing today?"

"Sir, outstanding sir."

"Great, you looking forward to the weekend?"

"Sir, yes sir."

"Awesome, looking good. Keep it up and enjoy the weekend. You've earned it."

The whole dialogue was mechanical and cold. Part of me wanted to answer LT Walker truthfully as I played the fictional scene in my imagination.

"Midshipman McGee, how are you doing today?"

"Sir, I'm hot. My balls itch. It's my senior summer, and I haven't been laid in over seven months. How the fuck do you think I'm doing, asshole?"

"Great. You looking forward to the weekend?"

"Sir, it will be all I have in me not to leave the yard, put on a bandana, and listen to Axl Rose as I permanently drive off into the sunset."

"Awesome, looking good. Keep it up and enjoy the weekend. You've earned it."

If only I had the balls.

Instead I played nice and followed suit. There was no need to rock the boat the day before my first real break of Plebe Year. Eventually our squad was complete and the inspecting crew made its way behind my squad and back towards the front of the formation.

"Second squad, atten hut!" quickly barked first squad's leader.

"First squad, atten hut!" followed the next squad leader.

The Platoon Commander marched back to his position at front and center of the platoon facing ahead. He drew his sword to a position of attention to acknowledge the senior officer in his presence. LT Walker then quickly saluted, said a few words, none of which we could hear, and was on his way.

Our platoon commander sheathed his sword, then performed a precise about face, and in one smooth motion, he was turned around facing us.

"Platoon," he started in his typical monotone dialogue, intentionally avoiding the slightest perception of emotion. "Great job today. I appreciate the attention to detail."

I knew it pained Theisen to say this. If it were left up

to his own devices, he would not even be halfway through our platoon's inspection. He'd still be smack dab in the middle of ripping everyone in his path a new asshole.

"Color Man is," he continued with a dramatic pause, "4th class McGee."

Color Man meant that I was subjectively judged as having the best uniform in the platoon that day. I was cautiously proud with a tinge of guilt. With Gonzo getting us out of room inspection later in the day, I had extra time in the morning to prep my uniform. It was a big advantage over my classmates. I also had the repetitive advantage of learning every dirty little uniform inspection cheat that Gonzo had collected in his four-year naval career. The "mop n' glow" on the shoes was my favorite. The trick made my spit shine shoes look as though they were mirrored.

"Great shoes always wins Color Man," Gonzo repeatedly said throughout the summer as he won Color Man in all but two of our uniform inspections of the summer. His dominance in this area pissed off detailers and classmates alike. Still, it was hard not to respect his acumen. This is what kept Gonzo respectability from residing in the toilet. Despite his foibles in certain areas, he really knew his shit in other important ones.

Gonzo actually did us all a huge solid in collecting the extra uniform inspection prep time. With my extra time, I would additionally have a chance to go into a variety of classmates' rooms and help them prepare for the inspection my room was exempted from. It would be a "hearts and minds" mission. With Gonzo as my roommate, I was continually trying everything that I could to stock up goodwill with my classmates.

Gonzo had been accountable for more forced pushups than any other member of our platoon. His humor, savvy, and wit kept him barely well-liked for the time being. He was always pushing the envelope of patience. I was continually trying my best to counter that trend. It was the only way I knew how to repay Gonzo for all of the times he helped me out over the course of the summer.

Following the few minutes it took the three overly anal-retentive Marine Corps Company officers to finally finish inspecting their platoons, we were collectively brought to attention as a plebe class. Noon meal formation continued as always with the mechanical marching and drum beat back into Bancroft Hall.

Parents seemed mesmerized by the process. To the untrained eye, noon meal formation looked like an impressive ballet of precision and discipline. Truthfully it was something you could train monkeys to do if you beat them hard enough over a six-week period. Luckily for the spectating parents, we were beaten just hard enough to look like we knew what we were doing. The spectacle lived up to the hype, despite the sacrifices every plebe made during the summer to make it happen.

Within ten minutes, we were back inside Bancroft Hall. The parents outside were left wondering how to occupy themselves between then and the military parade slated for the next morning. We were one step closer to the weekend. I could not wipe the enormous smile off my face.

✧✧✧

Mick, 2125 hrs.

By sundown, there was a giddy buzz throughout the yard. No one could contain the excitement of Parents' Weekend. Even the detailers seemed to ease off the throttle a bit once we got through room inspections. Underneath the red nametag and the generally hard façade, they were still midshipman. While their summer had not been as hard as ours had, it was still hard. I assumed they welcomed the break almost as much as we did.

As the night wound down, Gonzo made a miraculous recovery. He set his alarm for 0445 so he could get down to the corpsman the next morning and assure himself liberty the next day with an updated medical chit. All I could do was nervously pace around the room in excitement.

Mom, Aunt Nellie, and Bird would all be down the next day to see me. They would be piling into Yogi directly after Bird's morning surf session and zip up Route 50 to make their visit. Most families were already in town bolstering the Annapolis tourist economy and plotting out where they would sit for the next morning's parade. My family figured the only site they really wanted to see was me. They timed their arrival to coincide precisely with the start of my liberty and not a second sooner. I was the one that told them the parade would be lame. I didn't mind the lack of cheering section. Walking in a coordinated manner to occasionally break up the monotony of standing around and sweating your balls off did not seem like much of a spectator sport.

The utter lack of interest in all things plebian was fine

by me. The last thing I wanted to be over the weekend was a tour guide around the yard. This was likely the unfortunate fate for many of my classmates. For me, air conditioning, cable television, my CD player, and McDonald's would more than suffice.

I had been trading letters with Mom, Nellie, and Bird on a weekly basis. I kept them apprised of my situation, typically griping about Gonzo and his obnoxious mouth. Aunt Nellie wrote back the most, likely because she was naturally the most verbose. Mom wrote as best she could. Appropriately expressing emotions was not her strong point. She kept things short and to the point in fear that she might upset me or motivate me in an unintended way. Bird was even less verbose. His letters typically contained a brief summary of the week's surf report and occasionally a Polaroid picture of some random attractive female he spied on the beach earlier that week. Two weeks earlier, he also took a picture of his penis and somehow convinced the local tourist shop to embed it in an obnoxious souvenir picture holder called scopes. Kids hawked scopes to tourists on the beach. Bird and I hated them. The handsome douche bags that sold them were the worst. I could only imagine the shit storm that would befall me should my company officer or Gonzo stumble upon that trinket. Regardless, I kept it visible in the locked portion of my personal closet. Looking at it usually made me chuckle.

No one had made any hotel reservations for the weekend. That was typical for a few reasons. First, everyone in my family maintained bad credit and had maxed out any remaining credit cards the banks were too dim not to immediately cancel. Aunt Nellie was particularly bad.

She had a nasty antique addiction that kept her perpetually in financial peril, but she did have a complete 17th century silver set dating back to the British Empire. Reserving a roach infested motel room over the phone with a credit card was out of the question. On the bright side, fielding a proper dinette set should the Queen of England visit Ocean City on a whim would not be a problem. Second, Bird always carried obscene amounts of cash with him and could usually bribe a vacancy in virtually any hotel of his choice. Lastly, they were all lazy procrastinators and did nothing in life proactively. None of this concerned me. It was all expected behavior. I was just so happy to be spending time with them away from the academy.

We sang Navy Blue and Gold before mandatory bedtime. Every single person sang a little more loudly and with a little more pride that night. For as small a milestone as Plebe Parents' Weekend actually was, it was a nice break regardless. We thought about it hourly for the past six weeks.

As I sat wide awake in my bed, sleep seemed a long way off. My mind was racing. I knew that I would be tired come morning. It didn't matter. For the first time in multiple months, I could lie around and nap all day.

"Hey Mick, you up?" Gonzo interrupted my visions of glorious napping.

"Yeah man, what's up?" I replied in a non-whisper. N.D. was sleeping in the Ricketts Hall football facility. It was just Gonzo and me in the room tonight.

"Come out to the rooftop, I wanna show you something."

With that I hopped out of bed and followed Gonzo

out of the window. The rooftop at night was a magnificent view of the bay and the academy. Academic year was still a few weeks off. Being out on the roof was still relatively safe with minimal chances of being caught by upperclassmen. Sneaking out onto it became a nightly ritual for Gonzo.

"Pretty nice out here, huh?" Gonzo said. He repeatedly smacked the top of his unopened cigarette box. He peeled off the wrapper and pulled one smoke out. He flipped it and put the cigarette back in the box upside down.

"Gotta stash the lucky smoke, homey," he answered my nonverbal curiosity.

He extended the box to me, offering me one of his smokes.

"Thanks man, I haven't had one of these since before I got here," I said. I grabbed a smoke from the box. Damn I had missed this.

He pulled out a lighter and offered it my way. The wind was too intense for this gesture so I grabbed the lighter and lit it like an old pro. Bird and I would routinely light up smokes amidst intense ocean breezes so the roof top bay breeze was not an issue.

"Looks like you done that before, homey," admired Gonzo.

"Yeah man, menthols remind me of home," I replied. I went on to tell him about Aunt Nellie, and then an abbreviated version of my father's passing and my mother's subsequent depression. I withheld the full details of Bird, fearing he would never believe them.

"Your family sounds just as crazy as mine," Gonzo admired. It seemed surreal that he would actually be meeting them in a matter of hours.

We continued smoking silently for a while, eventually each enjoying our third cigarette. My lungs felt like I had just inhaled a chimney, but the lack of morning PT had me optimistically unconcerned.

"Mick," Gonzo interrupted the momentary silence. "I just wanted to let you know that you're a good guy."

"Thanks man, I appreciate it," I humbly returned. "I feel the same way about you. You've been a huge help to me this summer." I meant what I said.

"I know we didn't get off to a great start the first few days. I know how I can be a dick sometimes," he continued.

"Sometimes?" I said with a laugh.

"Fuck you, Wonderbread!" he sniped with a smile.

"No man, I mean it. You helped pull me through this stuff," I said to emphasize my gratitude. We both took in the view silently for the next five minutes.

"Here," Gonzo broke the silence. "Look at this, I want to show you something," Gonzo directed as he pulled a picture out from behind him along with a flashlight. He clicked the flashlight on and illuminated a picture of a young woman with an infant.

"This is my old lady Jennie, and that angel she is holding, she's my daughter," he spoke softly yet proudly. "She was born a month before I-Day. Her name is Marisol."

He handed me the picture. I vaguely remembered seeing this picture on his desk blotter. Gonzo had told N.D. and me that they were pictures of his cousins back home. I hadn't looked or thought more closely than that since Gonzo threatened to stab me every time I got near those pictures.

He then went on to tell me the full story. How he had dated the same girl for three years down in Norfolk. They met after his first long deployment and dated through several more. She got knocked up last fall. She's still down in Norfolk while he's cranking through the academy.

"They're trying to move out here. We just don't have the cash flow to make it happen. I'm making fifty bucks a month as a plebe. Annapolis is an expensive place if you're working a grocery cash register and you got another mouth to feed."

"So does the academy know about this?" I asked.

"The entire Navy doesn't know a damn thing," he answered. "Gotta stay that way. If they know I got a kid, I'm back to the fleet," he explained.

It was getting late, but I was completely sucked into the story. I knew what it was like to miss a dad. I really felt for Marisol.

"Can the Navy help you out here?" I asked.

"I'm not even listed on the birth certificate as the father," Gonzo's voice cracked and he quickly cleared his throat. "I don't wanna go back to the fleet, homey. They'll just send me back out to sea. If I can get them up here, I'll at least see 'em on the weekends."

"What about getting out of the Navy?" I asked. "I know you may not want to do that but—"

"Shit, homey," Gonzo interrupted. "I'd get out of the Navy in a heartbeat if I had the dough. Forty large, that's all it takes."

"What does that mean? I thought you could drop out of here up until start of junior year," I asked with budding personal curiosity.

"You get a free ride for two years if you come in as a civilian like you did. For the E-dawgs like me, it's forty grand to buy out if you leave before junior year. After that, it's sixty. If you don't got the dough, back to the fleet you go."

I breathed a sigh of relief. While I still resolved to never quit, it was nice to know that if I got kicked out for academics or discipline that I was still on a free ride till junior year.

"You want to get rid of me? Find me forty grand and I'll be out of your hair in no time."

His eyes began to tear up. "I'm so excited to see them tomorrow. I miss them so much, homey."

He took another deep breath, this time sans cigarette as he needed maximum oxygen intake to regain his slipping composure.

I vaguely understood the pressures of being a patriarch. It was complex. It was tough. It made things messy sometimes. With my own dad and grandfather gone, I partially related to the emotional weight Gonzo was feeling. My story had different context than Gonzo's did. I wasn't a father myself, but with each passing year, I felt greater pressure to fill the void of my own family's patriarchs. From that void, I could still hear their voices.

Suck it up, Mick.

"Mick, you can't say nothing about this tomorrow, or ever," Gonzo suddenly became firm. "You can't even look surprised or overly excited when you meet them tomorrow."

I nodded my head in agreement. "They're your cousins, end of story."

"Thanks, Mick," Gonzo replied with a hearty smack on the back that almost sent me tumbling to an unexpected death fifty feet below. "I'm going to need your help when the books come out," he continued with a sense of relief having ensured he was covered tomorrow. "Polishing shoes, folding clothes, cleaning rooms are all things I do well. Calculus and Chemistry is another story."

"I got you covered," I assuredly replied. "You cover the military stuff, I'll carry the nerd stuff, N.D. will carry the `if you mess with my room I'll kick your ass stuff," I added, cementing our post Plebe Summer roommate relationship and dare I say friendship.

"And Mick, one more thing," Gonzo chimed as I had already put one leg back through our window and into our room.

"What's that, Gonzo?"

"Puerto Ricans like Big Bird too, homey. I can hang on Sesame Street as well as any street," he continued with a smile, acknowledging that my outburst of a few weeks earlier was water under the bridge.

"Fuck off," I returned with a smirk.

Chapter 8

Enjoy it While it Lasts
Sunday, August 6th, 1995
Mick, 0732 hrs.

"Dismissed," ordered 2/C Foster to Foxtrot Company. He was one of a handful of upper-class midshipman unlucky enough to have to get up at 0730 with the rest of the plebes. Someone had to dismiss us for liberty. The rest of the detailers joyfully relished in the rare morning of extra sleep.

It was officially our last day of Parents' Weekend. Yesterday as planned, I spent most of the day in a hotel room in nearby Glenburnie. While most plebes' hotel rooms offered amenities like high thread count Egyptian cotton sheets and crab omelet room service, I was just happy to have air conditioning and complimentary HBO. I previously lacked these two things both at home and at the Naval Academy. The frigid air pumping out of our wall unit was more than enough to keep me happy.

Other than meeting the families of N.D. and Gonzo in our room shortly after receiving our first day of liberty, I avoided the academy and Annapolis like the plague. Bird managed to behave himself save for the instance when he was instructed to wear shoes by academy personnel. While entering Bancroft Hall barefoot, he chose to return in a pair of the only footwear he could find in Yogi, refusing to take the offer of my running shoes.

"Nah, Bunkie, I'll take these just in case I want to go boogie boarding," teased Bird, still holding onto his grudge against my occasional body boarding as he slipped on the fins I still kept in the trunk of Yogi.

I could only imagine what was being said in Spanish by Gonzo's full twenty member family caravan upon seeing dreadlocked Caucasian Bird entering our room in a penguin's waddle.

"Loco blanco," I recall hearing one of Gonzo's silver-haired aunts comment under her breath.

The first two mornings of Plebe Summer Parents' Weekend was filled with parades and other various forms of mandatory tourist performances prior to eventual lunchtime liberty. On Sunday, our final day of our respite, we were given the morning off to possibly attend religious services and then get a final afternoon of liberty before our weekend was over. Most of my friends were just planning to catch the afternoon matinee of Pulp Fiction a few miles off the yard at the Annapolis Mall.

I was indeed on a religious pilgrimage. It was not a journey to a traditional place of worship, or to see Pulp Fiction for the seventh time, but instead to surf my old breaks in OC. It had been too long.

Storm season was on the horizon and the typical early August "Lake Atlantic" was transitioning back into a surfable break. Powerful fall storms would be pumping in good surf right up until November. It was hardly the Endless Summer, but certainly better than hanging out in Bancroft Hall as a plebe.

In the handful of times I was permitted to call home, the upcoming storm season was about the only thing Bird could talk about. As with every year, hope sprung eternal as fledgling meteorologist Bird already had his scientific justification for why this was "the season not to be missed." He sounded like a junkie hunting for a fix. Parents' Weekend be damned, I was not going to miss it.

Over Parents' Weekend, there were three primary rules. Rule number one, just like the rest of Plebe Year, and the full year after that into our sophomore year, no civilian clothes. The only appropriate summer liberty attire was full summer whites, worn with spit polish detail. Rule number two, do whatever you like on liberty as a law-abiding citizen, but it must be within a thirty-mile radius of the academy. Anything outside of this radius was forbidden. Rule number three, stay out of trouble.

As we sped past the town of Easton, fifty-one miles away from the academy and thirty minutes into the drive, I had already broken two of the three short list of rules having well exceeded the thirty-mile radius and neatly hung my summer white uniform in favor of my more accustomed board shorts. Though I was not overly religious, I prayed that I could keep the third rule and stay out of trouble. I knew this was a 50/50 proposition given my temporary chauffeur.

The first thirty minutes of the drive lacked any resemblance of dialogue. Everyone in the car was tired of Annapolis and ready to get back to Ocean City, albeit my visit would be temporary. The lack of discussion was supplemented by the blowing wind coming through Yogi's rolled down windows, the steady beeping of Bird's radar detector, and copious amounts of loud Pearl Jam from the radio.

"Hey Bird," I said as I temporarily broke the dearth of conversation.

"S'up Bunkie," he replied after being lost in thought for a few moments, likely envisioning his forthcoming surf session a mere hour away.

"What ever happened to that chick Stephanie that I took to Junior Prom?" I queried as I went through a quick mental rolodex of attractive local Ocean City girls I had still presumed desirable, single, and available. It was a short list. It was the sad state of my love life, but it was all I had to work with.

"Dude, I heard that chick was boning that dude Meat that bounces up at Seacrets," Bird quickly replied, deflating all subsequent hope of romance for the weekend.

"Lawrence, that boy looks like Johnny Unitas, and with a name like Meat, I'd gladly play center for him," Nellie chimed in wistfully. "Best calves in Ocean City too," she continued her grocery store romance novel description.

"Mmmm, tell me about it," replied my mother wistfully. "That Stephanie is one lucky girl. Sorry, Mick."

"Fuck guys, LIMITS!" I yelled towards the back of Yogi and to the full attendees of the sexually promiscuous peanut gallery. With that last bit of dialogue, I pumped up the volume of Yogi's radio. The Pixies Surfer Rosa began where it left off on my favorite song, Gigantic. I hoped the song's lyrics would be predictive of the waves we would eventually ride later in the day. I closed my eyes to catch a catnap ahead of the surf that lay ahead.

Mick, 1545 hrs.

"I will be there once mooooooooooooooore." Pearl Jam lyrics echoed through Yogi's speakers and conveyed my deepest wishes. These lyrics were temporary. CD, tape, or otherwise, Bancroft Hall strictly prohibited music of any kind for plebes. I sat back and relished in the impromptu visualization my listening provided. Temporary imaginary waves would soon be replaced by very real and very agitated detailers.

With the blink of an eye, the morning and my final day of liberty was over. A storm camping offshore had merged with a front from West Virginia earlier in the day. Westerly winds cleaned up an already good swell. The surf session was indeed epic with glassy head high sets pumping in the entire time we were out there.

Unbeknownst to me at the time, Bird had bribed the lifeguards a couple hundred bucks to let us stay out for an extra thirty minutes before they had to clear the surfers out of the water for the oncoming tourists. Even after our temporarily purchased amnesty, Bird refused to get out of the water when prompted. For a fleeting few minutes, it felt like I had never left the shoreline. That felt good.

We eventually pulled closer to the Bay Bridge on our route back home. Bird stopped in a gas station strategically within the thirty-mile radius of the academy. It was just the two of us for this ride. We spared Mom and Aunt Nellie the burden of the three hour round trip to and from the academy back to the shore. It also meant not having to say another goodbye during a weekend and summer that was already filled to the brim with them.

I quickly darted into a bathroom stall and rushed to put my uniform back on. I already noticed new stains on my uniform shirt. It was a dubiously impressive feat. I hadn't even had my summer whites on for more than a half hour during the entire trip. I also worried that my general lack of attention to every small detail sans Gonzo's support would render me a giant bull's eye back at the hall. I knew that I would be right back in the suck of Plebe Summer life in about an hour.

In two minutes, my physical appearance was somewhat back to where it was at morning formation save a few stains. Mentally I was still lost in the waves. I left some sand on my feet as I slipped my white socks on and then my still glossy white leather shoes. They were still gleaming from their "Color Man" performance of a few days earlier. The irritation of sand in my shoes was an intentional reminder that I wasn't stuck on the yard today. It was a necessary yet lone memento of an epic day of surfing.

"So how are things really going, Bunkie?" Bird broke our post-gas station silence. "You know, with the Navy type shit."

"It's alright," I replied. "At least Plebe Summer is just about over."

"What about that Puerto Rican dude?"

"Gonzo? My roommate?"

"Yeah, the dude I met in the room. His granny called

me a "crazy white." He added quotation marks with his fingers to emphasize his disgust. "I took fuckin' Spanish too, you know."

"Gonzo's all right. He has his own drama shit going on."

"What kinda drama shit?"

"He's gotta kid, a big no no at the academy. If he gets found out, he gets the automatic boot. Sometimes I think he wants to. The forty large bail payment is just too much."

"What fuckin forty large bail payment?"

"It's nothin', just an expression. If you come to the academy as a prior enlisted sailor and decide to leave, you can either go back to being an enlisted sailor or buy out at forty grand. Forty grand would buy his way out of the Navy."

I could tell the dialogue was already confusing him.

Bird took a drag of his Marlboro and then stayed quiet for the next two minutes. He exhaled a cloud of smoke that filled the car cabin before making its way out of the window.

"Be careful with him, Bunkie. A desperate person does desperate things."

"Gonzo? Nah, man. He's a loud mouthed dick sometimes, but he's harmless."

"You say so." Bird turned his attention back to the ride.

I quickly attempted to change the subject. "It was good seeing Farm today, but he seemed a little down. What's goin on there?"

"Farm, yeah, that dumbass just got his second DUI," Bird explained. He won't be driving for a long time."

"Damn, why didn't he mention it to me?" I wondered

aloud. In a way I was insulted. We were friends.

"He lost his license and is fucking embarrassed. I also think he was trying to keep the heavy shit away from you. You know, you have enough to worry about."

I couldn't tell if that statement was serious or sarcastic. It was a fine line with Bird sometimes.

Silence pervaded our five-mile journey over the Bay Bridge, finally leaving Maryland's eastern shore in the rearview mirror. We headed over "oh shit hill," a stretch of road before the Severn River Bridge and eventually the Naval Academy on the adjacent riverbank. "Oh shit" was a commonly uttered phrase by mids upon getting the first vantage point of the Naval Academy after exiting Route 50. It was a common entrance point for mids returning from liberty and vacation. It had been the scene of a hor-rific accident less than a year earlier, prematurely ending the life of several well-liked midshipmen and only adding to its negative mystique.

Fuck me.

Mick, 1630 hrs.

"We have to talk, Micky," Bird said as he finally found an adequate parking spot on the yard for Yogi. He settled for a recently opened space between the chapel and the large white gazebo in front of it. It took us ten minutes to find the spot. The yard was filling up with returning plebes and sobbing parents. Luckily, we just missed the final rush to the yard at gate 8. I contemplated what I might do with my last thirty minutes of freedom. I wasn't about to go back to my room a second earlier than I needed to.

"Shoot," I quickly replied. It was an odd dialogue. In my lifetime with Bird I couldn't recall a single instance where he started the conversation with "we have to talk."

Sure, I had had several conversations that started with "we have to talk" but they were usually coming from my mom or Aunt Nellie to lecture me for bad behavior or from a soon-to-be ex-girlfriend initiating the "it's not you, it's me" speech.

"Epic day today, Bunkie," continued Bird from the driver's seat.

"Agreed," I said, reaffirming a blatant statement of the obvious and wondering where this conversation was going. "I really appreciated the surf session. Great to get out with the Fellas again."

Bird took a long sigh and scratched his dreads. He only did that when he was extremely nervous.

"Look, I don't know how to say this," he jumped right into the conversation. There was another pause and a scratch. "We have to stay apart after this."

"No shit, Sherlock," I replied. "I won't be seeing much of anyone back home until Thanksgiving."

"No, Micky, I mean for like the next four years," Bird interjected.

"What the hell is that supposed to mean?" I asked confused and angered. "So I guess I am officially not cool enough for you now?"

"No, it's not like that at all," Bird replied quickly.

"Then what exactly is it like?" I queried more audibly.

"You know my profession," Bird responded, "not exactly the type of thing a Naval Officer needs to be associated with."

"It's not like I didn't know that all along. Come on, man, you know that shit never bothered me as long as you stayed safe and kept me distanced from it. Are you still moping over that Danny Hudson shit?"

Bird's drug use had never bothered me. It never made him less of a person in my eyes. I distanced myself from it since I had seen firsthand where it had led his life. Bird may have been in his happy place, but that path wasn't for me. It's the reason I kept a partial distance from the Fellas.

"This time it's different," Bird spoke softly looking away from me and out of the rolled down driver's side window to avert an argument over the matter.

"How the hell is that?" I darted back looking for a heated argument.

"Look man, I am getting caught up in trafficking up in this area," Bird replied trying to diffuse the situation with as minimal dialogue as possible.

"What area is that?" I asked. There was ten seconds of awkward silence, until I figured it out.

"The fucking Naval Academy?" I screamed as I quickly contemplated punching Bird but avoided the temptation. "Oh yeah, that makes perfect sense, you asshole!"

"It's not like that, Micky, this one wasn't my call," desperately pleaded Bird.

"Bullshit, Bird, it's always your call," I fumed as I quickly exited the passenger side door. I forcefully slammed it shut.

"I wish I could tell you more but you know way too much already. I'm just trying to keep you out of trouble,"

Bird continued as he leaned across the front seat bench and yelled out of the passenger door.

I re-opened the passenger door. Bird thought I was coming back to speak reasonably. He sat back upright. I ignored him altogether and flipped the front seat down to access the back row. In my angry haste, I had forgotten my bag in the back. Bird sat back in silence trying to respect my anger.

"Quit doing me favors, asshole, I can cover my own ass!" I wanted to stay quiet, but my rage wouldn't let me. As I grabbed my bag of personal shit, I saw something I had unfortunately forgotten about. Directly behind Bird's seat on the back floor was my grandfather's rusty old tool-box.

The green toolbox was a family toolbox. It wasn't much to look at. It was the color of green dog shit. The toolbox wasn't very functional either. It was heavy, rusted, and half of the tools were broken with age or over use.

I had never met my grandfather. Pop Pop died just weeks before I was born. Stories of what a great father and patriarch he was lived long after he did. My mom often told me how much I reminded her of him.

That toolbox was our family's one possession that reminded me the most of the greatest man I never met. When my mom had reached a peak in her own addiction struggle, she sold most of our possessions for drugs. The memento came back out of retirement to save the day on more than a few occasions. Whether the tools were in the best shape or not, someone always had a picture to nail to the wall or a pipe to tighten.

We kept it in the back of Yogi just in case anyone needed it. Eighteen years after he died and my grandfather was still indirectly helping us out. That toolbox reminded me of what I wanted to be. Someone would eventually have to take over the role of patriarch. It had to be me.

"Mick, wait, please leave that. It's the only toolbox we got at the house . . ." Bird began pleading.

"You don't fucking deserve THIS!" I emphasized as I slammed the toolbox back on the floor.

"You know our house is falling apart, Mom will have my ass if I lose the toolbox," Bird continued his case.

"You know what, fine. Fuck it. Take it. Pop Pop is rolling over in his grave right now. I'm out. Have a nice life." I gave up on the toolbox.

I'll just grab it when I get back over Thanksgiving.

I slammed the door to emphasize my disgust and turned towards my walk back to the hall.

"Micky, WAIT!" I heard Bird calling as he leaned out of the driver's side window. Other words were screamed my way but I chose not to listen. Instead, I kept purposefully moving down Stribbling Walk, past the gazebo and straight for the Tecumseh Statue. I just hoped none of the detailers had witnessed the scene. Having my fellow returning plebes witness it was embarrassing enough.

I passed the Tecumseh Statue and arrived onto T-court. I could finally make out the music I had been hearing in the distance.

Rudolph the red nosed reindeer, had a very shiny nose
And if you ever saw it, you would even say it glows

Several large speakers were set up to loudly play Christmas carols to all returning plebes. Directly in the center of all returning activity, the intent of this soundtrack was not to rekindle happy childhood memories of yester-year visits from Santa. Instead, the soundtrack was meant as an ominous reminder that we would have to likely wait until the holiday season before we would see our families again. Depressing as that thought was, I wondered if I would ever see Bird again.

Fuck this place.

I temporarily considered leaving until my damn pride stepped in to prevent it.

I wasn't physically carrying Pop Pop's toolbox, but it remained in my heart. I needed to be the patriarch. I needed to find this version of the American dream. My middle class track was derailed the moment they put my dad in the ground. If I went back home it would only be a matter of time before Bird dragged me down into his shit pile. This incident only strengthened that notion in my head. I wasn't going to let shit like that happen. This had to be my path.

Be tough, suck it up.

Mick, 2140 hrs.

Later that night, Gonzo and I sat silently at our desks in the remaining five minutes of personal time. Bedtime formation was almost upon us. Plebe Parents' Weekend was already a distant memory. N.D. was still away from the room in football camp where he would stay until the rest of the brigade returned to initiate the academic year in another week.

Lucky bastard.

Despite all of my personal drama of the day, I had hoped he and Gonzo had a nice enough weekend. N.D. missed a good chunk of his time off due to football practice and Gonzo had to say goodbye to the daughter he barely knew. I slowly gained comfort in knowing the three of us were bonded in different shades of misery.

Puddles of mud and water canvassed our floor. We had just finished cleaning up the baby powder dumped all over our clothes and desks. This was a standard welcome back present from the detailers in closing out Parents' Weekend. The white powder was meant to accompany the Christmas Carols with a snow-like façade. The remaining mess on the floor was from the rest of the evening's festivities. Our detailers had been smashing us all night since returning from the final moments of weekend liberty. They ensured everyone in the company was completely covered in sweat and mud.

In some ways the beating and powdering was a favor of sorts. Generating angst towards my detailers was a welcome distraction from what went down earlier. The rest of our company mates scrambled to clean their muddy clothes and caked powder that covered our rooms. Gonzo gathered every piece of wet clothing in a large pile and haphazardly threw it into the shower in a sloppy heap. He anticipated the detailers would be too lazy to check for it when they made their way through for eventual bed checks after bedtime formation. It bought us five extra minutes of peace amidst the maelstrom of a day.

"We'll deal with the floor and that pile of shit tomorrow," Gonzo said.

We sat stoically at our desks. Exhaustion had wiped our emotions clean. At least we were dry. I glanced over to Gonzo. He was locked in a stare with his desk plotter. I had been doing the same. We were hypnotized by snapshots of better times.

My foot felt itchy in my sock. I reached into it for a scratch and felt a grain of sand. My recent shower still left some of the beach on my feet as a reminder of my day trip.

Fucking Bird.

Gonzo interjected while keeping his eyes fixated on the picture of his daughter.

"Hey man, didn't want to mention this 'cause it seemed upsetting, but you and your cuz all right?" Gonzo asked. "That was some argument you had earlier. I saw that shit on my way back. I think a lot of people did."

I exhaled in disgust.

"I talked to him for a bit. Your cuz, Bird. Called me bunkie ten different times. Whatever you guys were arguing about, he felt pretty bad about it."

"He fucking should feel bad about it," I said wanting to divert to another topic.

"None of my business, man," Gonzo said apologetically. He stood up and quickly moved towards his con-locker. He opened it and pulled out the green rusted toolbox.

"Here," Gonzo said softly as he slammed the box on the desk. "He wanted you to have this. He wouldn't let me leave without it."

I looked at it for a few minutes before opening it up to take in the smell of the tools. I saw a note in the box written on the back of a used bubble gum wrapper. It was neatly folded with the writing on the outside. I avoided the temptation to crumple the wrapper and just chuck the garbage in the trash. Instead I opened and read the impromptu note.

You were right. You deserve this.

I took a deep breath and bit the inside of my cheek to avoid crying in front of Gonzo.

"You know, Mick, I heard somewhere that the Naval Academy was a two hundred and fifty thousand dollar education," he paused only to look up with a smile, the first plebe smile I had seen in hours, "shoved up your ass a nickel at a time."

Yet again humor became my momentary stability.

Part III

Better Man

Chapter 9

March of the Black N
Tuesday, October 31st, 1995
Brigade of Midshipmen, 1810 hrs.

An open doorway became a temporary gateway of bizarre evening pageantry. First, a set of zombie plebes walked together in lock step unison. Then a male midshipman adorning nothing more than tighty-whities, black shoes, and a bow tie sauntered in. His arrogant smirk was accompanied by a cocky gait. Following closely behind was a pregnant nun. The black cloaked cross-dressing male looked like "she" might be expecting a basketball.

Halloween dinner was in full swing. The atmosphere in King Hall had a decidedly different feel than the typically mundane Tuesday evening dinner. Aside from mids proudly parading their makeshift costumes, not a single seat remained willingly unattended. It was one of the few mandated brigade events that all four thousand mids were more than happy to participate in. Hoots, hollers, and catcalls echoed across the jam-packed dining facility from all angles. It was a raucous atmosphere.

Though political incorrectness seemed to ooze from

the walls like slime, no authority figures were within eyesight. Per tradition, leadership was okay with letting the brigade blow off some untethered steam. The isolation and privacy of King Hall allowed for measured amounts of inappropriateness without much fear of public repercussion. The Baltimore Sun could only wish to be a fly on the wall at this event. Based on what happened a few weeks earlier, they didn't need to be.

Recent history had not been kind to the Naval Academy. The prior years were an emotional and reputational drain. In the handful of years preceding, a tragic holiday car accident and massive electrical engineering cheating scandal left a proud institution feeling less than perfect.

This year was meant to be deliberately different. The Navy's response to the few years prior was to get back to the core of their ways. That was achieved through amplified discipline. This translated into a new superintendent, a four star Admiral no less. It also meant getting "back to basics" in every facet imaginable. The discipline pendulum swung in the temporary direction of increased traditionalism. From the moment the upperclassmen joined the plebes to start the academic year they were suddenly doing a little bit less of everything fun. Less civilian clothes privileges, less driving privileges, the list went on and on. Everyone was generally a little crabbier because of it.

Something like the latest public humiliation was never supposed to happen. That unfortunate Air Force Game weekend incident had provided subsequent weeks of chaos for the brigade. First, there was the brigade wide drug test. Then there was the media circus that immediately followed. Suddenly the shenanigans of the "Double E" academic scandal a year earlier seemed like tidily winks. It had been hard to shake off the recent weight of what was potentially developing into the worst scandal in the history of the Naval Academy.

Despite having vampires and Spice Girls, the temporary bonding of Halloween dinner created a brief distraction that left everyone feeling ironically normal. Amidst the chaos of the impromptu costume parade, generous rations of fried chicken fingers were carted out in small metal bins to awaiting tables. Chicken "groins" were a brigade favorite and seemed a fitting celebratory meal.

The understandably distracted King Hall workers delivering the food were a little slower and sloppier than a normal service. No one seemed to notice. The surrounding festivities provided a tempting visual that easily pulled focus away from the tasks at hand. Even the plebes were permitted to talk and stand at ease during this meal. It was a rarely awarded privilege.

Showmanship naturally took over the event. Individually inappropriate costumes were soon followed by group themed attire. Most of these midshipmen groups took innocuous forms. Chewbacca and Han Solo were accompanied by an authentic looking Boba Fett. Later entrances became progressively more risqué. The Skipper and Gilligan were accompanied by a scantily clad Ginger. She was dressed less like an island castaway and more like a redheaded stripper playing the part. Her exposed cleavage bounced with each high-heeled step. It was a scene providing many male midshipmen a vivid visual for future fantasies. It was a stark contrast to how female midshipmen typically dressed.

At the fourth wing entrance of King Hall a commotion of activity was transpiring in the stairway. The now clandestine area behind entrances closed minutes earlier was just out of midshipman eyesight. This created a mysterious excitement around what might come next.

The closed doors aggressively swung open with a loud bang. A presumably male mid frantically sprinted through. His run was wobbly. He was constrained within a giant papier mache globe haphazardly painted white like the rest of his body. The large spherical costume resembling an egg was quickly chased by fifteen other uniformly costumed mids. The pursuing party was also painted white but had long white tails complimenting their all white attire. The egg never stood a chance against the much more mobile hunting party. A few minutes after the full visual unveiled itself, the group's ode to high school biology class dawned on most of the audience. The sperm chasing the egg routine was a fitting finale for such a sexually deprived congregation. The brigade applauded loudly for yet another brilliant showing by the Men's Water Polo team.

Just as the crowd seemingly had reached a climax, the grand finale was followed by one last encore. Across the nearly two football fields worth of dining facility, the area around the fifth wing King Hall entrance began creating its own buzz. What initially appeared to be a giant swarm of costumed bees was instead a sudden collection of roughly thirty midshipmen. All of them were proudly wearing bright yellow over their uniforms. Within closer proximity, the gaggle revealed a stitched black N on the lower left side of their yellow varsity sweaters.

Midshipmen varsity athletes were permitted to wear

blue varsity letter sweaters on occasion. Typically on Fridays or some other spirit related event. Those V-necked button down sweaters were navy blue with a yellow N.
The yellow N indicated lettering in a varsity sport. Every star stitched above that yellow N indicated a subsequent win over Army in the respective sport.

The yellow varsity sweater and those that wore it were of a different ilk. The bright yellow garment was a defiant trophy of the Naval Academy's most prolific rabble rousers. The stitched Black N was their scarlet letter. The full getup was the varsity uniforms of the "Black N," an all-star team of Naval Academy bad boys and girls. The sweater defined them.

Little was known about the Black N's history both in terms of the sweater and the collective underground society. The Black N was completely unsanctioned and virtually unrecognized by the academy's administration. Few outside the walls of Bancroft had even heard of it. Why would anyone at the academy wear their rival Army team's colors? Occasionally a modern era alumni Black N recipient would sport the sweater to a football game typically to the reception of confused stares or outright disregard.

Sporadic word of mouth narratives and verbal legend was the group's only genuine account of history. The Black N had been around since the early turn of the century. The original Black N letter had been sewn to midshipmen bathrobes up until the '80s when the more modern yellow sweater became one of the very few tweaks to a long history of tradition.

The Black N, though nefarious to administration in reputation, was most certainly earned. First, it required committing and getting caught for a disciplinary crime worthy of expulsion. This was typically characterized by getting busted in a transgression of alcohol consumption, unauthorized sex in the hall, or both. Second, it required that the midshipman be personally salvageable enough to avoid expulsion in subsequent disciplinary hearings. This was usually demonstrated by high academic performance, athletic achievement, or high leadership potential. Occasionally having a prominent alumni father didn't hurt either. Lastly, it required the highest watermark punishment of sixty days of military restriction. This was the maximum penalty for disciplinary action outside of outright expulsion. Restriction meant being secluded in your room save for meals, class, restriction muster, marching tours, and mandated labor around the yard. Most prison stints were not as intensive as one week of restriction much less sixty days of it. All of that was topped off with one hundred demerits on your service record.

As the brigade noticed the official entrance of the Black N's parade, everyone immediately rose from their chairs to provide a standing ovation. Most were secretly glad that they hadn't had to live through the experience themselves. In a night full of cheers, this one was the loudest. The great white buffalo was officially spotted.

Most of the Black N members were male, but a handful of legendary females had also earned a spot in the ranks. More than half of the members wouldn't even graduate. Some would elect to leave the academy to avoid future punishment. Some would get kicked out on subsequent transgressions. It was a temporary and transient bunch. All of them held their head high on this night. Halloween was their one night to wear their badge of honor in public as midshipman, only to then be hung up in closets until the next year's march. That was assuming they'd make it that long.

Though every Black N was admired, some were the stuff of legends. A handful had actually earned a star above their N, indicating the award of a second Black N. It had been rumored that in USNA history a midshipman had actually won two stars on their Black N, but the details of the stories ended there. Most mids categorized that history as mythical. No one could definitively prove it.

Heads were held high and the Black Ns continued their march amidst their adoring fans. As the group came within earshot of friends within the audience, personal acknowledgment came in the form of loud name recognition. One such mid seemed to be extra popular. It was the lone plebe in the rank-agnostic bunch.

"NDeeeeee! You're the fucking man!" and various other tributes seem to rattle out every forty-five seconds or so.

N.D. Okafor kept his eyes in the boat. His cool smile was the only visible show of pride. N.D.'s Saturday post game performance during the Air Force game weekend a few weeks earlier had given our class its first folk hero. Three months into Plebe Year and N.D. was already a living legend within Bancroft Hall.

Chapter 10

Daddy Issues
Thursday, August 24th, 1995
Bird, 11:30 p.m.

I wiggled my toes in the sand filled floor. I looked upward and momentarily forgot I was indoors. Fuck, I was high that night. I wasn't alone. Most of the tourists in the massive bayside Ocean City nightclub were already too drunk to notice whether they were inside or out. The stage lighting effects within the massive main-stage pavilion coupled well with altered mind states. The dark ceiling looked like the night sky. I needed to level set my brain. I stepped quickly to the exit. I needed a breath of fresh air and a view of the actual night sky.

Outside, in the open air portion of Seacrets nightclub, I took in the views of its bayside location. I squinted a bit harder for focus and could eventually spot the living room light of Mom's house faintly shining across the bay. A few straggling smokers enjoyed a puff in the open night air. I quickly joined them amongst the handful of grass-roofed huts selling alcoholic frozen beverages and Red Stripe beer. I always enjoyed the smoking tourists' reaction to a redheaded Rastafarian joining their horde.

"Aww Christ, hon, not another one of these guys bumming for smokes," complained the overweight blond to her date. She puffed away on her Menthol Kool. Her perfume was strong enough to cut through the smell of heavy cigarette smoke. She had lipstick on her teeth and a large salsa stain on her zebra print tank top. I began internally guessing which land locked shitty suburb of Baltimore she hailed from.

"Not to worry, I got ya covered," I kindly reassured. I wasn't even trying to bum a smoke. I had enough challenges forthcoming in the night. I didn't need to create a new one outside. I visibly pulled out and lit my own smoke and took a deep drag. I bowed forward just hard enough for my red dreads to dramatically whip forward in my downward motion. I let out a silently smoky exhale and gracefully made my exit from the group. I didn't look back to see their reaction to my theatrics. I spent half a cigarette aimlessly wandering the sands of the club's outdoor space by myself.

Hours earlier, the outdoor premises had been packed like it was Spring Break on the bay. The many outdoor bars and tables situated around and in the bay water was a siren to drunken assholes with jet skis and pontoon boats. The action hadn't dissipated at sundown, it had instead moved indoors. A few empty cups floated in the bay as a reminder of the day. I finished my smoke and flicked the butt into an empty drink glass left on a dinner table abandoned hours earlier. I grabbed a fistful of nachos off a half-eaten plate. It must have escaped a busboy's attention earlier. The cheese had long since congealed to its solid state.

"Fuck it, munchies," I rationalized to myself. "Now I need a drink," I continued my logic and made my way back inside.

Bouncers in bright orange shirts lined the handful of exits to the outdoor space. They were enjoying a temporary break in the action and flirting with whatever girls would give them the time of day. Most of them were meatheads that Micky and I knew from Decatur High. It wouldn't be long again before the magic mixing bowl of drunken chicks, thugs, hillbillies, and locals were prodding the guardians of safety back into action. Welcome to Seacrets in August.

As much as I hated to admit it, I loved Seacrets. Almost all of the locals did. Seacrets employed many locals. It was owned by a local. It even provided locals a much cheaper menu of its decent food once tourist season died down. Seacrets had certainly facilitated me getting laid on more summer evenings than I can remember. They even had killer Jamaican Nachos. They were infinitely better when they hadn't been sitting on a table for an hour.

There were plenty of good reasons for me to be hanging out there on a Thursday night. They didn't matter. This Thursday was about business. I made my way towards a familiar silhouette behind a large bar within the indoor stage area.

"I'll take a Pain in De Ass!" I yelled to an obese man behind the bar amidst a sea of other customers. His large frame kept most of the liquor bottles and margarita dispensers behind him hidden from sight. His pants were centimeters from falling off his sweaty ass crack. He dutifully continued collecting discarded plastic cups. I continued getting the silent treatment from Baby Huey.

"HEY! BAR BITCH!" I yelled with enough authority to preclude the excuse of not being loud enough. The bar back continued his work, diverting his attention just long enough to extend his right hand behind himself with a middle finger. I guess he heard me after all.

"Fucking Hemorrhoid. LET'S GO!" I yelled fully intent on grabbing his attention.

The large man swung around with the grace of an angry hippopotamus. The rage on his face washed away instantly.

"BIRD!" he joyfully exclaimed. "What's up, man? Long time no see."

"How 'bout that fucking Hemorrhoid, Bunkie?" I said with a scowl.

The lowly bar back stared back perplexed. He hadn't yet earned the right to be a drink fetching beer bitch.

"Man, I'm just fucking with you, Bobby!" I said breaking character with a laugh. I thought acting like the rest of the thousand plus drunken tourists might nab a smile. Farm's older brother was not quite sharp enough to appreciate all of my humor. Bobby wasn't necessarily slow, but he was a far cry from the fast lane.

Bobby's blank face eventually transitioned back to a smile. The rusty sprockets in his brain finally churned enough to garner the reaction I was initially hoping for. That great sense of humor is what made him a long-time friend of the Fellas.

"You're an ass, Bird, a real pain in the ass," Bobby said with a chuckle. He briefly looked left and right to make sure no one was looking. He grabbed a plastic cup and made his way to the frozen drink machine. He pulled hard on the frozen piña colada spout, filling the cup just enough to save room for the strawberry daiquiri topping the drink off. He snuck a sip before making his way towards me.

"Bird's always on the house when I'm around," Bobby said slamming the frosty cup on the table and almost breaking it in the process. He threw a straw in to complete the gratis order.

"What?" I screamed. The band on stage had just resumed their set and the club's volume had suddenly tripled.

"On the house," Bobby yelled into my ear.

"Thanks, Bunkie, you A'IGHT" I hollered above the music. I was truly gracious. I desperately needed a little extra buzz.

I chucked the straw to the sandy floor below and chugged the frosty mug half way down. I soon keeled over and painfully squinted through the searing pain of a brain freeze. I had forgotten a lesson learnt many times over in a 7-Eleven parking lot.

"Lick the roof of your mouth with your tongue," Bobby loudly instructed me in response to my comical display of discomfort.

That was Bobby. One minute you wondered if he could tie his own shoe, the next minute he was pulling Dr. Science shit out of his ass.

"I see a lot of brain freezes on this job," Bobby continued, "lots of drunks drinking lots of frozen drinks."

"Oh, right," I said having not immediately realized the connection. "Makes sense." Slowly my drink induced migraine subsided.

I could already see Bobby's manager looking over. I had seen that glare many times over in my own professional experiences. I tried to stay quiet long enough to get Bobby back on the job before he got into any more trouble.

"Bunkie, your boss is givin' us the evil eye, you should get back to work," I prodded Bobby along. His job wasn't much, but it meant something to him. Eventually he'd do something stupid to lose it. I just wasn't going to let it be tonight. Besides, how could I give up the free drinks?

The band finished their cover of Foreigner's "Hot Blooded" and continued the set into the next overplayed '80s radio hit.

"Play some fucking BUFFET," yelled the same hefty blond that was too cool to smoke with me ten minutes earlier.

"Mamama my SHA RONA!" the lead singer belted out in defiant fashion. The band was lame, even by non-peak weeknight Seacrets standards.

I remained leaning against the bar while Bobby eventually returned to his professional responsibilities. He wiped down the messy bar with a wet dishrag and then carried two crates of dirty dishes back to the washing station. Eventually somebody puked on the dance floor and he had to quickly tend to that.

The music played loudly. The air smelled of sweat, alcohol, and dry ice smoke. I finished the second half of my drink in a much more reasonable manner. I welcomed the warm buzz of alcohol that soon swept over my brain. It complemented my weed buzz nicely. I tried to distract myself watching a handful of drunken assholes painfully strike out with the night's local selection of loose women.

"So I'm surprised you're here, given the act," Bobby said tilting his head towards the stage. He had apparently made quick work of his cleanup duty and successfully slipped behind me under the veil of loud music.

He wasn't referencing the general shittiness of the band. True, they did suck, as did most bands that played weeknights on the tail end of tourist season.

"What brings you out tonight?" Bobby asked loudly in his second break from professional responsibility in the past fifteen minutes. His manager was back to pacing back and forth in frustration. The bar was crowded. The dirty dishes were backing up.

I leaned over and cupped my hand over my mouth as he drew his ear closer to it.

"Business. Family Business," I answered Bobby's question.

Bobby let out a concerned exhale. His meek brain struggled to find the words to break the awkward silence.

"Here," I commanded Bobby. "Give this note to my good buddy the bassist. He'll know what to do from there.

Bird, 2:00 a.m.

Seacrets' parking lot was as big as a mall parking lot. The large crowd inside had only filled it half way. Tourist season was winding down. On a big 4th of July weekend, it would be packed to the gills. I'd have to wait until the next month's "Dark Side of the Moon" party to see a half way decent crowd.

DJ Batman wasn't even here tonight and that guy practically lives here.

I took one last drag of my joint by the bushes on the lot's perimeter. It was timed perfectly. My temporary isolation was soon over. The masses meandering in the dance area finally migrated their way out of the club at the bouncers' closing time prodding. I flicked my roach to the street and watched the orange tinder skip across the pavement.

I could hear a chorus of car doors slamming shut. I was distracted by a rustling in the bushes twenty yards closer to the club. I walked ten paces to see if the commotion was worth watching.

As I drew closer, I was not disappointed. A small crowd of drunkenly hot chicks surrounded their guest of honor. Their bachelorette party had officially reached its down turn. The woman of the hour was keeled over in the mulch below. Her projectile vomit was stained red from five too many daiquiris. The red splatter had already ruined her veil. The giant penis pendant on her necklace swung back and forth with each heave.

"That your date for the evening?" I heard a sarcastic query over my shoulder.

I didn't need to turn to know who had snuck up on me. I was pissed that I let the shit show in the bushes distract me.

"Seems to be more your type, fucktard," I said in reply before turning around. "Isn't that why you play these gigs?"

"Is that any way to talk to your father?" the portly and

sweaty man said. His red curly hair was peppered with gray and his pot belly comically protruded in a Hammer-jack's T-shirt that was at least two sizes too small.

"So when are we going fishing, Pop?" I returned the sardonic line of questioning.

"You know that's not my thing," he returned with a smug smirk.

"No shit, Joe," I reaffirmed a blatant statement of the obvious.

Fishing was certainly not Joe's thing. Neither was being a good husband or father. My mom kicked his ass to the curb more than a few times. Eventually, everyone's least favorite boomerang didn't return. I had been essentially fatherless since grade school.

Well before I had been born, Joe had a history of hitting Mom. They had met at a local rock show in Baltimore where his band had been playing a set. At that time he wasn't quite so washed up and defeated by life. Mom was enamored with Joe's ambition towards being a professional musician. Unfortunately for all of us, Joe was a far better abusive husband than bassist. He often took that out on us. My fist clenched just thinking about it.

I pulled the fat envelope I had stuffed in my pocket. When passing my note to Bobby hours earlier, I briefly considered just having him pass the envelope along to Joe back inside. Then I imagined how easily Bobby might misplace a grand in cash stuffed in an envelope. I stuck with my initial game plan.

"Here you go, dick," I said as I tossed the stuffed enveloped to Joe. He wasn't expecting it. It bounced off his fat belly and tumbled to the ground below. He scrambled to the ground like a seagull after a dropped Thrasher's French fry.

"Now get the fuck out of here," I further instructed.

"Well, I guess my career as bassist for Johnny and the Ocean City Rockets has officially passed," Joe said with a smile, still crouched down on the ground below gathering his spoils.

Joe's gig with the Rockets had been a short one, just like the rest. All of the gigs were just charades. Every few years, Joe would find himself in debt. Gambling was the most common culprit. He was an even shittier gambler than he was a father. He'd start taking gigs locally in Ocean City as a way to get in front of my mom. He hoped that her pity would float him a few dollars. Her love was unfortunately blind like that. After Joe tried one too many times to additionally mooch his way back into Mom's house, I took over the responsibility paying him off. All of this was unbeknownst to her. That was exactly how I wanted to keep it. Joe couldn't care less. He just wanted to get paid.

"Good, now go crawl back into the hole you popped out of," I replied, anxious to get away.

"You know, Bird, you and me, we ain't that different," Joe said just as he stood back up.

"Go fuck yourself, Joe," was about all I could muster as I continued my walk back to my ride. I saw Farm's truck fifty yards away on the other side of the parking lot. Bobby was driving and Farm was riding shotgun, still dejectedly without a license. I couldn't wait to join them.

"You surf. I play bass. You have a bad haircut," he continued. "Other than that, we're basically the same. Apple and the tree, you know, all that shit."

My desire to leave was replaced by a stronger yearning to punch him in the face. Luckily my weed high tended to make me less violent.

"We are NOT the fucking same," I stopped in my path and quickly corrected Joe. His notion was not original. I thought about it often. It was a cancer in my life. I just wasn't going to give him the satisfaction of acknowledging it.

I gladly took the responsibility of being extorted. The payments were worth not being reminded that I was genetically linked to this cock knob. That's why I took on extracurricular drug gigs, riskier gigs. It's why I became a drug dealer in the first place. I was an ex-con before I was of legal age to drink. I couldn't afford Joe's payout working the whack-a-mole game on the boardwalk, and I sure as shit wasn't finding a respectable desk job any time soon.

"There should be enough in there to keep you back up in Baltimore County for a while. Thousand bucks," I stated in hopes that he would quit counting the money and just get the fuck out of my life.

"Inflation's a bitch," he said without looking up as he finished his count, "but this looks to be about right." There was no formally assigned payment amount. He was just mentally figuring out how much gambling he could pay off with this trip. I assumed it was enough to keep him out of our hair until next summer.

"So are you," I replied. There was not much more to say.

Joe nodded in feigned gratitude and turned to walk away. As big of an ass as he was, he understood the nature of the transaction. Neither of us was there to rekindle a father and son bond. It never existed in the first place.

"Hey Joe," I called out as he made his way to whatever shithole he was crashing in that night. "How much to get a permanent Ocean City Restraining Order on you? Hypothetically speaking."

"What, are you too chicken shit to hire a hitman or just kill me yourself?" he turned his head and replied with a smile.

"Don't tempt me," I returned. I wish I had the lack of morals to just off him. It had certainly crossed my mind over the years. It would have been cheaper than our current arrangement and a hell of a lot more satisfying. Unfortunately killing my own father was just too big of a pill to swallow. I had enough fucked up shit in my life to deal with. "Just name your price, dickhead."

"Ha, I may be poor white trash, but I'm too rich for your blood," he taunted.

"Try me," I persisted. "I can be awfully industrious with the right motivation."

Chapter 11

Monday Morning Blues
Monday, September 11th, 1995
Mick, 0600 hrs.

I had been conscious for fifteen minutes and had completed precisely nothing that I had intended to for my morning ahead. It was problematic. Monday morning was perhaps the absolute worst time of a typical plebe's week.

The weekend was ever so painfully behind us. Plebe liberty post Plebe Summer boiled down to a half-day off the yard and the temporary permission on Sunday to use our bed for napping in daylight hours. This was assuming there was no home football game slated and you hadn't been scheduled to stand watch, an assigned security duty, which seemed to happen at least once a month.

Despite its brevity and miserable inadequacies as compared to what normal college freshmen enjoyed on weekends, plebe weekend liberty was still glorious. Saturday meant a day away from having to be a plebe and on Sunday a chance to catch up on sleep. It was McDonald's versus a bland King Hall dinner and seeing a movie versus reading about it in the paper. It was the one spot in the week that was sane and about the only thing keeping Plebe Year from driving me completely crazy. I had been a midshipman at the Naval Academy for a little longer than ten weeks, and I had no idea how I'd survive ten months. Although Plebe Summer was seemingly behind us, we quickly learned that academic year life as a plebe was not much better.

Monday mornings and their inevitable transition from a temporary weekend oasis to the doom and gloom back in Bancroft Hall were the worst. As for most college freshmen, Monday morning harkened the end of the weekend and the initiation of a week of classes. This was dreadful enough as is. As plebes, the dread of Monday morning classes was the tip of the iceberg.

In addition to attending class, plebes had a long litany of military and plebian obligations. These included learning a professional military topic of the week, usually focused on a major force element of the Navy or Marine Corps and memorizing weapons forward to aft on various naval vessels and ground assault vehicles. These topics were tested weekly and failure to learn them meant losing liberty the following weekend. It was also potentially making a plebe's individually assigned upper-class chain of command look bad. These were both highly undesirable outcomes. Passing this test, though not tied to academic transcripts, was a major priority of each plebe's week.

There were also the obligations that I could only characterize within the "man, it sucks to be a plebe" genre. We were obligated to know the full menus of the next three meals in King Hall. We were to have three news articled read and prepared for discussion topics with upperclassmen at mandatory company breakfast. We were even re-quired to memorize the number of days until every ma-jor vacation, graduation, and 2nd class ring dance. Most importantly, we memorized the number of days until the plebe class could finally climb the Herndon monument. Plebe Year officially ended by replacing the plebe Dixie cup hat atop a greased down twenty foot phallic symbol with a midshipman hat. Regardless of what the count was, that day in late May the following year felt like a thousand days away.

Most of our plebe classmates were up at 0530, waking a full hour ahead of USNA reveille for all midshipmen at 0630. Plebes were expected to be knocking on their as-signed upperclassman's door for their first "come-around" of the week immediately upon the reveille bell. A come-around was intended as a twenty-minute training, and occasionally scolding, session with an upperclassmen. For plebes, it was the mandated way to start every weekday morning. Since come-arounds could last right up until 0700 formation and formation ran right up until break-fast, plebes needed to essentially be prepared for a full hour of harassment by the time they left their rooms at 0629. All of this slated to happen well before a full day of academic classes initiated a few hours later. These were the factors that got most plebes up at 0530 on a Monday. Only the prospect of a good break would get me up volun-tarily at that hour.

Unlike Plebe Summer, where squads were almost entirely comprised of plebes, the academic year's squads consisted of two to three mids within each respective class. Each upperclassman was assigned a plebe to train, and the upper-class military grade, which we all received in addition to our normal academic grades, was partially contingent on how well their assigned plebes did on various military competency tests, inspections, and evaluations.

Monday and Tuesday's come-arounds were slated with a sophomore mid, also known as 3/C midshipman or "Youngster." Wednesday and Thursdays were slated for 2/C mids, and Friday was reserved for final "sign off" with a Firstie. All of this activity culminated on Sunday afternoon when the official professional development quiz was administered brigade-wide on the previous week's topic. This was typically done after Sunday night's mandatory evening meal.

N.D. was already up and at his desk by the time I was out of my bed. We spent fifteen minutes of mutually silent study of our computer screens. N.D. exchanged love emails with his girlfriend while I checked the scores of the previous night's Orioles game. Our silent basking in the blue electric glow emitted from our computer monitors was interrupted by Gonzo's eventual awakening.

Gonzo rose out of his rack quickly, sitting up with a sense of urgency as though alarmed. His face still had the imprints of his cotton woven blanket on his rack, also known as a blue magnet for its color and tendency to pull any under-slept mid back into his or her rack. Without speaking, he jumped out of the top bunk and immediately charged to his computer.

"You homies gotta see this shit, man," he finally broke his silence with surprising enthusiasm for being so early and so immediately out of bed.

N.D. and I both walked over to Gonzo's desk, interested in what he had to show us. Gonzo was typically lethargic in the morning, still maintaining his late night smoking habit on the roof despite now being permitted to smoke once Plebe Summer had ended a few weeks earlier. His serendipitous energy had us intrigued.

"Check this out," Gonzo continued with a mesmerized stare at the computer screen.

On Gonzo's screen was a perfectly real picture of a slightly attractive, albeit a little rough around the edges, nude woman performing a lewd act on a glass Budweiser bottle.

"This Bud's for you, Mick," Gonzo said laughing audibly.

"Maaaaan, that's just wrong, dawg," chimed in N.D. with a smirk.

Gonzo then proceeded to show us what else he had found online the night before. The second picture was an animation of Fred Flinstone receiving fellatio from Jane Jetson. The last was what I could only tactfully describe as a "Tijuana Donkey Show."

The past three weeks, though hardly the time of our lives, did uncover the magical world of personal computers and the internet for Gonzo and me. N.D. had several years of history using a computer. He came from a family of college professors and a life growing up around academia. Gonzo and I were in completely uncharted territory.

My mom could barely afford to pay the electric bill much less finance a computer. Aunt Nellie blew all of her money on antiques, and Bird received most of his news from grocery store tabloids or random stuff he made up in his head. Any money that I had made at Shorebreak went immediately towards my surfing habit. My high school had a computer lab, but the utilization of those machines was strictly reserved for typing class and sneaking in games of Doom. I had only heard of the internet and email when I arrived to Annapolis on I-Day.

Gonzo was simply too old to have experienced the internet growing up. His birthday was three weeks shy of the maximum age cut-off date for admission into the academy. He had already turned twenty-one despite being a plebe. This meant his last time living at home was circa 1992 right before he decided to enlist. It took his family until 1991 just to get a Nintendo. A computer was a pipe dream. Once in the Fleet, Gonzo's pittance of hard-earned money went towards smokes, alcohol, and aftermarket parts and accessories for the automobile he could barely afford. A computer wasn't even an afterthought.

We received our computers the week following Plebe Parents' Weekend: it was Gonzo's first and my second. My family did at one time have a Tandy computer from RadioShack that hooked up to Aunt Nellie's TV. It was occasionally used to play video games by Bird after a fun night on the porch. The new computer had been a nice consolation prize for having seen Plebe Parents' Weekend come and go. Once we figured out all of the joys the internet could bring in email, sports scores, weather reports, and of course, porn, Gonzo and I were hooked.

While I dabbled in viewing internet porn, Gonzo was a connoisseur. Three weeks into the school year and Gonzo was already in academic trouble in several classes. I truly believed Gonzo had visited every porn website on the internet.

"Dude, in all seriousness, aren't you worried about the come-around this morning?" I questioned as a futile attempt to rein in Gonzo's focus towards something more productive.

"Come on, homey, you think I need help studying about the Navy?" arrogantly replied Gonzo.

"I rode an Oliver Hazard Perry Class Frigate around the world, TWICE," he continued. "Not only can I give you the weapons forward to aft, I can show you where Senior Chief Stanton hid his porn magazine stash while underway and where to find that Filipino guy's bunk that can get you hooked up in illegal cock fights in Singapore."

I briefly thought about reminding Gonzo he needed to finish out the chemistry lab report he was already a week late on, but I figured it was a fruitless endeavor.

"Besides, Mick," Gonzo chimed in one last time to his defense, "this morning's come-around is with Hacksaw, so no worries."

3/C Matt "Hacksaw" Hackett was a former Napster like many of Gonzo's enlisted buddies. He had also played varsity football as a linebacker the year earlier. He had to quit playing after blowing out his knee in the previous spring's practice. Hackett was also roommates with two other sophomores on the Navy football team, one of whom was the starting quarterback. This was the same quarterback that racked up over two hundred yards rushing and three touchdowns in our team's season opening road win against SMU over the weekend. Hackett had already long since been informal with N.D. That courtesy was extended to the rest of his room. We were already on first name terms with Hacksaw.

While the SMU Mustangs were hardly the locked and loaded team they were in the early eighties, there was still optimism behind the win. Starting the season with a road win was a stark contrast to the 3-8 record of the season prior. The offense garnered most of the praise and attention during a 33-2 blowout, but the defense was equally stout. Leading this dominating effort had been none other than the Navy's new starting defensive end, freshman N.D. Okafor. He had recorded three solo tackles and a sack against SMU. While N.D. was hardly a big man on campus living life as a plebe, it was fairly safe to assume that his football teammates would have his back in the hall, especially after the game he just put out.

All of my chatting with Gonzo had further distracted me from my task of preparing for the morning ahead. While a Hackett come-around would certainly help my cause, by 0620 I had done nothing more than check sports scores and screw around on the internet with Gonzo.

Still in my boxers and a T-shirt, I quickly grabbed a copy of the newspaper outside of our room door and read the first article I laid my eyes on. I was in a rush. It was an article about Newt Gingrich whining about how everyone was going to lose Medicaid subsidies. It was neither the most compelling article nor one I'd want to talk about. I had to make due. Between that article and whatever dialogue I could make up about the Oriole's game last night would have to suffice as my three articles of the day. Thankfully, I always knew how many days to various milestones as prescribed. I was constantly counting them in my head as a way of generating optimism. Hopefully no one would ask what was for dinner that night since I hadn't studied my meals for the day. Part of being a great plebe was studying. Part was correctly guessing what upper-class wouldn't ask you on a given day. I had hoped that I had guessed correctly.

"Almost show time, boys," N.D. said. It was 0625.

I hadn't even begun to get dressed or groomed. Thankfully, Gonzo and Plebe Summer had prepared me well. Within three hurried minutes, I had brushed my teeth, dry shaved, and completely gotten dressed in uniform. We stepped out of our room. It was completely inspection ready as prescribed. Upon entering the P-way I could see virtually every plebe in the company making their slow dreadful walk down the center of the hall. We squared our corners as we each individually reached our assigned upper-class rooms. The weekend was long forgotten.

Mick, 0630 hrs.

Simultaneous knocking immediately followed the dreaded Monday morning reveille bell.

"Sir, Midshipman fourth class McGee and Gonzalez reporting for come-around, sir!" Gonzo and I simultaneously belted out as I knocked on 3/C Hackett's door. Gonzo tone had much less enthusiasm than my own.

Gonzo and I then performed a few quickly executed squared turns and assumed our required position standing alongside the wall directly outside our upperclassman's room. Hacksaw's room remained dark and silent even after the reveille bell and our subsequent knocking.

Upon reveille bell, all midshipmen were supposed to be out of their beds with all overhead lights turned on. This was virtually impossible to monitor, save for the plebes who all had to be dressed and awaiting come-around directly at the bell. Primary wake up auditing responsibility for everyone else fell on the shoulders of the firstie assigned watch for the day. Typically, no firstie in their right mind would actually attempt to enforce mandatory 0630 wakeup on fellow upperclassmen. 1/C Darren Clarkson, however, was not your typical mid.

"Come on, reveille means reveille, guys," he spastically called out to open air in a frustrated tone directed towards Hackett's closed door, the darkness beneath the bottom crack providing evidence that everyone was likely still asleep. Gonzo and I were just relieved that he wasn't yelling at us. This was a rarity as he made a daily hobby of shitting on plebes.

Clarkson then eventually peeked his head into Hackett's room after first tentatively opening the door. The room remained silent though he continued, "You are supposed to be setting an example for your plebes."

A minute of silence passed without the slightest hint of movement behind the darkened and likely comatose room. Clarkson just stood silently in front of the open door, plotting his next move. He was clearly not going to let this situation go. His normally greasy and pasty white face began to grow red with passive-aggressive anger.

"Come on guys, rules ARE RULES!" Clarkson elevated his voice and tone to feign a level of authority while simultaneously flicking on the room's overhead lights.

After some brief rustling, which we could not view from our vantage point standing on the wall, Hackett's door aggressively swung open. Hackett's large framed silhouette devoured the diminutive and pencil-necked Clarkson. If this had been high school, an atomic wedgie would have surely followed the recent cadence of events, but the Naval Academy was a far cry from high school. I could only imagine in my head how great it would have been to see Clarkson's elastic underwear band ripped over his head.

A brief stare down ensued until the temporary awkward silence was broken.

"Fuck off, Clarkson, we're not plebes anymore," Hackett said as his disheveled hair and PT gear clearly indicated that this come-around would be the cupcake Gonzo had predicted.

Clarkson and Hackett's eyes met briefly enough for Clarkson's minimal survival instincts to kick in. He wisely chose his best option, passive aggressively leave in a visible huff. Hackett stayed behind with a slowly shaking head.

"That guy is such a tool," he said in a subtly frustrated tone as he reached back into his room and flicked the lights back off. "Who the hell does that guy think he is?"

Clarkson was the only firstie clueless enough to flick the lights on any upperclassmen, much less on the starting quarterback of the football team after a season opening win.

"Clarkson would carry a lunchbox to sex, if he had sex," I chimed in and immediately wondered if I had taken the joke too far.

"Not to worry," Gonzo interjected, "when that dude

hits the fleet, he's gonna get thrown over the side of the boat while he sleeps, I'll make sure of that."

We all enjoyed a good chuckle at that notion, wondering exactly how much jest was behind that threat. I suspected very little. Gonzo hated Clarkson to the moon and back.

"What do we got this morning?" Hackett queried as both Gonzo and I offered our sign off sheet for this week's come-around topics.

Per protocol, all plebes required completion of sign off sheets for the week's come-around topics. Each assigned upperclassman was to sign off following assured demonstration of plebe competency for a week's given topic. Each plebe needed signatures from their weekly assigned third, second, and first class mids. Failure to obtain these signatures meant Sunday's test would be automatically assigned a failing grade.

"Alright, I got this," Hackett stated calmly as he grabbed both of our sign off sheets. He briefly glanced at each sheet and then threw them on the floor, each individual's sign off sheet at our respective feet.

"Step forward over the sheet," Hackett commanded. It was odd hearing any military command from an otherwise placid upperclassman. "Now take a step backwards."

Gonzo and I followed the orders despite being a little perplexed by their intent.

"Good," Hackett complimented our adherence. "Now if anyone asks, you can say you went over these sheets with me twice this morning."

He then quickly stepped inside and grabbed a pen to provide the required autograph a day earlier than expected.

"Shove off," Hackett declared. He was an upperclassman but not far enough removed from plebedom to forget what a solid favor a light come-around was, especially on a Monday morning.

Gonzo and I then happily left our posts along the wall and quickly sprinted to the middle of the P-way. We were moving as expeditiously as possible back to our room. We both knew that staying in the hall any longer than needed meant we'd be sitting ducks for any roaming upperclassmen.

N.D. had not been so lucky. He had been in a separate squad as Gonzo and me. N.D. had the unfortunate luck of drawing 2/C Darnell Woodson, also known as "Dr. Doom" for his come-around. N.D's youngster was out with the flu. Not missing an opportunity to shit on an unattended to plebe, Dr. Doom was happy to fill the void. He volunteered to cover the newly available days with his own come-arounds.

I turned the corner on the homestretch to the room. I came close enough to notice Woodson's shaved baldhead glistening underneath the fluorescent overhead lights of the P-way. Luckily his task at hand kept him gainfully occupied enough to ignore me and Gonzo.

Dr. Doom was a self-imposed nickname intended for plebe intimidation but unintentionally cemented his persona as a target of angst for plebes and upperclassmen alike. The Doc was hardly intimidating and almost always highly annoying despite generally having good intentions. N.D. had gained instant brigade-wide admiration after a strong weekend football game. I imagined this popularity might be bothersome to Doc.

"Weapons forward to aft, GO!" Woodson's voice echoed around the corner and was audible from our open doorway. I used the extra time provided by Hackett to continue my examination of last night's baseball scores in the sports section of my paper. Gonzo continued his electronic quest to find every possible inappropriate website on the World Wide Web.

"The mark fifteen Close-In Weapon System twenty millimeter Phalanx CIWS." I could hear N.D.'s matter of fact response midstream as he continued his checkup with Dr. Doom. He was as good a plebe as he was a football player. Even Doc knew this as true, despite his twinges of social jealousy.

"Do you know what year they back-fitted all of the Hazard Perrys with the C-whiz?" Doc continued his line of questioning, immediately interrupting N.D. the moment he knew his previous question could not stump him. While Doc enjoyed highlighting areas of unlearned professional knowledge, he loved demonstrating his endless repository of prior-enlisted knowledge and sea stories even more.

"Nineteen eighty eight, NINEteen, Eighty, EIGHT," Doc emphatically answered his own question, knowing full and well that no plebe would just randomly know that fact, nor were they required to.

"In the fleet, you gotta know this stuff," he continued on his soapbox. "Sailors don't care if you were a hot shit football player, still gotta know your shit."

His prior enlisted service gave him a sense of superiority in very much the same way it did Gonzo, but that is about where the comparison stopped. Gonzo arrogantly pushed the envelope in thinking he was entitled to lessened adherence to plebian rules. Doc conversely relished in any opportunity to enforce the Naval Academy's many rules and regulations. Though some of this variation of perceived entitlement came by way of current rank, I doubted Gonzo would ever be one to overly harass plebes when given the opportunity.

"Sailors care about cigarettes, cars, and the honeys," Gonzo calmly spoke as N.D. made his way back to the room after finally being shoved off. "Just do your job and nobody's gonna mess with you. Doc don't know shit about shit."

Formation time approached, my stomach grumbled. Despite my intense hunger, I would have gladly skipped the forthcoming breakfast if given the chance.

Mick, 0735 hrs.

"Brigade, SEATS!" boomed over the speakers equipped within King Hall, USNA's massive dining facility. All four thousand mids sat in unison. A feverish noise and emotion swallowed the temporary stillness of a non-denominational chaplain blessing. At least a quarter of us were surely damned. The upperclassmen immediately dug into the plebes who sat rigidly on the front four inches of their chairs as required.

"Mr. McGee," 2/C Severson shouted from across my squad's dining table. Unlike Plebe Summer, the shouting was not being driven by angst. Severson got most of that out of his system over the summer. Shouting was instead required just to penetrate through the overpowering noise of King Hall breakfast.

"What did you read in the paper this morning?" the grilling began.

Seated directly across from Gonzo and me were our squad's three second class, flanked on either side at each head of the table by two youngsters to our right or two firsties to our left. The ratios of upperclassmen to plebes were far less generous after Plebe Summer. Plebes went from outnumbering upper-class at tables at a five to one ratio to being now outnumbered three to one. There was little room to hide from the inquisition.

"Sir, I read about the Orioles game last night," I began my answer knowing I could narrate a ten-minute conversation about a baseball game in my sleep.

"Bor-ing, next," 2/C Severson interrupting a diatribe I suspected would not see itself to fruition.

"Sir, I read about Ray Miller, the Oriole's pitching coach," I began on my next narrative. This one I hadn't actually read, I just figured I'd make up a story and talk about the Oriole's pitching staff for five minutes.

"Next!" Severson interrupted again, "what non-Orioles story do you have for me today? Ya'll haven't shut up about that shit since Cal broke the streak last week."

Severson was referring to Cal Ripken's recent breaking of Lou Gehrig's consecutive games played streak. It had been torturous being such an Oriole's fan and yet not able to see Cal's 2,131st game on television. All I could do was hear about it in the papers the next day and get pissed off every time I was reminded of it. The best I could do was collect the front page of every sports section I could get my hands on. There was a stack of them back in my room's personal locker.

"Sir, I read a story about Newt Gingrich and his critique of Medicaid funding," I began on the only story I actually did read that morning.

"Fucking liberals are ruining this country," chimed in our squad leader 1/C Houston Smith. He was known as Smitty to everyone but the plebes. We all called him Smitty behind his back.

"Them and all those Latinos, ain't that right, Mr. Gonzalez?" Smitty continued his interruption and deflected it towards Gonzo. I couldn't tell if he was being sarcastic or was just that big of a pompous ass. It was often hard to tell.

"Sir, no sir," Gonzo chimed back quickly to our squad leader. "My fellow Hispanic and Latino Americans are the fabric of this great country, sir." He eloquently continued his reply, "And one day we'll outnumber the Caucasians, SIR!" He stopped his aggressive response, smartly avoiding escalating things further. He was figuratively biting his tongue so hard that it was bleeding. Smitty was ranking mid at the table. Plebes especially were forced to maintain appropriate reverence, even if said upperclassman was an asshole.

Smitty sat at the head of our table with his typically arrogant grin. His hair was cut high and tight yet his uniform was at least a size too small. His pudginess stretched his polyester blend uniform shirt to its maximum capacity. His sarcasm was tough to read, often sounding antagonistic and almost always inappropriate. He generally made everyone at the table uncomfortable.

"Isn't that inspirational, I'm getting all misty down below," Smitty replied, quickly blowing off Gonzo and transitioning to the next topic of his liking.

"Hey Castiglio?" he continued. "Did you finally get engaged this weekend or what?"

"Yeah, Smitty, that crazy chick at the party was all over me," 2/C Tony Castiglio replied in a thick New York accent, his broken nose and Guido charm completing a perfectly substantiated stereotype. On cue with his equally obnoxious mouth he added, "I got engaged in a sixty dollar motel room above Chick & Ruth's all weekend long." He followed that statement with a few obnoxious moans and hip gyrations for anyone mistaking this conversations reference to engagement as having anything remotely to do with the promise of matrimony.

"You plebers get engaged this weekend?" Smitty then queried to the three plebes in our squad. Gonzo and I were joined by the squad's loan female, Summer Harris.

"Sir, seems like a question that somebody who didn't get engaged might ask, sir," Summer calmly replied. The entire table erupted in laughter. I tried not to laugh too hard as to not make my crush on her blatantly obvious. Most mids, inclusive of upperclassmen, failed miserably at this task.

Thankfully Summer had a quick enough wit that she could utilize her amazing humor to deflect the typical inappropriateness she was met with at the meal table and everywhere else for that matter. It had become routine.

While the formality of Plebe Summer kept most meal dialogue politically correct, the at-large academic year brigade seemed to care far less about such niceties. It was so loud during meals that any superior officer roaming about would have a hard time catching the breakfast dialogue unless they were within an immediate earshot.

Perimeter doors began to bust open all around us. Seemingly hundreds of King Hall workers simultaneously emerged through the swinging doors connecting the dining hall to the kitchen. They carried carts full of filled tin feeding trays carrying our morning meal.

"FLAP STICKS!" Smitty proclaimed exuberantly upon seeing the meal on the surrounding trays.

Flap sticks were the breakfast version of corndogs. They were comprised of a "sausagesque" meat filling surrounded by a deep fried blueberry cake. It was a unanimous breakfast favorite. My mouth was already watering at the sight. Summer was one of the few people I knew that abstained from eating this garbage of a breakfast. They might as well have fed us ice cream.

Eventually the meal cart made its way to our table amidst an impressive ballet of King Hall workers hustling out the morning meal. The trays were quickly dropped to the table. Before I could even smell my pending breakfast's aroma, all but save a few straggling workers had already disappeared back into the kitchen area. It would be the last time we would see them until lunch. They would not return to clean until we headed back up to our collective company areas. I can only imagine what slobs they thought we all were.

Smitty grabbed the tray the moment it hit the table and immediately grabbed three flap sticks for his own plate. It was not uncommon for the upper-class to eat first. Though seniority's eating order was up to the squad leader, most of them made the plebes eat last. Smith was the only firstie that actually grabbed his entire meal, inclusive of seconds, before anyone else had a chance to eat. It was par for course. It meant that the plebes would all likely get one flap stick. Luckily Summer let Gonzo and I split the lone flap stick she refused to eat.

By the time I took my first bite, Smitty was already throat deep in his second flap stick. He was obnoxiously smacking his lips and chewing with his mouth open. He ate with the manners of a junkyard dog. It made my blood boil just listening to it.

I looked a few tables down and peered at N.D. with envy. Unlike most plebes, the football team was permitted to sit at brigade varsity meal tables. Otherwise known as "fat tables," the extra portions received were the football team's way of ensuring assholes like Smith didn't steal their starting defensive end's breakfast. Unlike Smitty, N.D. could hardly afford to lose any more weight. As it was, his opponents in the trenches typically outweighed him by at least fifty pounds.

Luckily Gonzo was the typical lightning rod of upper-class attention for the rest of the meal. I scarfed down my first flap stick while everyone was still distracted by my roommate. Soon after the first meal bell rang, subsequently permitting plebes to excuse themselves from the table.

"Sir, permission to be excused," I quickly asked Smitty. Though I had the half of Summer's gifted flap stick left on my plate, I graciously took the opportunity to get away from the snake pit.

"Get outta here. Shove off!" Smith replied with his mouth still half filled with the remnants of his third helping of breakfast.

My early meal exit would afford me one last opportunity for morning peace and quiet. My stomach was still
far from satiated. A stale granola bar out of the remnants
of my summer care packages would fill me up back at the
room. As I exited King Hall, I made my way to the stairwell
to initiate my morning poo tradition. I contemplated how
glorious a peaceful five-minute morning dump would be,
sports page and all. It made the grumbling stomach worth
it.

"A fitting luxury," I mumbled to myself. "I already live
in a world of shit."

Chapter 12

Fucking Falcons
Saturday, October 14th, 1995
Mick, 1050 hrs.

"Go Navy, Sir, Beat Chair Force, Sir!" was repetitively echoed up and down the 5th wing stairwell in Bancroft Hall by the hundreds of plebes filing downward to street level. Air Force week was quickly approaching its climax, with just a few hours remaining until a highly anticipated gridiron tilt against our brothers in arms at the United States Air Force Academy. Saturday was game day. The yard was abuzz with energy, and within Bancroft Hall, it was palatable.

Most casual observers of the Naval Academy would assume that Army constituted the fiercest football rivalry amongst all service academies. What those casual observers often overlooked was just how much the entire Brigade of Midshipmen and Army Corps of Cadets hated the Air Force Academy.

The Army Navy football game was certainly a rivalry of epic proportions with history and tradition that was second to none. Air Force staked a claim on our collective hearts based on the sheer hatred of everything and any-thing related to that farce of an academy. The Army game was akin to a fierce sibling rivalry amongst fraternal twins. The Air Force game was instead a fistfight with the annoy-ing neighbor that lived down the street.

Anyone associated with the Air Force Academy would defensively draw upon an abundance of similarities be-tween their school and the rest of the academies. Yes, they were a military institution. Yes, they were academically rigorous with many of the same high standards for admis-sion. Yes, they had uniforms, ridiculous curfews, and mil-itary rules that no other civilian college could even begin to understand. Yes, they were required to serve a five-year service commitment post-graduation. That however was where the comparisons typically stopped.

The Air Force Academy was a different animal. Their dorms had air conditioning and modern fixtures. Their uniform standards were much more relaxed as well as virtually every other facet of military discipline. They had more personal liberties. They wore their hair longer. Worst of all, their Plebe Year harassment did not even last the full year. Their "Plebe recognition" happened a full two months earlier than Navy's.

"Those guys are a bunch of fucking pussies," Gonzo so eloquently summarized the comparison earlier that morning. His hatred stemmed from a similar distaste for all things Air Force in his enlisted days, exponentially compounding the typical level of Falcon hatred.

Unfortunately, Air Force did have one heck of a foot-ball team. In recent memory, Air Force had Navy's num-ber in our gridiron rivalry, winning all but one meeting in the past decade. This was the one difference every "zoom-ie" was quick to mention. This smug arrogance in football dominance was the one area they could hold over our head. This is precisely why the game meant so much. It was the one chance every year to steal the single meaningful bragging right they held so dear.

Hope sprung eternal down by the bay. We were in a new season. We had a new offensive scheme, dumping our aerial passing attack of the previous coaching regime and replacing it with a potent triple option rushing attack. This was a playbook brought compliments of an entirely new coaching staff, some of whom were stolen from the Air Force Academy.

"Air Force don't know what they got coming their way today," confidently remarked Gonzo as we both put on our covers and made our way to "march over" formation.

"Can't wait to see N.D. out there today," I replied.

"Homey's gonna give 'em all they can handle," Gonzo added.

Gonzo and I headed towards our company's formation point in the middle of the pavement on the now blockaded Cooper Rd., just steps away from its final turn on King George St. and about two hundred yards from the visitors' gate of the Naval Academy. Fellow plebe D.J. Green had already been in the spot ahead of everyone else as mandated for all company flag bearers. While Gonzo and I were more than happy to have avoided the assignment of company flag bearer, D.J. gladly embraced it. By the time I arrived to the formation, D.J. was already stoically hoisting our 11th company flag as a visual reminder of our mandated rendezvous point. As I looked up the street, I could see twenty-five other company flags preemptively staged up the road and completing the assemblage of all thirty-six company formation spaces. Within minutes, an organized mass of humanity would be marching in unified cadence.

With five minutes remaining until march-over formation, all of our company's plebes had assembled in a small cluster awaiting our upper-class company mates to join in on the pending festivities. Save for the football players and cheerleaders, almost all other members of the brigade were required to participate in the roughly one-mile Saturday morning march between the Naval Academy campus and the off-campus Navy Marine Corps football stadium. With every formation and subsequent mandatory march, no one particularly enjoyed being there. Most normal college students were tapping their recently iced keg. We were instead stuck manning a mandated parade.

Within minutes of our plebe class's arrival, the upperclassmen started to filter their way into our meeting area on the street. I could see the discipline spectrum between "dig-its" and "dirt-bags" play out right before my eyes.

Dig-its like Severson and Dr. Doom were always the first to arrive. They embraced the rules of the academy with open arms and tried to hold themselves to the same standards they enforced. While guys like Dr. Doom didn't always successfully adhere to those standards, the effort was always there. For better or worse they were "Joe Mid".

Dirt-bags like Hackett and Castiglio arrived at the last possible second. Castiglio was visually demonstrating the effects of hard partying the night before. Hackett had artfully constructed an "I don't give a shit" look accentuated by a partially untucked uniform and shoes that hadn't been shined since Plebe Year.

All of the plebes were mandated dig-its. We didn't have the luxury of choosing much variance on the matter. All of us had various opinions on the merits of both ends of the dig-its and dirt-bags pendulum. Those opinions typically aligned with our own preferences towards the military discipline spectrum.

Gonzo vehemently shunned anyone even close to dig-it status. I instead cared more about consistency on the spectrum. While Hackett had already provided us several favors and get out of jail free cards on come-arounds, I also silently respected guys like Severson despite his occasional propensity to make our lives difficult. I just wanted goods as advertised.

"Alright guys, form up, form up," 1/C Matt Duggan stated as he frantically paced. He was our company commander, the highest ranking mid in our company. He held ultimate accountability for our timely attendance and dutiful participation in the march-over festivities.

Unlike normal company formation during the academic week, march-over formation was much less structured and organized. There was no required place to stand, there was no mandated squad structure, and no formal accountability reports from squad leaders. This provided plebes the chance to assemble at the front of formation in a solidified cluster and stay as far away as possible from our most antagonistic upperclassmen. Gonzo and I strategically placed ourselves in the middle of the formation flanked by a full row of fellow plebes to our left and right and a complete row of plebe buffers to our front and back.

"Come on gang, it's time." LT Walker applied additional pressure, "Let's GO!" Beneath his eyes were deep dark circles. His infant daughter was born a week earlier and this was literally the first time we had seen him in almost two full weeks. Not typically known for being testy, his newborn-induced insomnia had visibly pushed his typically patient persona. I knew in my heart that Gonzo would have killed for the opportunity to suffer from newborn insomnia. He never said it overtly, but the thoughts and conversations around LT Walker's newborn secretly irked him.

"Hey Castiglio," Duggan whispered, trying to not draw attention to the matter, "where the hell is Smitty?"

Castiglio tilted his head back towards a set of park benches forty yards from the formation. There was my fearless squad leader, 1/C Smith. His head was buried deep in a public garbage can. He was likely the victim of the same locomotive that smacked Castiglio in the head the night before. As soon as Smith heard the orders of attention coming from the various companies, he lifted his head out of the trash receptacle. Mid-heave, he wiped off his face and quickly hustled his way into the back of formation. He futilely tried his best to sneak in unnoticed. Everyone in the company serenaded him with hoots and hollers as he made his way back into formation.

"Yeeeeeaaaaaah, Smitty," Castiglio loudly chimed in. "GET SOME!"

"Lock it up, guys," Duggan chimed in before the raucous drew too much attention. Joining the roughly four thousand person assembly, we initiated our commute to the stadium.

"Foooooooorwaaaard," Duggan ordered. "MARCH."

We immediately fell into cadence as the drums initiated the marching band's musical accompaniment of Anchors Away. Within minutes we had passed the main gate and made an immediate left on Randal St. heading directly towards the brick paved thoroughfare.

Our company made its way up Main Street. Each of the many bars and restaurants along our path hung a series of large blue and gold navy flags. It was a visual show of support for the home team. The flags flapped in unison under the power of slight wind gusts. They undulated as though they were moving to the very same cadence dictating our own pace of movement. Underneath these flags on both sides of the street were an eclectic mass of tourists taking in the scenery and festivities. It was hard not to get caught up in the excitement.

Downtown Main Street was as full and as festive as I'd ever seen it. We didn't get to see it very often. Plebes were restricted from leaving the yard on any day other than Saturdays. I had the unfortunate bad luck of drawing watch the previous Saturday. Standing watch as a plebe was just like being a mall security guard, minus a weapon and weekend liberty. This was, therefore, my first chance to see historic downtown Annapolis in two full weeks.

Candy began to rain from the sky. The observing crowd of spectators began tossing handfuls of penny candy in the direction of the passing brigade. Abstaining from the very minor temptation of grabbing for the candy like a six-year-old, I instead calmly let the candy bounce off my head like sugar coated hail.

"Cadence!" yelled a marching upperclassman from

the back of the company. The lack of accent or any other distinguishable verbal characteristic made it impossible to determine who was generating the command. The drum cadence generated two hundred yards farther into the march remained clearly audible and perfectly suitable for keeping time. The upperclassmen however refused to let the plebes casually enjoy any experience.

"Left. Left. Lefty, right, left, right," D.J. Green dutifully answered the order as an attempt to quickly keep the peace.

"Screw that, get a fucking slam cadence!" drunkenly interrupted Smitty. I had already heard enough of his obnoxious yelling daily over the past two months to quickly distinguish his voice. I could also smell his thick stench of puke and alcohol despite his position six rows behind us in the marching formation. I could only imagine how badly he reeked to those within closer proximity.

Slam cadences were just like a regular marching cadence but had the added flavor of personal insult. I avoided them like the plague. It was simply too risky a proposition. If the cadence was lame, I'd lose respect from my fellow plebes. If it was too risqué, I'd have an upper-class aggressively lecturing me at the stadium. Gonzo, on the other hand, was in his element and typically had two or three already scripted in his head before we ever took our first step in the march.

"Look to your rear and what do you see," Gonzo immediately engaged on cue as expected.

"Look to your rear and what do you see," the company energetically replied.

"Dr. Dooooooom staring at me."

"Dr. Dooooooom staring at me."

"Doctor Doctor, don't be blue."

"Doctor Doctor, don't be blue."

"Eventually you'll get laid too!"

Before the company had a chance to repeat the last line of Gonzo's poetic masterpiece everyone save Dr. Doom erupted in laughter.

"Hey FUCK you, Gonzalez," Doc belted out from the back. "Yo' ass is mine back in the hall!"

"Hey, LOCK it up!" Duggan commanded. He likely would have had a much more colorful response had we not been surrounded by several hundred civilian fans at the time.

I looked immediately to my right. Gonzo looked as though he had grown a full inch in the past two minutes.

Mick, 1315 hrs.

The temporary exuberance of a season opening blow-out and a second win just a few weeks later were quickly replaced by the dread of three losses in four games. That stretch included a dominating performance by Virginia Tech just a week earlier. The Navy rooting crowd was not yet ready to throw in the towel on the season. The desperation of this game compounded the emotions behind an already fierce rivalry.

Most college football stadiums predominately memorialized player names like "Namath" or "Unitas." Navy Marine Corps Memorial Stadium instead immortalized victorious battles like "Iwo Jima" and "Midway." Not even the great Roger Staubach, Super Bowl MVP and NFL Hall of Famer, could crack that starting lineup. While it would be next to impossible to replicate the level of heroics named in the stands, the Navy football team was certainly demonstrating their own level of high valor. Despite being down early, we were still very much still in the game.

It was 4th down and three yards to go from Navy's twenty-three yard line. Even though they were well within their kicker's field goal range, the Air Force Falcons decided to go for it. The Falcons had dominated the entire first half of football in every possible facet save the scoreboard. A couple of hometown slanted officiating calls and a big red zone fumble had kept Navy within just one score of the lead. With less than two minutes remaining in the first half, we were only down 14-10. The Falcons were essentially choosing the chance to put us down two scores as opposed to taking the more assured seven-point lead via field goal. There would be a tidal wave of momentum to take into the second half for whichever team could prevail on this next play. It was the biggest play of the game so far.

The Falcon's offense approached the line of scrimmage. The clock continued to tick down to the final minute. The Navy Marine Corps stadium was as loud as it had been all day. The midshipmen section roared particularly loud with virtually every midshipmen standing, screaming, and stomping in the bleachers. As soon as Air Force's quarterback approached his center to get the snap, he signaled time out. Both sides of the ball gathered up one last time to strategize during the last utilized timeout of the first half. This play carried enough gravitas that a couple extra seconds to think the game plan through seemed perfectly logical.

The game delay gave us all a minute to collectively catch our breaths. I began to notice that while the majority of my fellow midshipmen were quite passionate Navy football fans, a scant few others were the farthest thing from it. Most of these mids were either reading books, writing letters, or waiting to use one of the five stadium payphones within public access of the stadium's interior. I could not fathom going to my own college's football game and not caring about it, but also understood how football wasn't exactly everyone's cup of tea. For those mids, the academy had found yet another way to sap the fun out of a Saturday afternoon.

"Damn Mick, I gotta take a leak, homey," Gonzo yelled across Summer towards my general direction, "but I can't miss N.D.'s big shot to make the play of the game."

"Looks like you're stuck then," I yelled forward keeping my eyes fixated on the playing field, completely immersed in the game.

I was additionally thrilled to be sharing the game with Summer, who was sitting directly between Gonzo and me. Being squad mates all semester had brought us all closer together. I was trying my best to play it cool and continue hiding my obvious attraction towards her. I was sure Summer could already sense my romantic affection for her. She was far too savvy not to. While I had received no immediate physical indication of mutual feelings, she remained sitting next to me during the first half despite having to listen to Gonzo. It was a sign of encouragement. I had hoped and suspected that our increasingly random

excuses to spend time together were becoming more fre-
quent not by chance. A big fourth down and various romantic mysteries had my heart thumping. Not only was I
a significant football fan but the rumored promise of free
brigade-wide weekend liberty passes pending a victorious
outcome made this game doubly exciting for me.

The Falcon's quarterback again stepped under center
quickly after he broke their huddle following the timeout.
Their entire offense remained set on the line of scrimmage. Seeing my roommate out on the defensive line of
scrimmage with a chance to make the biggest play of the
season was surreal. Navy's number 99 wore that number
proudly as the only plebe class of 1999 on either side of
the field that was currently starting. Gonzo and I were
likely N.D's biggest fans in the stadium that day. His parents were watching the game back home in Nebraska. A
deafening roar returned and echoed through the stands
as the players assembled on the line of scrimmage. Just as
the hair on my back rose, the ball snapped and the play
initiated.

The Falcon quarterback took the snap from center,
and as per typical triple option protocol, faked the give to
the full back up the middle to the strong side of the field.
Then the quarterback and weak side motioning slot back
quickly countered their lateral path and ran directly back
to the sideline and towards the short side of the field. N.D.
and the weak side corner back had stayed at home in their
positions long enough to be in perfect position for the defensive stop. The quarterback ran directly towards N.D.
like a gazelle prancing towards the teeth of a starving lion.

The crowd pre-emptively grew louder seeing the play

unfold. N.D. was typically a Venus flytrap and the fans recognized the advantage of the situation unfolding. As the quarterback came within an arm-grasp's reach, N.D. poised himself for the tackle. The quarterback flicked his wrist quickly towards the pitch back but kept the ball in a brilliant fake. N.D.'s eyes were tricked out of place for a split second long enough for the quarterback to quickly tuck the ball and cut up field. N.D. was caught flat-footed and completely whiffed on the tackle. The cornerback had committed coverage to the pitch back. Once the quarterback made his way past N.D., he had a clear path to the end zone. Twenty-three yards later, Air Force was up two scores ahead of the half. A collective sigh was followed by a thoroughly muted home crowd. The few hundred Air Force Cadets that had made the trip out with the visiting team were bouncing with excitement on the opposing side of the stadium. The home side of the stands remained standing in disappointed silence. From our side of the stadium, we could hear the big rig diesel engines barreling up Interstate 50 in midday weekend traffic a half a mile down the road.

"FUCK!" Gonzo screamed out loudly well after the majority of the home crowd muted, many of them looking back in his direction with an air of inquisitive scorn. Gonzo sat down quickly amidst a sea of midshipman uniforms.

Luckily for Gonzo it would be nearly impossible for any curmudgeonly alumni to assign responsibility towards his recently loud public profanity. Most of said alumni were older and a bit more of a wine and cheese ilk. They would just as soon give away their wives' game worn mink coat than stand for anything in the football stadium that remotely smacked of unruly fun. Earlier in the game, I had even observed one such alumnus yell at the Navy fan sitting in front of him. The fan had been cheering on a critical third and short play for the defense and his standing enthusiasm was blocking the old man's seated view. I imagined he was the same type of guy that read books at football games fifty years earlier. The circle of life played out right before my eyes.

"Alright Mick, make way, I gotta hit the head or I may just give you a golden shower," said Gonzo hastily as he made a quick run for the men's bathroom, not waiting for the half to end.

The internet and its wonderfully diverse offering of pornographic content continued to expand Gonzo's working vocabulary. By the time he made his way up the aisle and towards the restroom, the first half had expired. I had already heard my fill of Gonzo's inappropriate jokes and phrases. While I typically found most of his humor hilarious under different circumstances, it was not helping my vibe with Summer.

As soon as Gonzo left my immediate sight, I quickly turned my attention back to Summer. I tried my best to generate a friendly and rational conversation versus listen to Gonzo quote Andrew Dice Clay with a Puerto Rican accent. I knew that any conversation I had with Summer in front of Gonzo would be replayed, critiqued, ridiculed, and remembered for weeks to come in the privacy of our room. I took aim at a rare opportunity, not knowing how long it would last. Eventually Gonzo would return to his seat with a fist full of nachos and an empty bladder.

"So you had said your mom was coming into town in a few weeks?" I asked trying my best to solicit conversation and appear to be the thoughtful and listening type of potential suitor.

"Momsssss," Summer responded. "Plural."

"Huh," I said not fully processing.

"I have two moms," she continued.

"Wha—," I stopped short and then I put things together. "Oooooh, I get it now," I continued feeling more awkward by the second. I could actually feel my penis shrinking.

"So you're adopted," I continued, soon after wishing I had kept my mouth shut and ridden things out silently until the second half kickoff.

"Sort of, but not exactly," she said.

I stopped and stared forward for a minute. My mind was spinning. All I could muster was, "Aaaah, I got nothing."

Suddenly Summer burst out laughing, I imagined at least partially from my humorous look of silent perplexity. It was a visual posture that I rarely took.

"So you know how I grew up in Northern California," she began her fascinating soliloquy with a coy smile and the flick of her hair. Her face slowly lit up as she told her story. I imagined it wasn't one she told very often, especially to male midshipmen.

The bleachers around us had suddenly cleared out. The mids made their way up the stands to wait in line for either stale hot dogs or an unoccupied urinal. The game's temporary hiatus dwindled as the halftime clock ticked away. Summer and I had been provided a serendipitous but temporary opportunity to have an open and private conversation.

I sat mesmerized by her story. Summer lived the first six years of her life in a commune. Her biological parents had met at Berkley. As students they got heavily caught up in the local scene and eventually became a couple. Sometime around the summer of 1970, they both left college early in favor of commune living about two hours north of Oakland. Seven years later, they had their first and only child.

"By the early '80s," she continued her story, "my dad got sick of the scene and took off."

There were sparse random recollected memories of her father. She was not even sure if her biological parents had even ever been formally married. Most remembered details of that time had been wiped clean from her memory long ago. At least it was presented that way in her narrative.

"Some people said he eventually took off to Alaska to become part of a professional fishing boat," she said now looking off into the field toward no one in particular. "Some people said he ran off with another woman and became a Reagan-era working schmoe."

"What does your mom say?" I asked in genuine interest.

"She won't even reference him by name," she answered. "And I haven't seen or heard from him since two weeks after my sixth birthday."

Her mom left the commune with her immediately. Not surprisingly, such painful memories precluded them from ever returning.

"We ended up moving farther south to Salinas," she went on. "Mom got a job as a yoga instructor at the local YMCA and for a while we shacked up with Pap."

Summer's mom spent just four years in Monterrey after a childhood of moving around as a Navy brat. Summer's Naval Officer Pap used his final tour of duty as a teacher at the nearby Naval Post Graduate School as a way to finally settle his family down.

"After a year of living with Pap, Mom met Lizbeth while teaching yoga," she explained. "She was the director of the local Y at the time." Her voice and our dialogue became louder as the Navy Drum and Bugle Corps performed their halftime show to temporarily empty stands.

"So Elizabeth, that's your second mom? I asked.

"LIZbeth, yes, she is my adopted mother," Summer replied, "and a great one at that."

It was clear in her posture that Summer meant what she said about her feelings towards her adopted mother. She told me that it was surprisingly Lizbeth, not Pap, who had been the impetus behind Summer joining the Navy.

"As to civilianize me after a life in the commune," Summer recollected, "Lizbeth forced me to take up a traditional sport, and that is how I picked up soccer."

Later in Summer's youth, Lizbeth helped gather recruiting letters and videos that helped Navy women soccer's star freshman player land an appointment at the academy during her senior year of high school.

"She also convinced my mom that I could date and have a television," she added.

Her story helped explain why despite being one of the smartest plebes in the academy she was woefully unaware of virtually anything related to pop-culture. She had not seen Star Wars nor did she know who the Cosby family was.

"The more I hear about her, the more I like this Lizbeth character," I jokingly interjected.

"If she is anything, she's a character." Summer smiled and then enjoyed a genuine laugh.

"My family is chock-full of characters as well," I said in an attempt to capitalize on our rapport.

"So tell me about these McGee family characters," she said flirtatiously looking me in the eye.

"Wow, I don't even know where to begin," I replied and taking a deep contemplative breath, I tried my best to stall my answer. While I could instantly rattle off hundreds of crazy stories about my family within random episodic tales, it was much more difficult to contrive a cohesive narrative appropriately edited for Naval Academy sharing. Having an adopted lesbian mother may seem like a bizarre family quirk amongst the homogeneously Caucasian and traditional majority of midshipman. It couldn't hold a candle to a cousin that not only sold drugs, but also sold them directly to the Naval Academy. I remained silent though only moments remained before it would appear awkward.

"Come on, they must be tame as compared to my fucked up family," thankfully Summer interjected.

"Oh, don't be so sure," I replied. "Fucked up families are going around a lot these days."

"Whose fucked up family?" chimed in Gonzo who had his rear end in my face as he headed back to his seat after returning from the concourse with a large container of nachos. I artfully dodged one cheesy projectile as Gonzo slipped on a large conglomerated mess of empty peanut shells. He had made the mess himself thirty minutes earlier.

"My family," I chimed in quickly. While I was worried about revealing too much of my family's past, I quickly became doubly worried that Gonzo might hear the story of Summer's adopted lesbian mother. That was the last thing any of us needed.

"Yeah, your family is pretty fucked up, man," Gonzo verbally recollected to Summer. "He's got this one cousin," he continued chuckling and displaying a more natural Puerto Rican New Yorker dialect. "That's a red-headed white dude that got dreads and calls himself Bird."

I then narrated the story about how Larry Parsons' one and only basketball season in junior high landed him his permanent moniker. My story about Bird, and the brief verbal description by Gonzo was enough to satisfy Summer's queried justification for family insanity.

We all heard the crowd applaud as the Navy team took the field. My moments of privacy with Summer would have to wait for another time.

Mick, 1455 hrs.

The seats throughout the stadium began emptying steadily well before the conclusion of a 30-20 disappointment against Air Force. As the game's final seconds ticked away, many of the fans that had the freedom to leave the game already did. The matchup was not nearly as close as the score had indicated. By mandate and tradition, all midshipmen remained in the stands until the bitter end. It was an early lesson in "going down with the ship."

"A toast to the host of men we boast, the U.S. Air Force!" the Air Force Cadets concluded the singing of their school's Alma mater. "Wooooo!" the cadets erupted in unison with their fists victoriously raised. The song's not-yet-completed tune blared on from the corner of the visitor side stands, directly across from the Brigade of Midshipmen. What sounded and looked like the peak of a southern evangelical biblical service was to the cadets a triumphant exclamation point concluding their final sung verse. It was an audibly obnoxious and self-indulgent show. It perfectly summarized just about everything we hated about that place.

There just seemed to be more reverence and dignity in the singing of our own "Navy Blue and Gold." Per the game's tradition, we sang our song first as the game's losing team. Aside from the emphatically loud last line of singing, the majority of the following Air Force song was barely audible given the scarcity of visiting fans and cadets. Over top of the several blaring horns, I could audibly interpret very few lyrics throughout the song. About all I could make out were some references about rainbows and a pot of gold. I couldn't tell if they were singing about a football game or a box of Lucky Charms.

"I guess by the time that academy got started they just ran out of good Alma Mater lyrics," I verbalized to no one in particular as a way of venting. Catching myself in the act of being petulant, I quickly ceased my sudden outburst. As tempting as it was to be a sore loser, the Naval

Academy was too prideful a place to be anything shy of a good sport. Gonzo and I instead silently sulked our way to the parking lot with the remainder of my shipmates. All of us were dreading the next year of gloating Air Force cadets had yet again just earned over us.

Chapter 13

Drowning our Misery
Saturday, October 14th, 1995
Mick, 1535 hrs.

Within thirty minutes of the traditional post game singing, the brigade relocated from our section in the stands to amidst the grass and pavement of the stadium parking lot. The air smelled deliciously of cheap beer and grilled hamburgers. In what felt like a wake, moods improved as alcohol consumption increased. Just about every midshipman of legal age was collectively drowning their sorrows being provided via their company's tailgate.

Tailgate tents were staged in pre-assigned company areas throughout the parking lot's exterior. The company tailgate was yet another example of Naval Academy-mandated fun. Every member of our company had to pay annual wardroom dues of twenty-five dollars, inclusive of the plebes.

If you paid for it, you might as well enjoy it. That was always my logic.

As plebes, we made fifty dollars a month. Our wardroom dues were like a mortgage investment. Instead of home equity, we received cheeseburgers and an occasional pepperoni pizza after the game. No plebe of any age was permitted to drink during their first year at the Naval Academy. Gonzo was already well past his twenty-first birthday. It killed him that he had to pay for beer he couldn't drink.

All of the firsties and second class in attendance had already changed out of their game mandated uniforms into more casual civilian attire. I had no idea where they did this but imagined they just snuck out of plain sight into whichever car backseat they could find quick access to. Service dress blue jackets and ties were long since traded in for jeans and sweaters. It was odd seeing our typically uniformed upperclassmen in regular clothes. It was harder to distinguish them from the rest of the tailgating fans. A few of the female upperclassmen looked much more attractive in their civies. I could only imagine what Summer would look like in normal clothes.

As Gonzo and I scarfed down our second cheeseburgers, we observed the drunken mayhem breaking out around us. Like clockwork, LT Walker ended his typical thirty-five minute stay with our company. He was likely off to change diapers or to simply take a nap. As soon as he was out of eyesight, several upperclassmen quickly assembled a beer pong table that had been stashed in the back of McVane's pickup truck. At the time he and Severson seemed a far cry from the Plebe Summer intimidators they were just a few months earlier.

The beer pong table was our company's prized possession. It drew mids in from other companies and even a few of the younger alumni looking to relive their old glory days.

Within minutes the table was standing. The cups were set and filled. The crowd around our company's tent tripled in almost an instant.

"Hey beer bitch," drunkenly slurred Smitty towards our general direction. "Go grab me a fucking <hiccup> beer."

I could not tell if Smitty was speaking to me or Gonzo, or anyone at all for that matter. He was so drunk before the game that I doubted he ever had time to sober up. He had already assumed the position as the first player in the oncoming beer pong tournament. He stumbled forward onto the table before catching himself with his outstretched hand. He knocked over three of the already filled beer cups set for the next match. Had the table not been there he would have surely been on the ground. His request for beer seemed particularly asinine considering he was standing in front of several pre-poured beer cups awaiting the first game of the beer pong tournament.

"I'm not your butler, sir," Gonzo retorted.

"Ooooo, look whose balls just dropped today," Smitty quipped. "Alright then, I've got my goddamn eye on you, chico," he continued swaying like a heavy weight boxer that was just took a hard right hook to the temple.

"Go get your own fucking beer, Smitty," Gonzo said without batting an eye. It was the same look he gave me just before we exchanged blows back in Plebe Summer.

If this dialogue had taken place back in the hall, all hell would have already broken loose. Most of the upperclassmen were either drunk, preoccupied, or both. Thankfully, no one outside of Gonzo and I seemed to notice the situation. Everyone had generally stopped listening to

Smitty before he even arrived to the tailgate in a stupor.

"Yo man, you gotta cool it," I quickly said to Gonzo as I firmly grabbed his arm and backed him away from the situation before it escalated into something more out of hand.

"Man, FUCK that guy, homey," Gonzo replied pointing back at Smitty and trying to wrangle out of my grip. Gonzo was still torqued up and ready to fight. Smitty had already forgotten where he was standing and was trying his best not to pass out or urinate in his pants.

Luckily I was able to walk Gonzo away from the circumstances and back towards the stadium.

"Smitty's a drunken dick, don't let that guy get to you," I said. "Totally not worth the trouble."

Gonzo finally stood still for a moment while continuing to breathe heavily. His adrenaline must have been firing on all cylinders. There was a part of me that just wanted to let him go just to see Smitty get punched in the face.

"Yeah, I guess," Gonzo said after taking a deep dismissive breath and eventually calming down.

"Look, why don't you head down to the locker room and see if you can catch up with N.D. and bring him back to the tailgater?" I suggested.

If anyone could use a friend after the game, it was N.D. In addition to his missed tackle before the half, the second half was even worse. There were three more missed tackles. There was even a bad personal foul penalty giving the Falcons a critical first down on third and long while the game was still competitive.

"Alright, I guess," replied Gonzo. "You comin' with me?"

"I'll hang back here," I replied. "Let me keep an eye on that drunken asshole and if he is still being a dick when you guys get back, we can bolt."

This statement was of course malarkey. The real reason I stayed behind was in the hopes that Summer might make an appearance at our company tailgate. I hadn't seen her since early in the second half when she wandered off to spend some time with her soccer teammates. I may have been totally misreading the situation but I felt like there were some sparks between us back at the game. I had even contemplated asking her out. Just thinking about it made the butterflies in my stomach frantically flutter.

Gonzo was still so torqued up from the drunken exchange with Smitty that he didn't even question my rationale for staying behind. Thankfully he did not yet know anything about my pending intent for an evening get together with Summer. He gathered that I had a bit of a crush on her, but that was the extent of his awareness. I certainly didn't want any dating tips from him. The last thing I needed was him saying something publicly inappropriate at the tailgater.

Mick, 2040 hrs.

By the time I got back to Bancroft Hall, the sun had set and evening was in its infancy. I had hung back at the tailgater until the bitter end. Summer never did show. She was likely hanging with her soccer teammates in an off-yard party at an illegally rented crash house.

Crash houses were not entirely uncommon. While it was strictly prohibited for any midshipman to rent or own any property, people did it anyway. These houses were typically split amongst five or more people to keep rent low. They were used strictly as party pads and a place to crash for visiting girlfriends. I wasn't yet cool enough to get invited to such venues, but N.D. had been through his football teammates.

N.D. and Gonzo never did show up to the company tailgate. They, like Summer, had likely found a cooler place to hang out after the game. I was secretly a little disappointed that they did not drop by to pick me up. I figured N.D. might have been hesitant as a plebe to drag along two other plebes to an off-campus party. Gonzo would have never let N.D. go to a party without taking him along too. That was likely how he made the invite list.

When I made my final squared turn arriving at my room back in Bancroft, I noticed that the door was closed. All room doors were mandated to remain open while unoccupied. Our room was either occupied or had been messed with. I quickly kicked open the door. My adrenaline was pumping as a way to prep me for what might lie on the other side.

The door swung aggressively open and locked into place with a loud "clang." If the hall hadn't been almost entirely empty at the time, it would have surely drawn undue attention.

"What the fuuuuuuuck?" I mused in disbelief.

Two mattresses were on the floor along with half of the contents of our unlocked personal closets. Clothes were strewn about everywhere as well as some of the shelves that previously held them. As I inspected the disarray further, I noticed that there were tiny shards of glass everywhere. As I followed the trail of glass, it ended at N.D.'s completely smashed computer monitor directly behind his desk on the floor. Looking at the extent of the damage, it had clearly been thrown versus accidentally fallen.

I didn't know whether to laugh, cry, or explode in a fit of rage. If it were physically possible to express all of these emotions simultaneously, I would have done it. Instead I stood still as though my feet were locked in cement. In shock, my body still debated which emotion would eventually take over the situation.

After a few explosively reactionary expletives, I immediately closed the door to hide the disaster zone and my ticking time bomb of emotions. Neither would do me any favors in the moment. I wanted to avoid any official attention from the mid standing watch. An official response from the academy may have hindered a subsequently unofficial retaliation. I wanted to keep that ace in my pocket for the time being.

I rummaged in Gonzo's desk and found his spare pack of smokes. I subsequently climbed through the window and lit my first stolen cigarette. I took a deep inhale and impatiently waited for the nicotine to calm my nerves back down to sanity.

After three smokes and thirty minutes, I climbed back into my room. The disaster didn't look any better, but at least my time on the roof calmed me down a bit. With a saner mind, I changed into my PT clothes and sat at my desk. Luckily my monitor remained unscathed. In a calmer state, I decided to check my email just in case anyone had dropped me a line on the incident. I was also procrastinating from picking up this mess in hopes that my roomies would eventually be back to help out.

I logged into my email and began perusing. There were thirty-eight new emails in my inbox. The first unread message was from some idiotic plebe that thought it would be a good idea to send an email asking the entire plebe class if they had found his protective goggles in plebe chemistry class on Friday. The next thirty-six emails explained various methods and places where he could shove those goggles. The last email in my inbox was from Gonzo:

> *Mick, N.D. is a Tasmanian devil. Girl dumped him.*
> *Gave him some booze. Bad idea. Trying to keep him*
> *out of trouble, he would not stay in room. May need*
> *your help tonight. Hang tight if you get this.*
> *-Gonzo*

Within an instant my room ransacking mystery was likely solved. At least the primary suspects had been identified. I glared upward to the ceiling rafter and saw a slightly out of place tile. I grabbed my chair and placed it directly below that misplaced square of rotted fiberboard. I wanted to inspect what had become of Gonzo's stashed liquor collection. He had procured it for us a month earlier while out on liberty. It was his gift for the room as a way to make Friday nights in the hall a little more bearable. Our Friday night cocktails had become a weekly tradition. N.D. had yet to partake as the football team stayed in a hotel on Friday nights, even before home games.

I stood on my carefully placed chair to peer above the tiles in search of our contraband handles of Jim Beam and Captain Morgan's. Aside from dust and a variety of rodent turds, there were no bottles within sight. Gonzo and I had a few Friday night drinks the night before and the bottles were far from empty. Now they were nowhere to be found.

Making myself useful, I began picking up the many pieces of clothing on the floor. Eventually I motivated myself to grab a dustpan and sweep up the shards of glass from the smashed monitor. Just as the room was looking like it had when I left in the morning for the football game, the door was kicked open. It slammed so loudly that I feared it might come off the hinges.

"Need your help, homey," Gonzo winced with N.D's arm draped around his arm.

Before I could verbally acknowledge my roommates, the overpowering smell of alcohol and vomit quickly wafted into my nostrils.

"Holy shit, what happened to you guys out there?" I quickly replied as my brain continued processing the shit show playing out before my eyes.

N.D. mumbled a few unintelligible phrases. He was nearly unconscious and covered in what I imagined was his own vomit. He was at least an hour removed from any level of coherency. As he and Gonzo made it through the threshold, I quickly took N.D.'s other arm and we carried him the remaining ten feet to the bottom bunk. Thankfully Gonzo still liked the top bunk. It would have taken a forklift to get N.D. to the top bunk given his current condition.

"How did you even get him up here to the room?" I

asked. Once the initial shock of their arrival passed, I became keenly interested in how things had played out. N.D. was a heavy carry with two men. I had no idea how Gonzo got him up to the fourth floor by himself.

"Snuck him on the elevator," Gonzo replied. "That's the least of our problems, homey."

Gonzo began his recollection of events. On Friday, N.D. had received a letter from his girlfriend like he did every week. Following his typical tradition, he opened it Saturday morning back at the hotel before the team loaded up the buses to commute to the stadium for the game. Usually these letters contained some girlish pep talk and other sappy garbage.

This Saturday's letter had been different. N.D.'s girlfriend had written a ten-page novel. Despite the niceties of compliments and regrets of fate's bad timing, it was the tantamount of a Dear John letter with pink ink and a postage stamp.

"That's some cold shit, man," Gonzo commented on the situation, "even for a blonde white chick."

I think everyone in the room shared the sentiment.

"Fuck-ing bitch," I commented angrily. I was genuinely disappointed for N.D. I was also ticked that this sorority girl in Nebraska may have had as much to do with our football loss as the opposing Air Force Falcon football team.

When Gonzo heard the story from N.D. in the locker room after the game, he decided the best place for N.D. was back at the room in isolation. His on-field performance and current emotional state wasn't going to win him many friends in the stadium parking lot.

"I thought a little buzz might ease the pain, know what I'm sayin?" rationalized Gonzo.

Before Gonzo could finish purchasing his vending machine mixers, N.D. was already guzzling the handle of Beam like Paul Bunyan. Once he polished off the bottle, he immediately broke out in a destructive rage. Unfortunately his computer monitor perished in a crime of passion.

"I tried to get him to calm the fuck down when I got back in the room," Gonzo narrated. "In an instant he was already out the door headin' to the Sinbad concert with his hot date," Gonzo continued and visually demonstrated that N.D.'s escort was the now empty bottle of rum he pulled out of a duffle bag on the floor. "I tried but there was no stoppin' that crazy train."

The comedian Sinbad was hosting a comedy show Saturday night on the yard at Alumni Hall. N.D. had bought tickets earlier in the week.

"How did that go?" I asked.

"We never even made it to the seats, homey," Gonzo smirked over his emotional stress.

On the way to Alumni Hall, N.D. had polished off the remaining quarter of the rum bottle. Mid-concert, in full uniform, they made their way down to the floor seats and finally found their row despite the audience darkness of the ongoing show. Before they made it to the seats, N.D. exploded with projectile vomit like the Exorcist.

"Holy shit, did anyone say anything?" I probed.

"Hell yeah, Sinbad stopped mid-set," Gonzo answered as his smirk remained. "I played like he had the flu and got him the hell out of there before anyone could stop us to ask questions. Everyone within five rows of us could smell the booze."

If it had been me being escorted out of Alumni, we might have been able to maintain anonymity in our escape. N.D., a burly six foot four African American plebe, was a little harder to hide. Their escape had merely bought them a few hours to a night at best to conceal the evidence and build a protective story around the incident before shit hit the fan.

"Here, let's get his uniform and these sheets in a bag, I'll wash them later tonight when everyone else is a sleep," Gonzo commanded.

Gonzo was in total control of the situation. I imagined he had seen enough of his friends' post deployment Dear John letters in the fleet to know how to handle conditions like these. He covered up the "crime scene" with the adeptness of a serial killer.

Thirty minutes post arrival, the room was clean, and N.D. was temporarily passed out. His lumberjack snoring was so loud that our room's glass pane windows vibrated with each exhaled breath. Based on my limited experience with high intensity hangovers, he was in for a long night. As a finishing touch, Gonzo poured a hefty portion of bleach in our garbage can and placed it by the bed. Hopefully this would be enough to protect the entire room from smelling like a bar should N.D. likely vomit again.

"I forgot to tell you the best part," Gonzo chuckled.

"What's that?" I enquired.

"The dude on the receiving end of the projectile vomit," continued Gonzo, "was a fucking full bird Air Force Colonel still in uniform from the game."

We both burst out laughing. It was the first time I had

done that since the game ended nearly ten hours earlier.

"Shit, at least somebody in the Air Force got dumped on today," I replied. It was one of the very few excuses to smile that day. It was a welcome yet temporary distraction from the loss to Air Force, the missed opportunity to further hang out with Summer, and the general craziness of the evening.

"Training day 107," Gonzo exclaimed as we finally hit the sheets for the night. "Down the shitter."

Part IV

Why Go

Chapter 14

Wiz Quiz
Sunday, October 15th, 1995
Mick, 1825 hrs.

Under normal circumstances, Sunday dinner was depressing enough. This week's dinner was even more so. The recent sting of the Air Force loss well outlasted the buzz of Saturday tailgates. Hangovers both literally and figuratively seemed to linger well into Sunday's required gathering.

I looked to my right and could see at the table next to me that D.J. Green was wearing boxing gloves at the dinner table. He had lost his weekly football bet with his upperclassmen, and now he had to pay the piper. He'd be eating this dinner and every dinner this week with mandated boxing gloves on his hands.

Plebes and upperclassmen football bets were a common way to make the season a bit more interesting. The plebe would be forced to pick Navy under a mutually agreed upon point spread. The payout of the bet typically related to getting additional privileges for the following week. Meal carry-on, which meant a plebe could sit, eat, and talk like a normal human being, was a very popular choice. I had won a bet a few weeks earlier and forced 2/C Castiglio to read our room a goodnight story out of "Penthouse Letters" before bed every night for a week.

On the flip side, the upper-class bets usually involved sadistic inconvenience or humiliation for the losing plebe. Truthfully, it was the only direction the bet could go. Plebes had very little privileges left to lose to begin with. Our upper-class were particularly sadistic in their bets as the past few years had been tough seasons for our football team. They all spent the majority of their own Plebe Years on the losing end of their own humiliating bets. This was a chance for restitution. It was also a nice insurance policy. If Navy lost, at least an upperclassman could see a plebe suffer as consolation.

My fellow plebes had little room to complain. This year's football team was off to a much better start. The plebes had been on the winning end of bets more often than not. My negotiated point spread with Castiglio kept me safe for the week. While Navy had lost, they hadn't lost by enough to surpass my well-negotiated fourteen point spread.

The Chaplain's traditional pre-meal blessing eventually transpired and was immediately followed by a surprise podium appearance by CAPT Vader Clemons, our newly assigned Commandant.

"Da, da, da, da, dada, da dada," the brigade broke out into an impromptu singing of "Imperial March." Darth Vader's theme song accompanied our own Vader as he expeditiously approached the podium.

While these sorts of visits were not entirely uncommon, they were typically driven by specific circumstances. I hypothesized that we would be receiving a pep talk following our disappointing loss to Air Force a day earlier.

"Brigade, immediately following completion of evening meal everyone is to report to their respective company areas for a mandated urinalysis, no exceptions. That is all." Vader completed his dialogue and abruptly left the main podium in the center of King Hall.

I could hear a fork clang as it hit the ground fifty yards from my table. Under normal circumstances, I would have had a hard time hearing the person talking directly across the table from me.

The faces of every midshipman I could see had the look of utter shock. It was a frantic silence. The weight of the negative energy was suffocating. For a plebe, Sundays were bad regardless. Air Force hangovers made them worse. With this news, we were likely sitting smack dab in the inner ring of hell. I looked across at 2/C Severson as he silently mouthed to an unknown recipient "what . . . the . . . FUCK?"

Vader's explanation was short and sweet. It held very little emotion and conveyed even less context. No rationale was given. It didn't need to be. Even the slowest of plebes quickly understood that this was serious business. Several midshipmen had likely been busted for drugs over the weekend, perhaps all in a single sting. It was the only scenario capable of driving surprise urinalysis of this magnitude. The nervous energy in the room was electric. Internal speculation was spreading like wildfire across the tables of King Hall. D.J. Green's boxing gloves suddenly became much less interesting than the emerging conversations at hand. My mind fixated on Bird and his revelation.

Within seconds my mind was racing. I immediately worried about Bird's potential involvement and whether I would be burdened by any future recognized association with him. It was the last thing in life that I needed right now. Then I started worrying about Aunt Nellie. She was barely equipped to handle Bird's first prison sentence much less a more protracted sequel.

I thought of my mom, and how my father's death pushed her towards the bottle. It had been several years and she still struggled to get away from it.

Would the same happen to Nellie given her past struggles? How would my mom survive? If Nellie again became a drunk, who would be there for Mom? Who would be there to take care of them with Bird in prison?

My mind raced. I could feel my pulse quicken exponentially as I became seemingly more irrational in my worries.

This was all speculative worrying. I convinced myself that it was my body's subliminal way of creating an internal sense of urgency. I knew that the power of the brigade rumor mill would have us all filled in before long. I had to figure out what happened as quickly as possible. It was the same biological wiring cavemen had when they had to kill what they ate. If my fate was going to be on the bad side of the truth, I needed to know what went down before everyone else did. Proactive damage control was far better than reactive emergency response.

By the time everyone was permitted to sit and eat, hundreds of conversations broke out simultaneously amongst a burgeoning mass of conspiracy theorists. Even temporary uncertainty was a nuisance. I drank a couple extra glasses of juice to gear up my bladder. I needed to get by the urinalysis quickly and find my way to a phone booth as soon as possible. I needed to know if Bird had any hand in this.

Mick, 2055 hrs.

Three male midshipmen meandered by the urinalysis check-in table in our company area. All three of them were chugging canteens full of sink water desperately trying to fill their bladders to the point of bursting. Every five minutes or so one of them would break out into an impromptu set of one hundred jumping jacks. The hope was that the internal jostling of the bouncing exercise would break the seal of a seemingly impenetrable bladder.

No one was going anywhere until the remaining empty cups on the table were filled to the brim with warm urine. The hallway would remain our mandated purgatory without exception until each and every one of us completed our urinalysis. Those were the rules as dictated a few hours earlier to every midshipman returning to company areas, upperclassmen included. I started to worry we'd be out there all night. I heard similar concerns whispered from the upperclassmen across the hall.

Drug tests were not that uncommon at the academy. Typically a handful of companies randomly tested every month. The military had long maintained a zero tolerance drug policy. The academy was no different. It was only natural to enforce it. Even the process of the drug testing itself was not foreign. Mids didn't need much instruction beyond "take this empty cup, fill it to the top, no funny business."

It was generally expected that urinalysis would happen to every company about once a year. 11th Company had already had ours just a month earlier. When it happened, no one even batted an eye. A Brigade wide test was apparently a different animal altogether. This was an extreme rarity from what I heard throughout dinner conversation that night from the upperclassmen.

The synchronized hallway clocks eventually hit 9 p.m. on Sunday evening. Order and discipline had long since worn out their welcome on the night. Nearly three hours of sitting on the floor and we already looked like a collective band of nomadic gypsies. Binders and open books surrounded my sitting area. The floor was the only logical alternative to my banned desk.

When we initially reported to our company area after Sunday dinner, LT Walker was there waiting for us. The company officers and medical staff administrating the urinalysis must have been tipped off well before the brigade was. Within a few days, everyone in the country would likely know about the scandal. It was the curse of an academy residing within thirty miles of Baltimore and Washington D.C. Major media outlets loved a juicy academy story, especially considering how much juice they squeezed out of the Double E scandal and various other shenanigans just a few years earlier.

Receiving orders immediately after dinner, the plebes

were additionally instructed to gather up our homework for the evening and immediately camp out in the hallway. As to not interfere with homework and group study, plebes were permitted to quietly chat as long as the conversation related to homework or professional military study for the next morning's come-arounds. It was the only fair way to compensate being prohibited access to our rooms. The evening's professional development quiz originally on tap for plebes after dinner had been postponed a day. It was one of the few bright spots of the experience.

After two hours of being stuck in the hallway, there was very little left in the way of chemistry labs and memorizing the weapons forward to aft of a CH-53 helicopter. Everyone was eagerly cheering on the remaining participants in the pubococcygeus muscle Olympics.

Throughout the evening, several plans and scenarios for getting to the nearest phone booth had raced through my mind. I knew my best bet was three floors down in our neighboring seventh wing where there was a large public phone room with private booths. My journey there would be quick, but getting there would be a problem. Plebes had mandatory bedtime at 10 p.m. As my pre lights out time was dwindling, I started making plans for sneaking down to the phones after hours. Nellie and Bird would both be up into the wee hours of the night. Nellie was a night owl, as was Bird when the next morning's surf didn't compel him to get out of bed early. I settled on sneaking down a few hours after midnight once most mids were in bed. If anybody questioned me, I would just say that I was checking in on a sick relative that I was up worried about.

I looked to my right from my seated vantage point in

the main hallway. LT Walker begrudgingly sat behind a recently set folding table. He seemed to be just as annoyed about losing his last free moments of the weekend as we were. On the table in front of him remained a handful of empty plastic cylinders. These were the last remaining urine receptacles that had yet to be filled.

Several enlisted corpsman helped facilitate the urinalysis. They were on loan from the on campus hospital known as Hospital Point. Hospital Point was staffed largely by military personnel. Their services for this evening included providing personal escorts from the table, to the bathroom, and back to the table with a warm cupful of urine.

"Is this social security number yours? Please sign and verify that the receptacle is clean of debris. Do not let the receptacle leave my eyesight at any time, including when you fill it," one of the four corpsman stated these phrases mechanically every two minutes or so. The utterance had been on a virtual repeat loop so many times in the past three hours that I had lost count. It reminded me of I-Day check-in. Occasionally the lone female corpsman responsible for escorting the female plebes in the company would break up the monotony with a slightly higher pitched voice narrating the same scripted dialogue.

The corpsmen were there to observe every gory detail of the process. This was inclusive of watching genitalia filling the containers. Strict mandates included that the bottles never leave the sight of the observing authority. This was to prevent tampering with the test.

"I wonder how that works for the female mids?" I whispered to Gonzo.

Gonzo let out a frustrated sigh and then a low voiced decree, "Fuuuuuuuuuck, this sucks. I need a computer to do my homework. This ain't the eighteen hundreds, man."

Being sequestered in the hallway meant our desktop computers would remain unused.

"Gonzo, I've never seen you do a lick of homework on a Sunday night. The porn you want to look at will still be there whenever the hell they let us out of here," I said in reply. Gonzo responded with a middle finger.

Gonzo had been temporarily occupied in completing his chemistry lab report when we first sat down. As usual, it had already been two weeks late. If he did not turn it in tomorrow, it would be his second flunked lab. It was a hit his already dreadful mid-semester GPA could not afford. As soon as he finished the report, he continued drawing pictures of naked people doing obscene things. It felt like junior high detention.

"Think of it this way," I whispered in return, "you could be that dude over there staring at his hundredth dick of the night."

Gonzo gave in and finally chuckled. "You would love that, wouldn't you, Wonderbread?"

"Man, fuck you," I replied.

"Hey, lock it up over there!" 1/C Derrick Clarkson yelled out breaking the mumbling chatter of the restless plebes. "Quit smoking and joking."

"In a night full of dicks, he is still the biggest," I whispered low enough to ensure it would not be heard outside of our gathered plebe group. A few chuckles followed and all Clarkson could do was shoot over a non-attributed scowl back towards us. "What a Joe fucking Mid," I closed with perfect showmanship to my forcefully captive audience.

The upperclassmen had only slightly better accommodations in the hallway. While they were permitted to talk, they were just as equally constrained as the plebes. Seeing the upperclassmen share in the pain of waiting was the one aspect of the whole experience that made it remotely enjoyable. Clarkson had been bitching all night about it, his snarls towards plebes was just his way of venting.

"My left ass cheek is asleep," I whispered my complaint to N.D. He smirked only long enough to acknowledge me before diving back into his English and literature reading assignment. He was likely the only mid inside Bancroft Hall still doing homework this long into our mandated "sit in."

N.D. woke up this morning to a bad hangover. Out of necessity, he nursed through it quickly. After careful consideration, N.D. had wisely assumed that he would not be able to contain the truth of the previous evening. We agreed with him when he asked us about it in the morning.

By early afternoon, N.D. finally decided to fess up to the previous evening's transgressions. He was smart. N.D. wisely chose to talk to the head football coach first. He knew that within academy brass, Coach would be the most likely to have his back. At the very least, Coach would likely be able to provide him with some level of preemptive damage control. It was in both of their best interests.

The confession ultimately garnered an immediate one game suspension from the team. His disciplinary trial, likely with the Commandant, was still pending but certainly on the near-term horizon. If the academy even decided to retain him, painful amounts of punishment lay ahead.

Underage drinking combined with the desecration of a colonel's uniform was nothing but a wild night as a normal college freshman. At the academy, it was tantamount to a capital offense. He had given us the blow by blow of the confession in the afternoon when he finally returned to our room. He had a look of total dejection. We hadn't spoken much since then.

N.D. was likely one of the few midshipman pleasantly surprised by the ordeal of the wiz quiz. It was the perfect bait and switch. There was no way USNA would be able to kick him out as their near term attention and ire would likely be much more focused on the pending drug scandal at hand. Comparatively speaking, drug shenanigans made a night of underage drunken debauchery look like child's play.

In typical N.D. fashion, he dutifully put his head down into his reading assignment and kept trucking along. It had been a bad weekend. His girl, the game, the comedy show, it was all a collective disaster. Homework still needed to be done, plebe duties still needed to be met. It was about all he could control at the moment—being the best plebe possible.

At 10:30 p.m. the men's bathroom door aggressively swung open. The last holdout of the night finally caved. Midshipman 3/C Turino walked back into the hallway and victoriously held a filled urine receptacle high in the air. His sample had a pale tint to it, compliments of fourteen canteens of imbibed water. Regardless of its testability, that last filled sample received a loud chorus of cheers and jeers. LT Walker's table was finally cleared of empty canisters. Everyone was either happy to head back to their rooms or pissed off at Turino's bladder of steel. I was just happy that I'd have a chance to get a catnap before calling Nellie and Bird in a few hours.

Mick, 2235 hrs.

"God damn the pusher man," Gonzo said as he finally entered our room in an ode to Steppenwolf. N.D. was already brushing his teeth in the sink by the time we had all roommates safely in our room.

The wiz quiz had finally ended. We had thirty minutes to take care of our final evening tasks and hit the sack. We were already a half an hour past normally mandated plebe lights out at 2200 hours. Thankfully our company at least gave us an hour extension so we could wrap up what needed to be done for the night.

Most plebes felt slighted by the evening interruption as it cut into normally important study time. For our room though, Sunday night was rarely used for productive activity. Since we were forced to sit in the hallway and at least consider homework for a few hours, our room was feeling proactively ahead of the week. Even though he griped about it all night, Gonzo had benefited from the mandated study focus the most. His chemistry lab was done, and I actually saw him read a lit novel for twenty minutes. It was the first time I had ever seen that happen. Normal circumstances would have had him consumed all night on the computer surfing porn or playing his ten thousandth game of "Minesweeper."

I was just happy to finally be back in the room. Night-time room occupancy was one of the very few plebe safe havens. Although the upperclassmen were relatively tame to us all night, the pressure of having them cohabitating the hallway with us was enough of a buzz kill. My first order of business of the night was setting my alarm. I had to prep for my evening phone call to Bird. Setting an alarm for 2 a.m. just didn't seem natural. I felt thankful for the opportunity to do it. For most of the night I had worried I'd be stuck waiting for filled urine receptacles till morning.

The passing evening had me thinking more calmly than earlier, but my mind was still racing in internal debate.

Pure coincidence. Just because there was a drug bust this weekend does not mean Bird was necessarily involved.

I took a deep breath and released a full exhale.

This is Bird we're talking about—FUCK!

Hopefully my evening phone call would bring my mind some peace.

"N.D., I forgot to ask you earlier, did you tell your mom and dad what went down last night?" I asked. We hadn't had much of the opportunity to discuss his problems given the unexpected events of the evening. The hallway didn't feel private enough to chat about it.

He spit his used toothpaste into the sink and took another quick sip of water. "Nah man, I'll save that one for tomorrow. I was gonna call tonight but those plans got spoiled by otha shit."

N.D. didn't get back into our room until just before dinner. By the time he was afforded the opportunity to convey the most basic details of his day. From the sounds of things, he was in hot water. The fallout would likely be harsh once the pending disciplinary proceedings played out in the days to come, but the coaches assured him he would avoid expulsion. It was about his only silver lining of the weekend.

Gonzo seemed unusually mum as compared to his normal self. I figured he'd have a lot more to talk about considering the past weekend we just had. Maybe he was just exhausted.

Our door suddenly opened without a knock. All conversation immediately ceased. While it would only be another day or two until the entire brigade would know of N.D.'s comedy show extravaganza, we still wanted to keep things quiet while we could.

Smitty's head peeked through the door with his characteristically arrogant scowl. There was something different in his look. It had a rare sense of seriousness.

"Gonzalez, we need to talk, shipmate," he said with a slightly perturbed tone.

A room entrance by an upperclassman this late in the night was highly uncommon. Most upperclassmen were especially respectful of study hour and lights out. Entering a plebe's room without a knock was an even greater rarity, typically reserved for bed checks for the firstie standing watch that evening. I knew that Smitty already had watch three days ago. He had complained about it endlessly at Thursday morning's breakfast. This was a less than official visit.

Gonzo calmly stood up from his computer desk and headed towards the door. I thought the inappropriateness of Smitty's impromptu entrance would have had Gonzo primed up for a few witty retorts. Instead Gonzo's gate was dutiful and uncharacteristically timid. Once they were both past the threshold, the muted conversation began. The evening was strange enough already. I felt as if I was living on another planet.

"Gonzalez, do we have an understanding per our discussion earlier?" Smitty queried Gonzo in a hushed tone. Although the conversation was intended as private, I was able to catch a few words here and there. I looked towards the sink and I could tell N.D. was eavesdropping just as intently. We both had no idea what was going on.

"Yes, sir," Gonzo replied quietly.

"If not, I'll have my fucking eye on you. Got it?"

"Yeah, I got it."

N.D. and I stared at each other silently in disbelief, each of us wondering what Gonzo was up to now.

"What the fuck?" I silently lip synched without noise towards N.D. hidden from Smitty's vantage point. From the look on N.D.'s face I could tell that he was feeling the same.

The conversation ended abruptly without the fireworks I was expecting. I was relieved and perplexed all at once. Gonzo walked back in the room and sat down at his computer desk as though nothing had happened. N.D. and I wore the same stunned look. It was quite an accomplishment considering the past twenty-four hours.

N.D. left his post at the sink and walked to the door

to peek outside. He wanted to ensure there were no unintended listeners in the hallway. After the night we were all having, smart money left nothing to chance.

"Yo man, what the FUCK was that about?" N.D. stood over Gonzo's desk chair once he saw the hall was clear.

"Don't worry about it," Gonzo replied staring straight ahead at his computer screen. "Not about your shit show last night."

"You sure about that?" N.D. shot back.

"Yeah," Gonzo said convincingly looking N.D. in the eye after finally removing his eyes from the computer screen. "I'm sure, man."

"So we're cool?"

"Yeah, we're cool."

I was decidedly becoming less cool by the moment. If Smitty's conversation had nothing to do with last night, then what was it about? It was bad enough N.D. found himself in the situation he had. I could only imagine what might be going down with Bird. The last thing I needed was added drama from Gonzo. I felt as though Bancroft Hall was imploding.

Within twenty minutes, we were all laying on our racks like nothing had transpired. I grabbed my alarm clock one more time to ensure the alarm was set for 2 a.m. I already knew there would be no sleeping until I left for the phone room. I was literally waiting for the rest of the brigade to fall asleep so I could finally deal with my issues. There were enough of them going around that night.

Chapter 15

Stranger on the Phone
Wednesday, October 18th, 1995
Bird, 9:15 p.m.

"HELLO? Who is this?" Mom answered the phone antagonistically. She made a habit of it.

A few awkward moments of silence were accompanied by her condescending scowl of contempt.

"No, I am not interested in a credit card. Are you interested in some toothpaste?" Instead of simply hanging up the phone, the alley cat played with the soon to be slaughtered mouse.

"NOoooooo? You say you already have toothpaste? WELL, I already got credit cards. Seven of them. Take your no interest payment bullshit somewhere else, hon. Goodbye!"

That was the second time this week I heard her use the toothpaste bit on the phone. I didn't know if her material was getting more repetitive or if we were just getting more telemarketer calls these days. She stole the bit from me. It was my own smart assed way to tell those dicks selling the scope photos on the beach to fuck off. Most of them were too stupid to even catch onto it.

The phone rang again. Nellie was still floating around it since her previous telemarketer spar.

"HELLO? Who is this?" There was mom's loving charm, right on cue.

"What? Bird? Yeah, he's here." She passed the wireless phone my way with a look of disappointment. She was already amped up to hop on the next telemarketer.

I grabbed the phone and ran upstairs to my bedroom and slammed the door behind me. Even in my late twenties, Mom loved to eavesdrop on my calls.

"Bird," I acknowledged my entrance into the conversation. I tried to play cool. The phone slipped in my hand. My palm sweat made my grip a little slippery.

"So I take it you made up your mind?" I had no time to bull shit. Time for that had passed.

I waited.

Fuck!

I let out a deep breath and suddenly felt lighter. "That's good to hear, Bunkie."

I was plotting a three-man job. The previous bust realigned our distribution plans and a drive to Indiana suddenly became a drive to Nevada. To make matters worse, my normal driving partner, Farm, had a fucking suspended license. I needed a second driver to split the drive. I was down to my last option.

"So you're cool with the deal?" I asked only because I had to. I still couldn't believe this fuck head was getting forty grand. He wasn't even fucking driving.

That's the riskiest fucking job.

Chapter 16

Jacked
Wednesday, November 8th, 1995
Mick, 1334 hrs.

"Attention on deck," casually interjected midshipman 4/C Chris Bowers.

The entire second floor classroom of plebes in Chauvenet Hall stood with limited enthusiasm. They were tiredly going through the motions of military formalities. It was an atypical reaction to an order. Under normal circumstances, the attention on deck order would have snapped everyone into rigid attention. We were in a safe haven of perhaps the least military and most boring classroom on the yard. Our Wednesday calculus class had officially begun.

"Hello class, sorry I'm late," Professor Samuel Kapenen said as he haphazardly scrambled through the classroom door. "Please, have a seat, so we can get started."

The classroom looked like any other sterile civilian college classroom. There were the standard four rows of tables for roughly thirty students, accompanying office chairs, a less-than-clean chalkboard, and an unenthusiastic class. Save the fully occupied room and its uniformed occupants, all mandated by military order, there was little else visually differentiating the environment. The students obediently listened and everyone standing at their spot in one of four rows of tables adjusted themselves in a seated position. There was a feeling of collective disappointment amongst the group. We were all but one minute away from the magic "five-minute rule" class cancellation. We would have killed for a few serendipitously awarded minutes of free time. There certainly was a scarcity of it.

"Damn, so close," I whispered over to N.D. We were both sitting next to each other at the far right end of the back table.

"Z burger naptime," N.D. whispered back in reply.

The aptly named Z burgers were academy lingo for cheeseburgers. They were a Wednesday lunchtime tradition and a favorite amongst the brigade. They also ensured that the afternoon's classes would be a slog as the several thousand calorie meal of hefty cheeseburgers and fries made staying awake in class extra difficult. Today would be no exception. The first class after lunch was almost always the hardest.

This afternoon's calc class made consciousness particularly tough. Our company's upperclassmen had instituted "back to basics week" since Sunday evening. This meant "all calls" on the chow call front and a full week of mandated early wake ups. It was all done to ensure no plebe ever got too comfortable in their plebedom. It sucked, but at least I was used to this type of shit. I had been dragging ass all week.

Professor Kapenen had an uncanny ability to tease the

threshold of the five-minute rule to us on a regular basis. Timeliness was never his thing. The professor's hair was a white disheveled mess of a bird's nest as usual. His over-sized brown corduroy sport coat completely clashed with the red plaid shirt worn beneath. The shirt was already halfway untucked. His mismatched white tennis shoes glided him dutifully towards his classroom podium. He had told us earlier in the semester that he needed to wear individually mismatched sneakers to treat his physical condition of uneven leg length. Dr. K was like a living and breathing mad scientist.

Despite his appearance and general proclivity toward physical disarray, Professor Kapenen was actually a decent professor. He had also collected enough awards and grants to seem quite impressive to the math nerd community. I'm sure that is why the mathematics department turned a blind eye towards his undisciplined style. I also felt his counter style to the academy's spit polish brand was refreshing. He was a nice break from the majority of my professors that were still uniformed officers.

We were four minutes late into our lesson, Professor Kapenen wasted no time jumping directly into it. He placed on his desk a briefcase spilling over with disorganized clusters of class documents. He immediately spun towards the black chalkboard. Within seconds white dust was filling the air as the white chalk furiously scratched the black board. Professor Kapenen began his hour-long dive into mean value theorem. He could have spent the entire afternoon talking about it if given the opportunity.

The Naval Academy was one of the few universities where skipping class was strictly prohibited. As midshipmen were considered military personnel, going to class was considered a job. Missing class meant dereliction of military duty. Dereliction of duty was considered worthy of restriction. For those of us that would have otherwise skipped this afternoon's class in civilian college, sleeping was a fair compromise.

I looked over to the seat next to me. N.D. was already fast asleep, as were several of our classmates. All plebes battled narcolepsy in class. It was an unfortunate side effect of the physically and mentally exhausting demands of plebe life. The tolls paid leading up to November were heavy. Most plebes were running on fumes heading into the last few weeks before our first Thanksgiving break. It seemed like we were still a long way from that finish line.

Most of the professors were annoyed by the narcoleptic plebe phenomenon but let it pass on most occasions. A smaller minority of them were incensed to no end by a snoozing student. Kapenen was one of the few professors that didn't really care one bit if mids slept through his class. His theory was that ultimately the midshipman was responsible for learning in any manner that they could. As long as a mid was passing their class they could be Rip Van Winkle.

Calculus was the one class that N.D. and I shared on our academic schedule. He spent most of his days sleeping through it. N.D. looked comically big passed out on the swivel seat attached to the table. His massive arms were folded, strong chin buried in his barrel chest and long legs spilled out in front of him. With all of his heft, one wrong movement and he would tumble to the floor below. The balance was impeccable. It was the pose he immediately struck when he took his seat to initiate class. From his assigned back row, he would remain a snoring statue until the end of class bell rung. Even when asleep he was a great athlete.

I didn't blame N.D. for sleeping. He had aced the Advanced Placement exam for the first two semesters of calculus back when he was still in high school. He could have woken up and pulled an A+ on the final exam on the spot if needed. It was laughable that I ever considered myself the Brainiac of the room. N.D. ran circles around Gonzo and me academically.

Football was back on track for N.D. He had paid his atonement back to the team in the form of a one game suspension. He was back on the field a week earlier against Notre Dame. Despite the team's loss, N.D. played like his old self and certainly held his own against an extremely talented Fighting Irish offensive line. His bad game on the field and off it during Air Force weekend had long since been forgotten by the team and coaching staff.

Unfortunately for N.D., the academy brass had not been quite as merciful as the football team in terms of forgiving his Air Force weekend's transgressions. Although the drug scandal certainly deflected some of the negative attention he would have otherwise received in isolation, USNA still came down hard on N.D. He had been given the class of '99's dubious honor of earning the class's first Black N, and all of the punishment that came with it. That shit platter special included restriction, marching tours, and a cancellation of both Thanksgiving and Christmas leave.

N.D. had been on restriction for the past two weeks

and was not yet half way through his penance. He had a brutal forty-three of his assigned sixty days remaining. His past weeks had been filled with daily morning inspections, surprise musters, weekend marching tours, and impromptu working parties usually in the form of outdoor garbage clean up. He could only leave his room for meals, class, and football. It was all par for course on restriction. Luckily as a plebe, restriction wasn't much worse than regular plebe life. Aside from lack of weekend liberty and a few extra musters there was very little else cramping his plebe lifestyle. N.D. was taking it all in stride.

N.D. had managed to knock out most of his assigned ten hours of marching tours during the weekend of his one game football suspension. I had been hanging in our room while he had been marching with rifle in hand on the red brick terrace four stories below our window for four straight hours. He looked comical marching there by himself in his exceedingly tight formal dress blues with the rifle hanging loosely from his broad shoulder. He had already gained ten pounds since the end of Plebe Summer and his uniforms were increasingly making him look like a stuffed sausage. His rifle was a toothpick against his massive frame.

Thanksgiving holiday was meaningless for N.D. He would still be on restriction when we hit that major milestone. His turkey dinner would have to be in King Hall. In some ways, N.D. not going home for Thanksgiving was a relief. He was still not over his break-up. I think subconsciously the last thing he wanted was to be around his old life with his emotional wounds still fresh. Although, I'm not sure he consciously saw the situation that way. I imagined that he didn't. I never had the balls to ask him. He was a friend for sure, but there were some boundaries I was not yet ready to cross with him. My room's destruction over Air Force weekend was proof enough to me that this topic might be one to avoid for a little while.

"So as the theorem goes," Kapenen droned on speaking directly to the chalkboard with his back faced to the class. "Here is the one point at which the tangent through its endpoints to the arc is parallel to the secant."

My mind quickly drifted to daydreams of Thanksgiving and the hopes that decent waves would still be around when I finally had a chance to return home in a few weeks. Eventually I grew tired of those daydreams. I decided to give into temptation. I crossed my arms and tucked my head similarly to N.D.'s standard posture. I had learned from the best. Within seconds, I was fast asleep.

Mick, 1430 hrs.

The end of class bell nearly knocked me out of my seat. Another calculus class had come and gone and I was none the wiser.

"Dismissed," Kapenen chimed in as the bell ringing ceased. "See you guys tomorrow."

Everyone save N.D. and I had already made their way out of their seats upon the class bell. As usual everyone in the room had somewhere else to be and was in a hurry to get there. Punishment for tardiness in any variety was enough to keep all plebes perpetually rushed to where they needed to be next. Our daily lives were designed to create this perpetual stress.

I wiped off the drool stain from the side of my face and noticed its stained landing spot on my right shirt collar. The T-shirt beneath my crew neck T-shirt was drenched in sweat. I had outlasted N.D.'s consciousness by about ten minutes in class.

"Don't forget Friday's quiz, ladies and gents!" Professor Kapenen's voice volume rose as to compete with the building commotion of classroom exodus. "It's on mean value theorem! We just spent an hour talking about it!"

I looked over at N.D. who had similarly been spending the last five seconds waking up his brain. "Shiiiiiit," I mumbled over to my partner in crime.

"I got you covered, man," N.D. said with smirk. He was nearly as good a teacher as Kapenen was. At least I knew he'd show up on time.

Calculus had been an hour of my life I wished I had back. I completely forgot that we had a quiz slated for Friday. I had to budget some study time between now and Friday to have N.D. teach me the lesson I just slept through. I blamed my learning discrepancy for the past hour more on lunch's Z burgers than Professor Kapenen's droning, though both played a part.

I regained my senses and quickly remembered I had scheduled a haircut back in Bancroft. Smitty and Severson had been on my ass for the past week to get a haircut. I had to hustle. My appointment was just over five minutes away and the barbershop would take at least that long to briskly walk to. If I were three seconds late for my scheduled appointment, it would be given away to one of the many waiting walk-ins. There were always at least three mids in the barbershop at any time cherry picking appointments.

"Alright man, I'll see you up in the room after practice," I said to N.D. as we walked down the stairwell towards the Chauvenet Hall exit. N.D. had a chemistry lab and then was off to football practice. This would likely be our last rendezvous before the evening.

"Later, dawg," N.D. replied in his typically calm and cool fashion. "Hit me up on that mean value theorem shit tonight. You'll be ah'ight," he said as he made his way down the Chauvenet stairwell towards his adjacent Michelson Hall basement chemistry lab. The basements of both buildings were all connected and could be commuted between without stepping outside. He had a short commute to his next class.

Hearing N.D.'s reassurance made me a feel a little better about sleeping through class. If there was one advantage of N.D. on restriction, it was that I had much more access to his tutoring skills. I think N.D. actually enjoyed the task. The last two weeks spent in room restriction had him bored out of his skull.

"Mick," N.D. hollered up the basement steps as I approached the door threshold. "Don't forget your cover, man."

"Shit!" I blurted loudly as I turned around just before I left the building without my hat. That was a cardinal sin in terms of plebedom, especially in the midst of midafternoon class and the hundreds of upperclassmen that would be more than happy to let me know about it. N.D. just saved me from an almost certain public thrashing by random upperclassmen. Before the upperclassmen flooding the stairwell could even attribute my expletive, I was sprinting back up to the second floor to grab my cover hanging outside of the classroom. It took me two minutes just to figure out which one was mine. The hat rack outside my previous classroom had no less than twenty covers hanging on them. Each one looked exactly like my own.

I finally made my way out of the building and onto the Severn River facing cement terrace between Chauvenet and Michelson Hall. I looked out to take in the view. My rush had subsided. I knew my hair appointment would not be met. I'd have to roll the dice as a walk-in.

Off in the distance I could hear someone singing Pearl Jam songs loudly in T-court. It was a welcome distraction.

Guess another plebe lost a football bet.

The unseasonably warm November day was bright and sunny, leaving a glistening reflection across the river. If I hadn't been mired in the suck of being a plebe, I might have appreciated the beauty of the view a little more. Looking at the Severn River Bridge, the first path leading homeward towards the eastern shore reminded me of my family. Then my mind wondered to Bird.

Bird if anything was resolute in his promise that we should avoid each other. My several attempts to contact Bird after the wiz quiz were all fruitless. I would end up chatting with Nellie who always had some ridiculous excuse as to where Bird was or why he couldn't talk on the phone. I knew it was all bullshit. A few times I could even hear Bird and Farm playing Tecmo Super Bowl on the Nintendo in the background. Bird was a creature of habit, I knew exactly where he would be at any given time, typically aligning his presence with the status of the latest internet surf report. I gave up trying after two weeks.

Word back on the yard was mum from all angles in terms of October's drug scandal. Whatever exactly had happened had been cleanly swept under the rug for the time being. All of the local media outlets had blasted the story about the brigade-wide wiz quiz for the entire month of October. It was yet again bad press for the Naval Academy, but I'm sure it had helped sell a few extra newspapers in the process. After a few weeks without having more than the story of massive urine collection, the newspapers moved on to other titillating topics. Even the brigade had seemed to place the situation out of sight and out of mind.

I had not completely forgotten about the scandal. My worries of Bird's involvement, especially after the intentional avoidance of all of my calls, had not gone away. Although lessened, speculative fears still festered deep inside.

I continued to keep my ear to the ground on the situation. Gonzo was my finger on the pulse in brigade gossip. Even if he wanted to, he couldn't keep a secret from me. N.D. unknowingly kept me in the loop on what was being said amongst his fellow restrictees. His new life on restriction and its mandated restriction musters kept him in constant contact with the academy's most notorious "criminals."

Click, clunk

A four-foot by four-foot cement block audibly responded to my step. The entirety of Radford terrace between Chauvenent and Michelson was comprised of hundreds of these blocks. About every random fifth block was either broken or misplaced beneath and would tilt then clank when one of these imperfect squares was stepped on. It was an audible landmine.

Click, clunk

In the middle of the terrace was a beautiful yet broken water fountain. It had been shut down for several weeks. Cold weather, however, was not the guilty party. The culprit instead was the residual effects of last year's firstie class hopping into and subsequently damaging it after their last mandated march during commissioning week. N.D. had heard the story immediately following one of his late restriction musters.

Juxtaposed against the natural beauty of the Severn River, the fountain was the perfect metaphor for the academy in general. Spit polish and surrounding scenery could never completely hide the brokenness below the superficial level. Eventually I'd hear what went down with the drug sting.

Click Clunk

Mick, 1507 hrs.

I was drowning in the collective buzz of twenty hair clippers feverishly doing their duty. The Naval Academy barbershop was operating at peak capacity in its typical midday, midweek frenzy. I sat in the lobby brooding over my lost appointment. Despite being just six minutes late, my appointment had since been given away to a walk-in.

The Naval Academy barbershop was a testament to

hard work and efficiency. Nearly every single chair in the small and crowded room beside the waiting area operated at full capacity from opening to close. Each of the roughly fifteen barbers cranked out ten or more haircuts a day. A few of them also had jobs across town and would cut hair off the yard after hours as well.

I could see Mr. Jones, or "Jonesy" dutifully initiating his tenth haircut of the day. He was not only the top barber in the establishment, but also its manager. There were a variety of characters working at the shop. Each barber had their own reputation, personality, and proclivity towards creative liberties with any individual's haircut.

There was really only so far you could take the three styles of buzz cut, flat top, and a "tune up." This was not the place to test out the trendiest hairstyles. If you needed an officer or an upper-class to get off your ass for your sideburns being too thick or your neck needing a shave, this was your place.

The barbershop appointments had as of this year transitioned from manual sign-in sheet to computerized scheduling. It was the only way I had known, but for other mids it was still an adjustment from the pen and sheet appointment scheduling system. Regardless of the switch, the chairs were without exception completely booked.

Jonesy and the desk receptionist had not done anything wrong with my cancelled appointment. Tardiness by anything more than a minute meant a lost chair. They had not done anything they wouldn't have done to anyone else. The barbershop was one of the few places on the yard that treated all mids, plebes included, completely fair.

There was no limit on how many haircuts any one

mid could receive. Most mids took a haircut every other week. Some mids had a standing haircut appointment every week. This privilege was reserved for those mids that knew precisely when the next week's schedule would appear online. I never quite cared that much about haircuts. Even though I had been a mid for several months, twice a month haircuts still seemed insane to me.

It had been three weeks since my last haircut. When I finally did get around to making an appointment a week ago, my procrastination had precluded me from getting a reputable barber on schedule in the time I had available. Rather than rolling the dice on a bad haircut with one of the notorious barbers, I decided to take my chances in the next week.

Since Monday I had not heard the end of it from my upper-class. Had I not been a plebe, I likely could have gone a third week without a haircut. I was not that lucky. Thankfully I was able to lock down a decent appointment at the witching hour, with Jonesy no less. That was of course until my tardiness had blown my opportunity and relinquished me to walk-in purgatory.

Gonzo had his own set of clippers back in the room. He religiously gave himself his own buzz cut on the Sunday leading into the week. While administering his own haircut, he would go on and on about how crappy and unsanitary the clippers they used down in the barbershop were. He would always try to convince me to let him cut my hair. I avoided that offer like a plague. I also knew of his not so secret monthly tradition of shaving his pubic hair with the same clippers he was proposing to use on my head.

"Makes it look an inch bigger," he used to say during his monthly trim downstairs.

I was resolved to stay in the small waiting room lobby and test my chances as a walk-in. Calculus was my last class of the day. I had the rest of the afternoon off.

"McGee!" the elderly receptionist behind the counter blurted.

"That's me," I calmly replied. I figured she could have just approached me directly since I had just spoken to her five minutes earlier. Just like everything else at the Naval Academy, personal touches were rarely a strong point.

The receptionist then confirmed the worst nightmare of any walk-in. With her slim wrinkled finger, the she pointed over to the Filipino gentleman with a chair midway down the left hand row of barbers. I had drawn Jack.

Jack was a tremendously nice man. He had been previously enlisted in the Marines and spent the past two decades as a barber at the Naval Academy. He always seemed happy to get whatever customer he could get, most of them plebes. Upperclassmen avoided him altogether, save a handful of overzealous wannabe Marines.

It's not as though Jack was a bad barber. Quite the contrary, he was actually very thorough and careful with every cut. Jack's biggest critique was that he gave but one haircut—the notorious high and tight. This haircut was a favorite amongst Marines and dreaded for everyone else. It was a short flat top with skin tight and high sides.

"Hey man, how you doin'? What you want today?" Jack asked in his usual amicable tone and thick accent.

"Just a little off the sides," I hopelessly explained. "You know, just a trim."

"Okay, high and tight," he replied joyfully reaching for his clippers. My three weeks sans haircut had him eagerly racing for his tools of the trade.

I was about to contest, but it would have been pointless. It was the very reason a haircut from Jack was often used as payment on lost plebe football bets. Within seconds, the locks I had managed to grow back in the past month were sitting on the floor.

Mick, 1517 hrs.

I had spent fifteen minutes waiting on standby for a haircut. The actual deed only took about ten minutes. Though I wholeheartedly attempted to avoid it, I caught a glimpse of my new hairdo in the mirror. The only hair I had left on my head was a small short patch at the top. It looked as though I had been given a Mohawk and then decided to shave off the back half. It was trademark Jack.

"WHOOOOAAAA!" I heard a loud and familiar female voice behind me as I exited the barbershop. "What the hell happened to your hair, dude?"

I didn't even need to turn around to realize who it was. I wanted to crawl in a hole. The last person that I wanted to see my hair like this was Summer.

"Hey, Summer," I replied, quickly thinking of some conversation topic to divert attention from my hideous head of hair. "You guys ready for Army this week?" I asked. The women's big soccer game against Army was just days away. I figured it might be the only topic salient enough to divert attention from my ridiculous hair.

"Sure are, devil dawg," Summer wittingly quipped, correlating my haircut to the epitome of Marine Corp hair grooming standards.

I tried to laugh it off but deep down realized the attempted appearance of humor looked contrived. Summer could sense the same.

"So my mom and Lizbeth get into town tonight," she diverted to a different topic as quickly as possible.

"Cool," I said graciously jumping at the opportunity to change the subject. Summer looked a little disheartened by my abbreviated response. A month earlier, I was pandering to meet her family's matriarchs, now I seemingly couldn't care less.

Though Summer and I remained friendly, the past month had been a strain on our formerly burgeoning relationship, potentially imaginary as it might have been. Shortly after the N.D. fiasco, I heard through the rumor mill that Summer was unofficially spoken for. Summer and company mate 3/C Matt Hackett had delved into the "Dark Side." My prospects of doing the same were quite limited.

"Dark siding" meant midshipman dating each other within the walls of Bancroft. Dark siding was a slippery slope in the academy's eyes. When trapping four thousand college kids to a single geographic location, there had to be some allowable relationships with the opposite sex. Full prohibition of such habits would be grounds for anarchy. This meant that reluctantly but necessarily allowing such behavior had to be done with serious thoughtfulness.

While midshipmen were not entirely prohibited to

date one another, there were strict bounds. Plebes could date plebes. Upper class midshipmen were permitted to date other midshipmen as long as they were not plebes. No one could date within the same company, and especially not the same squad. By those guide posts 3/C Matt Hackett dating 4/C Summer Harris within the same company and squad was about as out of bounds as you could get in terms of dark siding. As their relationship was strictly prohibited by academy standards, it was largely left incognito. Summer had not even officially disclosed its existence to me, although she knew that I knew.

I had heard about the clandestine relationship from N.D. only because Hackett's many remaining friends on the football team had mentioned it in the locker room. Not being one to immediately accept a rumor, particularly of a friend, it didn't take long to surmise the reality of the situation. My declining room visits to Summer often found Hackett spending private time there in the evenings. I had spotted them a few times in town together and their not so coy flirting in all squad related functions had all but confirmed an unfortunate hypothesis.

What made the situation particularly awkward was that I actually had no ill will towards Hackett. I had always viewed him as a really great guy, though a bit of a meathead. He had been nothing but friendly to me since even before his relationship with Summer. His lackadaisical attitude towards plebe training within our company and squad meant that he rarely if ever sent scorn my way. He was one of the very few upperclassmen I could say that about. Since he treated every plebe in my squad in the same manner, there was no possible way his relationship with Summer could be correlated as preferential treatment in the professional setting of our squad. This was the primary reason the academy dating rules were established in the first place.

It wasn't like Summer and I were even close to dating to begin with. I had no grounds to feel like a jilted lover, but I couldn't help but feel that way. My unrequited crush on Summer combined with my utter lack of sexual activity in the past several months of life had my penis overruling my brain. I couldn't stand the idea of their dating. Though rationally I admired Hackett as a person, my raging hormones made me hate his guts. It had also cooled my desire to maintain anything beyond a superficial relationship with Summer. It was petty, but I couldn't escape the fact that deep down I was just a sexually frustrated male with a bad case of blue balls.

Sexual frustration was one of the primary reasons the modern era academy could be such a harsh and lonely place. The ratio of males to females had continuously improved in recent history, but at the time remained at best five to one. The historically male dominated sausage party that was Bancroft Hall still smelled like breakfast swine.

The academy had over a century of male-only enrollment. The first class of female graduates wasn't until 1980. Fifteen years later, progress had been made, but the introduction of the first generation of male and female co-existence was certainly still evolving. It was an impossible situation to avoid. Even if every female midshipman did date a fellow male mid, it meant four others had to take their chances outside of the academy walls. With just a few days a month to access downtown's pool of available women, the statistics of the situation generally led to further frustration. It was an exercise in sexual futility. To most male mids, the handful of attractive female midshipman that did share Bancroft Hall was like waving a steak in front of a pack of hungry dogs.

This situation was no picnic for the female midshipman either. While having the odds disproportionately in their favor seemed like dream come true from the other end of the table, it also opened up a world of distraction. Any remotely attractive female midshipman could almost bank on being pursued, harassed, and generally annoyed by every mid on the short end of the dating stick. While I had seen Hackett in her room more steadily over the past month, Summer had a constant flux of unwelcome male mids of all ranks visiting her room since the day she took her first Oath of Office. I was just one of the few male mids smart enough to realize that my relationship pursuits at least in the near-term were severely limited.

"Hey, you wanna grab some coffee?" asked Summer.

"Sure," I replied. It was the very last thing I wanted to do sporting my new high and tight, but old crushes die hard. I made my way across the hall and headed to the Naval Academy bookstore.

The Naval Academy bookstore was attached to the Naval Academy Midshipman store. The "Mid Store" was the center of all things commerce in a midshipman's life. It had the staples of sundries and snacks. It also offered retail electronics, jewelry, and the plebe forbidden fruit of civilian clothes in a single mega-store. It was all housed under one roof and directly connected and within the interior of Bancroft Hall. It was one of the few places a midshipman could blow their money while still trapped within the mandatory boundaries of the yard. Although the tax-free products were all very well priced, the complimentary coffee in the bookstore was about the only thing free in the whole place.

"Aw shit, looks like somebody got jack'd!" I heard familiar chuckling from around the corner as we entered the bookstore. My nightmare was confirmed as Gonzo aggressively rubbed my head in an endearing yet slightly taunting embrace. I immediately made plans to shave the rest of my head as soon as I was able to escape back to my room, even if it meant using Gonzo's pube-laden hair clippers.

"Check out my new kicks, yo," Gonzo immediately changed the subject as though he had read my subconscious intentions. "The new color Air Maxes are IN," he said proudly displaying one of the shoes out of the newly purchased box as if it were a trophy.

"Compliments of Louie, I take it?" I queried.

"Fo sho," Gonzo said calmly with a smile proudly tossing the shopping bag over his shoulder, nearly hitting me in the head in the process.

Gonzo had bought his third pair of expensive shoes of the semester. Any one pair would have cost almost two month's pay considering we made fifty bucks a month. To avoid this cost prohibitive situation, he did what many mids did and illegally used his midshipman charge card to procure his consumer desires. While the midshipman charge card was intended to cover uniform items and school books, one of the cashiers in the mid store affectionately known as Louie would charge anything one's heart could desire. I had given up lecturing Gonzo on the wrongs and potential implications of these practices.

"Did you ever look for the mouse traps I asked about earlier?" I asked while still on the topic of mid store purchases. As the cold weather came, so did thousands of rodent refuges from the outdoor spaces surrounding Bancroft. We had been hearing nightly stampedes of mice skitter across our rotted ceiling tile for the past two weeks.

"Shit, sorry, Mick, I honestly forgot," Gonzo replied with a feigned snap of the fingers as though his professed amnesia actually frustrated him.

"Remember, man, you owe me. I bought the last three bottles of scrubbing bubbles," I reminded him. Not wanting to sound like a miser in front of Summer, I quickly changed the topic. "Speaking of mice, did N.D. tell you the story about the dude on his football team that ate a dead mouse on a bet last week?"

Summer opened her mouth and furrowed her brow in a look of interest and disgust.

"Yeah, he told me before calc class, said the dude's been at hospital point for the past two days and just got back."

"What is going on with the men of our class?" Summer replied and then quickly shot her eyes at Gonzo. "Speaking of which, dude, what was going on with you and Bill the Goat?" She was more excited about that question than she was interested in his newly acquired sneakers or my haircut.

"Oh, that? That was nothing," Gonzo quickly dismissed the question as his eyes glanced downward. "Gunny has Smitty and his fat ass doing mandated morning PT with Castiglio since he failed the sit-up portion of the PRT. They brought me along and were just fucking around. It was stupid." He glanced onward refusing to acknowledge it any further. I was his roommate and could not solicit much more of a response to the situation than that. I knew the look. I had been given it a few times before.

Monday morning's squad breakfast had started with Smitty brandishing a Polaroid of Gonzo. He was naked and riding the giant statue of Bill the Goat. The picture was taken outside of the swimming and physical education facility, Lejune Hall, during what must have been in the wee hours of zero dark thirty the night before. Smitty had been steadily referencing it and showing it around as a way to taunt Gonzo at tables all week. I was stunned that Gonzo hadn't already punched him over it, especially considering their past history. Gonzo shrugged it off and acted like nothing happened.

"Alright, I gotta bounce, puntas," Gonzo announced as though consciously ejecting himself from the mid store and discussing the issue further. "I'm late for class." As soon as he got behind Summer and out of her peripheral eyesight he put his fist in front of his mouth and started stroking it up and down. With his tongue, he poked inside his cheek to compliment the angle of his stroking as to mimic a blowjob.

While the sexual inappropriateness was trademark Gonzo, that was the first time I had heard class ever rush him anywhere. Something just wasn't quite right with him, but figuring that out was a priority that would not outrank having to un-fuck my haircut.

"I'm gonna take care of this debacle," I said as I rubbed

my newly shorn head and gracefully exiting my squad-mate's informal coffee gathering.

"I don't know," Summer said with a smile. "You could actually make that look good."

I cursed Summer in my mind as yet again she made my heart skip a beat. The thought of Gonzo's pubes, either on Bill the Goat earlier in the week or in the clippers about to cut my hair, temporarily left my mind.

Chapter 17

Joking and Smoking
Friday, November 17th, 1995
Mick, 1245 hrs.

"What is long and hard," Summer queried with a dramatically sexy pause, "and has cum inside it?" Every heterosexual male within an earshot of our squad's lunch table collectively breathed a little faster waiting for an answer. It was perfect showmanship.

"A Cu-CUM-ber!" she replied as the anticipation reached a crescendo. Several dirty mental fantasies faded with the corny joke's disappointing end.

"That's bullshit, Harris!" Castiglio immediately commented. "You can't blue ball the whole table like that heading into the weekend!"

"NEXT!" Smitty belted out.

Friday meals were normally more outlandish in general. This one felt different. There was a raucous feeling in the air with Thanksgiving vacation on the horizon. Jailbreak was in sight for the inmates. There was a weird frenzy to it, like at any moment a song or a riot could break.

Most professional obligations for plebes tended to be

lax on Fridays. The only major Friday activity was telling table jokes. Every plebe was required by their upper-class to have at least one joke prepared for lunch on Friday. It was treated like any military obligation. Forgetting a joke would be treated no differently than forgetting to make your bed in the morning. As such, joke selection and presentation were two very important aspects of a plebe's life.

The flavor of those jokes was largely up to the discretion of the table's upperclassmen. For some squads in our company, there was a PG limit to table jokes. Levels of religious conviction and military professionalism typically drove the various echelons of joke discretion. As Smitty and Castiglio ran the roost at our table, it was 110% "no holds barred."

"Alright, quit bullshitting around, McGee," Castiglio obnoxiously prodded. "You're stallin'!"

"Okay, okay, sir, here it goes," I took a deep breath and let it rip. "What has two legs and is bloody?" I asked trying my best to myself create a dramatic pause.

"Well . . ." Smitty interjected, "we're waiting."

"A half a dog," I replied trying my best to interject any level of comedy into an admittedly mediocre joke.

"SUCKED!" Smitty belted to break the dead silence of a flopped joke.

"Damn, McGee," Severson replied across the table. "You should really have somebody check out what's going on inside of that nutty shaved head of yours." Severson rarely participated in table joke Fridays as Smitty and Castiglio so seldom gave anyone much of a chance to speak during the plebes' weekly performance. I wasn't sure if he was being serious or not. I didn't care.

The upperclassmen especially liked table joke Fridays. It was a no lose proposition for them. If a plebe's joke was good, they had a good laugh about it. If the joke was poor, it opened up a perfect opportunity to verbally abuse them. Regardless of the jokes, the plebes were infinitely entertaining.

While I loved telling jokes, I hated table joke Fridays. Smitty and Castiglio wanted table festivities to be as inappropriate as possible. As long as they were not directly forcing us to tell any inappropriate jokes, there was little culpability they had towards our jokes' level of suitability. It always put me in a precarious spot.

Most dirty jokes that I knew were either racially or sexually oriented. As a white male, there was no way I could tell them at the King Hall table setting without potentially saying something entirely inappropriate. At least not with what I felt comfortable being held accountable for.

Summer was a female. She could somewhat press the envelope of the sexually oriented jokes without much threat of retribution. She was the only girl in the squad and basically set the standard for what was appropriate for a female audience. As she was the one telling the joke, of course anything she said would be appropriate. It also didn't hurt that she was extremely attractive and perfectly played on her sex appeal and charm with every joke that she told. By this point in the semester, she was practically untouchable.

Gonzo had plenty of racially-oriented Hispanic jokes in his quiver, but stuck squarely to his sweet spot of smut. His arsenal of dirty sex jokes was endless. Even before getting access to the joys of unsuitable material on the internet, Gonzo had stacks of dirty joke books that he had previously memorized cover to cover. While some people memorized biblical text, Gonzo had memorized verbatim four hundred and seventy-six unique jokes about Asians. Lacking my discretion, he held nothing back. His performances on table joke Fridays were stuff of legend.

"Alright, Gonzalez," Smitty finally broke the silence in the aftermath of my ill humor. "Salvage this shit show."

"Yes, sir, Mr. Smith," Gonzo dutifully replied with a smirk.

He then inquisitively looked over towards Summer then the rest of the table. "What's the difference between a woob and a hockey player?"

The entire table busted out in hoots and hollers waiting in eager anticipation for Gonzo's punchline. Though his jokes almost always pushed the envelope, the audience was in for a special treat. He had chosen the most officially off-limit topic in the academy.

"Woob" was short for WUBA. Though the academy had many different acronyms, WUBA was by far the most taboo. WUBA stood for "Women Used By All" or in some small circles "Women with Unusually Big Asses". Many of the male midshipmen referred to all female mids as woobs. Some of the female mids even embraced the name. For just about every mid its utilization was almost always tongue in cheek. Humorous intent or not, it spoke volumes about how many light years away the academy was from gender equality. Despite its unfortunately accepted existence in the collective midshipman vernacular, I had yet to hear it officially used in a King Hall table joke. Only

Gonzo would have that type of brazen audacity.

"Come on, Gonzalez, you went there, now finish it," Castiglio prodded. "What's the difference?"

Gonzo's delay I imagined had little to do with hesitancy. He, like Summer, had mastered the dramatic pause. I sat in my chair and squirmed. Sitting sandwiched between Gonzo and Summer on the plebe side of the table, I began to worry where he was going to take this. I did not like being caught in the crossfire.

"So, what's the difference between a woob and a hockey player?" he reiterated for dramatic effect.

He then looked over to me with a two-second stare, then over to Hackett for an equally long stare, then finally to Summer with a smirk.

"A hockey player only handles one stick at a time," he finished his perfectly inappropriate joke. The table immediately erupted into laughter. By this time almost everyone at the table knew about Hackett and Summer, and working a joke that also included a little roommate ball busting was just icing on the cake.

My world went red. Without thinking, I jumped from my chair and immediately punched Gonzo on the side of the head. The momentum of the punch tumbled Gonzo and I onto the floor where we immediately began wrestling and punching. Several plates and a carton of juice went with us. Chaos erupted at our table as Hackett also jumped across to get into the action.

I could not exactly remember much beyond that. The fight only lasted about twelve seconds. At least that's what I was later told. The rest of the mids quickly jumped into action. Fortunately at the academy there is no shortage of males willing to jump into a good scrap, whether to join it or just to keep the peace.

Luckily for Gonzo, I punched him before Hackett had a chance to get a hold of him. By the time the fight was broken up and Hackett was appropriately restrained, Summer was nowhere to be seen.

"Gonzalez! McGee!" our company commander 1/C Matt Duggan quickly commanded. "Get your asses up to see Gunny in company area NOW!"

Mick, 1305 hrs.

Gunnery Sergeant Daniel Ortega enlisted in the Marine Corps while he was just seventeen and never looked back. It had been rumored that he was forced to enlist by a judge that gave him the ultimatum to enlist or go to juvie after a failed attempt to hotwire a car. Sixteen years later, he was begrudgingly stuck as a desk jock playing number two to LT Walker as our Company's Senior Enlisted Representative. It was a job with few benefits beyond a prime location to the company's soda machine.

He had done two stints at the Marine Corp's famed Parris Island, one as a new recruit, one as a drill instructor. He did countless deployments including several stints in the Middle East. He had been trained in just about every fighting discipline the Marines had to offer. He was a steely-eyed killer, he was a snake eater, but above all things he was an infantry Marine. Being stuck babysitting a bunch of underage ring knockers that would soon outrank him was about the last place he wanted to be.

Gonzo and I reported to his office after our scrap, as instructed. We exploded our way up the stairs without speaking or making eye contact. Upon arriving to Gunny's door, we hit the bulkhead and waited for Duggan to make his way up the stairs.

"What do you go-hards want?" Gunny yelled out from his office desk upon hearing our arrival.

"Had a bit of a scrap, Gunny," Gonzo sounded off. "Duggan's on his way up to tell you all about it."

"Ooh rah, devil dawg," Gunny replied. "God knows Duggan loves to TALK about fighting."

Gunny above all people appreciated the fact that every now and then a man needed a punch in the face. I was sure that he had his own list of people in our company requiring such a treatment.

I looked at Gonzo in my peripheral while keeping the appearance of looking straight ahead. I didn't want to acknowledge his existence. Gladly, I could already see that his eye was rapidly swelling shut. It was compliments of my swollen right fist. My knuckles throbbed in pain with each heartbeat. I had not even bothered trying to stop the bleeding from my swollen and split lip. I wiped the moisture on my chin. I didn't need to look at my palm to know that it was covered in blood.

"Not another word out of either of you!" Duggan chimed in as he finally arrived on our company floor following a slower jaunt up the steps than Gonzo and I had just completed. "You two stay there, Gunny will deal with you when I'm done catching him up on your recent shit show."

As the office door shut behind us, a private conversation ensued. The adrenaline of the fight had yet to wear off.

Behind closed doors, I could only imagine what was being said. I could not have cared less. My preoccupied mind was still seeing red. Most college freshmen were trying to find private time with a coed. I was plotting where I could privately resume kicking Gonzo's ass without interruption.

The door suddenly swung open and Duggan stormed out without stopping or saying a word.

"Gonzalez! McGee!" Gunny called through the opened door. "Get your asses in here."

Gonzo filed into the office, and I followed behind him.

"Have a seat," Gunny offered us the two seats directly facing his desk. His office was a perfect reflection of his own appearance, simple and clean. There were very few decorations in the office. LT Walker's office was plastered with awards and personal pictures. It looked like an Applebee's. Gunny Ortega's looked as Spartan the day he moved in. There was not a single picture, not a single memento. He didn't need pictures to remind him that he was a Marine. The notion of any extra horizontal surface just meant one more thing to dust, polish, and shine.

"Looks like you two both got in a car accident," Gunny observed smirking as Gonzo and I reverently grabbed our seats.

"Gunny, it was all my fault," Gonzo replied before I had a chance to muster up an excuse. He opened his mouth to further explain his contrite alibi.

"I don't want to hear it, Gonzalez!" Gunny interjected.

I remained seated in my chair silently bleeding.

"Gunny, I . . ." I began my own interjection.

"I don't want to hear it from you either, McGee!" Gunny snapped before I had a chance to finish. It was at that moment that I realized how ridiculous the two of us looked sitting there with battle wounds and tattered uniforms.

"Look, I don't give a shit about the fighting," Gunny continued. "Next time just don't do it in front of four thousand people in King Hall. Use some fucking sense next time."

Gunny then looked over to Gonzalez. "You think you're headed to becoming an officer, but you're a long way from it. You pull a comedy routine like that in the fleet in front of a female officer and you'll be kicked off the boat so fast it will make your head spin. You pull a comedy routine like that again here, and I'll be looking for a private spot to kick your fucking ass."

Gonzo and I sat there in silence. My blood pressure began its march back down to normal. I realized how fortunate it had been Gunny and not LT Walker that we had been ordered to report to. We could have very easily landed ourselves right alongside N.D. in restriction muster days before Thanksgiving break.

"I'll handle LT Walker," Gunny explained, almost reading our minds as we began thinking about the fallout of the day's events. "Duggan will definitely have something to say to him, and the last thing I need is a half a day of disciplinary paperwork and three weeks of Kumbaya training for the rest of the company."

I wasn't sure if Gunny was doing us a favor or just

avoiding everything he hated about the academy. Not wanting to look a gift horse in the mouth, I just wanted to get the hell out of there as soon as possible.

"I'll talk to Mary Poppins when he gets back from changing shitty diapers," Gunny went on in an obvious jab at LT Walker's propensity to shrug work in lieu of fatherly duties. "In the meantime, you guys stay away from company area for the afternoon and away from each other. Is that understood?"

"Yes, Gunny," Gonzo and I replied in unison.

"Now get out of here, you're bleeding all over my office, and I have enough shit to keep clean already."

Gonzo and I rose from our seats. I again avoided eye contact. My desire to immediately fight had subsided, but I was far from forgiving what had happened.

"Gonzalez, next time you want to tell potty jokes, do it in your room," Gunny instructed. "McGee, same goes for you the next time you and your sweetheart want to roll around on the floor together."

Mick, 2205 hrs.

By the time I was finally forced to interact with Gonzo again, it was plebe lights out. We had just sung mandatory "Blue and Gold" in the hallway with our company classmates. We were all singing extra loud to the end of another long week.

After my two afternoon classes, I hung out at the library and then caught a Friday night movie at Mitscher

Hall. It was a second run showing of Batman Forever. While the movie was an expected disappointment, the price was free. It also helped me blow two additional hours away from Gonzo. I came directly from the movie to Blue and Gold. I had avoided my room for nearly nine hours.

"Hey," Gonzo sheepishly mustered as I entered the door looking up from the blue glow of his computer screen. I put my bag down in front of my desk without acknowledging him or his attempted greeting.

N.D. was out with the football team in the hotel across town prepping for the team's final home game versus Tulane. As usual, he joined the team for a walkthrough practice at the stadium and then an afternoon of naps and film study back at the hotel. Miraculously the team had scrapped its way to a 4-5 record. A win on Saturday would have them knocking on the door of a winning season heading into our grand tilt against Army two weeks later. N.D. always appreciated the Friday night in the hotel with the team, especially since being on restriction. Since the team left for the stadium before lunch and headed to the hotel immediately after, N.D. had likely not even heard that his two roommates had themselves a battle royal in King Hall.

I continued giving Gonzo the silent treatment as I began disrobing my uniform and prepared for bed. Various parts of my body ached. My still throbbing right knuckles had me contemplating x-rays the next morning.

"Hey man, wanna go burn one with me?" Gonzo reached out again, this time offering his smokes with his left hand and pointing out to the window with his right.

I sighed. "Yeah, why not." I had no place better to be.

Final bed checks were still well over an hour away.

I let Gonzo crawl through the window first. The last thing I was going to do was give him the opportunity to push me off the roof. As I watched him climb out ahead of me, the thought of giving him a little extra shove briefly crossed my mind.

We both carefully crawled out to Gonzo's regular smoking spot. The nighttime view of the bay was equally as magnificent as it had been in the summer and fall, but somehow different. The wind blew harder and colder. The gentle caress of the summer bay breeze was replaced by the harsh bite of impending winter. The bay that was once a parking lot for multi-million dollar yachts was now an aquatic ghost town. It was the perfect metaphor for my feelings towards Gonzo.

"Here, take one," Gonzo offered his menthols and lighter.

I obliged and quickly yet unsuccessfully attempted to light my cigarette. After the third attempt, I was finally able to light my vice. I handed the lighter back to Gonzo and he had his smoke lit in one try.

"Once you go on a tour out at sea, you'll learn to light up in a full winter maelstrom," Gonzo humbly bragged. I was unimpressed.

We both sat in silence, awkwardly puffing away. Gonzo took a strong drag and then finally interjected with an exhale, "Mick, I'm really sorry for what I said at lunch."

"Yeah," I replied after blowing out two lungs worth of smoke. That was all the language I could muster. Several minutes went by without a spoken word.

"He made me do everything," Gonzo sheepishly broke

the silence.

"Who?" I asked confused as to what he was alluding to.

"Smitty," Gonzo answered. "Smitty, that fucker, made me do everything."

"Made you do what?" I skeptically replied. I was offended that immediately following a genuine apology he backed it with some cockamamie excuse.

"Everything, the joke, riding the goat statue naked, all of it," he replied. "He's trying to run me out."

I tried my best to be non-judgmental towards his confession. I didn't know whether to laugh or just continue the fight we never had a chance to finish earlier. I took a last drag of my cigarette and flicked it towards the ground four stories below. I watched the orange spark drop like a shooting star in the night.

The idea of Smitty running Gonzo out was not entirely far-fetched. Smitty even had motive considering the fistfight they almost got into the parking lot after the Air Force game. Still, the extent of that motive seemed a bit ridiculous. Smitty was certainly a hotheaded blow hard, but calculating an intricate plot to run out Gonzo seemed like a stretch.

"You got another smoke?" I asked temporarily delaying the roof top disclosure. Gonzo obliged and I quickly lit my next indulgence.

"Why would Smitty do all that?" I humored the story with a half-genuine question and followed with an exhaled cloud of smoke. Knowing that Gonzo was known to stretch the midshipman honor code, I anticipated what would likely be a self-serving tall tale.

"'Cause I heard something I shouldn't have," he answered.

"Heard what?" I continued my prodded investigation.

"That night N.D. went ballistic, at the comedy show," he began explaining. "I went down to the basement laundry room after everyone passed out to clean the puke off his sheets. You know, to cover up the evidence."

Gonzo took a drag of his own cigarette. The crisp November evening wind urged brevity in his narrative.

"When I was in the laundry room, that night, it was late. I assumed I was by myself. Who the fuck does laundry at two in the morning on a Saturday? I heard Smitty talking to some guy down by the phones in the basement outside the laundry room and by the 5th wing entrance. I couldn't make out what they were saying, but I definitely recognized one of the voices as Smitty."

He shifted his seat in a nervous fidget and then continued, "After a few minutes I heard a gang of firsties come in from liberty. They were hanging in the basement entrance so Smitty and this guy moved into the laundry room and continued what they were talking about. I imagined it had been a private conversation. They continued without knowing I was in the back cleaning the sheets. I had ducked down out of their immediate view. They assumed they were by themselves."

Another dramatic pause as though he was inviting me to ask questions about what he heard.

"So what did you hear?" I asked, humoring the cue.

"The drug bust—Smitty was in on it. They were talking about the bust and how shit was going down. The wiz quiz, all of it. They went on for five minutes until they realized I was sitting on the floor reading behind a few of the machines trying to stay out of sight."

"Wait a minute," I interjected. I simply needed to slow the train of narrative down as I was already drowning from the fire hose of titillating information. Questions entered my brain immediately seeking to authenticate his tale.

"Who was Smitty talking to?" I asked, half-heartedly.

"The cops? NCIS? DEA? The fucking drug fairy? How the fuck do I know, but this dude knew everything that went down that weekend."

In my logic I was beginning to correlate the story to Smitty's rationale. It wasn't totally implausible that Smitty would be involved in such activities. It also explained why Smitty was either trying to run Gonzo out or at least attack his credibility.

"So why are you telling me all this?" I verbalized my immediate mental query.

"'Cause that is only half of the story," Gonzo quickly explained. "The first bust was just a setup. A setup for a bigger bust, for something going down over Thanksgiving."

I remained seated still perplexed by why this mattered to me beyond absolving a bad joke between jilted lovers. The confession didn't fit the sin.

"Mick, they mentioned a Bird from Ocean City as the mule," he continued as he stared at the dark ground far below the ledge. "I heard them say it a couple of times."

The half of my face that was not yet frozen from the cold November air went altogether numb. My worst suspicions were substantiated in a millisecond.

"Your cousin, Bird, is he into any of that type of shit?"

I didn't know whether to cry, question, or just resume

the fight I hadn't finished nine hours earlier. I defaulted to yet another long drag of my second cigarette. My heart felt as though it had been ripped out of my chest cavity.

"So why are you telling me this now?" my questioning went back to interrogative logic.

"If the deal does go down, they'll just keep on running me out of dodge. It's not like they can just erase the information in my head. They threatened me after the fact. They even know about my daughter. All they need to do is disclose that information and I'm back out to the fleet. I could lose everything. If that bust doesn't go down, they'll suspect I leaked information, and it wouldn't take long for them to figure out Bird is my roommate's cousin," he explained. "Then you're implicated."

"I'm already fucking implicated!" I yelled out in a rage. My instincts had my swollen right fist clinched and prepared to break a few more knuckles. I realized that my anger was misdirected. Gonzo wasn't my problem. It was Bird. It was always fucking Bird.

Fuck it. Let him rot for a few more years in prison.

My mind played that scenario out in my head. While I would not be directly implicated if Bird were busted, the association would be very hard to live down. Then my mind wandered to the same worries I had the night the wiz quiz was announced. Nellie would go into a tailspin. No one would be there for my addict mother.

"Look man, I have been plotting this out in my head," Gonzo reassured me. "I think I might have a plan if you can help me."

I clenched my teeth trying to hold back the tears and my immediate instinct to blindly say yes. I couldn't tell if it was the cold or the emotions fucking with my thoughts. I instead decided to step back indoors. I needed private space to think.

Once inside, I looked in my half-opened con-locker instinctively. There it was—my grandfather's rusted old toolbox.

Being a man means a hell of a lot more than no tears and hard work.

I walked over to the toolbox and stared intently. Gonzo remained outside while he finished his cigarette.

Being a man don't mean shit if you can't protect the ones you love.

In all of Bird's months of silent treatment, he was just doing what he could to protect me. He was a fucking idiot, but the effort was there. I wasn't much of a man if I couldn't return the favor. My heart and mind wrestled. Both unfortunately were thawing out. I took a deep breath kicked the toolbox with all my might. A loud clang on the rusted tin was followed by an avalanche of well used and half-broken tools on the floor below.

I stepped back out of the window and onto the ledge. The cigarette I was previously smoking lay half burnt next to Gonzo. He picked it up, took a drag to get it smoking again. He passed it my way. I took one last drag and flicked it four stories below. I looked Gonzo dead in the eye.

"Diga me, ese."

Chapter 18

Unhappiness Factor
Tuesday, November 21st, 1995
Mick, 1955 hrs.

"Mr. McGee, you really have a 'fuck you' attitude," Smitty had told me earlier at lunch that day. He had been riding my ass all week as though he had suddenly re-focused the angst he had for Gonzo towards me. Whether it was critiquing my uniform or assigning me chow calls for the entirety of the week, Smitty suddenly had a keen interest in making my life miserable. It was a stark contrast to the atmosphere most plebes faced during a shortened week ahead of our first real vacation since becoming plebes.

It was as if he could subconsciously sense the plan Gonzo and I had been working on all weekend. Being the guy we were conspiring against, he made it extremely hard to feel guilty about it.

Even without the extra torment, I would have had very little difficulty feeling guilty about anything coming Smitty's way. He, like me, had somehow found his way into this drug mess. The details surrounding exactly how he fell into this situation remained unclear. Those details mattered very little to me. In one way or another, he had entered a dangerous world. I had been pulled into it as well, as had Gonzo. Whether we liked it or even realized it, we were all playing with fire. One of us, if not all of us, could come out of this weekend badly burned. It was a risk I decided I had to take.

It was the night before Thanksgiving leave, a night that every plebe dreamt about all during I-Day and the entirety of plebe existence since. It was the night before the day most of us could finally return home. At the end of the summer, we had been reminded with fictitious snow that it was a long ways off. We had been forced to memorize the days up until it, yet with the count officially down to one, I looked towards the milestone with dread. There would be no return home for me over Thanksgiving break.

While most of my classmates would soon be relishing in the joyous taste of turkey and temporary freedom, I was setting forth on a much different journey. Per Gonzo's scheming, I would spend all of my vacation trafficking drugs across the country with my ex-con cousin.

Despite the sudden cancellation of my visit to the shore, I was anxious to get the extended weekend moving. Drunk with fear and a few swigs of Gonzo's contraband alcohol stash, my mind was squarely fixated on the trip ahead of me. I had spent the previous weekend and most of the short week second-guessing and poking holes in Gonzo's proposed plan. It seemed so ridiculous at first blush. It took Gonzo most of Saturday to convince me to even consider it. It took the rest of the weekend convincing Bird to join in on it.

Back in Bancroft, talk of vacation plans and trips home sickened me. My stomach was nauseated with resent. By 8 p.m. I had had my fill of the constant vacation talk. I made my way outdoors where I could clear my head.

Five hundred yards outside of the hall, the Triton Light Monument held water from the seven seas in honor of the USS Triton's trip around the world. What was the significance of the journey? When did it happen? Why did it happen? I sure as hell didn't know. It was sad that my brain had become wired this way.

Triton Light was like any of the other many monuments on the yard. If an upperclassman asked me about it, I knew just enough about it not to get shit on. We were all half-assed tour guides in the making. I was just happy that for the time being it was a private spot away from everyone else.

The Triton Light had other meanings to midshipman outside of military history. It's location on the easternmost corner of the yard also marked the intersection of the Severn River and the Chesapeake Bay. It was often used as a visual landmark for navigation of the many watercraft midshipman piloted during nautical training. It was a recognized meeting point around a rare enclave of parking along the seawall. It often became a pickup and drop off point for various automobiles. I knew that my privacy would be temporary.

For me, the Triton Light was special beyond its temporary privacy. It was also the spot on the yard that felt closest to the Delmarva shoreline. It was a place where I could look across the bay and know that my home was just a short jaunt across the Eastern Shore of Maryland. There were times when I would look out and could practically smell the boardwalk, at least in my imagination. On this night, the shore seemed like a lifetime away. This would be the closest I would get to it until Christmas, if I weren't apprehended first.

I looked out to the distant lights of the Chesapeake Bay Bridge, the nearest connection point to Maryland's eastern shore and the gateway for Bird's first leg of a very long pending journey in the early morning. I closed my eyes and took one last deep breath of the salty air.

"Don't let me down, Bird," I whispered to no one.

Mick, 2035 hrs.

The line of midshipman outside of the phone room extended ten midshipmen deep. They were all anxiously waiting for one of the occupied phone booths to open up. Sometimes this line could take five minutes, other times closer to an hour.

The line outside of the phone room was a great window into the collective emotions of the brigade. During Plebe Summer, audible eavesdroppers could hear complaining, threats of escape, and girlfriend baby talk. As the brigade reformed, those conversations were intermingled with upperclassmen tall tales to friends back home and pathetic pandering to whatever random girl gave them the time of day on Saturday night liberty. On the night before Thanksgiving break, I was surely the only mid in line lacking an ear-to-ear grin.

Under normal circumstances, plebes waiting in line would be strictly enforced to maintain silence. Most of us read books or did homework. On this particular night, those rules seemed lax. I heard two fellow plebes adjacent to me chatting away without fear of consequence. They were both heading home in a day and it was all they could talk about. My mood being slightly different, I maintained my thousand yard stare.

Fuck them.

Other than the internet and Saturday liberty, the pay-phone was a plebe's lone connection to the outside world. A handful of the highest-ranking firsties were lucky enough to have private phone lines accessible in their room, but that was limited to five leadership billets amongst over one hundred within a company. The idea of a plebe using a firstie's phone was laughable.

Plebes were never permitted access to private phone lines on the yard. It had been rumored that a few vacated classroom phone lines within the academic buildings were still active despite their lack of attached phones. Gonzo had told me a story of a NAPS friend that would carry a phone with him to pirate access to these lines to make free long distance calls. The location of these lines was shrouded in mystery. For those theoretically lucky enough to find them, there was reluctance to give up the location of their pot of gold. I had never actually seen such lines, and to me they were merely a white unicorn. Phone calling cards used to make paid long distance calls constituted the entirety of my upcoming Christmas list to Santa. I had spent at least half of my fifty dollar a month salary on them. If I had a girlfriend, my Visa card would have been maxed out by AT&T.

I was lucky enough to slip into an open phone after only about ten minutes of waiting. I plopped into the recently opened phone booth as soon as it was available. The wooden bench seat was still warm from the last long-sitting occupant. The glass on the phone booth door was slightly opaque. I couldn't tell if its lack of full transparency was driven by excessive grime or the steaming humidity of the seventh wing phone room. Even though the seventh wing of Bancroft Hall had only been renovated a year earlier, the phone room already had visible indication of excessive mileage. The smell of sweat, tears, rotten food, and stress-induced flatulence permeated throughout the room of roughly twenty adjacent phone booths jam packed within the large but crowded rectangular room. The potpourri of odor smelled as though I was living in a shoe that had just stepped in dog shit.

"Please enter your calling card number, followed by the pound sign," the automated dial in voice instructed through the phone's sweaty earpiece.

Dutifully I obliged and then dialed Aunt Nellie's home line as instructed by a familiar automated voice.

"Thank you." Then the computerize voice paused while the system processed my security entry. "You have twelve minutes remaining."

Shit, I hope I can get Bird on the phone before Aunt Nellie potentially drains my last minutes of long distance calling.

I closed the booth door in want of privacy and collective annoyance of the ridiculously happy calls I could hear in the booths next to me. The glass tinted further with heat-induced fog.

"Hello," Nellie's voice answered my call on the second ring.

"Shit," I exclaimed under my breath.

"What was that?" Nellie queried in slight annoyance. She must have heard my profanity. With my luck, I sat in the one phone booth that actually had decent audio reception. Under most circumstances the voice on the other line was running at half volume or crackling with static.

"Nothing," I replied. "Hey Aunt Nellie, good to hear you," I desperately tried to salvage my previous transgression with a quick complimentary diversion. "Is Bird around?"

"Sure," she said bluntly. The tone and brevity of her response was expected. I had broken the news to her a few days earlier that Bird and I would be missing Thanksgiving dinner and the entirety of the holiday weekend. I almost burned an entire calling card listening to her give me shit about not being around for my depressed mom. She almost talked me out of my own scheme. Luckily by the time of this call she had given into defeat, realizing that even her well executed guilt trip had been futile.

Nellie was right to be mad at Bird and me. Even though the weekend surf trip was a fictional excuse, it was hardly the first time Bird had blown off a major holiday to go surf. This missed Thanksgiving was certainly one of the most brutally inexcusable. Prior missed birthdays, Mother's days, and even an epic Christmas surfing adventure had her collectively steamed.

"LAAARRRRY," Nellie yelled out seemingly signaling Bird. A few seconds passed without answer. My heart fluttered in nervousness.

Come on, Bird, don't let me down, man.

"LAAAARRRRY, get your ass down here. I'm not a goddamn switch operator. It's Micky. Pick up the damn phone," Nellie yelled. "Good luck on your little surf trip this weekend," she said quickly before abruptly passing the phone over to Bird. The salutation was ripe with sarcasm and one last jab of guilt before we hit the road. Bird grabbed the phone from Nellie. In lieu of picking up the phone line upstairs in his room, he came all the way downstairs to ensure Nellie didn't hang out on the line to silently eavesdrop.

"What up, Bunkie?" Bird answered on the other line. The question was merely a charade. He knew why I was calling. He had to play it cool in front of Aunt Nellie with her suspicion of bullshit already at a heightened level.

"We good for tomorrow?" I asked.

"Yup. You know the time and place," he said cryptically. He didn't want to audibly give up even the smallest details of the trip to a surely spying Aunt Nellie.

"5 a.m. sharp at the corner of King George Street and Baltimore Annapolis Parkway," I dutifully answered. "You know where that is, right?" Even these small details stressed me out. I double-checked everything. I couldn't imagine what I'd be like once we were illegally carting drugs across the country.

"Alright, I'm in my room. We're private. Look, man, you still want to do this, Bunkie?" Bird asked, sensing my trepidation. "I can always use Farm if I need to, that was the original plan anyway."

"That was a DUMB FUCKING PLAN!" I caught myself yelling and then lowered my voice as to not attract undue attention in the phone room. "Fuck Farm, man, he has a DUI on record. You get pulled over, you are fucked. I just can't believe that was your original plan. I love the guy, but DUI or no DUI, there is no way Farm's pulling this off. Bird, you fuck this up, you're in jail, or worse. You need me on that truck. End of story."

As if he needs an explanation about how I am saving his ass.

Five seconds of silence ensued.

"You still there?" I asked.

"See you tomorrow, 5 a.m.," he answered before immediately hanging up the phone. Despite the days passing since convincing him to participate, Bird still audibly demonstrated reluctance towards the plot. It was a worry.

With a click and a dial tone, the call was finished yet my nerves remained buzzing. I imagined they would stay that way all weekend. I exited the booth and headed back to the top floor of the fifth wing. There were ten minutes left until 10 p.m. lights out. With a long weekend of travel ahead, I intended to grab some extra shuteye by actually going to bed directly upon lights out.

Few plebes slept very well that night. Excitement for the weekend ahead had us all on edge. No one slept more poorly than I did.

Part V

The Distance

Chapter 19

Toothache
Wednesday, November 22nd, 1995
Mick, 0420 hrs.

My morning alarm clock went off like a bomb. Although I had attempted an early lights out the night before, it took me until well after midnight to actually quiet my mind down enough to sleep. I never did know exactly when my slumber began. My night ended up being a long string of fifteen-minute naps awaiting the dreaded call to duty. Whether I had slept for three hours or forty-five minutes, my dreams were long. Bird, Gonzo, Ocean City, my father, they had all been a continuous cast of characters in my anxious dreaming.

As I grabbed the clock to verify that it was actually 4:20 a.m., it took but a millisecond to know the time of reckoning had finally arrived.

I looked across the room and noticed N.D.'s bunk was also empty. After a few seconds of knocking the cobwebs out of my brain, I remembered that he had a 4 a.m. football practice preparing for Army and an earlier wakeup than I did. With the big game a week and a half away, the football team was preparing extra hard for the tilt. The class of '96 did not want to be remembered as a class that had lost to Army all four years of their stay by the bay. I peered out of our room's partially frosted window. I could see the soft glow of the football practice field's lights turned on for practice. I would eventually pass them on my way to sneaking off the yard.

I didn't need to wonder what Gonzo was up to. Our neighbors were likely able to hear his incessant snoring, which only seemed to worsen as he had gained back the weight he lost over Plebe Summer. Gonzo had not budged at the sound of my alarm. He didn't need to. His next role in our plot was still over four days away.

We had never disclosed our plan to N.D. We both agreed that it would be best to keep him out of the shenanigans at hand. His single Black N had him in deep enough trouble as it was. Even mere association with this exercise would certainly send him packing home to Nebraska, regardless of how many sacks he could generate against Army.

I dressed quickly in PT gear and grabbed a pre-packed travel bag. Toothbrush, caffeine pills, four pairs of clean underwear, a few borrowed CDs, and a carefully folded service dress blue uniform completed my travel ensemble. I smacked Gonzo to wake him up. My initial gentle nudge was not enough to rouse him. Perhaps I was just looking for an excuse to hit him.

"Gonzo, yo Gonzo," I loudly whispered before smacking him again. "Wake up, man."

"What up, Mick?" he finally replied groggily rubbing his eyes.

"We cool? You got me covered?" I asked frantically re-alizing I needed to leave immediately in order to get to the rendezvous point in time.

"Yeah, man. Sunday, I'll be waiting at the bus stop at noon for that dude Farm in your piece of shit brown Old-smobile. I'm there, man, no sweat."

"Cool, what about this morning?" I continued my grilling as a way to combat my apprehension.

"You gotta bad dental case, homey. You'll be there all morning," Gonzo answered, this time with more clarity as the morning phlegm cleared his throat. My morning for-mation and class absence alibi was covered.

"Alright man, I'm out," I replied and turned towards the door with my bag.

"Yo Mick," Gonzo called out as I turned for the door. He had sat up in his bunk and extended his open hand asking for a soul shake.

I obliged as I could feel the nervous sweat on both our hands.

"Good luck, homey," he said as he released his tight grip. "Remember, stick to the plan and we're all good."

I didn't know whether to punch him or hug him. While our collaborative plotting had made me want to kill him a little less, we were still a long way from friends. I turned around and exited the door. I refused to talk about the plan any further. I had spent the past five days obsess-ing over it.

As I entered the hallway, it took me a few seconds to realize I was still squaring my corners per plebe regula-tion. Quickly I untucked my shirt and pushed down my socks. If a random upperclassman spotted me, I wanted them to think I was one too. If someone from my company spotted me, I would just play it off as being half-asleep and having to use the bathroom badly.

I expeditiously made my way over to the Company Mate of the Deck's watch stand in the center of our floor. It was the podium where all plebes and youngsters had to stand when individually assigned CMOD watch, which happened a few times a month for each of us. We were all mall-cops in training. That watch didn't formally post for a few hours. What was then an empty podium had contained what I had been looking for. I grabbed the academic log and flipped to the current page. Grabbing the pen at the desk I logged "McGee, Dental" and then listed out all of the classes I would be missing for the day. I wasn't thrilled having to lie about my absence, but frankly that was going to be the least of my worries this weekend.

"In for a dime, in for a dollar," I whispered as a way to placate my nerves.

I quickly hustled over to Summer's door. We hadn't spoken since the joke incident on Friday.

Summer had been alone in her room for a few days. Her one other roommate, Christie Grinkle, had been out on early leave presenting recruitment pitches to high schools in her home town. Only a select few plebes, with impeccable academic records, could be eligible for that privilege. We were both in the same English class together and she had been yammering on and on about it for weeks.

I took a deep breath and grabbed a folded paper note tucked away in my sock. I squatted down and slid the note under the closed door, hoping desperately that Summer would be the only person to see it. Not knowing what was coming on the other end of the weekend, I had some things I wanted to say before shit potentially hit the fan. I had worked on the note between plotting sessions all weekend. It read like a seventh grade love letter:

> *Summer,*
> *I'm so sorry about the way I reacted to Gonzo's joke on Friday. I hope that it did not cause you any undue attention or embarrassment. I guess he really got under my skin because I really do like you. I never had the guts to say it before. I thought it might make things awkward, especially if you are in another relationship. Then I thought, how could things get any more awkward than they already are? There, I said it. I like you. Whether you like me back or not, just know that I am really sorry and under stand if you want to ignore me for a while. I hope you have a great Thanksgiving break. Mine is looking a little crazy.*
> *-Mick*

Suddenly the hallway bathroom door swung open, someone must have been using the restroom before I originally left my room. Quickly, I darted towards the stairwell in a desperate attempt to avoid detection from anyone within my company.

I sprinted down the steps and eventually out of Bancroft. My heavy breathing was less stressed once I reached outdoors. The cold hit me in the face like a ton of bricks. Quickly I realized my initial escape plan was already flawed. Wearing shorts and a T-shirt outdoors at 4:30 a.m. the day before Thanksgiving was a bad call. It made me wonder quickly what other critical details of the scheme had Gonzo and I overlooked. My mind again began to consume me, just as it had all night.

I immediately amped up my running pace to generate extra body heat. As a way to supplement the exhaustion distracting my brain, I began mentally replaying my recollection of what I had written to Summer.

After the third time reciting it in my head, I temporarily considered running back up to the room to take the letter back. William Shakespeare I was not. I looked at my watch. It was 4:40 a.m., and I was at least a mile's run from my rendezvous point with Bird. There was no turning back for the letter. Soon there would be no turning back on this journey.

Mick, 0456 hrs.

Before 5 a.m., finding an escape to the other side of the roughly ten-foot wall surrounding the land facing perimeter of the yard was a necessity. It was about the only way to exit the Naval Academy without being caught by a variety of on-patrol police officers, aptly named "Jimmy Legs" by the mids. The majority of "hops" over the wall took place at several opportune heights along the fence's perimeter. I had taken the lazy man's route of sneaking behind the Naval Academy visitors' center. I was willing to stomach a brief swing around the wall's ending and attached fence over the icy cold bay water below. It was slower but a fair trade for the less likelihood of being caught by the Jimmy Legs who often kept an eye on the top of the wall for sneaky culprits. Around the wall's ending point I adeptly made my way onto downtown Annapolis' single strip waterway. The strip was aptly named Ego Alley for the massive boats frequently making their pass up the watery public runway. On the other side of the wall, I was smack dab in the middle of historic downtown Annapolis, which was ideal. While warmer weather would have surely drawn a few tourists out of bed early for sunrise views, cold morning Annapolis was a ghost town. It was a route that was a little more circuitous, but kept me better hidden in my premature holiday departure.

After a cold ten-minute jog, I finally reached my rendezvous point at the corner of King George St. and Baltimore Annapolis Parkway. I stood with my hands on knees heavily sucking wind. The sting of the cold had subsided several blocks back, but the sheer exhaustion induced by my running escape had consumed my body's senses. My lungs burned with the sting of the cold air. I quickly caught my breath while taking a brief glance at my watch. It was 4:58 a.m. and I realized my adrenaline had carried me faster than anticipated. I was a full two minutes early to my pickup point. My escape plan thus far went off without a hitch.

I looked at my watch again. It was 4:59 a.m. The previous minute seemed like an eternity. While the small likelihood of a company officer or off base personnel driving by at this hour was slim, sitting at a corner so directly close to the often used academy staff access gate #8 left me feeling exposed. It was a chance I was willing to keep as trade to keep Bird's meeting spot as simplistic as possible. I impatiently glanced at my watch's face. Another minute had passed. It was time to go.

"Come on, Bird, let's fucking GO," I frantically whispered to myself. "FUCK!" I shouted in frustration before regretfully realizing that screaming profanities while trying to avoid detection on a publicly visible corner was not an ideal practice. I began pacing back and forth trying hard to control my rising blood pressure. I could feel my pulse throb in my right fist. It was still slightly swollen after slamming it against Gonzo's head days before.

The notion of Bird running late was hardly a surprise. In my entire relationship with him, the only thing he ever showed up on time for was solid morning surf conditions. He was even born two weeks late.

I quickly heard the hiss of brakes from behind my back. I was caught pacing in the wrong direction. I quickly turned anticipating the worst case scenario.

"Mornin', Bunkie, time to rock and roll!" Bird screamed through the rolled down passenger window of a well-used box truck. It was the only way I could possibly hear him above the clanking diesel engine.

I quickly obliged, wanting nothing more than to get off the corner and out of plain sight.

One worry transitioned to the next, none of which were irrational. "Are you sure this shit pile will make it across the country and back in four days?" I screamed as I shut the door, again competing with the volume of the loudly running engine.

"Yeah . . . probably," Bird answered in a lower voice

and then a quick chuckle. Once I closed the door behind me, I thankfully realized the truck's primary cabin did an adequate job of blocking the magnitude of engine noise. At least I would have a somewhat quiet seat to sleep in when I wasn't driving.

Bird put the truck in drive and we were off to the races before I could even notice his bizarrely uncharacteristic appearance.

For starters, he was wearing my black and white faced Orioles ball cap backwards. It was one of my favorite belongings from back home. I couldn't take it with me as possession of any civilian attire, even hats, was strictly prohibited for any plebe. It was the first time I had seen Bird wear any type of ball cap on his head.

"What's with my hat?" I asked.

"Can't stand the sight of this," he replied removing the ball cap and running a hand over his cleanly shaved head. "White guys with dreads don't make the most inconspicuous mules."

Then there was the home green #33 Celtics Larry Bird jersey, a Christmas present from me three years ago that I had never seen him wear. "Then what's with the jersey?" I continued my curious grilling.

"Oh this," he said. "This jersey is my good luck charm. I have trafficked three times in this jersey and haven't been caught yet," he confidently narrated as though he hoped his lucky jersey would attenuate my visible look of nausea and fear. It didn't.

"Good to know my presents go to good use," I sarcastically replied with an eye roll. I pulled on the seatbelt, trying to buckle in for the long haul. I yanked three times and could not get it to budge.

"Oh yeah, forgot to tell you that both of the seatbelts rarely work," Bird stated in a matter of fact tone. "It's kind of like jerking off," he continued. "If you pull on it long enough, eventually it will come."

"Fuck it," I said with my arms raised in defeat. "Who needs automobile safety when you have such a secure and safe mode of transportation."

"That's the spirit," he replied calmly without acknowledging my cynicism, even though he surely noticed it. We had yet to make eye contact.

As we started making our way towards the appropriate interstate route, I had more time to take inventory of my broader surroundings. Once I felt safely distanced from the yard, I rolled the manual passenger side window all the way down so I could fully put my head outside the passenger cabin. While I had trepidation towards what I might see, I felt the intense need to further inspect the truck's side panel advertisement. I had entered too abruptly to initially remember my ride's finer details. When I finally stuck my head out of the window, my anxiety level raised another notch.

"Ocean City Amusement Maintenance Company? What the fuck is that?" I asked.

"We're a private outfit. We work on Trimper's amusement rides. Occasionally we need to go out of town for specialty repair items," Bird explained his fictional company tuck and our alibi for driving it.

"But the paint job looks like a three-year-old did it," I commented on the work's utter lack of quality. "Looks like shit."

"Adds authenticity," he retorted. "Makes it look like more of a local yocal's truck."

"And that's a good thing?" I asked with growing concern.

"It's all part of it," Bird coolly answered the question as though he knew it was coming. He could see I was perplexed by the vehicle choice. While I thought that I had a heavy influence on the trafficking plan, Bird already had squared away some details that would still be left as a surprise during our journey. We simply didn't have the time on the phone to hash out every little detail of the excursion. Even if we had the time, it's not like Bird would have taken much more advice than I had already given him.

"Look Micky, if this shit isn't for you, it's not too late to back out," he said finally looking over to me. Normally I would have associated this prodding response as reverse psychology. The seriousness in Bird's eyes had me believing the offer's credibility.

I looked forward and took a deep breath. Trying very hard not to show it, I briefly considered taking up Bird's offer. It was very tempting. Bird had been right. It was not too late for me to back out. I could have snuck back on the yard well before reveille and no one would have noticed that I was ever gone. I could stuff my face with turkey tomorrow and even get in a few cold weather surf sessions. Then my mind wandered back to the scenarios I played in my head at least a thousand times in the preceding week. If Bird got busted and went back to jail, it would tear my family apart.

"Fuck it, drive on," I said with a quick smack of the truck's dash. It knocked the broken door of the glove compartment onto the floor.

"Don't worry about that, it's a piece of shit," Bird said assuaging my assumed guilt of breaking the vehicle's interior. It was the least of my worries. I was just hoping the entire diesel-powered piece of shit would stay in one piece over the next four days.

After about forty minutes, we were getting on Route 70 just west of Baltimore. It was our initial gateway to the west. In my entire life, I had never been west of Maryland.

"Westward ho!" Bird yelped as he merged off the exit and onto the interstate.

By about Route 70, I felt calm enough to look for distractions. Ten miles into the interstate and the reality finally set in that there was a long ride ahead. I quickly started looking for entertainment options.

"Yo," I nudged Bird who had his eyes fixated on the road. "This truck got a sound system?" I took inventory of the truck's radio. Several of the knobs and buttons were already missing. I guessed the answer was no.

"Nah, man," he said breaking his outward stare. He had already been driving for well over two hours having started his day farther east in Ocean City. He looked tired. "But check this out, Bunkie, I'll hook you up."

Bird rummaged in his overflowing backpack in between us on the truck's bench. It had been likely over stuffed to conceal drugs of personal use. He pulled out a well-worn Sony Discman.

"Well I guess one of us can listen to music," I said, not liking the prospects of sharing one set of headphones betwixt the two of us for four days.

"On the contrary, Bunkie," Bird said with a proud smile.

Bird pulled out a set of foam earphones. The headset's ear pieces had the foam ripped off and had been instead enclosed with paper Dixie cups. He plugged his makeshift speaker contraption into the Discman. He hit play and after a two second delay of screeching and churning, the interior disc gained mechanical momentum to spin within the device. Soon out from the Dixie cups came a rather good sounding bootleg concert cd of the Dead coming through the homemade speaker system.

"Dude, you are like stoner MacGyver," I said. It was the first chuckle I enjoyed of the day.

"Nah, I just read about it in Playboy last month."

Bird was about the only guy I knew that read Playboy for the articles.

"What about batteries?" I asked.

"I got you covered," he quickly replied reaching below his seat. In a brown paper bag that I immediately recognized, was the entire collection of batteries Aunt Nellie kept in the fridge.

I almost mentioned that Nellie would not like the theft, but then I suspected as mad as she was about us missing Thanksgiving vacation, the batteries would have done little to make her anger any incrementally worse.

"Hey, can we listen to this?" I asked Bird pulling out of my bag one of the few CDs I had brought on the trip. My entire collection had been left at home, but N.D. kept a few extra CDs in his football locker. He lent me the new GZA CD and a few others as a Thanksgiving weekend loner.

"Sure, man," Bird obliged.

As soon as the CD spun Bird asked, "What is this crap?"

"GZA the Genius," I replied. "It's the new Wu-Tang joint. Came out a few weeks back. My roommate let me borrow it."

"Jizzy the Genie?" Bird queried. "Fuck that, I'll go insane listening to that shit across the country." Quickly he opened the Discman and threw the CD out of the window like a Frisbee. Before I had a chance to react negatively he said, "Don't worry, I'll buy you a new one to replace it for your homeboy."

Soon GZA the Genius was replaced with a Bob Marley concert album. It was a fitting compromise.

The harmonious tunes were jamming out of the Dixie cup speakers. Bird was jamming an imaginary hand drum better known as the steering wheel. His head bopped back and forth to the beats. If his dreads were still on his head they would have been swaying in full glory.

I closed my eyes in an attempt to catch some sleep before it was my turn to drive later in the day. After an hour of trying to slumber, I realized it was a pointless endeavor. I looked down at my wristwatch. It was 6:30 a.m. Formation back at the academy was only thirty minutes away. For better or worse, I was in the thick of it. An hour and a half into my ride, and I couldn't turn back even if I wanted to.

Chapter 20

Go West Young Men
Thursday, November 23rd 1995
Mick, 0500 hrs.

Both of my sweaty hands were firmly fixated on the wheel. We had officially eclipsed the first twenty-four hours of our journey. We had crossed the Iowa Nebraska border a few hours earlier. Bird laid beside me passed out against the passenger door. The drowsiness of my wake-up an hour earlier had yet to wear off. I did not feel safe enough to release my death grip on the sweaty steering wheel. The desolation of early morning driving was like a deadly lullaby. I was craving the energy boost of sunrise.

Bird and I were in the middle of a cannonball run to somewhere yet to be determined in Nevada. Bird reluctantly had to wait until Wednesday morning to pick me up. We had one less day of travel than he had initially anticipated. The complexities of sneaking me out on Tuesday weren't worth gaining the extra day of travel time. With a Wednesday departure, there was no time to waste.

The only stops we would be making over the long weekend would be for gas fill-ups and drug pick-ups.

Our sustenance would be strictly provided by gas station convenience stores and whatever food Bird decided to pre-pack for the journey. That was not much other than three large bags of cool ranch Doritos. We resolved that we would urinate in water bottles if we could not hold out until our fueling stops. Bird had even brought a few pairs of adult diapers in case we needed to go number two. That was motivation enough to avoid eating. Thus far, my diet had strictly consisted of Mountain Dew, Slim Jims, and Juicy Fruit gum. Bird and I had also each burned through about two and a half packs of smokes between the two of us.

Our initial plan was to drive in six-hour shifts. We had hoped catnaps between shifts would be enough to carry us through the next four days of driving. It took us about two shifts to realize that scheduling was pointless. Sleeping in the truck was hard to do on cue, so the two of us both stayed awake for most of the first day's drive. By dinnertime yesterday, we just agreed to drive as much as possible before needing sleep. Bird caught a few hours before midnight and then I slept between gas stops through a few hours in the early a.m. We switched shifts somewhere in eastern Nebraska around 4 a.m. Bird was bummed I was not awake for Winterset, Iowa, the birthplace of John Wayne. It was about the only thing going on in Iowa.

The first day of the drive was an eternity. The twists and turns through the small mountains of the Pennsylvania Turnpike transitioned to the rolling hills of Eastern Ohio. Ohio eventually leveled out and led to the long flat jaunt across Indiana. The drive slowly became as mundane as the roads we were traveling.

Even though we had barely spoken between I-Day and our road trip, our first day of driving was one long awkward period of silence. The first hour of feigned niceties and critiques on music selections eventually transitioned to long stretches of the silent treatment.

Thankfully the sheer boredom of the first day on the road had temporarily placated Bird's intentional muting and the nerves in my stomach. By the time we passed Chicago, Bird was a regular chatty-Cathy, and I could have been trafficking uranium rods to South America without a care. For a few hours of mutual consciousness during the first evening of the trip, the journey felt more like one of our many surfing road trips to the Outer Banks than a devious excursion involving criminal behavior. It wasn't until morning that my angst picked back up. Temporarily attenuated apprehension of drug deals were replaced by the fearsome possibility of Bird or me falling asleep at the wheel.

As I chugged my second Mountain Dew of the morning, my eyes widened from the caffeine. We had drained the first case of soda in our cooler and would need to restock at the next gas station. Shortly thereafter, the rising sun of Thanksgiving morning provided enough renewed vigor to resume the more comfortable practice of driving one handed. Bird remained in slumber. We were still several hours from our next required gas stop.

My temporary relaxation afforded me enough time to take full inventory of my surroundings in the driving cabin's first morning light. The 1986 GMC 400 diesel box truck was just as shitty as ever. The gears often stuck. There was a sizable crack on the passenger window and too many rips and cigarette burns in the faux leather bench to count. Thankfully there was enough discarded garbage strewn about the cabin to temporarily camouflage these flaws from obvious sight. The trash ironically made the cabin seem less flawed.

The truck's diesel engine seemed to slowly rattle louder with each passing hour. I could not determine whether this was actually happening or if my mind was sadistically playing tricks on my ears. The odometer confidently indicated this hunk of metal had been in service for 264,987 miles. I just hoped it would last a few more thousand miles. In the paranoid stretches as a passenger along the Pennsylvania Turnpike, I had read the owner's manual cover to cover just to ensure I knew every possible danger sign of possible engine failure. It did little to assuage to my fears, nor did it when I read it a second time in Indiana.

My eyes eventually became bored with inventorying the small cabin and settled back into my dazed stare into the road. They remained there until they were finally distracted by the flicking sound of Bird's lighter. Before I looked over to Bird, I instinctively reached in my pocket to grab another cigarette.

"Dude, what the fuck are you doing, man?" I screamed when my eyes finally noticed what Bird was lighting.

"Relax, Bunkie, this helps wake me up," Bird groggily replied as he executed a long morning stretch of his arms and lit joint in hand. "Besides, if you can't take me smoking a road J in east bumblefuck, Nebraska, just wait till we are hauling enough grass to put both of us in prison for the next decade."

Bird was right. A road joint was the least of my worries. He had smoked hundreds of joints in front of me in the past. If anything Bird's impromptu smoke was good practice easing my tolerance for being around drugs again. The academy had me well out of practice. It wasn't like this was the first time Bird smoked a joint in the car. It was a daily practice back home. It just felt more devious with my nerves on high alert.

"We gotta keep pushing," Bird repeated his mantra of the first full day of driving. "Drug distributors don't take rain checks, Bunkie."

Bird rolled down the manual window on the passenger side and I followed suit on the driver's side to air out the smoke. The marijuana provided a nice air freshener to the building stench of the main cabin. Between our own body odors and excessive beef jerky induced flatulence, the cabin had slowly cultivated the smell of a high school gym locker with a clogged up toilet. Eventually the November wind became too cold and we rolled the windows up.

"Pfffffffft." Almost on cue Bird reinvigorated the stench. We were resolved to roll the windows down again and sit in the cold for a few more minutes.

Mick, 1015 hrs.

"Click, click, click, click."
"Click, click, click, click."
"Click, click, vROOOooom."
After two failed attempts, the engine fired up on Bird's

third turn of the ignition key. I sighed in relief as we sat waiting for the truck's engine to warm up. Given its visibly lackluster condition, the sound of the engine successfully starting up was a sound I nervously awaited every time we stopped for gas.

"Eh mon, gotta go to work," Bird said in an ode to one of our favorite *In Living Color* skits. He instinctively pulled the seatbelt before remembering that neither in the cabin worked. He smiled with a giggle and then made an imaginary clock punching motion with his hand. I had ended my long shift through the Nebraska cornfields, now it was Bird's turn. Within the dusty confines of a dilapidated rest stop, our gas tank and cooler was refilled to capacity. I took a large bite of newly acquired beef jerky and a swig of Mountain Dew. We were back on our way to the long straight road to the middle of nowhere.

Like the quoted television characters in our favorite sketch comedy show, Bird was a man with a myriad of former and active professional responsibilities. He had held a long track record of short lived stints across a wide array of Ocean City, Maryland's shittiest tourist industry jobs.

Bird's first job was as a putt-putt golf store clerk. He picked up the gig when one of Aunt Nellie's neighbors offered fifteen-year-old Bird a job at one of the courses his family owned. I remember how cool I thought it was getting free rounds of golf, not to mention just knowing the guy handing out the bent clubs and painted golf balls. Unfortunately, that well was drained when one day after work Bird was caught peeing in a pirate-themed lagoon adjacent to the 16th hole.

In his "golden era" of employment, Bird had worked

countless delivery routes for a variety of boardwalk pizza and sandwich shops. He would typically use his tasked
"takeout delivery" as a venue for simultaneous drug delivery. "It was like getting paid to deal drugs," he used to
say, not realizing the irony that he already received pay for
dealing drugs.

Fountain drink cups were Bird's favorite decoy. He
could carry a quarter pound of weed in a fully loaded
four-cup cardboard drink carrier on the back of his mo-
ped without looking the least bit conspicuous. Those delivery gigs worked out well until he accidentally delivered
to the pizzeria owner's mother a pepperoni pizza with an
unintended ounce of stink weed on the side. He thankfully avoided arrest, but his reputation soon began preceding
him. Once word was out among the local takeout owners,
Bird was blacklisted from that very convenient delivery-
man cover story.

After over a decade in the Ocean City service industry, Bird had exhausted virtually every part time job imaginable. With the exception of Trimper's rides and games
and the handful of local surf shops, which were all considered sacred ground, there were a scant few places on the
boardwalk where Bird hadn't already worked.

Over time, as employment prospects steadily slimmed,
Bird was eventually known to the locals as simply a drug
dealer. To his friends he was a drug dealer that surfed. It
was a reputation that carried with him whether running
into his neighbor at the grocery store or getting harassed
by the local cops.

Nellie would torture herself over what Bird might
have been like under different life circumstances. What

if he hadn't been arrested? What if his biological father hadn't been such an asshole? There were plenty of plausible excuses for his lot in life.

Respectable careers required commitment, but so did the ocean. Lifeguard stands needed to be filled on a consistent basis. Fishing boats left port daily. A burnout looking for a dime bag could always wait an extra day if clean pipes were breaking on 45th Street. Bird was destined to be a drug dealer. He considered it a privilege.

That's not to say that dealing drugs was a stable or consistent paycheck. Every few years the heat would dial up on Bird and he would spend a bit of time on "walk about." This usually came in the form of out of state employment.

There was a stint as a snow groomer at a Maine ski resort. It was one of the few places you could surf in the morning, ride the slopes in the afternoon, and spend the night smoking joints in the grooming cat on the resort's dime. Then there was the stint as a Northern California "farm hand." His lessons learned there in traditional horticulture were his retirement plan. He often speculated and dreamed for the day when weed would be a federally legal cash crop. No matter what the career path or however temporarily invigorating it was, it never lasted much past the next good day of waves.

His unreliable career path was one of the few predictable things about Bird. Bumping up the corporate ladder was hardly his style. This is precisely why this whole cross-country drug deal made zero sense to me. Why would a small town drug dealer happily getting free rent at his mom's beach place ever want to risk decades of jail time just for a few extra grand? It just didn't add up.

I had been subtly grilling Bird the entire trip. I couldn't bull him over with questions right away. Not only would he have never answered them, he might have thrown me out of the truck altogether. While driving across the country on Interstate 80 was one thing, hitchhiking across it was entirely another. Preserving my aura of feigned interest, I figured enough hours had passed for me to ask another question without much suspicion.

"Hey man, I gotta ask. What is in the back of the truck?" I queried, breaking the silence of the first thirty minutes since leaving the last gas station.

"I was wondering when you'd ask that," Bird replied before returning to dead silence. The acknowledgement of the question was not a guarantee that he would answer it.

"Look man, I'm not the kid with his ass in the sand anymore. Quit treating me like I am," I pleaded.
I couldn't be. I was the one that convinced Bird to let me join the trip in the first place.

"I know, Bunkie, you're all grown up now," Bird complimented sarcastically.

"Yeah, so spill the beans, what's in it?" I continued.

He rolled down the window a quarter of the way down and lit the first cigarette out of his newly bought pack of Marlboro Reds. Upon taking the first drag, he paused a minute. Savoring in the inhaled cigarette smoke and the curious tension he let out a drag and then an answer.

"Lions, tigers, bears."

"Oh fucking my," I replied, not passing on the temptation to quote Dorothy. "Cut the shit, Bird."

A few more moments passed and I asked again, "No,

really man, what is in the back?" I knew this would be the last time I could ask lest I would look like I was being nosy.

"It's all part of it, Bunkie," he said with a smirk. "It's aaaaaaaaall part of it."

Mick, 1855 hrs.

Greenery transitioned to cornfields and cornfields transitioned to deserts and then into mountains. By mid-afternoon of our second day on the road, I had begun feeling the proximity of the west coast, ironic as it was still hundreds of mile away. The past few hours were a visual marvel. Statuesque mountains dominated the Wyoming horizon until twilight's darkness eventually veiled them. The sights were particularly breathtaking given the prior twenty-four hours spent in flatter America. It was hard to feel anything but small in their presence. I had never realized what a big place America was.

Existentially my feel of minuteness in the mountains complemented my matched feeling of smallness in the overall plan. After thinking of a question every two hours for the past day and a half, I began to realize how little I knew about our journey.

We continued heading south by southwest across Utah. I took one of my periodic glances over to Bird. He was once again fast asleep, catching a few hours of shut-eye while he had the chance. Collectively we had managed about six hours of sporadic napping between the two of us. Despite being nauseated from utter lack of slumber, a slew of questions continued to rifle through my head. I figured enough time had passed to resume my subtle interrogation of Bird and our game plan.

In the several planning conversations shared with Gonzo the weekend before, and strategically timed questioning of Bird, I had managed to garner only the basic details of our caper.

After driving our vehicle across country, we would stop in a to-be-determined location in Nevada. Bird would be informed of that location via pager at or around sunset on Thursday. Once at the pre-assigned rendezvous point, we would have a packing crew load our drug payload. Bird continuously refused my requests to detail what was in the payload.

Our truck would finish the packing process in a matter of a few hours. The harrowing leg of the journey would begin early Friday morning. Bird and I would then cart our fully loaded truck on the eastward bound journey back to Annapolis. Once in Annapolis, we'd take care of the drugs and Smitty in one fell swoop.

It was an ambitiously crazy blue print especially considering the abbreviated driving time. I poked holes in it the moment Gonzo pitched the details of it a few days earlier. I made several attempts to come up with something better. It was a futile effort. Reluctantly, I gave up pushing back and figured it was the best plan we could muster.

I lit the last cigarette of my third pack while rolling down the window to facilitate aeration of the cabin and also to calm my spinning head. Bird began to stir and awaken as we hustled our way through the stunning Utah mountains. They looked more like a Hollywood backdrop than natural scenery.

Construction forced an otherwise double lane stretch down to a single lane on westward Route 80 in opposing traffic. I noticed the accompanying orange crossover sign a little too late. I aggressively shifted lanes and barely missed the orange safety cones blocking the stretch of the closed highway currently under construction. The quick traffic maneuver coupled with the sudden visual of oncoming traffic startled my passenger's wake up.

"Whoa! What's going on, Bunkie?" Bird quickly queried in a suddenly panicked posture induced by fear. The opposing direction single lane traffic had him believing we were on the wrong side of the road.

"Relax, Bird," I interjected to help calm his wake up down a notch. "This is just construction, we're all good. We're in Utah."

"Oh, shit, Idapimp," he replied taking a big yawn. "Looks like we are making some progress."

"Idapimp?" I asked having guessed the phrase to be derived from Bird's prison vocabulary.

"Yeah, Bunkie, Idapimp, neighbor of Idaho. It's what I like to call Utah," he proudly proclaimed.

I couldn't even intelligently come up with a reply. We rode in silence for the next hour. Thirty-eight hours into our ride we had exhausted the niceties of small talk.

"So what happens when we hit Nevada?" I asked suddenly breaking the silence.

"Bunkie, I already told you that we'd get next steps when we hit Nevada later tonight. That's all I know," Bird replied. I could smell his bullshit from a mile away.

"Come on, man, enough of this crap, Bird. I'm in this.

I gotta know what's going on," I quickly shot back. I finally became fed up with the ambiguity of our journey.

"Listen, Micky, this is serious shit. We get pulled over now, you're just an innocent academy kid looking for something to do over an otherwise lonely Thanksgiving weekend. On the way back, it's the same story. Hopefully wearing the uniform on the return trip will give you a little extra cover. The less you know about what's in the back the better. We get busted in the process, you play dumb. That's the plan, stick with it, listen to whatever I say. End of story. Understand?"

"Yeah, I understand," I smugly replied as I shot my eyes back forward to the road. I suddenly swerved six inches over into the opposing traffic lane. I wasn't sure if it was anger, distraction, or exhaustion that pulled my attention from the wheel. The blaring horn of the oncoming big rig quickly snapped me out of daze.

I quickly flicked the turn signal upon seeing a rest stop advertised a mile ahead. We still had about fifty miles worth of gas in the tank, but I had had enough driving. If Bird wasn't going to disclose the basic details of the trip, I wasn't going to break my neck pulling double shifts behind the wheel. I had already accumulated a majority of driving time on the way out. That was half of my value in the plot, to give Bird an extra driver more reliable than Farm. The other half of the plan was what Gonzo and I were doing with the drugs back East. It was time for Bird to start pulling his weight.

I pulled the truck to the diesel fuel pump and tossed the keys onto Bird's lap. He tossed me a hundred dollar bill for gas and food.

"Hey Bunkie, this dry air has my lips chapped. Can you score me some ChapStick while you're in there?" Bird asked as I exited the main driver cabin.

I took the cash without responding. I dutifully headed to the interior of the rest stop. No sense in wasting time or raising suspicions. I reloaded our caffeine, smokes, and beef jerky rations along with another pre-paid gas tank. The expenses left me enough change to also procure Bird's requested ChapStick. With a smirk, I told the cashier to hold tight and decided upon the cherry tinted lip gloss on a kiosk close to the register.

"Here you go," I said upon entering the passenger cabin. By the time I had made my way back to the truck, Bird had already successfully fired up the engine in warm up.

"Thanks, Bunkie," Bird graciously responded, immediately covering his lips with much needed lubricant.

As he fixated into his own thousand-yard stare, another leg of our journey initiated. While his lips were now moisturized, their brilliant red coloring was enough of a laugh to keep me up a few more moments.

"You look cute," I commented back to Bird who was amusingly perplexed by my compliment. Before giving him time to register or catch on to the joke, I shut my eyes temporarily soaked in the happy buzz of retribution. It wasn't the turkey and NFL football games I'd be otherwise enjoying back home, but it was at least something.

I was fast asleep before Bird would even begin to notice his red lips.

Chapter 21

Friendly Neighborhood Store
Friday, November 24th, 1995
Mick, 0015 hrs.

"Winnemucca, muthafucka!" Bird exclaimed as he hopped back into the driver's side door. It was the first jubilant energy the cabin had felt in well over twenty-four hours.

We had finally been given our pickup site. Bird had been anxiously checking his pager since the moment we crossed the Utah Nevada border in the fading dusk of Thursday evening. An hour into Nevada and he was beginning to look anxious, which helped my nerves very little. Finally the page came and Bird was instructed via a gas station pay phone to rendezvous at a truck stop gas station mid-way between Winnemucca and the smaller Nevada desert town of Lovelock. It was the first trip details I had gathered in well over a day.

Daylight's exit a few hours earlier was a drain. The flat desolate stretch of desert-bound Route 80 felt like a never-ending straight away. The buzz of discovering our journey's official midway point was a much needed jolt of energy.

I looked over to Bird in the driver's seat. He was wearing the same garb he had shown up with on Wednesday morning. His green Celtics jersey and accompanying Orioles hat looked just as ridiculous on him as it had when I first saw it. The shaved head had grown on me. The red Chap Stick was icing on the cake. Even after discovering my prank, Bird proceeded with his lip moisturizing routine. It made him look like a drag queen moonlighting as a sports enthusiast.

With a more clarified mission, a re-energized Bird was full of vocal observation. I diligently studied the map trying to triangulate our potential stopping point.

"See those small shrubs over there on the side of the highway?" he queried energetically.

"Yeah," I replied with substantially less enthusiasm. In the evening under the illumination of headlights, they were barely noticeable.

"They grow even in the desert," he continued. "They get their water via radiational cooling."

"You mean dew," I returned in a sarcastic tone. "Thanks for the lesson, Dr. Science."

The map indicated Lovelock was about an hour east of Reno and our gas tank looked up to the task. I realized Bird would be finishing the remaining leg of our westward journey. I forewent my next caffeine pill and instead tried to sneak in a few hours of shuteye before reaching our first extended stop in nearly two days.

"Wake up, Bunkie, we're here," Bird said. He continued shaking me out of my slumber.

I rubbed my weary eyes and instinctively grabbed a

soda and a cigarette before I could even remember what state I was in. It was my breakfast of champions despite the clock showing it was a quarter past midnight.

It was hard to recognize any specifics about our stop. Bird already parked the truck while I was still asleep. From what I could gather, we had found the gas station between Lovelock and Winnemucca more quickly than what I expected. Surveying the area there were very few visual landmarks with the exception of a standalone garage, a convenience store, and a few rundown gas pumps. We were otherwise completely surrounded by the desert night. I could barely make out the highway in what I guessed was at least four miles away. The hum of passing truck engines on the still busy interstate was barely audible. We might have been the only paying customers this station had seen all day. Dealing drugs was likely the only way this place kept the lights on.

I stepped out of the passenger side of the cabin and nearly tumbled to the ground. I forgot how dead my legs had become from sitting predominately in a box truck for then well over forty hours. I caught my balance before falling. A herd of six black kittens randomly skittered over my feet. They must have come from the standalone garage in the corner of the property.

"Well, you're just full of luck today, aren't you?" Bird queried, verbalizing the superstition rattling in my mind. I tried my best not to think about it. Cursed was the last thing I wanted to feel before taking the wheel of a truck packed so tightly with drugs that we would be, as Bird put it, "Federally fucked" if caught.

A hanging bell clanged against the greasy glass entry

door. Bird and I entered the convenience store and payment station. I immediately headed for the snack aisle and, per traditional rest stop routine, grabbed a few candy bars and chips. Judging from the cleanliness of the glass door entrance, I thought the hotdogs for sale might have been a bit too risky. My gas station diet was in full swing as I approached the vacant counter. It was a far cry from the leftover stuffing and turkey sandwich I'd be helping myself to if I had just stayed back home.

"That'll be tweny dollars," I heard a deep voice coming from the back of the store.

"Huh?" I asked feeling a bit perplexed. I hadn't even been rung up yet.

"Tweny dollars," repeated the large bearded man behind the counter.

"You must be Grizz," Bird interjected before I had the chance to say something stupid.

"Yup, that's what they call me zippy," the burly man replied nonchalantly in a deep booming voice. He was a hulk of a man, standing nearly six foot six. His arms looked like pythons and his gut like a boulder. If he were fifty pounds lighter, I would have guessed he was a professional football player. He may have very well been one in his younger years.

"Grizz, Fox?" I surmised verbally. It was my feeble attempt to insert humor in the conversation. In his wife beater, I noticed our new friend's tattoos. A grizzly bear was on the right arm, a fox was on the left.

"Great guess, Sherlock, tweny dollars," he repeated his mantra. "Didn't Grandma feed you enough turkey today?" Somehow Grizz didn't strike me as the family Thanksgiving dinner type.

I looked over to Bird who was carrying a large gym bag filled with what I assumed to be a large quantity of cash. I hadn't even noticed the bag on the trip out. He must have hidden it under the passenger bench out of plain sight to avoid the threat of rest stop robbery. He reached in his pocket and slapped a twenty on the counter.

"I'm Bird," he proudly exclaimed assuming his identifier as the scheduled mule might change the tone of the interaction.

"Well no shit," Grizz replied in seeing the #33 Celtics jersey without the slightest indication of humor. "You got the cash?"

"Yeah, right here," Bird replied with an audible strain. The hefted bag of bucks landed on the counter with a slight thud. I could only imagine how much money was in the bag.

"Alright, hang tight and I'll call the loading crew. They'll pick you up and take you and the truck to the prep site," Grizz explained as he made his way back to the rear of the store where I assumed he'd be using the station's office phone to dial up his crew.

Three minutes later, he made his way back to the counter. In that time, I had already scarfed down my twenty dollar Snickers bar and bag of salt and vinegar potato chips. For a second I considered a Pepsi to wash it all down but decided against it in lieu of having to deal with Grizz behind the counter. I couldn't wait to get out of the store. Things were feeling progressively more unsafe by the moment. Even Bird was acting fidgety and nervous, and he had well over a decade in the drug game.

"Alright, they're on their way to pick you up. Be here in five minutes. What are you leaving as collateral?"

"Collateral?" Bird asked a little surprised. He had just blindly handed over what I assumed was well over six figures in cash.

"Yeah, what are you leaving as a deposit to ensure nothin' goes down at the load up?"

"What's the going rate for something like that?" Bird queried.

"Five grand," Griz answered quickly. "Cash".

"Shit man, that bag is all the heavy cash that we have," Bird replied.

"Then I guess your travel buddy stays with me," Grizz instructed.

"Look man, nobody told me anything about collateral," Bird began arguing back.

"He stays with me," Grizz repeated in a serious enough tone that even Bird knew it was the final offer.

My heart sank to my stomach. I did not like at all the idea of staying in this store for five more minutes much less in a multi-hour solo hostage situation with Grizz. I quickly shot a panicked glance over to Bird.

"Then I guess it's a deal," Bird reluctantly agreed, confirming my nightmare was soon to be a reality.

"Alright, you two hang tight while I make a few more calls," Grizz ordered as he picked up the bag of cash and swung it over his shoulder one handed as though it was a pillow. "And if there is any funny business out there, we got problems."

As soon as Grizz left our eyesight, I immediately dug into Bird.

"WHAT. THE. FUCK?" I loudly whispered to Bird. "No WAY I am staying here."

"Look, Bunkie, stay cool and stick with the program and you'll be fine. It's all part of it. Besides, this is a major drug deal, not Enterprise Rent-A-Car. What the fuck did you expect?"

"I didn't fucking expect to be held hostage by psychotic Grizzly Adams!" I continued in a panic. My frantic dialogue inadvertently escalated beyond whisper.

"Listen Micky, play it cool and you'll be fine. I won't let you down, I promise. I'm sorry you have to do this but we don't have another choice. This is what you signed up for."

I remained silent. Bird was right. The only thing we could do given our circumstance was to follow our orders. Even on vacation, I felt like a plebe.

As Grizz stepped behind the counter, the door's entry bell clanged again. Two white males entered the station. One of them was tall and lanky, the other short and squatty. Both of them were wearing baggy jeans, T-shirts untucked, and about twenty grand a piece in gold and diamond jewelry. They looked like a thug life version of Laurel and Hardy. If this had been Ocean City, Bird would have surely chimed in with some colorful commentary. The fact that he didn't only built on the dire gravitas of the situation.

The taller escort patted Bird down and then gave quick thumbs up. The shorter escort stepped in front of Bird. He pulled up his baggy shirt exposing a handgun tucked in the front waste band of his boxers just to let him know it was there.

"A'ight, time to bounce, homey," the lanky escort narrated.

"I got this man, just hang tight," Bird whispered before heading out of the door with his escorts. I heard the diesel engine fire up in the parking lot. They were on their way.

"Have a seat, friend," Grizz ordered as he positioned a folding chair within close proximity to where he was standing behind the counter. As I made my way around the counter, Grizz reached below the register and pulled out a sawed off shotgun.

"Sit tight and this will be over in no time," Griz commented with a smirk. Seeing that I was scared shitless was the first thing that had made him smile since we walked through the door twenty minutes earlier.

It was going to be a long fucking night.

Mick, 0300 hrs.

Cigarette smoke and the poignant stench of cheap perfume had devoured the interior of the gas station convenience store. It was a far cry from the fading aroma of turkey and pecan pie likely lingering back home at Nellie's house. All of the gas station's exterior lighting had been shut down since Bird was escorted out two hours earlier. I remained seated next to Grizz in the folding chair he had originally assigned me. I hadn't said more than three sentences nor budged beyond the effort required to grab my smokes. At this pace, I'd soon have enough Marlboro miles to buy a canoe.

One lone reading lamp behind the counter was our

only luminance in the interior of the now locked and closed convenience store. From the highway several hundred yards away, a casual observer would just assume this shithole was closed and empty for the night. It was not a comforting thought.

"You know, they should make a desert roadkill calendar," randomly mused Grizz. It was his first attempt at small talk in over an hour. "I think I've hit just about every animal in the desert at this point." Ironically, it reminded me of the same type of nonsense Bird used to drone on about. Clearly they smoked the same shit.

"You outta just go make one then," quickly encouraged Grizz's old lady, Marney. By that point in the evening, she had been the store's third occupant for the past hour.

Marney looked like a dragon. Her constant chain smoking had her blowing smoke every time she opened her mouth, even to speak. She looked to be about thirty-eight years past her prime. Her enormous fake breasts were about the only perky thing she had left on what I assumed was a retired stripper's body. She may have been younger than I was giving her credit. It was hard to tell. Hard living has a price.

The initial shock of Bird's unexpected departure calmed down after about thirty minutes. Grizz didn't say much. I surmised he wasn't in the business of making friends. The first hour of silence had me optimistically believing that his silence was more about being socially awkward and less about trying to intimidate me. Once Marney showed up, dressed to the hilt in black leather, a poorly colored blond perm, and shitty perfume, the mood lightened even more. Grizz avoided conversation with me but was a regular chatterbox with his girlfriend. I was slowly lulled into something less than a total panic attack. For a few minutes, I had even forgotten that I was a hostage.

In the last hour, the silence returned and the mood slowly changed. There was intensity in the air. It was exponentially building. Grizz's recent roadkill musings felt much less like small talk and much more like nervous bantering before having to do something unpleasant.

"Make the call," Grizz yelled over to Marney who had since gone to the fridge to grab a fresh Pepsi. He was pacing back and forth out of his chair. The wait had officially become too long.

She dutifully darted towards the back of the store. The immediacy of response was concerning. Marney disappeared into the storage room in the back where I assumed there was a desk and office phone. A few seconds later, I could hear her talking. The door muffled the conversation and I could only guess what dialogue was transpiring on the other end of the door.

The door to the storage space swung open and Marney had an entirely different look on her face. Small talk time had officially passed.

"No word, the boys are on their way," she calmly relayed to Grizz.

"Alright then, go set up the back for when they get here."
I wonder what the hell that means?

Not sure if "the boys" on their way included Bird, and if it did, what condition he was in. Then my mind wandered to scenarios where Bird wasn't in the arriving party. Those ponderings were even grimmer.

I did my best imitation of a statue, honed with months of practice as a plebe. I tried my hardest to not make eye contact with anyone.

Eyes in the boat.

As a mental distraction I tried to count how many blue bags of chips I could spot in the store.

One, two, three, four, five.

I counted silently. The distraction was minimal.

Suddenly a bright flash of light through the store's front windows temporarily illuminated the aisles of sugary junk food, chips, and tchotchkes. The boys had arrived. The lack of diesel engine sound meant Bird was likely not in the group. The door swung open aggressively and two large men entered the room. One was Hispanic and one was African American, both were built like refrigerators. Like the crew that escorted Bird, their general fashion sense included baggie clothes, jewelry, and not-so-concealed firearms. Neither of them looked very jovial at the moment.

My heart was beating at three times its normal pace and intense enough to bust right through my sternum.

"Alright boys, let's do this," Grizz rose from his chair. Before I had a chance to react, I was aggressively accosted by my two new escorts. Each grabbed me by the arm and pulled me roughly out of my chair along their desired path. If I hadn't been walking quickly enough to keep pace, they would have simply swept the floor with me. I was headed to the back storage room. Whatever Marney had prepped for me behind closed doors, I was about to experience it.

My escorts kicked open the door. A warm trickle of

urine soaked the front of my pants and ran down my leg. In the center of the storage room, surrounded by stored boxes of Fritos and air fresheners was a lone metal table. I had seen enough mobster movies in my lifetime to know what was coming my way.

For a split second in a panic, I tried fruitlessly to escape my escort. I caught one by surprise and wrestled an arm free. Before I could figure out what to do with it, my other escort wrangled me in a bear hug and promptly body slammed me on the metal table. My head smacked the back of the table with a loud thud. My adrenaline kept me from getting too woozy in what otherwise would have been a concussed state. I could hear the ripping of duct tape and quickly I was stabilized and incapacitated on the table. Tape was quickly wrapped around my head, chest, arms, and ankles.

"So Mick, I think you are smart enough to know what's going on here," Grizz said sternly. I realized his nervous small talk about roadkill was not about anxiousness, but excitement. Within my peripheral view, he looked like a kid on Christmas morning. He enthusiastically reached into a metal cabinet behind the desk and pulled out a very large, very old set of lock clippers.

"You know, I could sharpen these or just buy a new one, but that wouldn't be much fun," Grizz said putting the rusted blades of the clippers in my face. With my head stabilized in duct tape, I had no choice but to ogle at the nicked and rusted blades. I could hear them squeak as Grizz tried to squeeze the tool out of its rusted, locked position. I imagined it would take someone as strong as Grizz just to cut a paper plate with the well-used instrument.

"Now you are going to tell me what you and your little friend Bird are up to, or I am going to start trimming you up one appendage at a time," Grizz instructed with an heir of pleasant confidence. With the clippers in hand, Grizz was far from the strong silent type he had been for most of the night.

"Look man," I interjected with fearful desperation. "There must be some mistake. PLEASE, I DON'T KNOW ANYTHING, I PROMISE!" I pleaded loudly in tears. Since urinating in my pants a few moments earlier, I was hardly embarrassed about crying like a little girl.

"Rico," Grizz instructed to my Hispanic escort and pointed his finger to the table. "Let's do this. Time to cut up my second turkey of the day."

Rico calmly walked over to where I was bound and immediately grabbed my hand. He forcefully extended my right index finger. I recognized that I was now in a perfect homicide scene within a strategically secluded locale.

"I guess you know where we're gonna start, huh?" Grizz queried sadistically. "Some of that amnesia about Bird goin' away? Now fucking tell me where he is. I won't wait to saw off all ten fingers before we start sawing your balls off there, pee-wee."

"Look man, I'm serious. I know nothing!" I continued frantically begging. I knew it was futile, but I was just trying to do anything possible to buy time. "Bird is a fuck up. I was just along to split up the ride. I don't know a fucking thing. PLEASE stop, I'LL DO ANYTHING YOU WANT!"

"Anything?" Grizz replied with a smirk and a chuckle.

"Man, I sure wish Gay Ramone was here, we could have made his night real interesting!"

"Fuck it, just kill me," I begged. I didn't want to give them any more time for sadistic creativity.

"Nothin'?" Grizz asked one last time. "Alright then, that's how it's gonna be tonight." Grizz tightly gripped the clippers with both hands and squeezed much harder than before. I could see the blood pumping through the protruding veins in his biceps. The instrument squeaked again but remained locked. He grunted in effort for a third attempt.

"FUCK! What the fuck is wrong with these things?" he screamed in disgust before slamming them on the floor.

"I guess we should have been better about cleaning the blood off after using them last time," Rico tried to calm Grizz.

Grizz shot back an angry glare. "Well then get me a fucking knife, dipshit!" Grizz commanded.

I could see Rico exit the room in my peripheral. His hunt for a sharp object might have bought me a few more minutes with my fingers. I prayed he'd find another faulty sharp object. No such luck. Within a few minutes, he returned with a hunting knife I imagined was previously retail merchandise.

"That'll do the trick," Grizz replied.

Rico got back to business and quickly gripped my extended finger while the rest of my hand was pinned down in tape. It was their way of giving me one last feeling of terror before doing the deed.

"PLEASE!" I begged one last time in the midst of hysterical crying.

"Yo Griz, we packed, homey!" I heard muffled behind the door. Grizz stopped within two feet of the table.

"Huh?" he yelled out to the closed door. "Dante, is that you?"

The door swung open. I could hear the diesel engine humming in the parking lot outside. I wanted to lift my head to take in the scene further, but the duct tape kept me solidly in place.

"Yeah, man, all done. Those fucking animal statues were a bitch to weld, man. Took two more hours than anticipated," chimed in who I assumed to be Dante. He had suddenly become my best friend in the whole world.

"Then why the fuck didn't you call or pick up the fucking phone?" Grizz chided.

"Sorry man, I guess we just got caught up in the scramble and forgot," Dante said in his best attempt to excuse himself.

"Yeah, well next time make sure it doesn't happen. Opie over here almost lost a few digits. He's lucky my lock clippers got stuck," Grizz stated.

Grizz then pointed over to Dante, signaling with his hands to cut me loose from the table. Dante quickly grabbed Grizz's unused hunting knife and cut me free from my bondage. "Looks like it's your lucky night, holmes," he muttered as he cut me loose.

In anger, I considered saying something stupid. "Thanks" was all the compromise my good sense could come up with.

"So we're cool?" I cautiously asked Grizz.

Grizz looked me in the eye and then slapped me on the back. "Yeah, we're cool. Just business, ya know?"

"Yeah," I replied and then deeply exhaled, "business." I hopped off the table and returned to the main retail space of the closed convenience store. I was able to recognize Bird's silhouette behind the steering wheel of our now fully loaded truck. I was so relieved he was still alive. I wanted to jump in the car and kill him myself.

"You guys better hit the road," Grizz instructed. "Lots of highway, not much time."

"Yup," I said in a deflated voice. It was hard to muster up anything more enthusiastic than that given he had just moments earlier come inches away from cutting off critical body parts. I stormed out of the front door without saying anything else. I hoped it would be the last time I would see anyone in that store.

I hopped on our truck's running boards and swung open the passenger door.

"Hey Bunkie, ready to roll?" Bird yelled with a wide grin from the driver's seat. It was the only way to hear him above the increasingly loud engine.

I sat down and looked forward without acknowledging his presence. The Nevada desert felt a long way from Ocean City.

Mick, 0655 hrs.

"Hey Bunkie, wake up," Bird shook my incapacitated body in the passenger seat. "Almost time for your shift." Gentle nudges for wake ups were pointless three days into our journey. As the sun rose in the Nevada desert, it brought with it a visual sign of a new day. Bird was just finishing his driving shift and our morning's first tank of gas.

I stretched and rubbed the sand in my eyes. I had slept hard despite only being out for a handful of hours. My clothes stuck to my sweat covered body. I was so tired that I didn't immediately remember what had happened back at the gas station mere hours before.

The memory quickly rebooted in my brain. I temporarily wished it had all been a nightmare. As I wiped the morning clamminess from my forehead, I could feel the remaining glue left behind by the duct tape. Then I smelled the dried urine on my pants. The night before had unfortunately been very real.

I hadn't fully disclosed to Bird the full details of my night with Grizz and his crew. Part of me never wanted to retell it. I knew if I had last night, Bird would have either done something really stupid to retaliate or lectured me about how this is what I signed up for. Neither of those scenarios was more appealing than just grabbing some sleep as soon as I was physically able. Despite having a near-death and near-neutered experience pumping adrenaline through my veins, it took all but twenty minutes for me to close my eyes and get some sleep when Bird and I finally hit the road in the wee hours of Friday morning.

The rising desert sun provided an illuminated view of the Nevada wasteland. It looked like a sunward facing surface of Mars. The desert was a harsh place, in more ways than one. What minimal life existed in the cold, hard sand had to fight daily just to stay alive. There was something relatable to it given the last five months of life.

My conflict of emotions hadn't resolved with sleep. On the one hand, I was still quite angry with Bird. On the other, it was hard not to see the silver lining. We were both still alive. My fingers and balls were intact. My unresolved emotions helped distract my outright panic that we were barreling westward across Route 80 with an unbeknownst to me amount and variety of illegal drugs. It was like hitting my hand with a hammer to distract me from the pain of a broken leg.

"Man, I feel like I have been staring at those mountains for hours now, and I don't feel any closer to them," Bird broke the morning silence trying to generate enough small talk to wake me up.

I continued my study of the referenced horizon. Utah's Salt Lake looked like it had suddenly migrated west of its barrier mountain ranges. The rising sun had brought with it massive mirages.

As we hit the western outskirts of Salt Lake City, we finally stopped for gas.

"Alright man, gotta move quick," Bird instructed as he pulled into the rest top gas station. "Sitting ducks are eventually dead ducks."

We both exited the car with a stumble. Our legs were getting progressively deader with each subsequent gas stop. We'd need crutches by the time we hit the east coast. Bird headed into the store to pay cash for the gas and load up our dwindling food supply.

"I'm heading to the bathroom," I said to Bird once he exited the store with a bag full of beef jerky and caffeinated beverages. I left my watch station at the pump and jumped into the passenger cabin to grab my toothbrush.

"Micky, put on your uniform," Bird suggested before I had the chance to exit the truck. "We may need it."

The thought of wearing a military uniform for the remaining eastward portion of the drive was an unpleasant one. One of the many simple plebe pleasures of Thanksgiving leave was the opportunity to wear civilian clothes after not being permitted to since I-Day. Normally I would have protested, but it was one of the few trip planning elements I had contributed. My logic was that a police officer would be more likely to cut us a break if I was in uniform. It was admittedly a stretch, but I was willing to do anything that incrementally enhanced our chances of not getting caught. I reached back into the truck to dutifully grab my service dress blues.

After a bath in the sink, and a scrub of my fangs, I was back in uniform. I was a Navy man in the middle of the desert, literally and figuratively.

Chapter 22

Curtis
Sunday, November 26th, 1995
Mick, 0115 hrs.

It took most of Friday and Saturday, but after a few rounds of catnaps and a full two days of driving, Bird and I were back on amicable terms. The silent boredom of that much driving had made conversation a necessary element of our sanity.

"Man, it's hard to believe that it's been a decade since I was in school," Bird verbally pondered in the early morning hours of Sunday. We reminisced over various mutual acquaintances of Decatur High School. Decatur was Ocean City proper's only public high school. Though I did not graduate from there myself, I spent enough time surfing with Bird that I at least felt like an honorary alumni.

Bird's recollection of graduation had been a year off. He had only been nine years removed from graduation. The road and exhaustion was playing tricks on our minds. An hour earlier, I had momentarily recollected our three days of prior driving, even though it had been four. We were exhausted to the point of delirium. Even our ability to perform simple mental mathematics was compromised at this stage in the journey.

Despite our malfunctioning brains, optimism increased with every state's eastward departure. In jaunting along Interstate 80 East, I had taken on the practice of imagining how I would interact with the local prison population of each and every state we passed through. In the distance, the Ohio border became visible. Well-lit tollbooths dominated the otherwise black horizon. I mentally postured what hardened criminals from Cleveland might be like to bunk with.

Clunk, clank, clunk, psssst, buzzzzzzzz.

The warning buzz immediately snapped me out of my prison fantasies. From my passenger seat view, the yellow check engine light was immediately caught in my peripheral. My eyes scanned slightly right on the dash noticing the truck's sudden overheating. Thick black smoke precipitously poured out from under the hood. I was back to contemplating Indiana thug life behind bars.

"MotherFUCKER!" I cursed from the passenger seat. Bird remained silent, but quickly started biting his fingernails as he slowly guided the smoking truck off the next exit. He looked for the most visually concealed parking spot on the road's shoulder. I knew he was just as nervous as I was. It made me feel infinitely worse.

In the first hours of Sunday morning, Bird and I found ourselves stranded in the easternmost stretch of Indiana. We sat on the road's shoulder helplessly beside our broken down mule. We had quickly exited the truck as soon as it stopped in fear that it might explode.

After nearly four straight days of barreling across the

country with little incident, the elderly diesel engine decided to cry uncle. Just about a mile away from the Ohio border, we were sitting ducks.

Once we stopped on the shoulder of the off-ramp, it took the engine nearly an hour just to stop smoking. Bird and I sat on the side of the road, safely outside of our perceptions of a potential blast zone. We were freezing our asses off. Bird and I traded my service dress blues jacket as our only source of extra warmth. My back ached from my violent shivering.

We both kept our eyes on the hood, praying not to see flames. The potential warmth of fire was a very tempting yet still unwanted comfort. Though Nellie had long been a card carrying AAA member, a tow truck to haul our illegal cargo to the local repair shop was not a feasible option. Luckily the threat of detection with all lights off in morning darkness was minimal. Bird had wisely left off the truck's hazard lights.

It didn't take us long to realize that neither of us knew a thing about fixing overworked, mid-eighties era diesel engines. For about the first seven minutes and forty-five seconds after popping the hood and grabbing a flashlight, we tried our best to fake it. After futilely pulling on loose hoses and tightening fuel caps that we thought were suspect, all we had to show for our efforts was Bird's severely scolded left palm. We quickly realized that we needed either a really good mechanic or an escape plan into the woods before daylight broke. Bird had me pull all personal items out of the passenger cabin while he wiped down fingerprints in case we needed to make a quick escape from the police. I had begun wearing a divot on the pavement below with my frantic pacing. Time was ticking back in Annapolis.

Bird wracked his brain for phone numbers of anyone that knew anything about engines back home. I went on a quick foot journey looking for a pay phone. After a ten-minute walk farther along the exit ramp, I finally spotted a dilapidated phone booth in a closed Burger King parking lot. Lifting the phone from its hanging position, l sighed in relief as I heard a dial tone.

I eventually made my way back to Bird to share the somewhat good news. In my temporary absence, he had been passing time throwing rocks at a metal road sign. I could hear the metallic "ting" of rock hitting the sign several paces before I was close enough to see what had been causing it. After twenty minutes of criticizing the stupidity of the hobby, and two unsuccessful attempts to restart the engine, I reluctantly joined in Bird's game. Within twenty minutes, I was hitting the road sign on every third throw. Bird grew tired of losing and returned his mind to his mental search for mechanics.

"Guess I'll just have to call Curtis," Bird said after thirty minutes of panicked boredom.

I'd only met Curtis on one prior occasion. It had been so long before that I had totally forgotten he knew anything about cars. He was one of Bird's few friendly acquaintances from his prior prison stint several years earlier. Curtis' reputation as Ocean City's only skin head, accentuated by a swastika neck tattoo and a healthy criminal record, had relegated him to working as an un-certified mechanic twenty miles from the shore in the rural town of Pittsville.

Back in prison, Bird made quick friends with anyone

or any gang, regardless of how despicable their dogma, that offered him protection behind bars. White supremacy was about the only feasible option for a five foot seven, white, surfing, drug dealer from the beach. After being provided protection for his term, a few years later Bird honored a promise outside the pen to teach a newly freed Curtis how to surf. The one time we all went out together on a light day in Assateague, Curtis stepped in horseshit, got tumbled by a few bigger than average sets, and was back to the parking lot before the niceties of goodbyes. That was the first, last, and only time I ever met Curtis. As a teenager, he scared the shit out of me. I wasn't necessarily thrilled Bird was associating with him again, even for engine advice. It was the last hope we had.

Out of the darkness, Bird returned to the truck after making his phone call in the Burger King parking lot. He quickly opened the driver door and popped the front latch for one more look under the hood. I just sat on the road's shoulder, not wanting to get too interested or get my hopes too high.

After hearing some fiddling for a few minutes, the hood slammed back down. Bird quickly returned to the passenger cabin. With the turn of the ignition key, the engine sputtered and then miraculously turned over. We were back in business.

"CUUUUUURRRRRTIS!" Bird screamed at the top of his lungs. "My fucking MAN!"

I silently hopped in the cabin, still worriedly listening to the rattling engine and hoping that it would stay running for the next half a day of driving we had left. Formation back at the academy was about twelve hours away.

Mick, 0505 hrs.

"Why didn't you just call Curtis in the first fucking place?" I asked Bird. When he didn't answer, I figured he was being intentionally aloof. He was instead sleeping like a baby in the passenger seat. He must have passed out shortly after smoking his road joint five minutes earlier. He looked comical as the joint's cigarette chaser remained in his mouth even while sleeping. The last ashes of the cigarette found a final resting place on his lucky #33 jersey.

We barreled forward through Ohio trying to make up whatever time we could from our morning's delay. Engine be damned, I was going to put forth our best effort.

The engine's exhaustion had grown exponentially more audible since our breakdown, especially when climbing even the modest hills of Ohio. I had resorted to flat out pedal to the metal just to stay moving as quickly as possible. I stopped looking at the speedometer as the engine struggled just to keep pace with the morning's flow of returning holiday traffic. With every slight incline, the truck wheezed in protest.

In my temporary solitude, I struggled to remain conscious. Caffeine and nicotine had long since lost their efficacy. I resorted to plucking out my own nose hairs. The short burst of pain was just enough to rally my senses for a few minutes before I repeated the cycle.

My eyes remained singularly focused on the turnpike ahead. I could not tell whether my tunnel vision was driven by this focus, or if I was merely losing a fight against passing out. All I could see was the white dividing lines of my lane. I plucked another nose hair and then violently slapped my own face. I looked in the rearview mirror and could see a red handprint left behind.

Suddenly a blue and red light reflected in my driver's side mirror.

"FUCK! Bird, wake up, man. It's the cops!" I violently shook Bird as his cigarette and remaining ashes tumbled to the floor. He looked at me as though he had never seen me before. Getting out of his deep sleep at this stage of the drive was a process.

"Dude, it's the cops. Wake up, man!" I frantically continued my impromptu wake up call. Suddenly his eyes widened once the dialogue finally processed in his brain.

"Oh . . . shit!" Bird blurted in a panic. "Don't pull over right away, I need you to stall for another thirty seconds, man."

I dropped my speed down to thirty miles per hour and then deliberately swerved slowly over to the shoulder. Bird frantically scrambled through the cabin in the extra few seconds I bought him. First spraying about a half of can of air freshener in the cabin to get the smell of recently smoked weed out of the car. The stench of the car alone may have masked the scent. Next, he grabbed under the seat bench, pulled out a three ring binder, began frantically flipping through their pages.

"What are you doing, man?" I asked perplexed by the binder. He quickly clicked it open and pulled out a couple of documents.

"Alibi, Bunkie," he calmly replied without taking his

eyes off his search. "Quick, throw your uniform jacket on."

I stopped the truck and put it in park. I quickly fastened my top shirt button, tightened my tie, and finally grabbed my service dress blue jacket off the floor. It was a wrinkled mess with several stains and covered in cigarette ashes. I did my best to brush it off. I noticed the pin cap on the back of my ribbons had fallen off during the ride. Though I couldn't see it, I could feel the sharp point digging into my skin through my shirt.

"Alright, let me do most of the talking here," Bird said.

I could see the abnormally tall and slender state trooper approach the car. He was in winter gear but maintained the authoritative look of a drill instructor. With the "Smokey the Bear" trooper hat on his head and well-heeled jack boots, he looked to be about seven foot tall. His height allowed him to peer his dark brown eyes directly into the passenger cabin without looking up or having to utilize the truck's running boards. My heart rate had jumped up twenty percent with each pace closer to the truck. By the time I rolled down the window to address the officer, my heart was pounding through my chest.

"Good morning, officer. What seems to be the problem, sir?" I asked with the same reverence and decorum I typically offered my senior officers.

"Mornin', gents. I'm Officer First Class French. Could you please grab your license and registration?" he initiated his dialogue with a cold and authoritative tone as I scrambled to gather the requested materials.

I panicked when it dawned on me that the registration was very likely not in my name. Our truck was at best a borrowed if not outright stolen vehicle. I just prayed that

Bird had something forged in his name and that Officer French hadn't run our plates yet. Even if we were not immediately caught, a truck full of illegal drugs would not bode well in a police impound lot. Quickly, Bird handed me what I assumed was a forged registration slip. It was one of two pieces of paper he had been holding after scrambling through his binder. Officer French grabbed the document along with my license and military identification.

"Any idea why I'm pulling you over today?" he continued. I could tell by the sullen expression on his face that he was hardly happy to be working on a Sunday of a holiday weekend. He had already begun inspecting the registration.

"No, sir. I must have been distracted thinking about heading back to base today," I explained. "Kind of bummed my leave is over." It was the best excuse I could come up with.

"A Navy man, huh?" French lifted his eyes from the registration document. "I'm an Army grunt myself, not sure you want to hear my opinion of squids," he continued. His slight smirk was one that I had seen many times before. It was hard to decipher as either a sign of him softening or simply just being an arrogant prick. It was the same vibe I often received from upper-class midshipmen.

Bird was fidgety and looking to jump in the conversation right away. His leg shook vigorously from his seated position. I could tell he was getting annoyed by my excessive talking.

"Did you notice the construction zone you guys just drove through back there?" French continued. "Not only were you driving an oversized vehicle illegally in the passing lane, but you were doing twelve over the restricted speed limit in a double fine zone."

"I apologize, officer. I must have still been waking up," I continued with my own feeble alibi. It was total improvisation. Bird looked primed and ready with his alibi in hand, the second documentation he must have pulled from his binder.

"So what is a Navy man doing in land locked Ohio," French continued loosening up a bit as his eyes moved back towards our registration documentation.

"Took him with me to Chicago," Bird leaned in towards the driver's side window and interjected himself into the conversation before I had the chance to continue. "I had to run this cargo into Chicago for some specialty maintenance on some boardwalk equipment. Mick here tagged along for the ride to visit his college girlfriend while on Thanksgiving break from the Naval Academy. Cheap bastard wouldn't pay for a plane ticket."

"The academy, huh?" French chimed in. "Good lord, you definitely don't want to know what I think about ring knockers."

I tried my best to feign a chuckle. Deep down I wanted to let him know that he could go fuck himself.

"What boardwalk you coming from? Ohio seems like a long way from the ocean." French pulled back into his professional tone.

"Ocean City, Maryland," Bird quickly replied. "I have some antique rides in the back that needed specialty maintenance. I guess you could say that I took some of the boardwalk with me."

My mind was spinning on whether he really did have rides in the back stashed with drugs.

"No kidding," French replied. "I have been taking my kids to Ocean City for years. I love that boardwalk."

"Yeah, it's pretty great," Bird kept the dialogue's momentum moving forward. It was the first true thing he had offered.

"You guys go to Phillip's much?" French asked.

"Only every week!" Bird lied yet again. He hated that tourist trap. It was so convincing that I almost believed him.

"My family loves that place. All you can eat crabs. It's an annual tradition," French stated. "What rides you got in the back?"

My heart jumped to my throat.

"Why don't I open it up and give you a look," Bird said. I almost vomited right there in the driver's seat.

"That's okay, I'm not that interested," the officer said, thankfully not calling Bird's bluff. Bird had made a calculated yet successful gamble.

Bird handed him the paper he had been saving. "Every few years I have to take a few of the Merry-Go-Round animals to a specialty repair store in Chicago. Those animals are virtually priceless and there are only a handful of outfits that actually know how to refurbish them correctly."

"Farmer Amusements, Chicago, Illinois," French read aloud. "That's pretty cool. My daughters love that ride."

"Yeah, technically I'm supposed to be driving the whole way. Truth is that I tied one on pretty good last night while lover boy over here blew his cousin off for a night with his girlfriend," Bird proceeded spinning his web. "The truck's registration is in my name, but I needed a few hours of rest to sleep off this pounding headache."

"That's typical for a Navy guy," French quipped with a chuckle and then handed back our forged registration. "Next rest stop, why don't you switch back out and let this squid stick to driving ships. You guys have a great day."

With that French headed back to his vehicle and I let out the biggest sigh of relief of my life.

"Bird, that was some Jedi mind trick shit," I complimented in utter awe.

"Told you just to let me do the talking, Bunkie," Bird confidently whispered with a smile.

"The Merry-Go-Round, eh?" I said not able to resist the temptation of the query.

"The less you know, the better," Bird returned an expected response.

He slapped my back and I turned the ignition key. It fired up on the first pull. Things were definitely looking up.

Part VI

Paul Revere

Chapter 23

Boardwalk Reconciliation
Saturday, May 31st, 1980
Nellie, 3:10 p.m.

Cigarette in hand, I scrambled through my purse to find my lighter. It was an archeological dig through a pile of shit. Christ, I needed a smoke.

"Hey kiddo, you seen my light?" I quickly asked my eleven-year-old son. We were both frantically pacing down the boardwalk. Three blocks to go and we were already ten minutes late.

"Didn't you quit smoking?" he replied starting to huff from the physical exertion. He was pudgier than most kids. His asshole father had teased him about it constantly. I wasn't about to start.

"Larry, Mom's quit enough these days, smoking just ain't gonna be one of 'em. Not today," I replied trying to mask the annoyance of my tone. Booze and my ex-husband had been hard enough to stick through.

He looked up in silence.

"Well?" I prodded an answer. His poker face needed work, I could see the guilt as clear as day.

"I used it to light some firecrackers the other day and left it in my room," he explained sheepishly.

"Christ, Larry, you shouldn't be taking my stuff without asking," I replied with much less masking of my irritation. I was about to continue the lecture on the dangers of fireworks but stopped short. Scolding him on that would have only dared him to do it again in spite. In that way, along with the ginger hair, he was just like his father. I hated that Larry reminded me of Joe. I loved the shit out of him regardless.

As we drew near, I could see my sister Barb. Her permed curly blond hair was striking, even from a distance. She had always been the "pretty one." My nerves were fueling my cig craving. I found the first smoker I could find loitering on the boardwalk.

"Hey, I don't mean to bug you, but do you gotta light?" I asked the twenty-something leaning on the boardwalk rail across from the famous Ocean Gallery art superstore. He was hardly James Dean but the tautness of his Journey T-shirt had me wondering what it would look like crumpled on my bedroom floor. It had been way too long since I had been with a man.

"Sure thing," he replied in an exhale of smoke.

Before I could shamelessly hit on him, I could feel Larry's disapproving stare in the background. It wasn't the cigarettes he was objecting. Firecrackers or men, we both had our vices.

I puffed on the spark and exhaled in deep relief. "Thanks, hon," I replied and then turned before Larry killed the romance any further. I gave my new friend a flirtatious smile to let him know I was interested. Maybe

I'd catch him later when Larry was preoccupied in the arcade.

"C'mon, Mom, we're late."

"ALRIGHT! God, give your mother a break," I snapped before instantly feeling bad about it. Larry had been through enough. We all had. I took another deep drag of my vice. It didn't really help.

With one block to go, I panicked.

"Larry, I need to use the little girls' room, I'll be out in a sec," I narrated my excuse as I quickly handed my son a crumpled dollar bill in my purse and headed to the boardwalk's lone public restroom facility. "Go play some Space Invaders in the Fun City Arcade, and I'll meet you inside."

Admittedly, it was a lame excuse.

"C'mon, Mom, ya gotta grow a pair!" he tried his best to egg me on. As usual, he was much more aware than I typically gave him credit. The last few years stole what little innocence that might've been left in a typical fifth grade boy.

I took one last drag of my smoke and flicked it to the splintered boardwalk below.

"Stop being a litterbug, Ma," he preached again.

"Like I said, kiddo, I've quit enough these days. C'mon, let's go."

It had been just about four years since I had last seen my sister face to face. Despite our ten year age difference Barbara and I had been close most of our lives with rare exception. My time with degenerate ex-husband Joe, Larry's biological father, and an endless pit of destructive behavior, was that exception.

Joe had an uncanny ability to fuck up everything good

in my life. He met the naïve fantasies of my former twenty-year-old self. I was a girl desperate for attention and any deviation away from my likely path towards small town life. He was handsome and in a band. What can I say, he was hard to quit.

One minute Joe was buying me flowers. The next minute he was pissing our money away on gambling or drunkenly getting arrested for being an asshole. Every now and then, he would rough me up as a way to vent his frustration. Over time, he slowly began to realize what everyone else viewed as painfully obvious. His music career was wishful thinking at best. The building defeat left me all the more black and blue.

Dad hadn't heard about Joe's abuse until the day after our wedding. Two years of courtship outwardly seemed like a bliss. I was young. I thought we were in love. I wasn't too keen on hanging around the house or sharing my apprehensions with my family. The last thing I wanted was judgement. My sister told my dad about Joe's violence on our wedding day. It was more in spite than in help. I had it coming. I had been a shitty sister back then. The revelation prompted a fistfight between Dad and Joe on the front lawn hours before we were headed to our Niagara Falls honeymoon later that day. Like a barrel on the falls, it all went downhill from there and eventually shattered in a rocky mess.

The tipping point came a few years later when, against Joe's strongest wishes, I named our son Lawrence after my father. If he hadn't been too drunk to stand in the delivery room, maybe he would have convinced me otherwise. I was glad he didn't.

Seven years later in 1976, Dad was on the downward stretch of a three-year battle with colon cancer. Sensing the end was near everyone in the family paid their final homage to our family's patriarch. Barb drove in from out of town eight months pregnant, eventually giving birth to her son two weeks later. I was the last to say goodbye that day. I had been arguing with Joe all week over his refusal to see my dying father. No amends or closure would be made. When I finally showed to the hospital, I had a black eye and had been so high on drugs I was barely coherent. Dad died an hour later. Barb assumed of a broken heart. After the funeral, we spent the rest of the seventies apart.

About a year after Dad's death, I came to my senses and kicked Joe to the curb. It took a few times to finally stick. Barb, in resentment for what happened with Dad, kept her distance. Whiskey and prescription pills became my crutch to lean on. A few years later, I sobered up. Little Larry lost his innocence long before he should have. It was the cause of many a late night phone call to my sponsor.

Nellie, 3:45 p.m.

I stepped in front of the stroller beside my sister Barb. She must have been sitting there for at least a half an hour. I was surprised she hadn't already left. I wouldn't have blamed her. Upon Larry's unconventional encouragement, I mustered up enough gumption to walk the extra block from the arcade. It took a few seconds for her to recognize me. I was heavier, older, defeated. I was still a mess.

"Barb, I'm . . ." I tried my best to find words but my tears overtook me. "I'm, I'm . . . sooo sorry." It was all I could muster as I eventually erupted in sobs before she could even rise from the bench.

"I know, I know," she responded with an embrace. My emotional onslaught was not intentional. "Me too," she continued softly.

I shook in her arms like a scared child. I could feel her shoulders rise in our embrace as she took in a deep breath. I could taste the salt in the tears running down her cheek as our faces rubbed against each other. Full forgiveness would certainly take more than this, but it was a start.

Eventually our embrace ended. I could only imagine what the tourists on the boardwalk were thinking of the blubbery shit show. It would have made much more sense to invite her to our house, but I was still too ashamed to have her over to the crappy doublewide a few miles down the road in the rural outskirts of Berlin. It was all I could afford and I barely took care of it.

"And who's this little guy?" I said wiping the tears off my puffy cheeks. In all of the chaos, I had forgotten to acknowledge the one family member I hadn't met yet.

"This handsome little man is my son, Jimmy. Jimmy McGee," Barb said proudly.

"He is so handsome!" I replied in a crackling voice. Despite the blond bowl haircut, damn if he wasn't the spitting image of Dad. I started crying again. The little boy must have thought I was some type of lunatic. His eyes said as much.

"Larry, meet your new first cousin, Jimmy McGee," I

joyfully exclaimed to my son. He had been a good sport about all of this. I'm sure he would have preferred to be back home lighting illegal fireworks.

"Why don't you introduce yourself, sweetie," Barbara prodded her toddler. "Introduce yourself to your cousin, Jimmy."

God she loves to show off. For once, let her.

"Jim . . .ME . . . Mick . . . GEE," Barbara continued her encouragement.

"Jim . . . mmmee," the small boy followed along. Barbara continued the encouragement "Mick . . ."

"Mick . . . gee . . . Mc . . . gee." The toddler did his best to mimic his mom. He was a total pleaser.

"How's it goin, Micky?" Larry said before snorting loudly and spitting a large wad of phlegm on the boardwalk.

Chapter 24

Bonfire
Sunday, November 26th, 1995
Mick, 1430 hrs.

I stared intently at the spider webs in the ceiling's corner. I had been at this practice for well over an hour atop a tattered tweed couch that smelled of skunked beer. Despite my exhaustion, I was too hopped up on nerves and caffeine pills to sleep.

Bird and Farm were back to normal routine. They played Tecmo Bowl on the opposite couch on a well-used Nintendo Entertainment System that had likely been a midshipman's Chirstmas present nearly a decade earlier.

"Man, that's bullshit. No way Lawrence Taylor can block every goddamned extra point," Farm moaned. It was a complaint I had heard a thousand times before. Bird tried to respond but was interrupted by a monstrous yawn.

Bird and I had made our way to our second major stopping point. As promised, Gonzo had met Farm and Yogi earlier in the day. Farm figured that since he wasn't driving a car loaded with drugs that it somehow made driving Yogi on a suspended license less illegal in the eyes of a cop.

Go figure that fucking logic.

In the past hour, we had all collectively rendezvoused at our "staging house." It was a ransacked ranch home a few blocks away from Pinky's liquor store in West Annapolis.

Annapolis was a largely affluent town. Outside of the waterfront areas, however, there were numerous less prosperous neighborhoods. These areas scattered throughout the city were largely minority occupied, save a few cheap rental units. Those more than affordable rental units were the lifeblood of illegal Naval Academy inhabitation of the city. Though not permitted, groups of mids would routinely pool in to one of the many cheap rental units scattered throughout the city as a place to escape the Naval Academy on the weekend. They were typically the epicenter of sexual and alcohol activity, or so I had heard. I did not understand, however, how Gonzo had gained access to such a place. He had mentioned a friend of a friend scenario. The story smelled like bullshit. I was too tired to call him on it.

Upon arrival, Bird and I were immediately met by Gonzo and a group of four men in their twenties. They were introduced to us as cousins. The men were dressed in rather unassuming street clothes. None of them had a military haircut nor did they look remotely Puerto Rican. They certainly lacked visible resemblance to Gonzo. I again resolved that I was too tired to ask questions.

I had spoken very little to Gonzo and his crew since arriving. When we first showed up, we made small talk for a few minutes. Caught up in the buzz of making the truck drive safely to Annapolis, I retold my near castration from my new friend Grizz in Nevada. Gonzo eventually took the truck from us and positioned it in the back of the driveway towards the stand-alone backyard garage. Bird and I were immediately sequestered into the home's living room at the front of the house where Farm had already been playing Nintendo. Bird and Farm, like me, were no longer part of the plan for this stage of the scheme. Though Gonzo left a "cousin" behind to keep us company, his demeanor made us feel like he was more likely there to stand watch. It was apparent that the mantra of "the less you know the better" was not exclusive to my part in the plot. I was surprised Bird never raised a protest to this. I imagined he was just happy to have made the eastward mule trip without incident.

The plan moving forward was a not so simple bait and switch plot. At our current location, we'd take the drugs from the truck and stash them in Yogi. Then Gonzo and I would head for the yard with my drug-packed ride. Once Gonzo and I got Yogi on the yard, assuming we could pull it off, we'd switch the stash from my car to the trunk of Smitty's newly bought yellow Corvette. We knew he'd be on the yard all day given the impending drug raid scheduled for later in the afternoon. Gonzo had already stolen Smitty's car keys and made a spare weeks earlier. Bird would pull the then empty box truck to the sting location where Smitty would also be heading once the brigade had officially reformed from Thanksgiving leave at 1800 formation. Gonzo had heard this part of the sting's plot during his night in the laundromat eavesdropping on Smitty. We were betting on the likelihood that Smitty would not check his trunk on the car ride over to the sting. The cops would likely swarm Bird's empty truck intentionally parked by Smitty's less than stealth bright yellow 'vette. The K-9 unit would swarm Bird's truck only to be distracted by the redirected dogs sniffing the relocated payload in Smitty's ride. Bird would have an alibi as to why he parked by the sting. Smitty would be left getting pinched for something he had already been busted for.

"Serves a rat right," was a mantra justified over and over in my head.

It was a half-assed scheme, but it was the same one that convinced me to take this journey. I had been bought into it for a week. I wasn't stopping to question it.

For the past hour, Gonzo and his crew had been busy at work. They focused their efforts in the weathered backyard garage. I had garnered this intel on a few sly trips to the bathroom and a few quick glances through the blinds of the room's window on the driveway side of the house. Gonzo and his crew had Yogi stashed in the garage interior while the box truck's raised cargo door directly faced the open garage for quick payload transition into my car.

"Alright, Micky," Gonzo said as he remained in his civilian clothes two hours into our stint in the living room. "Get your uniform on, it's time to roll." It was time.

My palms glazed over with sweat as I heard the diesel engine fire up one last time from the side of the house. Within minutes, I was in my uniform and headed out to Yogi. Bird and Farm followed closely behind and prepared to assume their next duty in the box truck. Not knowing how all of this might turn out, I suddenly began to worry if this might be the last time I would see Bird for a while.

Bird quickly approached me and embraced me with a strong bear hug. It was something he rarely did.

"I love you, Jimmy," Bird said in the embrace, something I had never heard from him.

There was no cheek bite hard enough to hold back the tears streaming down my face. I had already lost my dad.

Mick, 1605 hrs.

The Gate 1 traffic was still decidedly light considering we were just two hours shy of expired liberty. Most mids were smart enough to delay their return to the yard from leave until after 5 p.m. All ranks wanted to avoid Mother B for as long as humanly possible.

By the time Gonzo drove Yogi into the line waiting for Gate 1 access, we had only a two car line ahead of us. I was in the odd position of passenger within the stalwart Yogi, just as I had been five months earlier on I-Day. The feeling of dreadful anticipation was eerily similar despite being contrived under entirely different circumstance. Gonzo sat behind the wheel without a bead of visible sweat. If he was stressed by the situation, he wasn't showing it.

I sat in the passenger seat in full uniform. While my service dress blues were hardly in as bad of a condition as they had been hours earlier with Officer French, I was still looked like shit. Gonzo was still disguised in civilian garb. His incognito approach was effective. His look sans uniform was decidedly older. Even people in our company would have difficulty recognizing him dressed in jeans and a burgeoning beard well past a 5 o'clock shadow.

Yogi was not a registered military vehicle, a requirement of any midshipman driving on the yard. DoD base stickers on the windshield were the accessory to have as a mid. Their possession was a privilege only afforded to 2nd and 1st class mids. Plebes weren't allowed to drive on the yard, nor were they allowed to wear civilian clothes. Even if we hadn't been transporting drugs onto base, mere association with Gonzo's transgressions would have been enough to get us all fried and placed on restriction with N.D.

The red brake lights of the Mustang ahead of us flicked off as the gate guard waved another guest onto the yard.

"Just zip it and let me do the talking," Gonzo ordered with a look of gravitas in his eyes. It wasn't the first time I had heard that.

"Good afternoon, sir, where ya headed to today?" the gate guard mechanically asked in the same robotic manner he questioned every car in line.

"Just takin' my cuz back to the yard," Gonzo explained. "This homey here is my cousin. Just bringing him back from Baltimore."

"Can I see your license, please?" the guard quickly requested, annoyed that he even had to ask.

Fuck.

"Yeah, here ya go," Gonzo obliged and quickly offered his license.

The guard looked at the license as though he was studying it for a test later in the day. He bent it to ensure its legitimacy and then read it a second time just to confirm he didn't miss any important details. Gonzo stuck his hand out of the driver's side window, non-verbally trying to rush the evaluation.

"So it looks like your license is from Virgina, but you have Maryland tags," the guard calmly observed with an heir of arrogant authority. The gate guards, with minimal military clout, relished any opportunity to exert a position of power.

I could feel my feet swimming in nervous sock sweat.

"Sorry about that, sir," Gonzo quickly replied. "It's my fault. I don't want to get my cousin into any sort of trouble. I was just driving my cousin's car and giving him a ride in return for a quick tour of the yard. Sad to say it, but his car is nicer than mine. Here is his registration." Gonzo quickly shoved my registration out of the car window.

Gee thanks. Now they know exactly who owns the car full of illegal drugs.

Like Officer French, the guard blew off review of any further documentation. I don't know if he was just being lazy or he felt bad for the guy that had a vehicle less appealing than a brown '86 Oldsmobile Celebrity. With a flick of the wrist, we were waved on. Gonzo slowly accelerated Yogi through the gate and we had officially smuggled drugs onto the yard. The successful entry did little to calm my nerves.

Once we were far enough away from the gate guard to hear the celebration, Gonzo exhaled deeply and then added, "*Whew*, that was close." He tapped his fingers on the steering wheel in a celebratory drum roll.

We pulled Yogi into the fifth wing parking lot just between Bancroft and Luce Hall. On the way to my drop off point, we could spot Smitty's car across the parade field.

"Alright, Wonderbread, you remember the plan. I'll stash the goods over there," Gonzo pointed to Smitty's car while he continued his mastery of the situation. "You go upstairs and keep an eye on Smitty. I suspect he will be in his room trying to stay cool and out of sight. He should be there until after formation. If he bolts early, you follow. If he heads to the car, get there faster. If all goes well, I'll see you upstairs before 1800 formation."

I obliged with a tip of the hat. I grabbed my lightly packed bag out of the backseat. It still reeked of cigarettes. If you sniffed closely enough I'm sure you could still smell the weed. Quickly, I entered Bancroft's fifth wing through the basement. Whizzing past the cobbler shop, I hustled up to our top floor room, squaring my corners all the way. My relief of our temporarily safe passage was quickly supplemented by fear of getting flamed for my sub-standard uniform. I'm sure there were upperclassmen just waiting to pounce on that.

"Go Navy, Sir, Beat Army, Sir," I belted out with each turn. I had finally arrived back to the yard just as Army Navy week was kicking off. All the while I wondered if I would be around long enough to see the game.

Mick, 1810 hrs.

As I frantically jogged past Triton Light, I was too pre-occupied and exhausted to gaze longingly across the bay to the Eastern Shore. Beneath the veil of evening darkness,

I struggled to keep pace with Gonzo. In an entire Plebe Summer together, I had never seen him move as fast in a blue-rimmed T-shirt and a pair of go-fasters.

Gonzo and I had made it through post-vacation formation and immediately changed into our PT gear. Gonzo had long since dropped the civilian clothes and the beard before he came back up to our floor for formation. He was back to looking like a slightly overweight plebe.

The frenetic energy of Army Navy week coupled with the close proximity of winter break provided a great distraction for our schemes. Smitty was right on plan and did not head out to his car until well after Gonzo had returned from his clandestine cargo loading.

After formation, Gonzo had the two of us excused from evening meal with a phony chit. It was some load of crap related to setting up an Army Navy week display on behalf of the Mothers Against Drunk Driving. Gonzo knew at least fifty plebes would show up for this volunteer opportunity given the offer of free pizza. He figured it would be nearly impossible to prove we lied and ditched given the likely lack of a muster or roll call.

Gonzo and I jogged amidst an eerily quiet yard. The rest of the brigade was occupied with the first Army Navy week meal in King Hall that we ditched. We had about thirty minutes to do what we needed to do. Everything was going as planned.

"Come on, Wonderbread, keep up the pace," Gonzo said ten paces ahead of me. "We gotta move fast to make this work."

The effects of the road trip were quickly catching up to me. I practically felt narcoleptic and struggled even mid jog to keep my eyes open. Suddenly my eyeballs just about popped out of socket. "What the fuck, man?"

As we rounded our unlikely jog around the chin up bars and towards the seawall parking, I was finally within eyesight of Yogi. Black spray painted lettering covered the entirety of the hood. As we approached, I could make out the phrase of the moment, Beat Army.

"What the fuck happened to my car, dude?" I questioned in shock. I assumed Gonzo and I were headed out to sneak and stash my car off the yard after switching out the cargo in Smitty's trunk. It would be quite difficult to drive inconspicuously, much less stash a graffiti covered car in downtown Annapolis for a week.

"The chit said we are volunteering for Mothers Against Drunk Driving," Gonzo answered with a steady glare. "Well?"

"What the hell does that have to do with this?" I asked wondering how Mothers Against Drunk Driving would have anything to do with us getting a spray-painted car off the yard. Gonzo never mentioned the details of that part of the plan. I just figured the MADD chit was an excuse to get out of evening meal.

"All part of it," Gonzo replied.

I was too angry to respond. My stare virtually burned a hole in the hood. Not only was I nervous about our evolving plot's prospects of success, I was pissed off that my wheels had been desecrated. Yogi was a piece of crap, but it was my piece of crap. My mind quickly moved towards the prospects of spray-painting the entire hood black. It would look terrible but at least a little less conspicuous.

"Whack!" A loud collision suddenly distracted my

racing mind. As my eyes moved towards the noise, I noticed Gonzo had just hit my passenger car door with a large wooden axe handle.

"What the hell are you doing?" I blurted just as Gonzo took a second whack at the rear passenger window. It partially shattered as glass shards covered the asphalt below. He took another whack on the passenger door with an echoing thud.

"Shit," Gonzo responded as his eyes darted quickly right. "Get down, get down," he ordered in a loud whisper. "Somebody's walking by. We can't let anybody see us."

I ducked down as ordered. We waited silently. Fearful of detection, I withheld angrily asking the thousands of questions worriedly bouncing in my head.

Gonzo quickly stood up and then tossed me the antique axe handle before I had a chance to talk. It had been stashed in Yogi's back seat, a trophy for winning the annual axe handle homerun derby game we played in Aunt Nellie's backyard. It also doubled as the bat for the contest.

"Go smash up what you can. I gotta take care of the rest of the paint. We need to roll in two minutes. Do what damage you can before somebody else rolls by, we need this thing look like a wreck," Gonzo commanded while shaking two cans of spray paint. "There are still some goods in the trunk. Smitty's Corvette had a smaller than expected trunk. We gotta move fast," Gonzo spoke above the hissing spray paint can.

"Goods in the trunk? What's that supposed to mean?" I asked in a panic as the new details processed.

"What do you think it means, homey? The drugs we couldn't squeeze in Smitty's trunk are still in yours," Gonzo explained quickly. He was finally beginning to look rushed.

"Why not dump that shit in the bay?" I asked. I was still trying my best to talk him out of whatever crazy plan we were currently executing.

"Drugs float, Mick. The fuzz will be back on the yard scouring this place tonight after the bust. Come on, man, you gotta trust me on this," Gonzo closed his argument, there was no time for further rationale or questioning.

Anger and desperation overtook my reluctance. I took my frustration out on Yogi, first smashing the driver's side headlight followed by two overhead whacks on the hood. Thunderous thuds of wood hitting metal echoed across the field in front of us. There was good reason my name had been burned into the side of the axe handle as two-time derby champion. Gonzo disappeared on the passenger side. He was squatting and spraying graffiti at a dutiful pace. Rage overcame me one last time, a culmination of the full journey. Without thinking, I took my angst out on the windshield of Yogi. The glass stayed in place but the point of impact rendered the driver's side portion of the windshield completely opaque.

"What the FUCK are you doing? I still need to drive this thing!" Gonzo interrupted my demolition job and quickly opened the driver's side door. "Get in on the other side, we gotta bounce. NOW."

I hustled into the passenger door before I had a chance to read what was spray-painted on its side. As the door slammed shut, Gonzo had already accelerated the car in reverse out of the parking spot. Jostled by the unexpected momentum, I fell awkwardly back in my seat. With a screech of the tires, we were quickly speeding down the side of the seawall, making our way past Rickets Hall and Rip Miller Field. All the while Gonzo drove the car with his head outside of the rolled down driver's window. It provided a convenient excuse for him not to answer the ten questions I threw his way in the first three hundred yards of driving. Yogi's condition all but guaranteed that the Jimmy Legs would pull us over as soon as they spotted us.

The road bent around Ricketts Hall and suddenly the visitors' gate was four hundred yards straight ahead. There was still a line of traffic coming into the yard. More than a few delayed flights and good excuses had justified a tardy return to at least a handful of mids still coming in from Thanksgiving break. I resolved to hold my breath until we passed through the gate. My heart rate reached a crescendo as we approached the guard stand.

"Oh God, please let us get through this," I prayed aloud with my eyes clenched tightly shut.

Instead of leaving the yard, Gonzo quickly turned Yogi right on Cooper Road and stayed on the yard. Out of the rearview mirror, I could see a sprinting gate guard yelling into a walkie-talkie. We had officially been spotted.

With another quick left on Porter Rd., I could hear sirens in the distance. Gonzo and I were suddenly speeding past Captain's Row and deeper into the yard's center. Knowing the Jimmy Legs were now in chase, Gonzo certainly was not paying much attention to the speed limit. Yogi howled as the growl of the struggling engine echoed off the pristine senior military housing.

"You're killing me, dude! What are you doing?"   I

asked, knowing full well that Gonzo was not going to answer.

Just like I had been with Bird, I was merely a passenger along for the ride.

He made a right onto Buchanan, the tires screeching loudly through the turn. It felt like we would swerve right into the superintendent's backyard. Instead we fishtailed and eventually accelerated forward. As we approached the end of the road, I did not feel the anticipated breaking. With a thud, we hopped the curb and were heading straight for T-Court.

A uniformed upperclassman was the first obstacle to block our path. I could hear the distant sirens getting closer. We only had a few minutes. Gonzo slammed the breaks and Yogi screeched to a stop twenty yards shy of the Tecumseh Statue. The firstie looked annoyed to see us. It was a better reaction than what I had been expecting. I looked through the back window. There were still no red and blue lights in sight, yet.

"WHOA! Who said anything about driving the car into spot?" the firstie aggressively questioned to Gonzo who already had the chit in hand waving out of the window. He luckily was too preoccupied with our car to notice the high-speed police chase closing in behind us.

"Sorry about being late, the tow truck dropped it off in the wrong spot. We just did what we could to get here ahead of the 1900 pep rally. Message to Garcia, sir," Gonzo apologetically explained as quickly as he could get the words out of his mouth.

"Just get the car where it needs to be," the firstie retorted. He pointed to another car parked in front of the giant

Tecumseh Statue. "In front of the statue, parked next to that other pile of shit. I don't care how it gets there. Just do it in the next five minutes."

His lack of sleeve stripes indicated he was not exactly the stickler to rules that a three striper would have otherwise been. Before we had a chance to proceed, he was already turned around and heading out. "Just make it quick," he yelled mid-walk without turning back. "You plebers are way late."

Gonzo accelerated the vehicle, this time remaining in his seat and navigating through the severely damaged windshield. The remaining journey was short. He didn't need to see much of where he was going.

He pulled the car to a stop. Through my side of the windshield, between spidering cracks, the intent of our location became clearer.

"You're stashing the car here? Next to another wreck?" I asked in a panic.

"Army Navy week, homey. Gotta have the right spirit," Gonzo replied. He tossed me a screwdriver. "Get the plates off. This thing needs to look as useless as the pile of junk next to it."

The referenced hunk of junk was what I imagined to be lethal car wreckage compliments of a drunk driver. It was part of a weeklong "don't drink and drive" message from the Mothers Against Drunk Driving. The wreck had similar decorations to Yogi. Beat Army and other prohibitory cautions against vehicular libations were spray painted across the entirety of its decimated steel body.

"That's a totaled automobile, Yogi is still running, how do we deal with that?" I continued my desperate interrogation as I furiously unscrewed the front license plate. I grabbed the license plate and tossed the screws behind me onto the white bricks of Tecumseh Court.

"Not totaled yet, we'll take care of that with the rest of the cargo," Gonzo explained without breaking his own frantic action. He had been fiddling in the interior of the car and then emerged with a small red gas tank.

"Gotta get on that license plate quicker, homey," Gonzo continued without breaking his practice of dousing the wheels and exterior in gas. "This thing's gonna blow soon enough."

"Blow? Wait! Where the fuck is the cargo now?" I asked as I grabbed Gonzo aggressively by the arm. I was partially trying to grab his attention and feebly stalling my cars inevitable destruction.

"Relax, homey. It's in the trunk, soon to be charred," Gonzo explained as I managed to get two of the four rear screws out.

"Did you gas it?" I asked.

"Gas what?" he replied, ineffectively trying to play dumb as I removed the third screw. The license plate swung down hinged on the one remaining screw. I quickly stood from my squatting position to more aggressively plea my point.

"The fucking drugs, man. I need to know it will all blow," I exclaimed pounding on the trunk. "Pop the fucking trunk!"

"Trust me, man, the shit will burn," Gonzo said with attempted confidence.

"That's a solid steel trunk, if they put the fire out fast enough, the drugs may not burn," I said making a final plea to ensure proper disposal.

From the corner of my eye, I could make out a familiar red and blue glow amidst the evening darkness. Two base police cars were speeding past Dahlgren Hall and bearing down on our location.

"You got one minute, homey, before those cops catch you and your car loaded with drugs," Gonzo further attempted to coax my blind acceptance. "Besides," he continued banging his fist on a gas covered Yogi. "This is a plebe's car, snuck on the yard with fake plates, and a VIN registered in your name. You'd be up a river before they even found the drugs, homey."

"There are no drugs," I finally stated despondently as my dreaded realization clicked in my brain. In an instant, my adrenaline deflated to defeat. I'd been duped the whole time.

The Jimmy Legs vehicles screeched to an abrupt halt at the end of Buchanan. In the minute it took them to spot our car, two overweight middle aged rent-a-cops came sprinting towards us. They were yelling the whole way but my spinning head could not make out what they were saying. I just stood numbly.

Gonzo stood in silence, his lack of immediate reaction validated my call against his bluff. His brain was processing as fast as it could to keep his scheme together.

"Yeah, but you still got those guys to contend with, no sense joining N.D. after you made it this far," Gonzo did his best to complete his plan as the base police made their way closer. "Tick-tock, Sherlock."

He was right. I needed to get out of there quickly. I fumbled through the last screw of the rear license plate. I tossed the screws and tucked the second license plate under my shirt. Gonzo pulled out a pack of matches. As soon as he saw the license plate's removal, he struck the flint. With a spark, the second strike dangerously lit the match.

"Bounce, homey, this thing's goin' up before we char the Jimmies."

Knowing there was no contesting, I scrambled in self-preservation. A brilliant flash of orange reflected in the many windows of Bancroft Hall followed by a loud explosion echoing off its stone walls. I had no idea where Gonzo scrambled off to. I just desperately sprinted back into the Hall where I figured I could hide in the anonymity of four thousand midshipmen.

I didn't need to look back. I knew Yogi was gone in a ball of flames.

Mick, 2229 hrs.

A loud slam bounced me out of my slumber. When I abruptly sat up in my rack, I could see the silhouette of someone entering my pitch black room, likely the individual that just kicked in my door.

"What do you know about the stench in my room, shipmate?" angrily chided 1/C Clarkson.

I remained sitting in my bed dazed. He aggressively approached my bed. As far as I could tell, I was the room's lone occupant. I rubbed my eyes and tried my best to groggily comprehend the situation. I shot a quick glance at my alarm clock, it read 10:30 p.m.

"What are you talking about?" was about all I could come up with, still dazed by the slumber I initiated as soon as I entered my room following Yogi's incineration three hours earlier.

"My room," 1/C Clarkson continued. "It smells like a pile of shit. What do you know about it?"

"I have no idea what you're talking about, sir," I responded honestly, not knowing what Clarkson was talking about. "It smells?"

"It smells like a plebe Army Navy prank and you sure seem like someone that might know about it!" Clarkson continued his contrived intimidation tactics. He looked like a petulant three-year-old throwing a temper tantrum.

"No idea," I replied.

"No idea, huh?" he continued. "Well, if I figure out that you knew something about this, I'm turning you in for an honor offense!"

"Sir, with all due respect, I have more important things to worry about than your stinky fucking room," I said standing from my bed and staring down inches from Clarkson less than intimidating presence. "Not sure what you are doing in my room after lights out."

Clarkson stood there silently and tried his best to seem intimidating. I could see a vein angrily pulsating on the side of his forehead. A bead of sweat followed down the side of his face. He quickly realized that he was in the wrong by being in my room after lights out.

"Watch it shipmate, I have my eye on you," he finished our dialogue and stormed back out of our door before spastically tripping over our garbage can on the way out.

From the hallway, I heard a familiar voice.

"Sir, good evening, Mr. Clarkson," was N.D.'s prelude into our room, a salutation not returned by what I assumed was a still steaming Clarkson. As soon as he entered our door, he couldn't wipe the smile off his face.

"Yo, what the fuck was his problem?" I asked.

"Maaaan, Micheals and Paulson stink berried his room," N.D. replied. "They collected a bunch of stink berries from the bushes on the yard last week. Then they smashed them jaunts up into a paste and spread it all over the horizontal surfaces of Clarkson's room. It dries clear. It'll take weeks to get that smell out. Unheard of, dawg, unheard of."

"Man, that's awesome," I said in a monotone reply. It was the best artificial excitement I could muster. I still felt half asleep, a condition I was sure would last several more days given my holiday journey.

N.D. approached and we smacked a high five into a handshake.

"Damn, dawg, good to see you," N.D. shifted the conversation sensing my lack of interest in stink berries. "How was Thanksgiving break? Wait, I don't want to know. You look like shit so it must have been pretty good."

"Uneventful," I fibbed. "What are you doing out so late in PT gear, shouldn't you be resting up for the big game?"

"Army Navy week, you know those woops can't fuck with the defense dawg. I'll be amped no matter what I do. No way I can sleep all week," N.D. replied. "Actually, I just got back from restriction duty. They had all the restrictees out cleaning up from the mess of the various pep rallies. Good thing we didn't have to deal with that exploded car in T-court."

"Nothing like free labor," I said trying to engage in small talk without seeming like I was losing my mind on the inside. "Wait, what exploded car in T-court?" I asked in my best attempt to play dumb.

"Dawg, what cave did you crawl into after dinner? The MADD car that exploded after dinner, you didn't hear about it?" N.D. responded, dumbfounded by my shaking head. "Damn, you must have had one hell of a weekend! Some asshole must have left one of the wrecks with gas in the tank. Somebody threw a match in, the rest is history."

"Damn, was anyone hurt?" I asked nervously hoping I'd get the answer I was looking for.

"Nah dawg, but T-court sure looks pretty fucked up. I'm sure they'll have the restrictees scrubbing the black off those bricks all the way up to commissioning week."

My reassurance of bystander safety was quickly replaced by the sense of severity in Gonzo's stunt.

"Did anybody get caught doing it?" I asked my next lingering question.

"Not yet, but I'm sure in time I'll have a new friend on restriction. You know the academy, they have eyes and ears everywhere." N.D. did little to attenuate my growing trepidation.

"You were right about before. My weekend was actually pretty cool. I spent all weekend partying pretty hard with my boys back home so I've been sleeping since after dinner to catch up. I figured everybody would be out at pep rallies so I could just sneak some time in before lights out. I didn't want to mention it because I figured you didn't want to hear about it," I quickly tried to change the topic.

"Yeah, I know," he said. "I was in here earlier and you looked like a corpse. Come to think of it, you still look like shit. Must have been a fun weekend."

"Any good Army Navy pranks today?" I asked changing the topic again.

"Man, these people are crazy. Somebody glued pictures from a gay porno mag all over Doc's floor. I also heard some dude in 2nd Battalion put a dead deer carcass in his 2nd class room. You know, typical Army Navy shit," N.D. described the shenanigans we had been waiting all year to see.

"We reap what we sow," I added.

"True dat, dawg."

"Hey man, have you seen Gonzo around tonight?" I asked.

"Nah dawg, that cat's been a ghost since he skipped out this morning. Hopefully nobody paid too close attention to muster," N.D. voiced his concern. He was even more in the dark than I was. "Everything cool with him?"

I didn't know if he was referencing his sudden absence today or our fight last week. "Yeah, everything's cool." I answered as ambiguously as the question asked.

"I'm headin' back out. We're going to pull Severson out of his rack and tape him to the Tecumseh Statue in his underwear. Wanna join the action?" he asked.

"Nah, I think I'm just going to go back to sleep and recharge for the rest of the week," I said declining the offer. Wrestling upper-class was not the safest way for our starting defensive end to be spending Army Navy week. Thankfully for N.D., I didn't think a Nebraska State wrestling champion would have too much trouble wrangling an elf like Severson out of bed.

"A'ight, I got some business to tend to," N.D. finished with a smile and a fist pound to his other palm. He headed off into a night of good old-fashioned mischief. If it had been any other day than today, I would have been right there to join him.

Instead, I slowly took inventory of Gonzo's side of the room. There was no typical pile of dirty clothes, and his desk was completely clean. I imagined N.D. had been correct in his observation. Gonzo had been a ghost.

With a new sense of adrenaline and a few hours of sleep under my belt, I sat in my bed waiting. I figured he would return before midnight bed check, and I wasn't going to miss his return.

Fifteen minutes later the door swung open.

"Hey Wonderbread, surprised to see you up. You must be bushed," Gonzo initiated the dialogue with small talk.

"Fuck you, man," I calmly retorted. I stared straight ahead. Deep below my anger boiled.

Gonzo immediately made his way to the con-locker and pulled out a black backpack. He tossed it across the desk and onto my bed. "Ten grand, cash. Christmas came early," he narrated as the loaded bag hit my bed and landed on the floor. "Fair wage for services rendered."

I just stared at the bag on the floor, not wanting to give Gonzo the satisfaction of seeing me pick it up. Instead I sat silently without saying a word.

"So there never were drugs on the yard?" I eventually asked.

"Nope."

"But the truck, the drugs, that was real," I continued

my grilling.

"Right again," he answered. "All we really needed was an extra driver in a pinch. You know, someone more reliable than that fat doofus Farm after our original mule got pinched and Bird volunteered for the drive."

I rose from my bed and calmly walked over to the door. I locked it and then stared intently at our rifle rack in the closet that stored our M-1 parade rifles. I was tempted to pull off the bayonet and give it the first action it had ever seen.

Sensing the inevitable scrap, Gonzo decided to add fuel to the fire. "Hey Mick, maybe you can take that cash and give your mom a few months off bussing tables in some shithole Ocean City restaurant."

I immediately charged Gonzo like a bull. His head and body loudly collided with his recently closed con-locker door. The impact knocked the sliding door off its tracks. I leaned my full body weight into my wrist. It was firmly pressed against Gonzo's throat. "What the fuck did you just say?"

I relished in his inability to immediately garner a response. He struggled in enough breath to say, "I wouldn't do that if I were you."

It only made me press my chokehold harder. It would only be a matter of seconds until he would black out and hit the floor. His eyes started rolling backwards.

Gonzo struggled one last time to gather enough breath for a final plea. "Would be a shame to see Bird and Aunt Nellie suddenly disappear . . ." He ran out of breath before he could finish his sentence.

I loosened my grip to allow him another gasp large

enough to finish the sentence he started.

"While you're here stuck on restriction," he continued.

Shocked by the statement, I loosened my grip so I could hear more. "What the FUCK does that mean?"

"My boy Griz, you met him. He does East coast work too. He even makes road trips to Ocean City every now and then," Gonzo continued as I suddenly let him go in disbelief. "Yeah, we can make our way down to Lewes to visit your mom. We know where she lives too. We do our homework."

We both took the next few minutes to regain our breath.

"Alright, I'm all ears now," I replied quickly trying to calm myself out of the sudden fear that overwhelmed me.

Gonzo finally stood upright after catching his breath. He slowly and confidently made his way to his desk chair. Once settled, he began his instruction. He knew his previous statement had made me suddenly enthralled with what he was about to say.

"So tomorrow, you're gonna turn yourself in for blowing up the car. Just say it was Army Navy spirit that got outta hand. If you're lucky, if they don't kick you out, maybe you can spend some time with N.D. on his last days of restriction," he said with a smile as he finally he rubbed his throat.

"And what if I don't?" I asked.

"Then you may not have a family to go to when you do get back for Christmas. And that'd be such a downer over the holidays."

I walked over to my rack to lie down. I didn't have anything to add to the conversation that wouldn't put my family in danger. Gonzo walked over to the sink area to turn on the shower as he disrobed. The psychopath continued as though it was just a typical Sunday evening. I half expected him to start showing me porn on his computer.

"Oh, and Mick," he summoned my laying body before entering the steamy hot shower. "You touch me again and I'll make sure Grizz really does cut your balls off," he said with a devious chuckle as he closed the shower curtain. "PLEASE STOP, I'LL DO ANYTHING!" he mimicked my final pleas a few nights earlier from behind the shower curtain. He was letting me know that he and Grizz were as tight as he made them out to be.

I rolled my face into my pillow screaming into it as loudly as possible in frustrated rage. I was helpless. I tossed the pillow in anger across the room. In the void vacated by my pillow sat a note. I immediately picked it up and opened it.

I'm single, you jackass . . . and I like you too.
-S

Chapter 25

Boring
Tuesday, November 28th, 1995
Bird, 2:50 p.m.

I impatiently sucked in my nicotine fix. I was freezing my ass off beside the pay phone of the local Dash In gas station situated at the eastern tail end of Route 50. There was at least a pack's worth of dried gum stuck all over the outdoor phone station as well as several humorous graffiti obscenities. I had drunkenly Sharpied the one about Farm's mom and her dick sucking skills earlier in the summer. He had it coming. The fucker stiffed me on an ounce for the third time in a month.

The ocean was a mile farther east, but felt much farther away. With a duffle bag, backpack, and awkwardly shaved head, I looked like a homeless skinhead. Curtis would have been proud. My foot had been tapping impatiently for the past five minutes staring at the phone.

The pay phone's ring nearly scared the cigarette out of my hand. Quickly I scrambled to pick it up.

"Yo," I spoke before even taking the care to listen. "Talk to me, you're late."

"Sorry, homey. These booth lines are unpredictable," spoke a voice on the other line. "You're all good."

"What about Mick? All's still safe after the fire?" I nervously asked. I still couldn't believe Gonzo had gotten Mick to believe his bull shit story. I guess he knew Micky all too well. The mere threat of family harm set him in place. That's how we manipulated him into the gig in the first place.

"So far plan B still sticks. He still seems convinced I was the mastermind. He's still buying the family threats. It was enough to get him to confess and cover for blowing up his car," Gonzo reassured me.

"What about the fall out? Is he in trouble?" I tried to ask without sounding overly concerned or panicked. I had repeated these questions in my head a thousand times in the past two days.

"We'll see, but I think we're alright. After he confessed about the car, the brass seemed to initially buy it. He gets his punishment from the Commandant next week. They're pretty pissed off. We fucked up a lot of bricks, homey, but look, nobody got hurt. At the end of the day, everything looks like an Army Navy prank spun out of control. Mick's a good mid, they'll throw him on restriction and that'll be the end." Gonzo's confident voice made the story feel credible.

"You sure about that?" I quickly followed just to make doubly sure.

"Yeah, pretty certain. He'll be fine. Likely missing Christmas but sitting on ten grand. Not a bad deal."

I released a sigh of relief and then took a drag of my smoke. I was still pissed Gonzo walked away from this with forty grand and Mick with ten. Mick had the riskier job. He deserved a bigger cut. Mick had told me the story about Gonzo and his kid when we were surfing over his Parents' Weekend. He also told me how Gonzo wanted to buy his way out of the Navy. I knew if I asked Mick to drive the drugs myself, he'd never go for it. I took a chance and approached Gonzo a month earlier. He was at the right place at the right time. At least it looked like Mick was going to end up okay.

"You still there?" the phone's earpiece reminded me of the conversation I had just mentally jumped out of. Despite the net positive outcome, my mind was still swimming in guilt.

"Yeah, I'm here. Look, keep an eye on things. If shit bubbles up before you head out, you know how to reach Farm," I instructed as a final point of emphasis.

"All good, homey. I'll keep an eye out while I'm still here. If all goes well, we'll never talk to each other again. Good luck laying low."

I hung up the phone before adequately responding with proper salutation.

"Where the fuck are Bobby and Farm?" I spoke aloud to myself. It was five minutes past the top of the hour and they were officially late. Farm may have been bugged out by the cop car in the gas station's parking lot. He was doing me a solid by driving while still on a suspended license.

Mick had been right. He was my only choice as a driver. Even I wasn't dumb enough to think Farm would have pulled off that drive without incident, DUI or no DUI. The rationale didn't lessen the guilt.

Fuck me.

Back beside the butt receptacle in the station's smoker's pit, I took a drag of my last smoke and flicked it on the asphalt below. My teeth began to chatter. I had been waiting outside the station for the past fifteen minutes. It felt like fifteen hours. The ocean wind knifed through my bones with each gust.

I searched for distractions. The heated interior of the gas station's convenience store would have been a welcome escape, but the asshole cop shooting the shit with the cashier knew me all too well. I didn't want him asking questions about my duffle bag. I didn't want him to see Farm driving when he shouldn't have been.

Guess I'll just continue freezing my balls off.

I heard a beep and several subsequent clanks. Some fucking local yuppie was fumbling around filling his Lexus. Even though I didn't recognize him, I knew he was local. Who else hangs in Ocean City past October? It took him three tries to get the gas hose back in the pump. He should have lived at the Jersey Shore. They pump the gas for patrons there. That shithole needed accountants and lawyers too.

I had tried boring on for size a few times. It just never fit.

Despite ditching half my classes for waves at nearby Salisbury State, I managed Dean's List my first semester of freshman year a decade earlier. I scored a 720 on the math portion of my SAT. My teachers and guidance counselors considered me a sort of a deviant savant.

It just took one party gone wrong to change all of that. Campus police busted me selling a few dime bags at a weekend party in the freshman dorms. That party also just happened to include the Dean's daughter. He wanted to make an example of me. Weeks later, I was in court. My previous criminal record landed me in prison. I never saw the spring semester. Boring was never to be.

I heard the welcome screech of tires speeding in the station's entrance. Farm always drove his truck like an asshole, even into gas stations with a recently suspended license and a cop car in the parking lot. His brother followed closely behind in their mom's decrepit minivan. It was the same van Farm drove to prom over a decade earlier. About two months ago, its sliding side door stuck permanently a quarter open. I knew they wouldn't fix that shit until they had to pass state inspection next summer.

Farm quickly parked the truck on the curb in front of me. He hurriedly exited the driver's seat to avoid evidence of driving on a suspended license. A quiver of my three favorite boards was already loaded in the back. I had left my single fin nine footer behind at Mom's house. Despite lacking a big red bow, I figured it would make a nice Christmas gift for Micky. Farm exited the truck and slammed the door behind him.

"S'up, Bird?" he provided his expected salutation.

"S'up," I returned. Five seconds of awkward silence ensued. "Here ya go, man," I broke the conversation stalemate and tossed the mostly empty duffle bag in his general direction. It bounced clumsily off his chest and landed on the ground below. Traditional sports were never his thing.

The bag was lighter than it had been two days earlier. A hundred grand evaporated quickly. Half was spent paying off Gonzo and Mick. Then there was the forty of "get lost" money to my degenerate father. The last roll of cash was all that was left in the previously fuller bag.

"It's all in there," I told Farm. "Ten grand."

"Dude, the Turd ain't worth one grand," he sheepishly replied as he tossed me the keys.

"Get yourself something nice," I said. I knew that I was entering a bad business deal. I wish I had more to give him.

Farm's half-wit brother Bobby finally made his way over from the minivan.

"S'up Bird?" he greeted me upon arrival. Originality was never a Farmer family strong point.

"Hey Bunkie," I replied as Bobby gave me a military style salute and made his way inside to likely buy some stale gas station donuts.

A few more minutes of awkward small talk and Farm could sense my desire for near term departure. He finally grabbed the duffle bag from the ground and struggled for some parting words.

"Good luck out there," was all he could come up with.

Farm hustled his way to the van to toss the bag in the back. Bobby fired up the engine. That fat fuck already had a mouth full of donut and a large smear of chocolate icing on his cheek. Farm made his way back over for one last goodbye.

"Hey man, you sure you need to do this?" Farm took one last shot to keep me around.

My eyes emphatically told him "yes" without saying a word.

"Alright man, then I guess this is it," he reluctantly gave up on any further speeches. "Title's in the glove box, tube's in the tank."

"Thanks, Farm," I replied, gracious that he had not

again tried to talk me out of leaving. I gave him a long hug. These goodbyes were becoming a habit. I hated that.

"You take care of yourself, Bunkie," I instructed with one last firm slap on the shoulder. "And if you hear from Gonzo or see my asshole dad tooling around here anytime soon, you know where to find me."

"In the ocean?" Farm said with a sarcastic smile. Humor was having a tough time taking the edge off the sadness.

Bird, 4:20 p.m.

The steady rumble of the boards clanking in the pick-up bed had lulled me into daydreams of surfing. It was a welcome distraction from my racing mind. The ocean was once again my mental safety net.

My musing was interrupted by my growling stomach. I hadn't eaten all day. I instinctively reached in my shorts to search for pocket change. In feeling a few loose bills of cash, I figured I had enough to at least buy a gas station hot dog. I immediately went on the lookout for convenience stores. I might as well have been driving in the deserts of Nevada. I lit up a half smoked roach lying on the seat bench space beside me. Farm had left it there. I was just stoked that the car lighter still worked.

I was about an hour into my drive and a few miles south of the Virginia state line. If Ocean City was considered a ghost town in November, this was its desolate outskirts. A few barns and grain silos were the only thing breaking up the flat farmland horizon. In November, it was miles and miles of brown.

I was speeding southward to the Outer Banks via Route 13. My immediate desire to put Ocean City further in my rearview mirror made my right foot a bit heavier on the pedal. My grumbling stomach made me floor it. My new truck's engine rattled in protest.

"One hundred fucking grand," I dejectedly spoke to an empty passenger cabin. It was merely the cost of services rendered. A few thousand miles, a truckload of drugs, and a little deception was all it took.

High value, fast moving inventory was the holy grail of any retail business. I still remembered that lesson from my freshman year business class several years earlier.

Supply and demand was the driving force of my recent weekend employment. When the October drug bust in Annapolis stymied established plans for November cross-country drug distribution, the supply of eligible cross-country drivers in the crew bottomed out. The demand for such services went through the roof. I was just being opportunistic.

I was never someone with heady professional ambitions. I had a long list of shitty food service jobs to prove it. Even in present day, I was satisfied hustling dime bags to tourists and my surfing buddies. When my father offered a new business deal in the parking lot of Seacrets three months earlier, that all changed.

Forty grand was that asshole's price tag to get lost permanently. I considered it a fair lump sum payment. It was better than paying him a grand every six months for two decades. I told him if he blew through that wad of cash and came back, I'd finally take his suggestion for a paid hitman. He knew that I was being serious. Mom was finally rid of that dickhead. It made all of this shit worth it.

Fathers were a tough topic in my family. I did all that I could to keep mine out of my life. Mick would do anything to get his back. I remember his dad's closed casket funeral. It was required given the brutality of the motorcycle accident. I remember wishing it were my dad in that casket and not his. Mick spent his teens looking for someone to fill that empty church pew next to his mom. I did a pretty piss poor job of it.

At the end of the day, Mick was still the kid with his ass in the sand. I knew one day he'd figure that out, if he hadn't already. It would eat him up. I pressed harder on the gas pedal.

A desperate person does desperate things.

I was going away for a while, a year, maybe longer. I needed to get lost and lay low. I'd let the next few months pass and ensure there wasn't any transaction spillover or future busts implicating me. Farm had stuffed two grand of cash in a plastic tube residing in the gas tank. We learned that trick from *Easy Rider*. I had enough dough to survive anonymously for a few months.

By spring, when things felt appropriately in the rearview mirror, I'd get a shitty under the table job. I'd rent out a room or some shitty apartment with cash. Maybe I'd sleep a few nights in the truck. I'd surf a great break. I'd be happy.

Mom would be pissed and sad, but she's lived it before. Mick, well, I just hoped one day he'd listen to my side of the story and forgive me. I wouldn't fault him if he didn't.

I finally caught a 7-Eleven in my peripheral and peeled into the parking lot. I had enough pocket change for a hot dog and some ChapStick. My dry lips were driving me crazy. I slammed the truck's door behind me and rushed towards the prospect of a fuller stomach and moisturized lips. I caught my reflection in the glass, looking at my own pale pink lips. I promised to avoid the red tints and smiled.

Chapter 26

Faithful
Tuesday, June 30th, 2015
Mick, 0605 hrs.

"Eddie and the boys, they still got it," Bird says as he flips my car radio off. A crooning Eddie Vedder is cut unduly short in a stirring live rendition of "Sirens". I wish he were patient enough to let me finish my favorite Pearl Jam song.

No such luck, more pressing issues at stake.

From my car, we hurriedly make our way over the boardwalk and onto the sand. Bird moves as quickly as he can. Age has made him a few steps slower. I guess it did the same to me.

The first orange sliver of sunrise casts a golden glow on the water as it peeks above the darkness of zero dark thirty. I lick my lips. I can still taste the remnants of the toasted scrapple, egg, and cheese sandwich I ate on the way to 12th Street. The ketchup and jelly always tends to stick to my beard.

It is a mediocre surf day at best. The solid waves of the prior weekend have lost their power. The offshore storm system is moving on while the winds shift back onshore. Most of the remaining sets are sloppy and inconsistent. Legendary big wave surfer Wally Froiseth died at the ripe old age of ninety-five yesterday and it seems as though the ocean is in mourning.

"Check this out, Bunkie" Bird says with a devious smile. "If these guys want a show, then I'm gonna give'em one," he continues as he pulls his pants down and proceeds to take a shit in the ocean. An old couple walking their dog catches the visual in their peripheral. Before they have a chance to walk over and scold us, we paddle out quickly past the breakers. It feels just like old times.

The local news van is parked in the closest spot to the boardwalk. It was there even before we had arrived that morning. An eight-foot hammer head shark had been filmed days earlier swimming in our current surf spot. It was the big news story of the prior week. Ironically the cameraman sets up his camera in front of Hammerhead's Boardwalk Bar. It will likely be the only hammerhead he'll see today.

Fear of Ocean City's most famous guest of the summer has people petrified out of the water. Bird's recent aqua-plop is a far greater danger compared to the typically placid shark. He certainly doesn't mind the irrational fear and general hoopla. It is a temporary oasis. In another day or two, most of the shore's visitors will be too distracted by selfies and tweets to even remember what was swimming out there days before.

June 30th has been marked with a large red X on my calendar months ahead of summer, just like it had been two decades earlier. My anticipation of that red X was

different these days. At a time that X was a point of de-
barkation, now it is merely a reminder of my family's annual beach vacation. Though enough time away from the
Delmarva shoreline has reduced me to being just another
tourist, it is sure as hell better than being a plebe.

Plenty has changed twenty years north of I-Day. Drug
dealing Bird is now a legitimate businessman. He hung up
his cleats in the drug game a few years back when meeting
his now wife. They are both running an organic farm a few
miles west in Pittsville selling cucumbers and carrots to
the hoity-toity restaurants of the surrounding Delmarva
shoreline.

"Why grow weed when I can get triple price for to-
matoes grown in local horse shit?" Bird recently told me.
I guess all that experience in local horticulture finally paid
off.

I was scared when my wife asked him to "bring some
greens" to our family crab steam a day earlier. Luckily, he
forgot the greens altogether. Instead he brought a bushel
of live blue crabs freshly nabbed from the Choptank River. He still had the balls to grab them barehanded from
the basket to the pot. I have long since transitioned to the
safety of steel tongs.

Throughout its long history, Ocean City has tried to
reinvent itself on more than one occasion. In the most recent twenty years, some attempted changes stuck, some
didn't. Places like Seacrets have become institutions to
tourists and locals alike. Yet the coastline is also scattered
with foreclosed luxury condominiums and shutdown golf
courses.

2007 and the subsequent Great Recession certainly did

some damage to the local Ocean City economy. The real estate boom of the mid 2000s saw rapid economic development right down the Delmarva shoreline. It all started when the mid-Atlantic LGBTQ community brought class, style, and great restaurants to the already excellent family beach of Rehoboth in the eighties and nineties. Dewey added a few more bars and became Spring Break for the Mid-Atlantic region Friday through Sunday all summer long. Indian River became a much fancier campground. The yuppies and D.C. wealth snapped up the largely private beaches of Bethany. Fenwick Island's oceanfront shacks flipped into four-story multi-million dollar mansions.

By 2005, Ocean City was primed to eat up the wave of wealth making its way south on the shore. Locals took out home equity loans to buy obnoxious luxury vehicles on houses that had tripled in value in just a matter of four years. Everyone became a real estate mogul in their own mind, prospecting on two to three beach condos at a time. Thirty foot fishing boats were bought by fifty-year-old divorcees with hopes of picking up the new twenty-year-old hostess at Hooters. All of them were scouting a wave that never came.

When the market collapsed, so did the effort to reinvent Ocean City, at least temporarily. Now that the dust has settled, Ocean City is almost exactly as I remembered it the first time I met Bird and Nellie on the boardwalk. Some of the hotels have different names, but the city is still largely as it has been in my lifetime. It is a small town, a waterman's town, a redneck's Riviera—it is perfect. For at least a few more years, my children have the chance to experience this place in the same way that I did. This makes me happy.

The Naval Academy also saw an abundance of change in twenty years. Phone booths are dinosaurs. No modern era mid is without a cell phone. Black flag, 90+ degree summer days are made infinitely more bearable with the installation of air conditioning in Bancroft Hall. Gonzo would have had a field day as a mid with the modern day internet capabilities of Bancroft and the internet's full bevy of porn websites.

There is also plenty about the Naval Academy that hasn't changed. Restriction and weekend watches are just as depressing today as they were in my day. Beating Army is just as joyous as ever, despite winning thirteen years in a row. Being a plebe still sucks ass.

In recent years, some pundits have publicly questioned the value of the Naval Academy. In the modern era Navy, ROTC programs and Officer Candidate School grads constitute the largest feeder of Naval Officers. Some say "boat U" is obsolete. I say bullshit.

Post-9/11, graduating the academy brings with it almost certainty of armed conflict. The applications are still stacked to the ceiling. Year after year, a thousand kids show up chasing the same dreams as once young war heroes, CEOs, astronauts, Super Bowl Champions, and a President. I recently heard one of Summer's soccer teammates was even a front runner for the first manned mission to Mars.

For those with the right grit and opportunity, those dreams will come true. Most of us alumni know those types of people. Some of us are those people. The Naval

Academy is a magnet for these types. That is the value of the Naval Academy. Putting up with the four year shit sandwich that is the life of a mid is merely the price of admission.

"Look to your left, look to your right, look across from you," I recollect Severson screaming at us in one of our first of many P-way flame sessions of Plebe Summer. "One of you will not make it to graduation." It is one of my only memories of my first night in Bancroft Hall.

Severson had been overly ambitious in his instruction. One less head turn would have sufficed as nearly a third of the twelve hundred and ninety six class of '99 sworn in on I-Day would never see graduation day. For those of us that did, our hat toss was extra sweet. Through all the chow calls, pushups, days on restriction, friends lost and gained, at least we had each other. Above all things we are faithful to each other. That will never change.

I received my first Black N for faith in a lie. In Plebe Summer an upper-class asked if I knew how many bricks made up T-court. I still don't know the answer to that question. After my bonfire shenanigans, I am just glad that sixty days restriction was my only required repayment for the hundreds of T-court bricks we ruined.

By the time I served my first day of restriction, Gonzo had already left the academy. We both confessed to burning the car the morning after the incident. On the second day of finals a week later, I came back to the room from my chemistry exam and Gonzo was gone. His locker was empty, his sheets stripped, his nametag pulled off our door. It was as though he never existed. Not a word of departure was spoken before the event. N.D. was stunned.

I would later come to find out that after he received his punishment, Gonzo decided to voluntarily leave the academy. Even enlisted midshipmen, who were typically sent back to the fleet upon resignation or expulsion, had this option. E-dawgs were good to go as long as they could use their own dough to pay off their financial commitment of $40,000 for resignation. The buyout option and the requisite money to do so was the whole reason Gonzo took on Bird's scheme.

All of this came days after losing a brutally heart-breaking game to Army by a single point via a ninety-nine yard touchdown drive with less than four minutes to go. The bitterness of the loss was only partially relieved by the fact that I did not get kicked out of school. I spent most of the following winter's Dark Ages on restriction muster.

It would be a few years before I saw Gonzo again. His resourcefulness would have served him well in the Fleet as an officer had it been directed differently. Instead, he traded glory for dirty money. It all caught up with him eventually.

Bird still lives in Nellie's house by the bay. Unfortunately, we lost her to cancer five years earlier. In my imagination, I can still vividly hear her laugh and smell her cigarette smoke.

My mother eventually found love and lives in Tulsa with my stepdad. He's alright, I guess, but no one will ever replace my dad. I miss him every day.

I turn off the outdoor shower below Bird's house following our morning surf session. I quickly realize that I forgot to pack a change of clothes before coming to pick up Bird earlier in the morning. I go to the closet in Bird's old bedroom. He let me stash my stuff there after my mom moved to Oklahoma.

In opening my closet, there is my old friend. Its yellow thread is as brilliant as ever. A neatly stitched Black N sits with two stars astutely sewn above of it.

Sex, drugs, and rock and roll, academy style . . . or rather drugs, sex, and rock and roll.

N'd

Acknowledgements

First and foremost I'd like to thank my many family and friends in Delaware, Ocean City MD, Annapolis, MD, Washington, DC, and Pittsburgh, PA for being so supportive of my writing aspirations. I love you all deeply. That sentiment extends especially to my wife, Stacy Conlin, Robb Wirts, Carolyn Menke, Robin Siddoway, Tanya Keetch and Carl Holsinger. Your input into the editing and production process truly helped this book become the best that it could be.

Thanks to Dream Oak Publishing for your faith in my story. Your commitment to artistic integrity and love of all things writing is a rarity.

I'd also especially like to thank the midshipman and Alumni of the U.S. Naval Academy. I meant every word of my last chapter.

When I was at the Naval Academy, I was fortunate to read two books that made me want to one day write my own. James Webb's *SENSE OF HONOR*, and John Feinstein's *A CIVIL WAR* remain two of my favorite books.

Life ambitions are a funny thing. I held the dream of writing a novel about the Naval Academy for many years after my time by the bay. I started typing on two different occasions in my twenties and quit both efforts within a couple of days.

On October 11, 2013 that distant dream became much closer to my heart. After battling recurring pericarditis and thoughts of my own mortality for a full year prior, I saw Pearl Jam play the concert debut of "Sirens", my all-time favorite song from my all-time favorite band. In dedicating that song to someone that tragically died well before his time, they inspired me to get off my ass and start writing. Somewhere distantly close, Michael was in the room that night. Thanks Fellas.